📖 Books should be returned or renewed by the last date above. Renew by phone **08458 247 200** or online *www.kent.gov.uk/libs*

**Libraries & Archives**

CUSTOMER SERVICE EXCELLENCE

UK

The Government Standard

Kent County Council

# The King's Corrodian

Also by Pat McIntosh

*The Harper's Quine*
*The Nicholas Feast*
*The Merchant's Mark*
*St Mungo's Robin*
*The Rough Collier*
*The Stolen Voice*
*A Pig of Cold Poison*
*The Counterfeit Madam*
*The Fourth Crow*

# The King's Corrodian

## Pat McIntosh

Constable & Robinson Ltd
55-56 Russell Square
WC1B 4HP
www.constablerobinson.com

First published in the UK by C&R Crime,
an imprint of Constable & Robinson Ltd., 2013

A copy of the British Library Cataloguing in Publication
data is available from the British Library

ISBN 978-1-4721-0105-1 (hardback)
ISBN 978-1-4721-0107-5 (ebook)

Printed and bound by CPI Group (UK) Ltd, Croydon, CR0 4YY

1 3 5 7 9 10 8 6 4 2

For Helen

# Author's Note

Ever since it became a kingdom, Scotland has had two native languages, Gaelic (which in the fifteenth century was called Ersche) and Scots, both of which you will find used in the Gil Cunningham books. I have translated the Gaelic where needful, and those who have trouble with the Scots could consult the online *Dictionary of the Scots Language*, to be found at http://www.dsl.ac.uk/dsl/

I would like to thank the Nagging Crew (you know who you are) without whom this book might never have seen the light of day.

# Chapter One

'The tale seems very improbable,' said Gil Cunningham cautiously. 'How should the Devil enter a house of Religious, and carry off one of its members?'

'Precisely my point!' said Archbishop Blacader in sour Latin. He gestured irritably at the nearest stool, and Gil rose obediently from his knees and seated himself. 'But it is not one of the Dominicans who has vanished.' He paused as if setting his thoughts in order, lifted a pewter goblet from the table at his elbow and gulped the red wine it held. In the shadows, Blacader's secretary, the rat-faced William Dunbar, drew his plaid closer about his shoulders. Gil maintained a pose of attention, wondering what the wine was; its scent was heavy and rich, cutting through the smells of wet wool and boiling kale.

They were in the Archbishop's own lodging in his castle in Glasgow, where Gil had been summoned almost as soon as the prelate's retinue had dismounted in the courtyard and shaken the icy January rain off their oiled-wool cloaks and leather hoods. A branch of candles and a glowing brazier made the chamber less dark and chill than it was outside, but that was all one could say. Blacader, plump and blue-jowled, garbed for riding in expensive, mud-splashed velvet and high leather boots, finished the wine and set the goblet down. Dunbar lifted the jug and refilled it.

'The man who has ... vanished,' pronounced the Archbishop at length, 'is named Leonard Pollock, and is a corrodian at the convent.'

'A corrodian?' Gil repeated, startled. 'With the Blackfriars?'

'The Perth house,' said Blacader reprovingly, 'has a very extensive provision for guests, given that it was once the preferred royal lodging in those parts.'

'Quite so,' said Gil. 'I hope they've mended the locks.'

The Archbishop ignored this reference to the unfortunate end met by James Stewart, first king of that name, taken unarmed while hiding below the privy in the royal lodgings of the Dominican priory at Perth, but his tone grew cooler as he continued, 'The Perth house is well able to maintain several permanent residents. Pollock, having been a member of the late King's household, was,' he paused again, apparently suppressing the first word which came to his lips, 'was lodged there some twelve or thirteen years ago, I am told, and a substantial endowment made from the Treasury for his keep.'

'His corrody,' agreed Gil. Blacader threw him a glance and took another gulp of his wine. Not claret, Gil thought, it seems heavier than that. Wine of Burgundy? Behind the Archbishop, Dunbar drew closer to the source of heat.

'By means of this corrody,' Blacader continued, 'Pollock has been supported since '82 in a private lodging next to the main guest hall, a commodious stone house of two chambers with a fine chimney and its own small garden.' Gil nodded, thinking of the guest hall of the Perth house as he had last seen it, smiling in the sunshine. A far cry from today's weather, he reflected, as the rain rattled on the window-shutters. Blacader glanced at the gloomy skies beyond the glass above and stretched his booted feet nearer to the

2

brazier. He seemed to be having difficulty framing his next sentence.

'And this is the man who has vanished, my lord?' Gil prompted. 'What happened, then? What were the circumstances?'

'Ach, there's no reason to it!' exclaimed Blacader. He looked over his shoulder directly at Dunbar. 'William, have you Bishop Brown's letter there? Let Gilbert have a sight of it. I took George Brown for a man of sense, Gilbert, but you may see for yourself what foolishness he writes.'

'Bishop *Brown*?' Gil, who had also taken the Bishop of Dunkeld for a man of sense, accepted the document which Dunbar produced from his scrip, and tilted it towards the candles. 'It tells us little,' he said after a moment. 'He writes of fire and black smoke, but says only that these rumours of the Devil are strong in Perth and the countryside, and damaging to Holy Church as well as to the Dominicans. You can tell he is agitated,' he added, 'his Latin is deserting him. There are no other facts.'

'And he asks for the loan of my quaestor.'

'That's what puzzles me, my lord.' Gil folded the paper carefully. 'What has the Bishop to say in the matter? Perth and the Perth Blackfriars are not in his diocese; they look to St Andrews, not to Dunkeld. How will Archbishop Scheves take it if I start sniffing round his archdiocese uninvited?'

'Hardly uninvited,' said Blacader. 'George Brown was at school with George Hepburn.'

'The Provincial Prior?' Gil raised his eyebrows. 'I mind him when I was first at the College here, when he was lecturing to the Theology students. A fine intellect.'

'Indeed.' The Archbishop drained his wine. Gil contemplated the situation. Presumably Hepburn, whom he remembered as a much-respected teacher, had asked his old friend to call in a favour, rather than making a formal request through the convent's own archdiocese, a request which was unlikely to be granted however it was couched, given the opposing politics both church and civil of the two prelates concerned. It was flattering that the Provincial Prior, elected master of the Dominicans in Scotland, should have called for him, rather than for someone within the archdiocese, but his position would clearly be precarious. And yet one did not offend the mendicant orders, he thought ruefully. He would have to go.

'It will need a man with a clear and open mind to make sense of it,' continued Blacader. 'The corrodian carried off by the Devil, indeed! I hope you can assist, Gilbert. Are you able to travel the now?'

'I am.' Gil was reckoning in his head. 'I can set out tomorrow, my lord, and be in Perth in three days, I suppose, or four, assuming the weather gets no worse.'

'Aye.' Blacader switched to Scots, a sign that the formal part of the interview was over. 'You'd need more time than that to prepare for sic a journey. I'd suggest you call it a pilgrimage, maybe take madam your wife wi you if she's in good health.' Gil looked up sharply, to encounter a significant glance from his master. 'These matters oft go smoother when there's a bonnie young woman involved, I'm told, even in Holy Kirk.'

'What has the Provost told him?' said Alys in some dismay, her colour rising.

Gil had found her in the little solar at the back of the house, the chamber made comfortable with two foot-warmers full of hot stones, her needlework on her lap. She was alone; her elderly companion Catherine, who was growing frail, had been persuaded to keep her bed in this weather, wrapped in blankets and surrounded by more hot stones, and Gil knew his assistant Lowrie

4

Livingstone was dealing with a sasine exchange out towards Partick. In the hall their small ward John McIan was rampaging about with a wooden horse while Alys's tirewoman Jennet gossiped with his nurse; the other servants were probably in the kitchen where it was warm.

'My thoughts too,' Gil admitted. 'He's perfectly right, I'd never have reached some of the conclusions I've found without your help, but I thought we'd kept it hidden from him. The Provost must have let something slip. Can you be ready to leave tomorrow?'

'Of course,' she said simply, though her quick smile came and went in gratification at his comment. 'How far is Perth? No knowing how long we must stay, I suppose.' She delved under the wide skirt of her woollen gown for the purse which hung between it and her kirtle, and drew out her tablets. 'Will you see to hiring the horses? We should have one sumpter beast at least, for six of us.'

'Five. I'll leave Lowrie here in charge of the house.'

'A good thought. Someone must have a care to Catherine and John and the maidservants.' She was already noting items on her list. 'You, Nory and Euan, Jennet and me. A donation of meal, and we should take that barrel of figs since none of us like them. Bedding. I suppose we'll be lodged separately? The women's hall is set apart?'

'I don't recall,' he confessed. 'I know they have one.' He lifted the smaller footwarmer by its ring, using the corner of his gown to protect his hand, and moved to the door of the little solar. Socrates the wolfhound, curled round the larger footwarmer, raised his head to watch him. 'I must clear up some of the papers on my desk before we leave.'

'Confession. We must all be confessed if we are to ride so far.' Alys made another note. 'If Father Francis will come to the house, will you make do with that, or

5

should I send to the Blackfriars as well? And Euan may call at my father's house and let him know while he is down the High Street.'

Gil nodded, reflecting that his father-in-law might come up to bid them farewell and safe journey. No point in wondering whether Alys would go down the High Street herself; she and her new stepmother existed on terms of the barest courtesy, the situation made worse by Mistress Ealasaidh's advanced pregnancy.

'But Gil,' Alys looked up from her list, the high bridge of her nose outlined against the grey light at the window, 'why are you sent for? If someone thinks they have seen the Devil himself, is it not rather a matter for Holy Church?'

'I don't know.' He closed the door and set the little box of hot stones down again, blowing on his fingers. 'The Bishop's letter was clear only on that point, that he wants me. The rest of the tale—' He pulled a face. 'Something about smoke and fire and a lost key, and how it's disturbed the peace of Perth and all the country round.'

'I can well imagine it has,' she said. 'I see why the Devil has been mentioned, but is it not simply a house fire? You said that Pollock had his own little house, like the old men at St Serf's here.'

'The Bishop said no more. *Vanished away in fire and smoke*, were his words,' Gil said, quoting the Latin. She nodded. 'No mention of the presence or absence of witnesses, nor of what the lost key should lock or unlock. And then the request for the loan of Blacader's quaestor.'

'And you have seen the mood in the burgh,' said George Brown, Bishop of Dunkeld, his round, good-humoured face creased with anxiety. He was interrupted by another flurry of yapping, and muzzled the little spaniel on his lap with one plump hand. 'Be at peace, Jerome! Bad dog!' he said in Scots.

'Oh, no, my lord, do not scold him,' said Alys. 'He's defending his maister. He's a very good dog.' Socrates, sitting politely by Gil's knee, turned his head and gave her a reproachful look.

'A course he is,' said Maister Gregor the Bishop's secretary, reaching to pet the animal, an indulgent smile on his sheep-like countenance. 'He's the best wee dog in Perth, aren't you no, Jerome?'

'Rob, this is no the moment,' said the Bishop.

'There was a gathering outside St John's Kirk as we rode by,' Gil said in Latin, 'with much shouting. I heard witchcraft mentioned.'

'And the man at the port tried to persuade us to turn back,' said Alys in Scots, 'to lodge wi the Franciscans instead.'

'One of our brothers was pelted with mud yesterday,' said Prior Boyd. 'It is urgent that we determine what has happened and whether the Devil or some mortal agency was responsible.'

'It would have been better to have conducted the exorcism immediately,' said the Bishop. His dog yapped again, and Socrates sighed and put his chin on Gil's knee.

'I confess,' said Gil, slightly apologetic, 'that I find it easier to believe in the mortal agency than in a physical action by the Devil.'

'The fact remains, Gilbert,' said Prior Boyd, 'the man is vanished, and there is no trace and no sign of him.'

'Start at the beginning, sir,' said Gil. 'How did you find he was missing?'

David Boyd, Prior of the Dominican convent of Perth and Gil's third cousin, glanced about his sparsely appointed study, straightened the stack of papers on his reading-desk with a longing look, lifted one of the books, contemplated it, and set it down again with precision. They all watched him in an extending silence; Gil wondered that Maister Gregor managed to hold his peace.

'On the morning of the second day after Epiphany,' the Prior said finally, 'our cook sent his servant with the man Pollock's morning repast, as was his custom. The servant returned to him saying that he had found the door barred and could get no reply. Fearing the man might be sick or injured, our cook summoned two other lay brothers, and they attended the door of the man's lodging with loud shouts and knocking. By this time,' some disapproval crept into the austere tones, 'our subprior's attention had been drawn to the matter, and he commanded the lay brothers to break down the door. This they did.'

Gil glanced at Alys, who was frowning intently as she followed the fluent, elegant Latin.

'So the door was barred from the inside,' he said.

His kinsman flicked him an irritated glance, and continued, 'All who were present, a considerable number, swear that when the door was burst open, neither smoke nor flame emerged. Nevertheless, when our subprior made an entrance he smelled smoke and burning, and called for the shutters to be flung wide for light. This being done, he perceived that there was no appearance of anything burned in the outer chamber, and that the door of the inner chamber, in which our corrodian slept, was shut fast.'

'It's extraordinary!' exclaimed Maister Gregor. 'It makes no sense!'

'Rob,' said the Bishop in warning tones.

'This was in daylight?' Gil said, glancing at the heavy sky beyond the high window.

'It was perhaps half an hour after sunrise by this,' said the Prior.

'After nine of the clock,' said Gil. 'So there was light enough to see by.'

'Our subprior,' resumed the Prior, inclining his head in agreement to this statement, 'setting his hand to the inner door, found it warm to the touch, but locked against him. He knocked and called to the resident many times, but on receiving no answer ordered that door broken down as well.' He paused, considered his fingertips again, then looked at Gil from within the shadow of his hood. 'You must understand that the inner chamber has no window. It once had one, that looked out onto the back gardens of the houses across the path that runs by the wall, as do the windows of the other houses, but the corrodian himself asked some years ago that it be filled in with stones and mortar.'

'Do we know why?' Gil asked. Alys glanced at him, then back at Boyd, waiting for the answer.

'He gave a reason which we felt to be spurious,' said the Prior remotely, 'but since he paid for the work to be done, the community allowed it.'

'So the inner chamber was in darkness,' Gil said.

'That is correct. By this time I had been summoned, and can speak for what happened when the inner door was broken open.' David Boyd paused again, and at length said reluctantly, 'In common with all present, I saw smoke emerge from the opening.'

'Smoke,' Gil repeated.

'How much smoke, Father?' asked Alys in Scots. Boyd looked at her, startled. 'Was the whole chamber full of smoke, or was it some wee thing burning?'

'No a great amount,' he answered in the same language, studying her intently. 'You understand Latin, daughter?'

'She reads it well,' said Gil.

Alys blushed and nodded, but persisted, 'Only smoke, Father? No flames? No smell of brimstone?'

'None,' he agreed with care. 'No evil smells at all, no stink of brimstone or aught else. Only . . .' He hesitated, shaking his head. 'I couldny detect it, but Brother William our subprior says there was a strange smell, kinna sweet, like nothing he had smelled before.'

'Pleasant?' asked the Bishop doubtfully. His little dog growled at Socrates, and Maister Gregor bleated faintly in protest at one or the other. The Bishop delved in the fur-lined sleeve of his great velvet gown and produced a titbit which he fed to the spaniel. Socrates ignored all this with dignity.

'Neither pleasant nor unpleasant, so he says,' said the Prior.

'And what did you find in the chamber?' Gil prompted.

The Prior shook his head again. 'There wasny that much furniture. A bed, a kist, a great chair, two stools. The bed was as it was made up by one o the lay servants the previous morn, hadny been slept in. The kist stood open as if he'd been looking in it; one of the stools had fallen over. But the chair—' He crossed himself, and went on resolutely, 'The chair was burned almost to ashes. It was a wee while afore we saw it was there; indeed, it was only when Brother Dickon recognised one o the arms we realised what the ashes were.'

'And the man Pollock was vanished away,' said Bishop Brown.

'Although the outer door was barred,' said Alys.

'I think there's a chimney,' said Gil. 'A fireplace, a hearth? Is the roof harmed at all? Thatch scorched, slates cracked?'

'The roof's tiled, and it's taken no hurt, though the tiles are blackened,' said the Prior. 'There's a wee hearth, but the chimney was blocked at the same time as the window, on the same docket.' He looked at Gil, and reverted to Latin. 'The community is much disturbed by

10

these events. I should be very glad to know the truth of the matter, in order to negate the rumours which abound in the neighbourhood.'

'And these are?' Gil enquired. 'Is it more than simply the tale of the Devil carrying the man away? Do other matters trouble you?'

The Prior bent his head, examining his fingertips.

'Folk must be looking for reasons why it might happen,' Alys said in Scots, 'what might draw the Devil to the house, and if they find none they'll make them up.'

He looked up at her, relief in his face for a moment at her understanding.

'Indeed,' he said. 'And little to the credit of the community.'

Gil was silent, considering this.

'I wish,' reiterated Father David, 'to know the truth of the matter. However unpalatable it may be, the truth is more nourishing than the poison of rumour or the sweets of wishful thinking, and *Truth* is, after all, the watchword of our Order. Moreover, if it was indeed the work of the Devil, exorcism will be required.'

'It should ha been done long since,' said Bishop Brown again.

'I'll want to see the lodging where this happened,' Gil said, with resignation. Across the small chamber Alys gathered her skirts together as if to rise. 'Though I suppose there's little enough to be seen now after, what, ten days?'

The two senior churchmen looked at one another.

'It has been sealed,' said the Prior. There was a pause, and then he continued delicately, 'As soon as it was perceived that something strange had occurred, and that it would be better investigated by someone from outside our house, we determined that all should be left as it had been found. Brother Dickon became quite emphatic on the matter, in fact, so Chapter ordered him to nail up the house. It is easily unsealed.'

'That will be a help,' said Gil. He remembered Brother Dickon, the senior lay brother of the house, who had been sergeant-at-arms to the late King James Third, and could well imagine him becoming emphatic. But why should it be *someone from outside the house* who investigated, he wondered. 'And I'll want to question everyone who witnessed the place being opened, and probably the rest of the community forbye.'

'I will give orders at Chapter tomorrow that all should cooperate with you,' said Boyd.

'And the man and woman in the house outside the walls and all, I suppose,' said Maister Gregor. 'They've all sorts to tell you, I'd ha thought.'

'The man and woman?' Gil repeated. 'Who are these?'

'They witnessed the Devil leaving the house,' said Bishop Brown in Latin. Maister Gregor nodded in assent, crossing himself assiduously. 'The woman is not reliable. She hears voices,' he said fastidiously, 'but her tale is borne out. Sir Silvester Rattray, the former Ambassador to England, a knight of my diocese and a supporter of Dunkeld Cathedral, in general a man of sense and not given to fancies, was lodging with his acquaintance Mistress Buttergask. Chancing to look out in the night, he clearly saw the Devil rise up above the house and fly away. And so did the woman. She has not hesitated to describe this vision to her acquaintance.'

'I can see she wouldny,' said Alys in Scots. 'Nor would it lose in the telling, I suppose.'

'Aye,' said the Prior. His voice was without expression, but his lip curled.

'I had best see the house now,' said Gil. He caught Alys's eye across the chamber; she nodded agreement and rose. The Bishop set his dog on the floor, where it

12

began yapping at Socrates again, and Prior Boyd rang a little bell on his desk.

'Brother George,' he said over the dog's noise to the young friar who answered it, 'show Maister Cunningham the corrodian's house, and send to Brother Dickon to open it up for him.'

'I'll just come along and all,' said Bishop Brown. 'Rob, you can mind Jerome till I get a look at this.'

'Will you not take us yourself, Father?' Alys asked in careful Latin. 'It would be good to have your witness also.'

The young friar looked startled; after a moment the Prior rose, saying, 'Very well. I can spare a few moments afore the afternoon lecture.'

'And the more of us there is the better,' said Maister Gregor anxiously, 'in case he comes back again.'

'In case who comes back?' asked the Bishop in wary tones.

'Why, Auld Nick! He could be waiting in there for—'

'Rob, he has more to do than hide in a shuttered house,' said his master. 'Whispering daft ideas in your ears, for one thing.' He swooped on his dog and thrust it into his secretary's arms. 'Bide here and mind Jerome.'

Bundled in their various plaids, the rest of the party emerged into the cloister, Socrates at Gil's knee. Rather than cross the wintry garden in the icy drizzle, they made their way round the walkway under the severe vaulting, past Chapter House and refectory, where the smell of stockfish cooking for the next meal floated out, past the high decorative windows of the guest hall, and through a narrow slype between guest hall and library.

'How big is your library, sir?' Gil asked.

'Oh, it's a good size,' said the Bishop, before the Prior could answer. 'Near a hundred books, many o them new print, besides the study copies o Peter o Spain and Peter Lombard. I borrow from it mysel, by David's grace.'

They emerged into the courtyard which served the guest lodgings. To their left was the guest hall, in which Gil hoped their servants were unpacking and making what comfort was possible in the big, chill building. Across the yard, facing them, was the elaborately worked facade of the royal lodgings, and on the right a row of doors and windows proclaimed a set of four small individual domiciles, each with a fenced plot before the door.

'Have you other residents?' Gil asked. 'Other permanent guests?'

'None at present,' said Father Prior. 'The other houses are used only at the pilgrimage season, nearer to St John's Tide. The gardens come in handy,' he added in Scots.

'The most o them stop no more than a night or two,' said the Bishop, 'for they're on their way through from Dunkeld and on to St Andrews. There's little in Perth to draw them.'

The nearest house was boarded up, with splashes of red sealing-wax here and there over the nails, and a well-executed image of the Virgin and Child chalked on the window-shutters. Its trampled little garden held a bench, a stone shelter stacked with kindling with a closed coalhouse beside it, and a rose tree, bare and spiky in the winter air. As they entered through a gate of palings, young Brother George came round the end of the royal lodgings, together with two stalwart lay brothers, one of them hefting a crowbar, the other carrying two copper lanterns. They bowed their heads to the company, but their backs were very straight.

'Dickon,' said the Prior. 'Here is Maister Cunningham and madam his wife. You'll gie him every assist in your power, I trust.'

'I will, Faither,' said the older brother. He was a wiry grizzled man with a scar across one eye, his bushy beard striped like a badger's head. 'Sooner we get to the roots

14

o this, the better all round, I'd say.' He nodded to Gil, raising his hand in something like a salute, gave Alys a considering look, and waved his underling forward. 'Brother Dod, shift they planks, will you?'

Brother Dod crossed himself, licked his lips, and applied the crowbar. Two or three mighty heaves dislodged the planks.

'You told us the door was barred, sir,' Gil said. 'Were the shutters barred and all?'

'Dickon?'

'Aye, Faither, they was barred,' confirmed Brother Dickon, looking up from the lanterns. 'He'd sealed hissel in well, which was no surprising considering the weather. It was the midst o that cold snap we had,' he elaborated to Gil as he closed the little door on the second lantern. 'Freezing hard it was.'

'It's open, er, brother,' reported Brother Dod. Brother George eased himself to the back of the group; the Bishop craned forward, clutching his episcopal cross for protection, but before Gil could speak, a small bell began to toll somewhere in the priory, with rapid light strokes. The Prior looked at the sky.

'Is it that hour already? Sirs, madam, I'll leave you. I've a lecture to deliver. Brother Thomas's words on the Lombard, honey to the soul, wasted on the— Well, I'll get a word wi you later, Gilbert. Brother George, come wi me.' He offered a general blessing and strode off, the young friar following him.

As the paling gate clacked shut behind them, Gil replaced his hat and said politely to the Bishop, 'I'd be glad of a moment to look about me afore we all crowd into the place, sir. Brother Dickon, I think you were among the first through the door? Can you show me how it all lay?' He gestured to Socrates, ordering him to stay with Alys; the dog sat down beside her, but point-edly turned his head away.

15

'Aye, well,' said Brother Dickon, 'there was little enough to see here in the outer chamber.' He stepped over the threshold, lighting Gil into the little house. 'All in order, as he'd left it when he retired, just the way you see it now.' He held both lanterns high, then moved to open the shutters. The grey daylight made little difference. 'There was a smell o smoke and burning, and Brother William our subprior found the inner door yonder was warm to the touch. We'd to smash the lock, as you see, maister, and then—'

'A moment,' said Gil. He stood still, looking about him. The outer chamber was adequately furnished, with a cushioned settle, two stools, a small table, a cold brazier. The walls were panelled with good Norway pine, the ceiling was of the same wood, and a small crucifix and several painted woodcuts of various martyrdoms hung next to the settle. Behind the door and on either side of the window were hangings cut down from a much larger tapestry. Gil moved to the window and sniffed at the woollen folds. They were musty, and rather damp, as could be expected when the house had not been heated for days, but the predominant scent was of smoke. He sniffed again, registering – was it woodsmoke? And incense? There was something else, something sweetish and unfamiliar, as Prior David had reported.

'Aye,' said Brother Dickon again. He gestured at the inner door. 'Will you see the worst o't, maister?'

The door swung in at his touch. Within was darkness, and a stronger smell of smoke and that strange sweetish smell, overlaid by incense. Gil took one of the lanterns from the lay brother and moved into the shadows, peering about him. As his eyes adjusted, the box bed emerged from the dimness, curtained in what looked like more of the same tapestry; beyond at its foot was a substantial kist, a stool beside it. Another stool lay overturned beside the dark hollow of the little hearth, and next to

16

that was the pile of ashes which must be the remnants of the great chair.

'And this is what you saw when you broke the door open?' he asked.

'This is what we saw. It's no been touched, maister. Well,' qualified Brother Dickon, 'it's been well smoked and sprinkled. Incense and holy water, to mak siccar. Forbye the kist was standing open, like as if he'd been searching in it for something, I closed it down mysel for fear o mice or worse.'

'I take it you checked behind the bed.'

'I looked there mysel. And fetched under it wi the crowbar and all. He was nowhere to be found in this chamber or the other, maister.'

'There was a great crowd at the door, I think?'

'There was.' The lay brother paused for a moment, reckoning. 'Ten or a dozen o us, by the time we got entry, and a course no all those cam in, several was still out in the yard. So he never hid hissel in the outer chamber and slipped out at our backs.'

'Nor went up that chimney.'

'It's still blocked. A slate across it, well mortared in place; I had Dod get a good look by daylight. Right neatly done. It's blocked this flue but no the one from the front chamber. There's a wee crack o light visible, but nothing like the full width o the flue. Forbye the man Pollock would never ha got up a chimney, the way he was.' Gil made an enquiring noise, still gazing round him, taking in the detail of the scene. Dickon asked: 'Did, er, did Father Prior never gie you a description?'

'No yet.'

'Ah.' Dickon lowered his voice. 'He'd be my height, I suppose, and a wee thing broader in the shoulders, but long since gone to fat. Twice my weight, I'd guess, and a course it had went for his knees and his hips, and his legs was swoled like tree trunks. He wouldny use a stick, which would ha helped him, so he gaed about rolling like a drunken sailor, and groaning the whole time, complaining o the pain. Made him right birky, so it did, though there's one or two said he'd aye been like that, a sour kind o man.' He bent his head. 'And here I'll ha to confess this at Chapter o Faults, for it's no charity to speak o the man so.'

'Have you seen enough, Gilbert?' asked the Bishop from the outer chamber. 'I'd best get back to my diocese, seeing Prior David's caught up wi his lecture, but—' His voice tailed off as he peered over Brother Dickon's shoulder into the dark space. 'Christ and His saints preserve us all,' he said after a moment, crossing himself. 'Is that the man's great chair, indeed? That heap of ashes? And yet the bed-curtains areny harmed? And truly no smell of brimstone or – or –'

'Aye,' said Brother Dickon baldly. 'Aye, it is, my lord,' he added with more circumspection. 'There's a wee bit carving off the arm there, where it hasny quite burned up. Here, watch yoursel, maister,' he added as Gil stepped forward incautiously. 'The boards is right waxy, all round about – I've no notion where it's come fro'. Watch and no slip.'

'I can tell that,' Gil said rather grimly, regaining his balance. 'We need lights in here, and plenty o them. What I can see makes no sense.'

'Indeed no,' said Bishop Brown. 'No sense at all. Why would the man set light to his chair, and vanish away like this, and leave the stool couped ower like that? And did you say the kist stood open, Dickon? And how would the chair burn to ashes and yet nothing else in the chamber catch light?'

Gil held the lantern high.

'The ceiling's marked above it,' he said. 'The flames have gone straight upwards, by the look o't, and not spread out at all.'

'The fire has been fierce,' said Alys behind the Bishop. He looked over his shoulder, and turned, putting a hand to her elbow.

'No, no, lassie, come away. It's no fit – no need for you to trouble yoursel.'

'Let her by, sir,' said Gil. He could hear the dog snuffling in the outer room. 'Her eye's acute, she might see things I'd miss.'

'I can see nothing,' she said decidedly, 'till we have more light. Why did the man have the window blocked, I wonder. It's like a storeroom in here. And Socrates thinks there are rats in the place.'

'I'd no be surprised. The window was afore my time,' said Brother Dickon, 'but I heard he was afeared o housebreakers fro outwith the Priory. Dod,' he called.

'Aye, Ser— Brother Dickon?' answered his henchman from the outer door.

'Away and fetch a couple o branches o candles. Six or eight lights, I'd say.'

The Bishop, nodding approval of this, stepped carefully into the inner chamber, holding his great velvet gown up about his knees.

'Well,' he declared, after a long look about him into the shadows, 'I canny see aught that tells us what happened in here, nor what's come to the man. I hope you can learn more, Gilbert, for I ken well you've a knack for it; that's how Blacader made you his quaestor. But I'll away now and be about my own duties. I'll hold you in my prayers, the both o you, but I'm no so certain it's right to keep your wife at your side, maister. I fear you may lead her into spiritual danger,' he added in Latin.

'We can keep each other safe from that,' said Gil in Scots. 'I wouldny dream o leading her anywhere,' he added. 'She's her own mistress.'

19

The Bishop grunted, gathered his gown tighter about him, delivered a blessing with his free hand and swept out, checking briefly in the house doorway as he encountered Brother Dod with his arms full of ironwork and wax.

Even with eight candles alight, the small space was gloomy and full of leaping shadows. Moving cautiously on the greasy floorboards, Gil peered behind the box bed, bent to look under it, craned to see on top.

'Tell me how the man lived,' he said. 'Lives. We have no proof of his death yet.'

'How he lives?' Brother Dickon, watching his movements, cocked his head to think about this.

'Does he take any part in the life of the community?' Alys asked. She was quartering the other portion of the chamber, touching the panelled walls fastidiously, peering into the empty hearth. Socrates was still in the outer room, blowing hard into a corner, the hackles standing up on his narrow back.

'Too much,' said Brother Dod.

'Dod,' said his senior warningly.

'Aye, but he did, Ser— brother. He was aye into things, peching about like a bellows, asking what he'd no right to ken. It's been fine and peaceful wi'out him.'

'Dod!'

'His food was sent across here,' Alys prompted. 'He never ate wi the rest of you?'

'No him,' said Brother Dickon unguardedly. 'No, he reckoned his corrody paid for a richer diet than the community gets, so he would have that served to him, meat and fish and all sorts we're no allowed, even on fast days. The amount of meat he ate in a day would ha fed my troop a week on campaign, I can tell you. And since the guest hall was empty this time o year it was carried to his lodging. It was the lad fetching his morning meat that found the place barred, ye ken, mistress.'

20

'So Prior Boyd said,' Gil commented. He set the light on the stool by the kist, lifted the lid, which creaked, and began to turn over the topmost layer of the goods it held. A remarkably good cloak, a bundle of parchments, more garments; several sets of tablets in their brocade or leather bags. Why did the man need so many tablets, he wondered. 'And after he'd broken his fast, what did he do?'

'As Dod says,' said Dickon reluctantly. 'He'd gae about the place, watching all what went on, asking ower many questions. Times he'd bring a stool out and sit afore his door in the sun, just keeping an eye. No this time o year, a course,' he qualified.

'*Ans que vent ni gel ni plueva*,' said Gil absently.

Brother Dickon looked closely at him, then said, 'Hah! Aye, wind and hail and rain aplenty here.'

'And if he seen aught that didny conform,' said Brother Dod in resentful tones, 'it'd be wi Father Prior by Compline, or else he'd be at your elbow, speaking o what he'd remarked, wondering what it was worth no to report it.'

'Is that so?' Gil turned to look at the two lay brothers: Dickon, against the light, rigid with disapproval, and beyond him the younger man swelling with remembered indignation. 'But what could he extort that way in a house o religion? You hold all your goods in common. There's no way to get coin or valuables to him in return.'

'Is that what happened to my good wax candles?' Brother Dickon asked.

'Might be,' muttered Dod.

'Privileges,' said Alys. 'Did – does the man go into the town?'

'No a lot,' said Dod in faint relief at the change of subject.

'He's no been fit for the walk in a year or two,' said Dickon. 'He's had one or two callers, mind, folk that comes to visit him regular.'

'I'll need their names,' said Gil. He tilted a set of tablets to the light. 'Unless they're in here.'

'Billy Pullar,' said Dickon thoughtfully, 'was one o them, and Jaikie Wilson I mind. Journeymen, the both o them, to different craftsmen o the town.'

'And Andrew Rattray?'

Both lay brothers looked sharply at him.

'He's no a townsman,' said Dickon. 'He's one o ours. A novice, poor lad.'

'Poor lad?' Gil queried. 'Why d'you say that?'

'He's in the jail,' said Dod. Socrates slipped past him, his claws clicking on the greasy boards, and began sniffing about the chamber.

'He's in confinement,' corrected Dickon. 'Ever since—' He stopped.

'Ever since what?' Gil asked.

'Ever since he confessed,' said Dod. 'Faither Prior said he was best shut away, even if he didny do it.'

'Confessed to what?' Gil persevered. Socrates was pawing at something among the legs of the fallen stool, snuffling hard at whatever he had found. Gil snapped his fingers at the dog, but was ignored.

'Confessed,' said Dickon heavily, 'at Chapter o Faults, to slaying our corrodian. Only since he couldny say clear how he did it or where the man's corp might be, Faither Prior isny convinced, but like Dod says, he reckoned he's best confined away fro his brothers.'

'He never mentioned—' Gil began.

'Gil! Look what the dog has!' said Alys in panicky French. Two strides took him to her side. She had brought her branch of candles over to light Socrates' investigation, and now was pointing and staring wide-eyed. 'A shoe! A shoe, with— with—'

'Oh, God,' said Gil, as the dog delicately mouthed his prize and came to offer it to him, his stringy tail waving

22

proudly. 'With a foot in it. And the,' he swallowed, 'the bone all burned.'

'A *foot*?' said Dod in disbelief. 'How can it be a foot? Is it his? Where's the rest o him?'

'That's what I'd like to ken,' Gil said. Alys freed herself from his clasp with a precarious smile, and he looked at her closely, then bent to receive the dog's find. It was, as she had said, a shoe, a well-worn sturdy item of local make, spread and twisted to accommodate the swollen foot which still inhabited it. In the light of the candles Alys still held, the flesh of the ankle showed black, crisp and shrivelled, and a spur of calcined bone stood out like a handle.

'Good dog,' Alys said shakily. 'Clever dog.' Socrates gave her a considering glance, then grinned, his teeth white in the flickering light.

'It's his shoe, all right,' said Dickon. 'Seen 'em often enough. But where's the rest o him? If he's been carried away wi the Deil right enough, why leave his foot ahint?'

'I think this heap of ashes must be him,' said Gil. Then: 'Bear up, sweetheart. Do you want to go outside? Aye, he's here, I'm afraid.'

The two lay brothers crossed themselves simultaneously, staring. Alys stepped back, away from the grey tumble of cinders, and reached for her beads.

'Christ on a handcart,' said Brother Dickon reverently.

'But what,' Dod swallowed, 'here, I've seen folk that was burned to death. It's no, it's no a bonnie sight, but there's a corp to be seen, no a heap o— a heap o ash like a bonfire. How come he's burned to a cinder and the house still standing round him?'

'That,' said Gil grimly, 'is what I mean to find out.'

# Chapter Two

'But how could it happen, mem?' demanded Jennet.

All the servants were agog, hanging on every word of the narrative which their master and mistress provided over the stewed kale and stockfish in pepper sauce.

The meal had appeared almost as soon as they emerged from the corrodian's lodging, but that was some time after their unpleasant discovery. Brother Dickon, recovering his self-assurance, had sent his junior for 'a wee brush, a couple shovels, a fair linen cloth out the sacristy and a good stout box'. When Brother Dod returned, the two lay brothers had set about lifting the heap of crumbling, flaking fragments with care, meantime muttering the *Ave Maria* interspersed with curt instructions. Gil looked anxiously at Alys, but she had retired to the doorway where the dog was leaning heavily against her knee, so he hunkered down to join the two men at their charitable task. It was he who found the several lumps of metal buried in the pile, small twisted things which glinted brassily when he rubbed the black deposit off, and a larger knot of dark iron.

'Well, well,' said Brother Dickon, cautiously sitting back on his heels, peering over his shoulder at the objects. 'Belt-findings, likely. And could yon be the missing key, d'ye think, maister?'

'I'd forgotten about that.' Gil turned the misshapen object. 'It's the right weight, certainly. But what a heat the fire must ha been, to melt iron like that.'

'Aye.' Dickon tipped another shovel-full of fragments into the box, and reached across the patch of ashes to lift another small object. 'How about this? A finger, maybe?'

Gil drew the candles closer.

'Aye,' he agreed, 'or from the other foot. Is there more of it?'

'Canny see any.' Dickon set the fine bone in the box beside the shoe with its gruesome content, and turned back to coax more crumbling scraps from the same area onto the shovel. 'No, I see no more, though there's a few teeth here. Brother Dod, easy wi that brush, I've no wish to swally Leonard Pollock's mortal remains.'

'Will we need to tell Faither Prior?' Dod wondered. 'And ring the passing-bell?'

'A course we need to tell him, daftheid!' said Dickon. 'The bell can wait, mind you, it's waited long enough a'ready, no to mention the proper prayers. But what exercises my mind,' he said to Gil, 'is where this is to lie till we get word to the Prior.' Gil raised his eyebrows. 'See, if it was the Deil indeed struck the man wi fire, then it's hardly fit for him to lie in the kirk. Faither Prior's the one to decide on that.'

'You could leave him here meantime,' said Alys, from the doorway. 'There are lights already, after all. Maybe the outer chamber would be better.'

'A good thought, mistress. And we'll ha two o the lads to watch,' said Brother Dickon, 'for either way prayers'll no hurt the matter. They can get their bite o supper after.'

'But also, brother,' she went on, 'if there's to be any prayers said, you need to get a mat or the like, to protect the friars' habits when they kneel. This greasy floor . . .'

'Aye,' said Dickon thoughtfully, looking down at his own knees. 'I'll tell you, mistress, my boots hasny

26

squeaked since the day we entered this lodging. Swimming in lard, it was.'

'Was it set cold?' she asked, rubbing her toe on the broad boards nearest her. 'Or did it still run?'

'Atwixt and atween. It's soaked well in by now.'

By the time they had contained the inseparable ashes of Leonard Pollock and his great chair, and set the box decently on a stool with the linen cloth to cover it, the little bell had begun ringing again and the members of the community were gathering from study and from daily tasks to wash hands before the evening collation, making their way half-seen in the twilight in their white habits and black cloaks, with sidelong glances at the fateful lodging. The meal, Gil knew, would be followed directly by Compline, which was begun in the refectory and ended in the priory church. He also knew that little or nothing was permitted to interrupt Compline. Informing Father Prior, he reckoned, would have to wait until afterwards.

The guests were not expected to attend the service, it seemed. A lay servant had carried in the dishes and helped to set up the table by the fire in one of the smaller chambers, promising to return later for the crocks. He was accompanied by the kitchen cat, a large black animal with a white bib and paws, who leaped onto a window-sill to inspect them all from a safe distance, established that Socrates knew how to be polite to cats, then sauntered impudently off when Gil called the dog to heel.

The accommodation which they had been allowed was more comfortable than Gil had expected, now that their servants, who numbered three house-servants and two grooms borrowed from Gil's uncle Canon Cunningham for the journey, had spent some time rearranging the sparse furniture and kindling the fire. Gil had still not worked out how they would arrange themselves for sleep; Jennet could hardly lie in the same chamber as the men. Perhaps Alys had the answer, he decided.

'How was the whole wee house no burned down?' Jennet went on now, mopping pepper sauce from her platter with a piece of hard bread. 'It makes no sense, unless it truly was the Deil carried him off.'

'Was it no one of the novices set fire to him?' asked Nory, Gil's body-servant. He was a skinny fellow in his forties, very neat in the suit of clothes he had had as a New Year's gift; he had been in Gil's service for four months or so and promised well. 'The lad 'at brought our dinner was saying they've one of the novices locked away, for that he confessed to killing the man. No that it's any great loss, he says,' he added primly. 'Seems he wasny well liked.'

'Aye, but the lodging was locked tight against thieves,' said Tam, one of Canon Cunningham's grooms. 'So how did he get in to set fire to the man?'

'And how will the poor fellow be rising from his grave at the Last Day, all burned to ashes as he is?' wondered the Ersche gallowglass.

'With God all things are possible, Euan,' said Alys.

'Aye, mistress,' agreed Euan, his long narrow face serious, 'but God will be having a lot to see to on that day. Maybe He'll no be bothered wi one man's troubles.'

'Aye, but if it was the Deil struck him down,' said the other groom, a wiry man called Dandy, 'then likely he's in the Bad Place a'ready and no need of judgement or rising up.'

Euan considered this doubtfully, and Gil broke off another piece of bread and dipped it in the sauce-dish.

'Did the fellow say aught else about the dead man, Nory?' he asked.

'Why, only that. He'd ha said more, I think,' Nory admitted, 'but their cook called him fro the kitchens, and he'd to go.'

28

'See what you can get from him later,' Gil suggested. 'I can learn little enough about Pollock from the friars. I think they're reluctant to speak ill o the dead, and there seems to be little good to say o him.'

'Will I be talking to the man and all?' said Euan hopefully.

'No, I've another task for you, though it will have to wait for the morning now.' Gil cast his mind back to the last time he had been in this guest hall. Out in the great chamber, its high ceiling now filled with shadows, then bright with summer sunlight, the elderly Infirmarer had tended to Tam and another groom while his assistant knelt over a dying man. 'The sub-infirmarer's an Ersche speaker, by what I recall. I want you to get a word wi him and any other Erschemen there might be about the convent, learn what you can about the dead man and about what's going on.'

'Och, yes,' said Euan with enthusiasm. 'I can be doing that. Never fear, Maister Gil, I'll get anything there is to be kent from them.'

'So what's to do the night?' asked Jennet. 'Is there tasks for us, or do we sit about the fire and tell pilgrim tales, the way my auntie said they did when she went to St Andrews?'

'The pilgrim tales, I think,' said Gil, 'but don't stay up too late. I'll try and get a word wi the Prior once he comes from Compline, unless he goes straight to his rest. They'll be up again after midnight to sing Matins and Lauds, after all.'

'Where does he sleep?' Alys asked. 'There was hardly room in that study, and I saw no door to another chamber. Does he have his own lodging?'

'He'll sleep in the dorter wi the rest,' Gil said, recalling his one sight of a Dominican's cell. 'It's a great long chamber, wi a row of beds at one end for the novices and the younger brethren, and the other end partitioned into spaces just big enough for a bed, two stools and a table, so the older men have a place to study. A Dominican Prior keeps no great state, even in a house like this.'

'Well, if you do get a word wi him, maister,' said Nory, 'I'll wager he'll no sleep much after he hears you. It's a troubling tale.'

Prior Boyd's reaction was much the same, though his reasons were a little different.

'You are certain the body was entirely consumed to ashes?' he said in his elegant Latin, and answered himself. 'Indeed, you would not say so if it were otherwise. This gives the matter quite another complexion.' He rose and took a jerky turn about his study. 'By what means could a fire be set inside a locked house – indeed, a locked chamber within a locked house – and such a fire, at that, a fire which consumed only the man's body and not the furnishings and hangings of the chamber, let alone the other timbers of the house. By what means, Gilbert?'

'I don't know, sir.'

'Nor I. But I fear the answer, truly.' Another turn about the room. 'I think we have to face it, nevertheless. Either it was the Devil carried the man's soul away, setting fire to his body, or it was,' he swallowed, 'witchcraft. And such witchcraft as speaks a practised witch, long sunk in evil.'

'Or it happened by some mortal means,' said Gil. 'As I implied before, I should prefer to consider either of these answers only if I can prove no other method.'

His kinsman studied him closely in the candlelight, and seemed to relax slightly.

'Aye. That is a better approach. How will you set about your inquiry?'

'I need to gather information, by questioning many people.' Gil ticked off the list on his fingers. 'The other

30

persons present when the lodging was opened. Those members of the community who had dealings with Pollock. A list of all the brethren would be valuable for that. The knight of Perth who saw something that night. The man you have confined because he confessed to the deed.' He paused, watching the Prior. His kinsman bent his head so that the shadow of his cowl hid his face.

'Aye, you must. I see that.'

'And yourself, sir.' Another pause. 'Perhaps we could begin,' he pursued carefully, 'by discussing Pollock himself. How long had he been lodged here? Was he a valued guest? Did he take a part in the life of the community?'

'All our guests are valued,' Boyd reproved. Gil waited. The Prior seated himself, and said at length, 'His corrody originated from the late King – from James Third. I suppose it was erected in '82 or thereby, to a good value.'

'Of which I believe he calculated every penny that was spent on him,' Gil said.

'Every farthing,' the Prior corrected, without expression. 'The man took some part in our daily life, by walking about and talking to the servants at their work, by sitting in his small garden in fine weather, by hearing Mass daily and also some of the Office, but . . .' He considered his next words and finally said, 'I did not feel that he immersed himself in our spiritual observance as a man should do at the end of his life.'

'Was he liked by the community?' Gil asked. 'Did the servants like him?'

'I suggest you ask them.'

'Thank you, sir, I will do that. Now, the novice who is confined.' His kinsman looked directly at him, and then away. What is going on here, Gil wondered. 'I understand he confessed at Chapter of Faults. When was that?'

'Andrew Rattray.' The Prior studied his folded hands. 'A very promising novice, indeed one of the most

31

promising in many years.' He sighed. 'On the day after the discovery, when I had already consulted with Bishop Brown and he had written to Archbishop Blacader, we held a Chapter of Faults as is our custom. I had noticed, indeed, that Brother Andrew was in some distress at my lecture the previous afternoon, but in my abstraction did not question him. Therefore it was a shock to me as well as to the rest of our brothers when he knelt before us and asked our forgiveness for causing the vanishing away of our corrodian.'

'In so many words?'

'In so many words. His Latin is excellent. However, when I questioned him, first in Chapter and later in private, he could give me no reasoned narrative of how he had done this deed, but only seemed convinced he was instrumental. I judged it best to confine him for prayer and reflection, to see if he might come to some sensible conclusion, but none has so far emerged, though he remains persuaded of his guilt. I have prayed with him daily myself.' The Prior contemplated his hands a little longer. 'I should find it very hard to believe the young man capable of witchcraft,' he said at last.

There was a bell ringing, urgently, clanging and clashing, and the dog was barking. He had slept in his shirt. Why had he slept in his shirt? Gil struggled up out of sleep into an unfamiliar place, Alys beside him up on her elbow, Jennet across the room exclaiming in fright. Through the dog's noise he could hear shouting, a word which spurred him into action.

'Fire,' he said, flinging back the clothes, groping for his outer garments. 'There's fire in the convent. I must go and help.'

'Mercy on us, we'll be burned in our beds!' said Jennet. Alys straightened the bedclothes and swung her legs out of bed, feeling for the tinder box on the stool

32

beside her. When she had a light she went to the chamber door and peered out.

'There is nothing to see on this side of the building,' she reported. 'The fire is in the convent itself, maybe? Socrates, quiet!'

'What is it, mem?' Nory's voice. Gil dragged on the leather jerkin he had ridden in and stepped into his boots.

'Fire somewhere in the convent,' he called, and bent to buckle the straps. 'You men rouse yourselves, we can lend a hand.'

Crossing the outer chamber he ordered the dog to stay and unbarred the guest-hall door. The night was cloudy, with only a few stars showing, but there was a red glow rising from behind the hall, over in the priory. The bell was still ringing, and as he emerged into the raw cold the lay brothers appeared, trotting in a tight disciplined group, rakes and hay-forks at the port and Brother Dickon recognisable at their head in the eerie light.

'Aye, maister,' he called across the courtyard, 'we'll likely be glad o yir help.'

Gil let the door slam behind him and followed, through the narrow passage by the library into the main cloister. A towering column of red-lit smoke full of sparks was visible from here, not rising from this range of buildings but beyond.

'The infirmary!' said one of the lay brothers. 'Ser — Brother Dickon, it's the infirmary!'

'Aye, lad,' said his superior. 'I've een in my heid.'

In the small courtyard by the infirmary building there was panic and disorder. Prior Boyd and another elderly man were planted stock-still in the middle of the courtyard, the one praying aloud, the other lamenting incoherently. About them friars ran to and fro shouting, their black and white lit wildly by the leaping flames which issued from the windows of the infirmary. The fire burned with a greedy sound, a snapping and crackling and roaring, and a heat which struck the face and hands. Someone was hauling on the handle of the draw-well, making the wooden mechanism squeal, while someone else hastened with a bucket.

Brother Dickon halted his troop at the entrance to the courtyard and assessed the situation.

'Dod, Archie, Tammas, get across and help them deal wi the roof,' he said decisively. 'Jamesie, Eck, go and get a bucket chain together. Maister, will you come wi me? I need to learn if that laddie got out.'

'My thought and all,' said Gil rather grimly.

'Rattray?' said Prior Boyd when Brother Dickon grasped his sleeve. 'Why, no, I— Our Lady protect him! James? Did Andrew get out?'

'Andrew?' His elderly companion turned a horrified face to the flames. 'Oh, David! Oh, Our Lady forgive me! I never – I never thought—'

'Where is he lodged?' Gil demanded.

'Along at the end,' said the elderly friar, wringing his hands. 'By the last window, in a wee cell by himself. Maybe he heard me shouting,' he said hopefully. 'Maybe he heard me shout "Fire!" or the bell or that.'

Gil did not pause to answer him, but plunged towards the burning building. It was a timber-framed structure of three bays, the red roof-tiles now cracking and shattering in the heat, the upper floor beginning to catch. The last window disgorged a furious blaze, flames licking out and upwards like dancing devils.

At his shoulder Brother Dickon bawled, 'We'll never get into that, but he might ha got out the cell. Here, maister!'

He produced a length of rag from under his scapular, and then another, dunked them in a passing bucket of water, handed Gil one. Tying it about his face, Gil followed him into the blaze, with a quick silent prayer to St Giles for protection.

He would have nightmares about it for years, he thought afterwards. The wet cloth helped, but the smoke bit at his eyes, obscured everything, and groping through a strange building amidst flames and roaring heat seemed to take more courage than he had known he possessed. Sparks and flakes of burning wood fell past him, a table in flames appeared before him and collapsed as he moved round it. Strange smells caught his throat, even behind the wet rag, as the infirmarer's stock burned.

He kept as close as he could to Brother Dickon, who suddenly dropped to his knees. Gil knew a surge of alarm, but the older man crawled forward, feeling from side to side, and he realised that the air was clearer near the ground and got down likewise. For what seemed like forever they searched the outer chamber in this way, the flames crackling round them, burning debris falling like snow, but when Brother Dickon opened a door in the far wall a great gout of flame rushed out, with a roar like a lion's. The Dominican rolled over, away from the door, and scrambled to his feet, half crouching.

'Run!' he bellowed, and stumbled back the way they had come. Gil rose, coughing, and followed him, and suddenly a dark shape loomed before them, one of the other lay brothers, grasping an arm of each with strong hard hands, pulling them towards the door.

They lurched choking from the building just as the far end collapsed with a great crash, flames shooting up into the night sky. Someone threw a bucket of water over Gil, which was when he realised that his hair and his hose were smouldering, and someone else held another bucket so that he could drink palmfuls of the water to soothe his throat.

'Did you find him? Did you find him?' It was the elderly Infirmarer, his hands shaking in the firelight.

'No, Faither,' said Brother Dickon hoarsely by his side. 'We went as far's we dared, and no sign o him. I doubt he's never got out o his cell.'

'But was he locked in?' Alys smeared more green ointment on Tam's brow. 'Or had he perhaps had a sleeping draught?'

'No to both.' Gil tipped his head back against the upright back of the settle. The two women had lit the fire again and it was warm here in the guest hall; he was already beginning to think of the place as a refuge. At his feet Jennet knelt over a pannikin of wine, swirling it in the firelight to infuse the spices she had added. 'Father James seems to have panicked, and simply run out of the building shouting "Fire!" It's fortunate that someone in the dorter heard him, or it could have spread to the main range.'

'It was burning fiercest at that end the building,' observed Nory. 'Where they said he was lodged, I mean. I doubt maybe it started there. Likely the laddie was owercome by the smoke and never knew what was happening, poor chiel. God send it was quick.' He crossed himself, and Dandy did likewise.

'We'll hope that,' said Tam, and flinched as Alys anointed another burn.

'Or maybe it was the Devil carried him away,' said Euan in portentous tones, 'like the other one.'

'Mercy on us!' Jennet exclaimed. 'There must be something badly amiss wi this place, maister, that the Devil can come and go as he likes! Should we maybe no leave here and lodge wi the Greyfriars?'

'This fire was very different,' said Gil. 'The one which consumed Pollock was confined to one place, almost as if it was in a brazier, and the rest of the house is near

undamaged. This one has destroyed the entire infirmary, like an ordinary house fire, and a fierce one at
that. If you lads hadny been here I think it could have
been worse. Father Prior may be a great scholar and a
famous preacher, but he's no man for quick action.'

'Aye, the Infirmarer was fair lamenting his ointments
and simples,' said Nory. 'He hardly kent which to grieve
for the more, all his way of life gone up in flames or the
young man that was trapped.' His tone was
disapproving.

Gil said, 'It's the shock. It takes folk strangely.'

'If the fire was so different from the other,' said Alys,
pinning a bandage on Tam's arm, 'so ordinary, could it
have been set a purpose?' She looked about her to see if
any burns remained unsalved, then considered Gil,
moving the candles close to the hearth.

'Surely never!' said Euan, shocked, and Dandy
muttered agreement. 'Who would do sic a thing in a
house of holy men?'

'The town's no so happy wi the Blackfriars, by what
we saw,' observed Tam, rolling down his singed sleeve.

'It could ha been,' said Gil grimly, ignoring them.
'Brother Dickon will come for me as soon as there's light
to see, though Christ Himself kens that's none so early at
this time of year. We'll search the wreckage, see if we
can find the missing laddie, see if we can learn aught
else.'

Alys made no comment, but tucked her hand into his
and held it tightly. He caressed the knuckles with his
thumb, and smiled at her.

'This is about ready, mem,' said Jennet, feeling the
side of the pan with a cautious hand. 'Have we beakers,
or that?'

Inspecting his boots and jerkin by daylight, Gil found
they were not so badly damaged as he had feared,

though they stank of smoke like everything else about him. He was buckling on the boots again and contemplating the fact that since he had an established income he could now afford another pair if Nory could not refurbish these for best, when Brother Dickon opened the main door of the guest hall and stepped in, shaking drops of rain from his sleeves.

'Aye, maister,' he said, rather than offering the conventional friars' blessing. 'How d'ye feel the day?'

'Hoarse,' Gil admitted.

'Aye, me and all, and the rest o the house. You should ha heard us croaking at Prime. And Brother Infirmarer canny help us, by reason o the fire itself, and all his simples consumed.'

'My wife has a receipt which might help. The most of what it asks is common kitchen stores, she tells me. She's gone hoping for a word wi the cook, now we've broken our fast.'

'Oh, aye?' Brother Dickon pulled a face. 'Good luck to her, though I'd say if anyone can get round Brother Augustine this morn, madam your wife can. He's no in a charitable state, what wi the broken night, and one o his best knives is missing the day and naeb'dy admitting to having lost it. A good cook, he is, and like all good cooks he's a wee thing.' He paused, considering Brother Augustine. 'Touchy,' he concluded.

'Alys can likely deal wi him.' Gil lifted his plaid. 'How's the ruin the day?'

'A sorry sight.' Brother Dickon turned back towards the door. 'I'd a wee look as soon's it began to lighten,' he went on as they crossed the courtyard, 'and it was still smouldering, but this rain'll likely ha seen to that. I've set my lads,' he ducked into the slype by the library, 'I've set my lads to make a start on the end by the door, where we searched a'ready last night, and you and I'll have a good nose about at the other end o the building, for the laddie never got out – or if he did,' he added grimly, 'he's vanished into thin air. He's no been seen.'

The infirmary was an ugly sight, as Brother Dickon had said. The further end had collapsed completely, the roof-tiles in a blackened layer over fallen timbers, part of a wall standing up like a broken tooth. The end by the door was still standing, though much of the roof had fallen in. Over all the reek of smoke hung, and the drizzle had laid the worst of the ash into a clinging slurry. Brother Dickon's little troop was working hard, habits kilted up, more wet rags bound about their faces to keep the ash out, their sturdy boots and thick leggings smeared with the stuff. Gil's two grooms were with them, and several young Dominicans, presumably novices of the house, their natural high spirits much subdued by the task. They had already amassed a number of stacks of different salvage, unbroken tiles, timbers only partly burned, a couple of pieces of furniture. Gil accepted a wet rag himself and made his way to the far end of the ruined building, assessing the task before them.

'The fire was fiercer this end,' he said. The lay brother grunted agreement. 'It's brought the whole structure down here, and yet the two couple o rafters at the other end are still standing.'

'Have to come down, mind. The whole thing'll need rebuilt.' Brother Dickon dragged a charred beam aside, and kicked at the remains of the wall below it, which crumbled obligingly. 'The laddie was in the end chamber by hissel, by what I can make out, and this should be the one next it.'

'Where would the Infirmarer have been?' Gil asked. Brother Dickon surveyed the scene, measured off a section and then another with his forefingers at arm's length, and finally sketched with decisive gestures a narrow chamber not far from where the door had been.

'About there,' he said. 'He'd be atween the patient and the door, if there was ever anyone kept there the night. Him or Brother Euan. No that Brother James would ha heard if the Last Trump sounded, bless him,' he added. 'He's no so good the day, wasny fit to rise for Terce. I hope he does better. Right, maister. If we can clear the tiles, and they great timbers, we should be able to— Have you ever seen a corp that burned to death?'

'No,' Gil admitted. 'Have you?'

'Aye. No a bonnie sight.' The lay brother bent to a blackened timber, and Gil tossed his plaid over a singed rosemary bush and hurried to take the other end. Fragments of tile slid away as they heaved. 'These tiles is all done, we'll get none fit to use again.'

They progressed sideways with the length of wood between them, and set it down some distance away.

'Tell me more about the man Pollock,' said Gil, rubbing wet ash from his hands, and stepped back into the ruins.

'Him? Why?'

'Because nobody else seems to want to talk about him,' said Gil deliberately, bending to gather broken tiles, 'and I'd say you were a man to gie me a straight answer. Is there aught like a basket we could use to fetch these out of the mess?'

'A basket.' Brother Dickon straightened up with care, stuck two fingers in his mouth and whistled sharply. One of his industrious team looked up, left his task and joined them at the double. 'Brother Jamesie, get to the store, will you, find two-three baskets. Sound ones, mind, that will hold these broken tiles. Should ha thought o that mysel,' he allowed as his henchman trotted off. 'Pollock. Well, it's right hard to say aught about him, maister, seeing we're enjoined no to speak ill o the dead, and him no buried yet either.'

'If he was still alive, what would you ha said?'

The lay brother's grizzled beard split in a grin.

'I'd ha warned you he was a sleekit, spying yadswiver,' he said promptly. 'We tellt you as much yesterday, how he'd go about the place, overhearing all sorts that was none o his mind, writing it down in his wee tablets and casting it up at a man later. He'd a go at me,' he admitted, 'wishing to call me into trouble for some language I used that was no seemly, but I preferred to take it to Chapter o Faults mysel, and so I tellt him. Wasny any great penance,' he added.

'Was he a man given to drink? Could he have been asleep when the fire started?'

'That's one thing he was moderate in,' said Dickon consideringly. 'I'm no certain I ever seen him fou, nor even a wee thing argumentative wi drink. He'd no need o a drink to start an argument,' he added, his tone souring.

'Had he any friend in the convent?' Gil asked. 'There's no other permanent lodger, is there? No other corrodian?'

'No. Faither Prior – no Prior Boyd but the previous one, Prior Blythe that's novice-master now – he put his foot down when there was to ha been another, said we'd enough to do wi one, we'd ha no more. That one went to the Greyfriars, I heard. No, Pollock had no friends in the convent, though he'd spend enough time talking wi one or another o the friars, getting wee favours of them, getting them to run errands for him.'

'Getting the friars to run errands?' Gil repeated.

'Aye.'

Brother Jamesie arrived with an armful of baskets, and a great sheet of tarred canvas folded into a bundle over his shoulder.

'See, we could stack them on this, Brother Dickon,' he said, 'easier to get them all out the road after. Or I suppose we can use them for backfill,' he added.

41

'We'll find a use for them,' agreed his superior. 'Good thinking, lad.'

'And Sandy Raitts is in a right passion, ower there in the cloister,' added Brother Jamesie, grinning. 'Seems the pilgrim lady wants into his library, and he's no for letting her in.'

'What have I tellt ye about gossip, lad?' said Dickon.

'She said she wanted to see the library,' said Gil with misgivings, and Brother Jamesie went red and ducked his head in apology.

'She was being right civil to him,' he assured them. 'He'll maybe no say anything that bad to her. Just he doesny like ladies ower much.'

'Jamesie!' said his superior sharply. 'Get back to work, and less o your prating.'

'Aye, but he doesny,' argued Jamesie. 'That's why he's been minding the library these two year and no out on the road, ken, so he doesny have to speak to ony ladies. How he managed afore he was tonsured— a'richt, I'm going, I'm going!'

'And so I should think! Gossip's a sin,' Brother Dickon reminded him. 'You'll ha to confess that.'

'Aye,' said Jamesie, bitterly. 'And if those better'n me ever confessed their faults likewise, I'd ha less objection.'

'Jamesie.'

At the warning in his superior's voice, Jamesie offered no more argument, but swung away to the section where he had been working. Brother Dickon glared at his back, but returned to his own task in silence.

'Did Pollock have other friends?' Gil asked after a moment. 'I think you mentioned folk who visited him from the town.'

'Aye, a few. They'd come and go freely enough in the outer yard, never tried to get inside the cloister that I noticed. I can let you have their names, likely.'

42

'Had he money of his own? Apart from what was paid for his keep, I mean.'

'Now that I couldny say.' Brother Dickon hoisted his first basket of sherds and made for the tarpaulin. 'But,' he paused before tipping the blackened mass out, 'he never wore the clothes that were provided him. Nor the shoes. Aye well clad he was, warmer than us this weather, and plenty coal and kindling to his wee house, more than my lads ever fetched to him.'

'Did you ever run into him afore?' Gil asked. 'When you were still sergeant-at-arms, I mean. Given you were both members o James Third's household.'

'I did,' replied Brother Dickon baldly. 'I couldny say if he minded me,' he added. 'I'm a wee thing changed since then. The beard makes a difference.'

'He'd hardly have enemies in a house of Religious like this,' Gil went on delicately, slinging broken tiles as he spoke. His companion produced a sardonic grunt. 'But did he have any particular unfriends about the place?'

'Oh, I couldny say,' said Brother Dickon. He shifted another handful of tiles, and paused, staring through the charred timbers below them. Gil paused too, watching him, as Dickon turned, very deliberately, threw the tiles into the waiting basket, and turned back to look closer. Then he crossed himself.

'Is that—?' Gil began.

'Aye, it is, maister. We've found our missing laddie.'

Gil picked his way to join the lay brother. At the far end of the building, the other men gradually stopped, straightened up, watched them. When Gil bent his head and removed his hat the two grooms did likewise, and one by one the whole group left their task, drifted out of the tangle of ash and timber, drew closer. The little group of novices stood shoulder to shoulder, staring in awful fascination.

43

'It's him, then,' said one. 'I hoped he'd— I hoped . . .'

'He'd ha turned up by now if he'd escaped the fire, Sandy,' said another. 'It was aye more likely.' He crossed himself, tears in his eyes.

His neighbour, a tow-headed muscular young man, said quietly, 'I wonder how he didny get out? Or was he maybe right at the heart o the fire? Could it ha started wi him?'

'Don't be daft, Adam,' said someone else roundly.

'He's deid, then,' said one of the lay brothers, possibly Brother Dod.

Brother Dickon gave him a look which should have shrivelled him, crossed himself again and began, *'Subvenite, sancti Dei, occurrite, angeli Domini.'* By the second phrase his cohort had joined in, and the novices followed. *Aid him, ye saints of God, meet him, angels of the Lord*: the prayer for the dead, to be said as soon as life departed. A bit late, Gil thought, staring down at what he could see through the criss-crossed beams of the roof. Nobody alive looked like that.

The body lay on its back, partly covered by a very singed blanket and black woollen habit. It was curled up and set into a strange, contorted position, the knees drawn up into the belly, the fists clenched before the face, but he could see enough of the face that he wished he could not. The lips were drawn back, the gums and broken teeth exposed, the tongue showing red in the shadows behind them. All the visible skin was blackened, presumably with soot; coppery curls as singed as the blanket clung about the brow where the skin had split. It had split on the backs of the hands too, and across the jaw, exposing rather cooked-looking flesh. There was a smell of singed hair, singed wool, burned meat, which— he found himself gagging, and turned away.

Brother Dickon finished the prayer, crossed himself and said with some sympathy, 'Aye, it gets to ye. Right, lads, we'll get him out o there, and then someone can let them ken we've found him. Have a care how you go, we'd no want bits falling off him.'

'Is that him right enough?' asked Dandy. 'Is it no some blackamoor?'

'No wi red hair,' said Tam. 'Whoever seen a blackamoor wi red hair?'

'It's the smoke, see,' said Brother Dod. 'It blackens all it touches, ye ken.'

In fact it took all hands, under Brother Dickon's competent direction, to clear the debris over the body and bring matters to a point where they felt they could lift it out onto the grass. By that time word had spread, the convent bell was tolling and the community had gathered, watching in sombre silence as the remains of the young man's bedstead were hoisted complete with the burned bedding and the blackened corpse, and carried out to set at Prior Boyd's feet.

He took a step back in dismay at the sight, and looked round for Gil.

'Is it him?' he said helplessly. 'It – you'd never ken this face, it's no—'

'I never met him,' Gil pointed out. 'Does nobody else ken him?'

'The hair's right,' observed Brother Dickon, standing at attention beside the exhibit. 'Naeb'dy else in the place has hair like that.'

'But he – and the teeth—'

'It's never Andrew, it's some blackamoor, for certain,' pronounced the subprior. One of the novices sobbed quietly.

'I suppose he was owercome by the smoke,' said Prior Boyd, still staring in horrified fascination. 'Poor laddie. What a way to—'

'No,' said Gil. Brother Dickon glanced sharply at him, and returned to staring over the Prior's shoulder.

45

'No? What d'ye mean?' asked Boyd.

'It wasny the smoke that slew him,' said Gil deliberately. He bent over the dreadful object, touching with care. 'See, his skin's blackened by the smoke, but there's no sign it entered his mouth. He wasny breathing by the time the fire took hold.'

'Not breathing?' repeated his kinsman. 'Why? He was well enough when I saw him after I spoke wi you, Gilbert. He wasny taken sick that fast.'

'No,' Gil agreed. 'Here's what killed him, sir.' The corpse was rigid, presumably from the effects of the fire, but if one looked from the side, as Gil had done when they lifted the bedstead over the broken wall, it was clear enough. 'Someone's taen a knife to his throat, and slit it wide open, like killing a pig. I suspect we ken why Brother Augustine's knife is missing.'

# Chapter Three

'A library, mem?' said Jennet warily. 'All full o books and that?'

'Yes, indeed,' said Alys, and thought longingly of the library she had known in Paris, with Mère Isabelle peering at her latest acquisition for the convent and demonstrating its delights to her pupil. *A complete copy*, she would say with satisfaction. *The entire work.*

'But is it safe?' Jennet persisted. 'They study a' kind o things, don't they no? Witchcraft and heresy and the like. And ackelmy, and the stars.'

'Alchemy,' Alys corrected. 'They study such things, true, but in order to prove they are wrong. The books can do no harm – they can hardly leap off the shelves and attack you.'

'Aye, for they're chained,' said Jennet.

'You may stay by the door,' Alys said, but was not surprised when her maidservant followed her into the library, sidling after her with an apprehensive gaze for the shelves.

It was not a large chamber, but it contained three big cases of books. There must be – she reckoned quickly – near 200 volumes, far more than Bishop Brown had said. A great collection. A row of reading-desks stood by the windows, with a big, broad-shouldered Dominican just raising his head to stare at her in surprise; beyond him was another man, getting to his feet from a writing-desk like Gil's, shock and indignation written all across his narrow face.

'You canny come in here!' he hissed. 'Shoo! This is no place for women! Go away, go away, shoo!' He flapped his hands at them ineffectually. The man at the reading-desk bent his head to his book, clearly not wishing to be involved.

Alys curtsied, aware of Jennet bobbing behind her.

'I should like to consult some of the books, Father,' she said respectfully.

'Consult? Women canny consult books – they canny read! It's naught for you! And if it's your fortune you want,' he added suspiciously, 'you can go elsewhere. I'm no having sic practices in my library.'

Alys met his eye, smiling reassuringly. He was a thin awkward man, with heavy dark eyebrows which twitched in agitation; his hands were trembling. He is afraid of us, she thought with incredulity.

'Mère Isabelle deplored such practices too,' she agreed. 'How can paper and print know what God has in store for us? I'll do your books no harm, sir, I'll treat them wi care. See, my hands are clean.'

'Go away!' he said, ignoring her words. 'Women canny consult books! They're all in Latin, they're no use to you.'

'Mère Isabelle?' said the other Dominican. He closed his book, marking his place with a tattered crow's feather, and looked more closely at Alys. 'In Paris? Do you speak of Isabelle de Marivaux? Is she still alive?'

'Indeed, sir,' said Alys, and curtsied again. 'I had a letter from her quite lately, written before Yule. I was her pupil for two years.'

'When you reply, gie her Henry White's greetings,' he said, and she bowed her head in assent. 'Alexander, we could let the lady consult as she wishes. If Mother

Isabelle de Marivaux taught her, she's fit to enter the library.'

'No – no, I'll no have it—' The librarian wrung his hands, almost dancing in despair. 'It's no right, it's irregular. The rules canny permit it, I canny allow it!'

'Away and ask Father Prior,' suggested his colleague. 'I'll mind your books while you're gone.'

'And leave you – and leave you –' Brother Alexander looked from White to Alys and back.

'She has her woman wi her,' White pointed out. 'Away and speak wi Father Prior.'

The librarian crossed himself, then darted past Jennet and out of the door, which thudded heavily behind him. Jennet sighed in relief, and let go of her beads.

'Now,' said White as the echoes died. He was older than Alys had at first thought, though his hair was still thick and dark round the tonsure; he had a penetrating stare, now bent on her. 'What did you wish to consult, daughter?'

'Albert the Great,' she said promptly. White's eyebrows rose.

'Indeed? His works are here. Which volume would you want, d'you suppose?'

'His writings on alchemy.'

White considered her carefully. 'Now, why would you want those?' he said after a moment. 'He never found how to make gold, you ken that.'

'I do,' she said. 'But I wish to learn more o the subject, and I knew you'd have his writings here, seeing he's—'

'One o ours,' he agreed. 'He's here. But I'll ask again: why would you want to read his alchemy?'

'I hope to learn more of his method,' Alys said, with what she hoped was an earnest smile. 'He was very clear on method.'

'Hmm,' said White. 'Method you'll find, but no summoning o spirits or the like.'

49

'*A daemonibus doctuture,*' she quoted, and continued in the Latin, '*It is taught by demons, it teaches about demons and it leads to demons.* He was very clear about that too.'

White frowned slightly, and after a moment turned to the furthest shelf. Scanning it briefly, he located a row of six disparate volumes carefully marked *A MAGN* on their fore-edges, drew out one and leafed through it.

'His *Compositum de Compositis,*' he said, handing her the volume. 'It's a beginning. You read Latin as well as quoting it, a course?'

'A course.' She carried the book to the nearest reading-desk, handling it lovingly. He watched with approval as she checked the spine and front of the binding, then opened the heavy boards and inspected the first leaf and the last where the list of the contents had been inscribed, keeping the place he had found for her with one hand.

'Does any here make a special study of alchemy?' she asked casually. He paused, on his way back to his own desk.

'No,' he said. 'That's no an interest o this house. A comparison of Brother Albert,' he nodded at the volume before her, 'and Brother Thomas on the Epistles of Paul, a new commentary on the Sentences, a wider study o witchcraft, but no alchemy.'

'Using one shining light of the Church to illumine another. Which is your own interest, sir?' she asked. Always a good way to engage a scholar, Mère Isabelle had said.

'The witchcraft is mine.'

'What do you find?' she pursued, trying to ignore Jennet crossing herself at the words.

'I find,' he said, watching her face, 'I find that there's no sic thing. It's no a popular stance, I'll admit, but I've concluded that the curses, the spells, the summoning o their Black Master, are all illusions.'

'But—?' she prompted, answering his intonation rather than any word.

'But those who practise such things are generally far gone in heresy and wickedness.'

'That makes sense,' she said. 'My husband would say the same.'

'You could try the Greyfriars,' he added, as if she had passed some test. 'I've heard they dabble wi sic things alchemical there.'

'Whereas here you dabble wi witchcraft,' she said.

'*Exactement*,' he said. There was approval in his tone, but he returned to his book without further comment. She drew her tablets from her purse and applied herself to Albert the Great, aware that Jennet had withdrawn to a position out of the draught from the door and had started on her spinning.

The book was a good manuscript copy of Albert's work, in a clear hand, with few of the abbreviations which could make reading difficult if they were idiosyncratic. The first section of the work she sought dealt with the forming of metals from sulphur and mercury, something she had always had doubts about, though she had never been able to procure enough of either to try them in the fire. She worked her way steadily through the three humid principles of sulphur without striking anything of use, but as she turned the page the door opened with a crash.

It was not the librarian who entered, but a much younger friar, breathing hard. He paused on the threshold, staring in surprise at Alys, then bowed briefly to White, as outside, the convent's small bell began to ring slowly.

'They've found,' he began, and crossed himself. 'They've found Andrew. In the, in the, in the ruins, Faither. They're lifting him now.'

'Ah.' White crossed himself too, bent his head and muttered a prayer. Everyone said *Amen*, and he closed

51

his book on the crow's feather again, and said to Alys, 'I should be present, if you'll forgive me. He was one o my pupils.'

'I'll stay here,' she assured him. 'We'll meddle wi nothing.'

Jennet, who would have clearly preferred to go and watch the excitement, cracked open the shutter of the window next the door, and peered out as the two friars left.

'They're a' running across the yard,' she reported, 'going out-by. Is that where the bit was that burned down?'

'Likely.' Alys crossed herself, murmuring a prayer for the young man whose life had ended in flames and terror, drew a deep breath and addressed herself to Albertus again. She had just caught sight of something useful – ah, there it was. Indeed, yes. *De putrefactione*, was the heading: Of Putrefaction. *Mors & vita ab igne fiunt* ... Death and life come from fire. Extrinsic fire, approaching a body – the similar element which exists in the body ... As she had found with other alchemical writings, the passage did not really explain what she wanted to understand, but it provided a new way to think about it. She groped for her tablets, drew the little stylus from the case and began to copy what she read, speculation whirling in her mind.

'They're a' coming back the way,' Jennet reported, an unknown length of time later. 'Oh, Our Lady save us, they're bringing the corp. You can see it, mem, it's covered ower wi a cloth but you can see where it's a' curled up. Where will they take him, I wonder? They'll no can wash him, his skin would all peel off wi the water like peeling an orange.'

'You ken a great deal about it,' Alys said, distracted. Processional singing floated through the open shutter, deep-voiced and sincere, one of the penitential psalms.

The singing was not as good as at Glasgow, where they had the resource of the College to draw on for voices, but the grief was unmistakable.

'My sister Bess helped the layers-out, after that row o houses got burned down in Ru'glen last year. She tellt me all about it. Gied her quite a turn, it did, when the skin cam off the first one she took a cloth to.' Jennet craned to follow the procession. 'Aye, they're taking him direct to the kirk. He can lie there till they coffin him, I've no doubt. Be an orra-shaped coffin, so it will,' she added thoughtfully. 'They never soften, see, if they're burned.'

The community vanished into the church. It was probably Sext by now, Alys considered; Gil would be at a loose end if they had taken the body with them and he had nobody to question. She half hoped he might come and find her, but he did not appear, and she applied herself to copying Albert's solid Latin prose.

She had just finished when the librarian returned, taking up his post at the writing-desk with a silent, resentful glare. Brother Henry followed him, and then several young men, very subdued, who all drew copies of the same text from the shelf by the door and looked about them for places, except one who drew out his eating-knife and began to clean the ash from under his nails. Brother Alexander, seeing this, drew a sharp breath and hurried across to him.

'Put that away! We'll ha no knives in here! There's no need o sharp knives in a library, it's no the place for it,' he ordered, his voice trembling with outrage. The young man looked at him, then down at his knife.

'Forgive me, brother,' he said in Latin, and put the blade away. 'I forgot.'

'And *you*'ll need to go now,' said the librarian, turning triumphantly to Alys. 'There's no room. The desks are all wanted.'

'Very well, sir,' she said, and curtsied again. 'I hope I may come back tomorrow?'

'We'll see about that,' he retorted, came round the desk and almost snatched the volume she had been working from. 'What? Where did you get this? How did you find it? You'll no get—'

'No summoning of demons,' she said. 'I ken that, sir. It was on yon shelf, third one down, at the end of the row of Albert's works.'

Henry White looked up and nodded briefly as she turned to leave. Jennet came forward from the window with relief, and exclaimed before the door had closed behind them, 'What's at greetin-face? He's like a man that's swallowed a lemon.'

'Maybe he has troubles we don't know of,' said Alys. She drew her plaid up against the rain, and turned towards the slype.

'Where are we going now, mem?' Jennet asked. 'Somewhere there's more folk to talk to, maybe?'

It took longer to get away from Blackfriars than she had expected. The friars' dinner was served, and that for the guest hall was carried in at the same time; after it she felt it necessary to dose everyone in the household with her cough elixir, and to send a flask of the stuff into the convent with her compliments and a placatory message to the Infirmarian. Dinner had been a silent affair; the men were all morose after their morning's work, the reek of smoke and – yes, burned flesh – which hung over them discouraged conversation, and Gil was disinclined to discuss matters, though he pointed out that it was Father Prior's decision as to whether he should investigate the death of the young man in the ashes; this would have to wait for a Chapter meeting.

'What's in that stuff, mem?' Tam asked as they made

their way out of the gate. 'Right tasty, it is, I'd never ha taen it for medicine.'

'That would be the honey,' Alys said, choosing her path with care over the muddy ruts in the roadway. 'Then there's pepper, and sage tea, and thyme. They were out of celery seed, so I had to make the sage tea extra strong.'

'Pepper,' Jennet said thoughtfully. 'Ye'd think it would bite, then, but it doesny. It's warmer than a comforter at your neck, so it is.'

'Where are we going, anyway?' Tam stared about him in the drizzle, and craned to see over the fence into the dyer's yard they were passing. 'No the best part o the town, this, is it? A' the stinking trades by the brig-end, a' these wee houses; it's no like Rottenrow.'

'This way,' said Alys with confidence, turning onto the path by the Ditch. She had made certain to get directions from the servant who carried out the empty crocks after dinner.

'Is it that woman that saw the Deil rise up from the man's house?' said Jennet, brightening. 'We'll can sit in her kitchen and hear it all from her servants, eh, Tam?'

'If she'll see me,' said Alys.

Mistress Buttergask was very happy to see Alys. She was a well-padded woman in a gown of good dark-green wool, hastily assumed over a striped kirtle to welcome her guest, with a very up-to-date black woollen headdress framing a round, sweet face. Her eyes were pale blue and rather vague, though Alys suspected they saw more than appeared.

Having rattled at the pin by the door of the neat stone-built house she had been directed to, Alys found the three of them warmly greeted and drawn in out of the rain, to the accompaniment of a stream of unceasing, welcoming chatter. Tam and Jennet were despatched to the kitchen along with two young maids and orders to bring in spiced wine and cakes, and herself led into a cosy, untidy solar where a small woolly dog had been yapping endlessly since she stepped into the house.

'Be quiet, Roileag!' said her hostess without effect. 'That's right kind in you, my dearie, to call on me in this weather, I was near deid wi boredom mysel and those two lassies driving me daft wi their prattle. Come in, come in, hae a seat. Gie me that plaidie, we'll just shake the rain off it,' she cracked it like a whip and droplets spat and fizzled on the brazier in the centre of the chamber. 'Hang it here, it'll be dry by the time you leave, you'll get the good o't when you go out again. Be *quiet*, Roileag! My!' She sat down opposite Alys and studied her with interest while her dog jumped onto her knee and growled faintly. 'And who did you say you were?'

'I'm Alys Mason, from Glasgow, at your service, mistress. We're lodging at the Blackfriars the now, while my man looks into this matter o the fellow,' she paused, choosing her words, 'carried off by the Deil.'

'Oh!' Mistress Buttergask breathed, the blue eyes going round with excitement. 'Oh, I can tell you—'

'I hoped you might,' Alys said, with a complicit smile. 'Prior Boyd has tellt us what you saw, a course, but I thought I'd as soon hear it from you.'

'And your man's looking into it, you say?' Mistress Buttergask tilted her head, frowning. 'Why would he need to do that? It's a' seen to, is it no? Though a course they couldny ha a quest on him, seeing there was no corp to examine. My – my friend said they'd no notion what to do in the matter on the Council.'

'Holy Kirk wants an inquiry,' Alys said. Their eyes met, and both nodded. What Holy Kirk wanted, Holy Kirk got. 'So I hoped you'd tell me at first hand what you saw, for I'm sure it was more than Prior Boyd ever said.'

'D'you ken?' Mistress Buttergask clasped her plump hands together. The dog Roileag lurched on her knee and complained, with a sound between a growl and a whine. 'I was certain that would happen. He never wanted to hear what I saw, you could tell that, only acause I hear things, he thinks I canny tell what I see wi my own een. It was only when my – my friend bore out everything I tellt them that they listened at all.'

'He saw it too?' Alys said. The other woman relaxed slightly at her tone, and nodded. Alys wondered if her neighbours were inclined to be sanctimonious about her 'friend'.

A tapping at the door heralded one of the young maids with a tray. It held two horn cups, which gave off a welcome spicy smell, and a platter of little cakes. Once she had departed, they had toasted one another, and Roileag had been fed one of the cakes, which she took under the chair to consume, Alys said, 'Are you close to the Blackfriars here? I'm all turned about,' she admitted, 'wi the way the path winds to come here. I'm not sure what way the house looks.'

'Aye, it's like a morris-maze,' agreed Mistress Buttergask. 'But that's the Blackfriars at the foot o my garden.' She nodded at the window of the little chamber, shuttered against the January weather. 'It's the outside wall o the very house, mistress.'

Alys rose and went to the window. It was deeply recessed; a new-looking crucifix had been hung on the panelling at one side of the recess, a print of the Annunciation on the other. She peered through the small greenish panes of the upper portion. The garden was long and narrow, the typical shape of an urban toft, and dismal in the rain, the kale shining dark green; at the far end was a fence, and beyond that, presumably on the other side of a path of some sort, was a well-built stone wall. Slabs of dark-red dressed stone, in many shapes and sizes, well fitted together in the same style as the front of Pollock's house, rose to a roof of what must be local slate. The wall extended right and left into the drizzle; further to her left the bulky shape of the Blackfriars' church loomed darkly, to the right the roof ended, showing where the row of small houses stopped, but the wall itself continued. She looked intently at the nearest section again, and made out the blocked window, on a level with three other little windows carefully shuttered against the weather. It was indeed Pollock's house which faced her, and those must be the windows of the other small lodgings.

'Tell me about it,' she said, returning to her stool.

Mistress Buttergask set down her beaker and clasped her hands again before her round bosom.

'Oh, mistress!' This was clearly a well-rehearsed tale. 'Oh, it still makes me that wambly to think on it!' She paused, considering her audience. 'I rose in the middle of the night, see, and when I'd done wi the jordan and eaten a bite out the dole-cupboard, I went to the window to see how the night was progressing.'

'The window looks the same way as this one?'

'It's the chamber above this.' On the word, they heard footsteps overhead, and chattering voices. Roileag yapped, and Mistress Buttergask smiled tolerantly. 'Och, those lassies, they'll be showing your servants where I looked out and what it was I saw.'

'Did you open the shutter?' Alys asked, one ear cocked for the responses above her.

'I did.' Mistress Buttergask nodded. 'I did that, for it was a mite stuffy in the chamber, for all it was so cold. Bitter cold it was, and a clear night, wi a hard frost. So I looked out,' she went on, regaining her narrative, 'and the moon was shining on the rooftops, and sparkling on the frost, right bonnie it was, and not a thing moving. And I was just thinking what a sight it was, wi the moon and the stars like jewels, when I seen this great black shape rise up fro the roof there.'

She waited expectantly. Alys obliged by saying, 'A shape? What sort of a shape?'

'Oh, my!' The other woman set one hand at the base of her throat and looked away, down at the floor beside her. 'What a sight it was! All hunched ower, ye ken, what wi carrying the man, but there was flames flitterin about it, and a pair o great red een. I crossed mysel, you can be sure,' she suited the action to the words, 'and woke Rattray, and got him out his bed to look. And he seen it and all, and bore me out when I tellt Father Prior,' she added, 'so he's no need to doubt me or shorten the tale. I was feart for my mortal soul, I can tell you, mistress, and Rattray's and all.'

'He hadny shortened it by much,' said Alys, studying her. There could be no doubt it had been a genuine account of something the woman had seen or thought she saw; she showed signs of distress now at the recollection. Roileag had jumped possessively onto her lap again, and now curled up firmly; her mistress stroked her fur, as if for comfort. 'Will I call your servants for more of the wine?' Alys asked. 'Or should you eat one o the wee cakes, to settle your humours?'

Mistress Buttergask drew a hand down her face and straightened up.

'No, no, mistress, I'm well. Aye, maybe a cake.' She accepted one when Alys handed her the platter, and nibbled it cautiously. 'It just cam ower me all o a turn, there, how we'd escaped sic a fate as that poor man. No matter what an ill-doer he was, it's no a thing I'd wish on anyone, to be carried off to the Bad Place and tormented by fiends the rest o yir life.'

Alys, appreciating the charity which underlay the statement, made no comment on its theology.

After a few moments her hostess said reflectively, 'And it's just come to me: none o my voices had a word to say that night.'

'Would they usually?' Alys asked, as being the most non-committal comment she could think of.

'Oh, aye.' Mistress Buttergask gave her a wary look. 'It's no – it's no like I hear sounds, you ken. It's like a voice right inside my head, telling me things, and sometimes I can picture them and all. There's my grandam now telling me you're a kind lassie, and well intentioned, but you've your own reasons for talking to me.'

Taken aback, aware she was blushing, Alys could only say honestly, 'Aye. That's true, mistress.'

'Och,' said the other woman, 'you're asking it for your man. Your man's work must aye come first, lassie, I see that.'

No wonder Prior Boyd had not wished to hear this woman, Alys thought briefly. Trying to recover her poise, she said, 'How long did – what you saw stay there? How long were you watching it?'

'Oh!' Clearly nobody had asked this before. Mistress Buttergask stared at Alys for a long moment, then raised her eyes to the window, her fingers moving as if she was telling her beads.

'The length of three *Aves*, maybe,' she said eventually. 'Or four. Proper ones, no the ones you say when you've left the dinner too near the fire.'

Not long then, thought Alys. Well under the quarter of an hour, but longer than I had assumed.

'And then what did it do?'

'Why, he rose up, and flew away northward. No fast, mind, I never saw his wings flapping or nothing, he just kind a floated off the way a buzzard does.'

'Could you still see the flames and the red eyes?'

'No, well, I never saw the eyes, would I, if he was flying away. And the wee flames had stopped and all, now you ask me.' She nodded. 'Likely they blew out when he flew off.'

'You've been blessed,' said Alys, hoping to offer some comfort. 'There's not many of us allowed such a vision. It's a dreadful warning.'

'That's what Rattray said,' the woman admitted. 'Likewise that he wouldny ha believed me telling it if he hadny seen it himsel, but men are like that, are they no?'

Alys smiled in agreement, though she had never yet tested Gil in that way.

'Is he in Perth the now?' she asked.

'No.' Mistress Buttergask deflated slightly, then recovered and said with faint defiance, 'He's out o the town the now, a week or more. At his other house. Wi his wife.' She crossed herself. 'She's doted, poor soul. She's older than he is, a good few year. She canny be left alone now, the servants has to wash her and that. No a happy thing.'

Their eyes met. Alys put a hand out and touched the other woman's wrist.

'That's hard,' she said. 'For everyone. Is he good to you?'

Mistress Buttergask turned her own hand to grasp Alys's a moment, then gestured around her.

'He feued this house to me,' she said simply. 'It's my own – I could sell it the morn.'

'That's generous.' With a need to change the subject, Alys suggested, 'Might I see the window where you looked out?'

The chamber above was low, with a slanting roof where panels had been fixed to the rafters of the house, and furnished with a box bed, a settle and two carved kists, the bed-curtains and window-hangings in red dornick with bright flowers embroidered on it. There was a man's doublet hanging on a nail near the bed, a pair of well-trodden pantofles half under the bed, a good furred gown thrown on one of the kists. Roileag scurried about the place, her claws rattling on the

61

polished boards, snuffling in corners and under the bed. Alys crossed to the window and peered out, past the crucifix and the woodcut of the Visitation which protected this view.

The window was set into the eaves, with a low sill, and offered a clear view of the roof opposite, of the red tiles with the blackened portion near the ridge, of the absence of any way into the convent or the house from this side. Alys could see nothing which offered more information, though she pressed her brow against the little panes to look up and down the line of the priory wall.

Mistress Buttergask was chattering on in her ear, pointing out the direction in which the Devil had flown, the way he had risen up from the house roof, where the moon had been.

'And your friend saw it all as well,' Alys said, drawing back into the chamber.

'Aye, indeed he did. Well, he was here at my side,' the woman qualified, 'just in time to see – to see *him* towering ower the wee house like a great hawk, and then to watch him flee away. I'd to tell him about the flames and the red een and that. But he saw it all, so he did.' She paused a moment, and sighed. 'It's been right strange, these past two weeks, what wi Faither Prior and then my lord Bishop wanting to hear the tale, and a man of law to write down all I said, and then the neighbours wanting to hear it and all.'

'None o your neighbours saw anything?' Alys asked. Mistress Buttergask shook her head.

'No, none o them. It was just a chance that I was up at that time and keeked out. I suppose they didny happen to do likewise. Come away down to the warm, lassie, it's chilly up here.'

The mood in the town was no better than it had been when they rode through yesterday – could it only be yesterday? Surly groups of men stood on street corners in the drizzle, gaggles of women had their heads together in doorways. The word *witchcraft* floated on the wind. Alys picked her way along the darkening Skinnergate and past St John's Kirk, hoping the two servants could obey her instructions and keep silent at her side long enough to get through the burgh. She was aware of curious glances, as a stranger in town, and also of Jennet peering at the stalls and booths they passed, nudging Tam to point out a leatherworker's display on the Skinnergate, but they reached the South Port without drawing undue attention to themselves, emerged through it and took the short path to the Franciscan monastery.

Its buildings were less ostentatious than the Blackfriars' foundation, with a low plain church surrounded by timber-framed structures, a hall and dorter and Chapter House, and a paling fence round about the policies. Alys had noticed it as they rode into Perth and had thought then how characteristic it was of the Franciscans with their vow of poverty.

'What, more friars?' said Jennet in discontent. 'Could we no get questioning someone wi a friendly kitchen, mem, same as the last one? Those lassies were right good company, weren't they no, Tam?' Tam grunted agreement, and she went on, 'Tellt us all what their mistress seen fro the window, and how the Bishop was there telling her no to pass the word on, and that wee dog o his stole a good leather glove and chewed it all to ribbons, and then picked a fight wi her doggie and all. Our dog would never do a thing like that.'

'No, indeed.' Alys led the way to the west door of the church. 'I may need you, if I can get a private word wi one o the friars, so don't stray.'

'As if I would!' said Jennet, offended.

To Alys's relief, she had gauged the afternoon correctly; at this time of year it began to grow dark well before the clergy began to think of their evening devotions. The church was busy, with lay people kneeling before one saint or another, several Franciscans moving among them in their grey gowns with the knotted rope girdle. I hope they wear enough under those, Alys thought irrelevantly. They could die of the cold. The Rule was written for Italy, not Scotland. She looked about her, and caught the eye of one of the friars, who made his way towards them.

'Can I help you, daughter?' he asked.

'Faither,' she said, and curtsied, aware of Jennet crossing herself, Tam muttering something like *Amen*. 'I hope so. I read something in a book lately, and I hoped someone here might explain it to me.'

'A book,' he said in disapproving tones. 'You can read?'

'My mistress is aye reading,' said Jennet proudly. 'Our maister says she's a great scholar.'

The friar shook his head. 'Better to leave sic things to the men, daughter, and mind your household,' said the friar, his disapproval deepening.

'Nevertheless,' Alys persisted, 'now I have this matter in my head, I'd as soon have it expounded.'

'What's this matter, then? What book were you reading in?'

'Albert the Great. He mentions the secret fire.' She watched the changes in his expression, keeping her smile as innocent as she could manage.

After a moment he said, 'Hah! I've no time to deal wi sic things the now. Bide here, lassie, and I'll see who I can send out to you.'

Seating herself on the stone bench at the wall-foot, she drew her beads from her purse and prepared to wait, the two servants beside her. In fact, it was no more than a quarter of an hour before another Franciscan came into the church by the friars' door, looked about, and made his way hastily towards them through the gathering shadows. He was a plain, bony man with a shaggy mop of greying brown hair and light, piercing eyes. She rose at his approach, and curtsied.

'The secret fire?' he said, without preamble. 'What do you know of it?'

'Only what Albert the Great writes,' she said. 'And a little I learned when I was still in Paris. I hoped you could tell me more.'

'Paris.' He peered at her, but shook his head. 'Never been there. What do you need to know? Why are you asking about sic a thing?'

She sat down, and patted the stone bench. He settled himself at a slight distance, still gazing intently at her through the gloom, his hands tucked into his sleeves.

'Albertus wrote,' she said, calling up the Latin phrases, '*Fire, coming into contact with a body, sets into motion—*'

'Yes, yes,' he said dismissively, 'that's elementary. In all senses, that's elementary. But the secret fire—'

'Is it different?' she asked. 'Does it operate by different laws, or the same ones?'

He grunted. 'Why are you asking this? What do you want it to do? What do you need it to do?' He looked beyond her at Jennet and Tam, and back again. 'Who are you, anyway?'

'That's Mistress Alys Mason,' said Jennet stoutly, 'fro Glasgow. She's marriet on the Archbishop's quaestor, that's looking into the man that's disappeared at the Blackfriars.'

'Only he hasny,' said Tam. 'Disappeared, I mean.'

The friar stiffened, and looked hard at Alys.

'How much did you find?' he demanded after a moment.

65

'One foot, still in its shoe,' said Alys. 'Bones of hands or the other foot. Ashes.' She considered him. 'You have heard o this afore, then.'

'Aye. I wondered, when word first reached us.' He turned his head, gazing into the chancel, or somewhere more distant than that. 'I read o't years ago – what was it in? Where was I?' He almost bounced round to face her again. 'Tell me about it. When was this found? There's been no word. We only hear the town's gossip the now, a course, wi them almost besieged in their house, but I'd ha thought—'

'Only last night,' said Alys soothingly, 'and then there was the fire, and the young man dead.'

'Aye, they've no to seek for their troubles. Tell me,' he ordered, crossing himself briefly at the mention of the death.

She described what they had found in Pollock's house, as clearly as she might. He listened intently, almost sucking in her words, nodding from time to time, and sat back when she had finished, staring into the distance again.

'Aye,' he said at length. 'I see what – and you wondered if the secret fire might . . . No. No, I think it wouldny work. See, it has to be sealed tight.' His hands emerged from the sleeves of his habit, for the first time, and described fragile glassware. 'The marriage chamber, you ken?' She nodded. 'Sealed wi wax, or clay, so the red man and the white woman may be—' He bit off his words, suddenly realising his surroundings. 'Any road, this wasny the same situation.'

'The chamber was sealed,' she said, in disappointment.

'Aye, but you canny seal a chamber the way you can an alembic. The windows, the door, the chimney, the air aye gets in.'

'All were blocked,' she said.

'Were they now? So the air was reduced, maybe,' he said thoughtfully.

'Like burning charcoal? But where did the flame come from? It behaved,' she paused, to choose her words. 'It never behaved like ordinary flame. To consume the man, and the chair beneath him, but never damage the rest of the chamber, surely that was no ordinary fire. That was why I wondered . . .'

'Aye.' He nodded in understanding. 'A good thought, but no our answer.' Somewhere above them a bell began to ting. 'I need to go. Where are you – no, you're lodged at the Blackfriars, I suppose. I canny come there the now. Can you come back here the morn's morn? After Sext, maybe?'

'Who should I ask for, sir?' She began gathering her skirts together to rise.

'Why, me, a course. Oh!' He shook his head, half irritated. 'Michael Scott. Ask for Michael Scott. No that I'm any relation, you ken.'

'D'you think he is?' Jennet speculated as they picked their way out of the church, past the people drifting in to hear Vespers. 'Any relation, I mean?'

'Of the wizard?' Alys said. 'Surely no. That Michael Scott was hundreds of years ago.'

'No, surely,' said Tam. 'I seen his grave one time, at Melrose, and they showed me where he split a great hill in three, just by the town.'

'It takes more than wizardry to split a hill open,' Alys said.

'That's what Canon Cunningham said,' Tam admitted, 'but the hill's there, just the same, all in three bits.'

# Chapter Four

Waiting on the stone bench outside the door to the Prior's chamber, Gil considered the situation gloomily. He had barely begun to approach the question of who might have killed Pollock, let alone how it might have happened, and now the community was shaken by this double disaster. No saying whether his kinsman would see it as obvious that he should investigate both matters; the novice's death might be considered an internal matter. And what was Alys doing, he wondered. He had hoped she might have some success questioning the lay servants, who would not have the same objections to talking to a woman as their masters, but after dinner she had dosed everyone in sight with her newly concocted throat medicine, which he had to admit had helped, and then she had disappeared without explanation.

There was someone with the Prior just now; he could not make out the words, but the mumble of voices seemed to be Scots rather than Latin. After a time one of them grew louder, as if the speaker drew nearer to the door. The latch stirred, and the door opened a crack.

'You're a fool if you think so, Davie,' said a forceful voice. 'It has to be dealt wi, and sooner than later.' Prior Boyd said something indistinct. 'Aye, I'll leave you.' The door flung wider and a tall Dominican emerged, checked briefly at sight of Gil, then flung over his shoulder, 'Here's your man waiting. Better face up to it, Davie.'

Nodding to Gil, he strode off, his white scapular flapping energetically. Gil rose, and tapped on the doorframe. Within the chamber, Prior Boyd looked up from a scrutiny of his clasped hands on the reading-desk.

'Aye, Gil,' he said wearily. 'Come in. We need to talk.'

'We do, sir,' Gil agreed.

Despite this, Boyd did not seem in a hurry to speak. He sat for some time, still gazing at his hands. Gil sat equally silent, waiting, and at length the Prior looked up.

'Henry has the right of it,' he said, nodding towards the door. 'It must be dealt wi, no matter the grief it brings us.'

'What, the boy's death?' Gil asked. His kinsman grunted agreement. 'Aye. It's a bad business, sir,' he added conventionally.

'Very.' The Prior rose and took a jerky turn about his study, hands moving wildly, clutching at nothing, until he thrust them into the opposite sleeves. 'I am able to see the implications of these events,' he said, switching to Latin. 'The convent is closed at night, the servants go home or sleep in their own quarters. It must have been one of this community who cruelly slew our brother and set fire to our infirmary. The conclusion is odious, but it is not to be avoided.'

'Very true.'

Boyd turned and gazed across the chamber, light from the window catching the silver hair about his tonsure.

'How do we proceed, Gilbert?' he asked helplessly. 'I have no experience of such violence within a community. It seems to me worse than the matter of our corrodian. I suppose there is no doubt that the young man was slain deliberately,' he added in faint hope.

'None whatever,' said Gil firmly. 'His throat was cut – you saw the wound yourself. I suspect he was killed while he slept, and then the fire was set, I believe to make us think it was the same circumstance as the corrodian's.' *Whatever that is,* he thought.

'But why?' asked Boyd in Scots. 'Why kill the boy, sic a promising novice, and why the need to make us think it was the same as the other?'

'I hope we can find out the answers,' said Gil. 'You spoke to young Rattray last night, I think. Did anyone visit him after that? Apart from whoever killed him,' he qualified, before Boyd could speak.

'Best ask the Infirmarer for that.' Boyd shook his head. 'If you can get sense out o him. Poor James, he's right shocked by the whole thing.'

'How was the young man when you saw him?'

The Prior returned to his desk and sat down, apparently as much to delay answering as for any degree of comfort. After a space he said, 'He was much as he has been since I confined him.'

'And how was that?' Gil persevered. 'I never met him. What sort of a laddie was he?'

'Oh, very bright. Very promising. A fine intellect,' said Boyd, and repeated the phrase a couple of times. Gil waited. 'But,' the Prior said at length, 'maybe too much sail on for his draught, if you take my meaning. No that steady afore the wind.'

'Devout?'

'Passionately. He'd asked for one o the wee figures o Our Lady to be in his cell wi him, and he spent a lot o the last weeks on his knees afore her.'

'Why?' Gil asked bluntly.

'Who can say? He did not, at all events.'

'And why did he claim to be guilty o the corrodian's death? Did he say the man was dead?' *Too many questions,* he thought, but Boyd bent his head and gave them consideration.

'When Andrew first confessed,' he said eventually in Latin, 'his words were, *Brothers, I ask forgiveness, for I*

71

*have sinned by causing the vanishing away of our corrodian.* This caused some consternation in Chapter, you may conceive, and I judged it well to isolate the young man and question him myself. I asked him many times how he had achieved this, but he seemed unable to offer any means, only repeating that he was guilty by reason of his hatred for the man.'

'Why did he hate him?' Gil asked.

'This he did not say, though I asked him repeatedly. I hoped the protection of Our Lady in the form of her statue might bring him to rational thought and proper confession, but this had not occurred when I last –' his voice cracked '– last spoke with him.'

'Did you tell him we had discovered Pollock's,' Gil selected a word carefully, 'remains? That the man wasny carried away by the Devil or anyone else?'

'I did.' The Prior contemplated his clasped hands again. 'He seemed astonished, as we all were. He repeated my words: *The man was burned to ashes? In his house?* Then he crossed himself, and said, *So he is truly dead.* Then he looked frightened, and flung himself on his knees before Our Lady and fell to his prayers. I judged it best to leave him.' He sighed. 'I wish I had questioned him more closely now.'

'He looked frightened,' Gil repeated.

'More than that. Horrified, perhaps. Aye, I would say horrified. Poor laddie. I feel I failed him.'

'Did he have enemies? Any who disliked him within the convent? Or any particular friends?'

'This is—' Boyd checked himself. 'I would have said this is a house of brothers, living together in harmony. Clearly this is not so, but I do not know of any enemies the young man had. His friends were the other novices, with whom he experienced great fellowship and amity.'

Gil, resolving to question the other novices, waited for a moment and then said, 'What opportunity could one of the community have to leave the dorter and go about the place by night, into the kitchen or into the infirmary?'

The Prior glanced at him, and back down at his hands.

'The Rule,' he said heavily, 'forbids it. Since we are clearly dealing with one to whom the Rule is an irrelevance, I should say every opportunity. The door is not locked. The stairs are shallow, and familiar. There was no moon last night, but each man has a lantern, to light the way down for Prime, or to go out to the necessarium. The only risk, I should suppose, would be in disturbing one of his fellows. Brother Augustine sleeps in the lay brothers' dorter, the kitchen servants sleep out in the suburb this side of the town, so access to the kitchen would be easy enough. You think that was the knife that was used?'

'It seems the simplest conclusion. Brother Dickon has set two o his men to search for it, though God knows it's a small enough thing to find in a place this size.'

The Prior nodded wearily.

'I have required at Chapter that the miscreant confess, and also that any who know or suspect anything come to me privily, citing the urgent need for confession and penance. If I receive any information I will pass it to you immediately, if I am able.'

Gil nodded.

'Thank you, sir. And the Infirmarer?' Gil said. 'Did he hear or see anything before the fire took hold?'

'Better ask him yoursel.' Boyd's mouth twisted in what seemed like grief. 'The sub-infirmarer will help you get a word. I think you had best not wait too long about it.'

The sub-infirmarer was the man Gil remembered, a tall fellow with a soft Ersche voice and a calm manner which was slightly fractured just now. The house two along from Pollock's had become a makeshift infirmary, with a fire blazing in the grate of the outer room, one lay brother tearing and rolling bandages and another pounding something in a mortar on a small table barely equal to the task. A covered dish set by the fire was producing an eye-watering scent of cloves.

It seemed to be the consulting hour, for three friars sat in a row on a bench by the wall while the sub-infirmarer himself listened to Brother Archie coughing.

'And it's still coming up black?' he said as Gil entered the house.

'It is that,' agreed Archie hoarsely, and coughed again.

'There's little enough I have to give you,' said the sub-infirmarer in vexed tones. 'Just this throat mixture of Mistress Mason's, and that will not be lasting for ever. And the clove decoction when it's cooled.'

'Easy enough to make some more o the throat mixture, I'd ha thought,' said Gil.

'Good stuff, it is, too,' Brother Archie remarked. 'Right soothing, for all it's full o pepper, she said.'

'Pepper has great virtues,' said the sub-infirmarer, measuring out a spoonful from the flask. 'Come back later,' he directed, as he tipped it into Brother Archie's compliant mouth, 'and you can have some clove decoction. And take care. If you get out of breath, you should sit down till it is passing off. I was telling Brother Dickon the same thing,' he added, seeing argument in his patient's eye, 'so you may be reminding one another of it.'

'Aye, right,' said Archie. He adjusted his black scapular and got to his feet. 'Thanks for that, Brother Euan.' He nodded to the waiting friars and to Gil, and picked his way out. Brother Euan straightened up and looked at Gil. 'Is it urgent?' he asked. 'Only there is these fellows,' he indicated his patients, 'and I must be checking on Brother James.'

74

'I was hoping for a word wi Brother James,' Gil said.

'Oh.' Brother Euan pulled at his ear. 'No so easy, maybe. Come ben, we'll see if he's improved at all.'

The inner chamber was also warm, with a fire burning in the grate. Thin daylight came in at the window and showed a kist, two or three stools, and two plank cots like the one Gil had slept in last night; in one of these the Infirmarer lay, propped on a hard backboard, and beside the fire, legs stretched comfortably to the blaze, sat Euan Campbell. As Gil stepped in he scrambled to his feet, an ingratiating grin on his face.

'Maister!' he said. 'I came for a word wi Brother Euan here, like you were saying, but he's as busy, what wi the fire. Minding the Infirmarer, the poor man, is the most help I can be for him. You see how he is.'

'I do,' said Gil, studying the sick man. He lay unmoving, limp against the supporting board, eyes half open, his breathing rough and rapid, and did not respond even when Brother Euan touched his shoulder and spoke to him. 'Sweet St Giles, how long's he been like this?'

'Since afore Terce, maybe,' said Brother Euan. 'He was fine after the fire, for all he was so distressed, but when we were all to be rising for Terce I found him like this. We were moving him down here when we set up after the Office.' He gestured about him to indicate his temporary quarters. 'I've dosed him wi what I can find in the kitchen, but valerian would be the best thing and that's hardly a kitchen herb.'

'Can Euan no go into the town for you?' Gil offered, with faint malice. 'If you gave him a list he could call at the apothecary. Or maybe the Infirmarer at one o the other houses would help.'

'I was never thinking of that,' said Brother Euan. 'It would be a big help. I could be making up a list, easy, and Brother Edward would give us coin for it.' He bent to his superior and shook the old man's shoulder more firmly. 'Brother James! James! Wake up, man!'

A crease appeared between Brother James's brows, and he swallowed slightly but did not seem to rouse. Gil hooked one of the stools closer with his foot, and seated himself by the head of the bed.

'A dose of the throat mixture, maybe?' he suggested. 'Milk? Water, even? Then you could get back to your patients. Euan, get a list from Brother Euan and get out into the town. And never a word out yonder of who it's for,' he cautioned. 'You can tell the other religious houses what's amiss, but best if nobody about the town connects you too close wi the Blackfriars.'

'Never fear, Maister Gil,' said Euan, innocence shining on his cheekbones. 'I'll keep all right, and never be letting a word slip. And when I get back,' he added, pausing in the doorway, 'I can maybe be getting a word wi another Ersche speaker that's here, so Brother Euan is telling me, that is a McIan and likely will be glad to hear o Ardnamurchan.'

In a little while Brother Euan returned with a beaker of warm milk. It smelled herbal, though Gil could not identify the receipt. With some difficulty the sub-infirmarer coaxed a few mouthfuls down his superior's throat, but finally he straightened up and said, 'That ought to be helping him, but I should see to the fellows out by. A strange thing, it is: those who assisted at the fire, they were fine last night when we finally retired, but the day they are presenting to me with breathing troubles, sore throats, pains here,' he rubbed his breastbone. 'And all our simples and linctuses gone up in smoke.'

'Where were you sleeping last night?' Gil asked. Brother Euan bent his head and crossed himself.

'We have been taking it in turns,' he said, 'while the poor laddie was confined. One of us was in the

76

infirmary the whole time. Last night it was Brother James's turn, and I was sleeping in my cell in the dorter.'

'Was that generally known?'

'Och, yes. I was talking about it after supper, for one, and we've been taking turn about ever since he was confined, as I was saying.' He shook his head and looked away. 'Much do I regret it.'

'You think you would have woken sooner?' Gil asked.

'I know it.' He glanced at his superior, who seemed slightly less withdrawn, and touched his ear. Gil grimaced. 'The laddie might not be dead if I had been there.'

'Whoever killed him might simply have waited for the next chance,' Gil pointed out. Brother Euan considered this, crossed himself again, and went back to the outer chamber. Gil lifted the cup and touched Brother James's shoulder as Brother Euan had done.

'A wee drop more?' he suggested.

The old man accepted two sips of the cooling milk, and then a third. Then he turned his face away from the cup.

'No more – now,' he whispered. Gil set the cup down by the leg of the bed, and took one of the thin dark-spotted hands. 'Who – who?'

'Who am I? I'm Gil Cunningham. The quaestor.'

'Ah.' Brother James's eyes opened, peering up at Gil. 'Oh, aye. Questions?'

'I have, sir. Are you well enough to hear them?'

'I'll no be – better.'

'I hope you will,' said Gil, though he doubted it. The hand in his tightened briefly, and the mouth twitched. 'What woke you last night, sir? When did you know there was a fire?'

'The light. Flames. Light.'

'You mean the light from the flames woke you?' A small nod. 'So the fire had a good hold already?'

'Aye.'

'So you rose and ran out to give the alarm?'

'Aye.' The old man's eyes closed, and after a moment tears leaked from the corners. 'Shame. Ashamed. Duty of . . .'

'You owed the young man a duty of care,' Gil supplied. The hand in his tightened slightly. 'But he was already dead. Whoever killed him set the fire hoping to conceal his deed. You did the right thing in raising the alarm quickly, or more of the Priory could have burned.' An idea came to him. 'Perhaps Our Lady made use of your frailty, to protect those still living.'

Brother James's mouth twitched again, but he said nothing to that.

'Can you mind last night, before you all retired? Who visited the infirmary? Faither Prior came to speak to young Rattray, I ken that, but was anyone else in the place?'

After a moment, Brother James whispered, 'Robert. Henry.' He swallowed. 'Sandy – Sandy Munt. Other Sandy. Librarian.'

'Five?' said Gil. 'Is that usual?'

'Four. Rheum.'

'Did anyone else speak to Rattray, apart from the Prior? Last night, or at other times?'

'Henry. Teacher. Confessor.'

'Right,' said Gil. He lifted the beaker of milk. 'Another wee mouthful?'

While the old man took another sip, and another, Gil considered the situation. At length, setting the cup down again, he asked, 'Did Rattray ever say anything to you about just how he caused the man Pollock to vanish?'

Brother James frowned, working the question out, but then whispered, 'No. Just – guilty. Spent his time – knees. Our Lady.'

'So Faither Prior said and all,' Gil said. He disengaged his hand from the old man's, and sat back. 'I'll leave you, sir. Brother Euan will likely send someone in to sit by you. God send you mend from this, whatever ails you.'

A very slight nod was his answer, but the hand he had released moved in what might have been a blessing. Gil said *Amen* and went out to the other chamber, where the line of patients was no shorter but the lay brothers were now working together on another herbal concoction. Brother Euan looked up from dressing a burn.

'George,' he said to the young friar under his hands, 'when I finish with this you can be sitting with Brother James for a bit. Can I help you more, maister?'

'Not the now,' said Gil, in answer to the tone rather than the question. 'I could do wi a word when you've the time, but later will do fine. Who would he mean by Brother Henry?'

'Faither Henry,' corrected Brother Euan and his patient at the same time. 'He is *Lector principalis*,' Brother Euan continued. 'And novice-master.'

'I seen him in the library the now,' offered the patient.

'Now there's a surprise,' said one of the waiting line.

'Robert,' said Gil, checking the names off on his fingers. 'Sandy Munt. And Sandy the librarian.'

'Robert Aikman?' said George. 'Second-year man, same as me.'

'Or Father Robert the subprior?' said someone else.

'And Sandy Munt's a first-year novice,' continued George.

'Sandy Raitt's the librarian,' said the third man on the bench.

'Now, he'll certainly be in the library,' said the first.

The library was comfortingly familiar, with its row of shelves and scent of worn leather bindings, and at this hour of the day, when most were free to pursue the studies which were a great part of the purpose of the Order, it was full. A few people raised their heads when Gil entered, but only the librarian continued to glare at him as he picked his way between the tables and reading-desks.

'This is a private library!' he hissed as Gil reached him. 'We canny have everyone running in and out! There was *women* in here this morning!'

So Alys did get in, Gil thought, schooling his expression. She didn't mention that.

'I am in search of Father Henry,' he said quietly in Latin. The librarian scowled at him, but someone at a nearby reading-desk looked up and caught Gil's eye – the tall, decisive man who had left the Prior's study earlier.

'I am Henry White,' he said, 'instructor of the Dominican young. How may I help you?'

'I hope you may instruct me, sir,' said Gil.

In the guest hall the Blackfriars servants had kept the fire going, and Socrates and the big black cat from the kitchens were sharing the hearth, at a cautiously formal distance from one another. Father Henry seated himself, refused ale, studied first Socrates and then Gil carefully, and then nodded.

'I had the pleasure of speaking wi your wife earlier,' he said. 'To something I remarked to her she replied, *My husband would say the same.* I see why she said it.'

Gil raised one eyebrow, but no further explanation was forthcoming. Instead the other man sat back, watching him for a moment, and then said, 'You want to know about young Rattray, I take it?'

'Among other things,' Gil agreed. 'Father Prior has given me one account of the lad, I'd like to hear another.'

'Hmm.' Father Henry looked down at his hands folded on his lap. 'A loss to the Order. A very promising young man.' He crossed himself and murmured a prayer. Socrates rose to sit down beside him, and nudged his free hand.

80

'Was he really?' Gil asked when he was done. 'Or is that simply what you'll say to his kin?'

'He has no kin, I believe,' said White, absently scratching the dog's chin. 'But aye, he was genuinely promising. The most o our intake is townsmen, you understand, but this year we've three sons o landholders, none o them baronial maybe but more cultured, more educated, than we generally get. Calder, Rattray and Mureson. Rattray's family held land over near Montrose, and I'd ha said he was the most able o the three, the most flexible in his thinking. An ardent soul, perhaps, burning ower bright for his own good at times, but wi a great grasp o the works o Brother Thomas, and a considerable understanding o church history. Some o the questions he asked in class were deep, very deep.'

'So what did you think o his claim to have caused Pollock's vanishing?'

After a pause, White said simply, 'I didny ken what to think.' Gil made a questioning noise. 'Oh, I never thought he had aught to do wi't in reality, but the boy was convinced he was instrumental, though he couldny bring himself to say how.'

'Couldny bring himself?' Gil repeated. That was not what Father Prior had told him. 'You mean he said as much?'

White looked down at the flagstones beside him, ordering his thoughts.

'I spoke with him more than once while he was – isolated,' he said. 'He was missing classes, after all. I wished to set him work. Each time I asked him, in so many words, if he could tell me why he was being kept separate from his brothers, he replied, *Because I am evil*.' White looked up and met Gil's eye. 'I showed him how no man is wholly evil, and how to find the good in himself and strengthen it to cast out the evil, but he persisted in saying that he was evil. I asked him in what

81

way, and he offered the disappearance of our corrodian as evidence. I asked him how he had achieved that, and he replied again: *Because I am evil.'*

'It makes no sense,' said Gil, and realised they had reverted to Latin.

'No. What is more, it makes a nonsense of years of teaching in logic and analytical thought. He should have learned to dissect a syllogism at fourteen.'

'Indeed,' said Gil. He paused, and said carefully, 'I believe you were also his confessor.'

'I was. This was not said under the seal of confession.' White also paused, and said with equal care, 'I think I may say to you that the young man did not confess anything to me which would help your investigation.'

Gil bowed his head in acknowledgement of this, and considered what he had learned so far.

'So we have a young man,' he said, 'intelligent, highly strung, emotional—?' White nodded. 'Who suddenly becomes convinced that he is evil and that he has therefore caused the corrodian to disappear, with no logical explanation for the belief.'

'A fair summary.'

'And the fact that Pollock had *not* disappeared, that his ashes were still in his lodging, was not known to anyone. What could the boy have been doing, to make him think he had caused this situation? Was his reading supervised? Could he have been lured into some of the darker mysteries?'

'I see where you are leading this,' said White, 'and I may say that I am working on the subject of witchcraft myself, and my conclusion, though there are those who disagree with me, is that there is no such thing, no power to cause harm by casting spells. On the other hand its devotees are invariably far gone in heresy and in the worship of the Devil.'

'Had you taught your students this?'

'I have discussed it with them.' He produced a reluctant smile. 'Andrew and his friend Sandy Munt argued the matter forcibly, but were unable to prove the existence of witchcraft to my satisfaction. *Everybody knows* is not proof. Indeed, what everyone knows is quite frequently erroneous.'

'Pollock was in the habit of extortion,' said Gil. 'I found Andrew Rattray's name among his papers.'

'*Was* he now?' said White softly. There was a short silence. 'I must question Andrew's fellows, the other students. Poor young man, I hope Our Lady has received him under her mantle, whatever he has been dabbling in.'

'I need to question them too,' said Gil. 'Let us not lose sight of the fact that someone slew this young man, unshriven, still in his confused state, and tried to conceal the deed by setting a fire which has seriously injured the community. That is murder and arson, which are both pleas o the Crown and capital offences. Whoever is responsible must be found, for the sake of his immortal soul and of his brothers.'

'Believe me, I have not lost sight of it,' said White rather sharply. They looked at one another, and after a moment White gave a slight bow. 'I agree. Your investigation should take precedence. I would appreciate it if you would send them to me when you are done.'

Andrew Rattray's fellow students were still in the library, though how much work they were doing was questionable. Their faces, as their teacher summoned them one by one, were a series of studies in surprise, well-concealed alarm and concern, but when Gil led the four of them through the slype and into the warmth of the guest hall without Father Henry they relaxed slightly.

'Tak a seat,' he invited. 'Will you have some ale?'

'I'd not say no,' admitted the nearest as they gathered stools and settled themselves, and the others nodded.

'Tell me your names, first.' Gil lifted the jug from the table, and one of the group sprang up to serve. Socrates, sprawled by the hearth again, raised his head to follow the movement, then settled again, nose on paws, watchful. The cat had left as they entered, sauntering out towards the kitchens with the air of one whose neighbourhood had been invaded by undesirables.

'Sandy Munt,' said the one with the mousy hair and the round face.

'Sandy Mureson,' said the one with the jug. One of the landholder's sons, Gil recognised, accepting a brimming beaker.

'My name's Adam Calder,' said the tow-headed one nearest the fireplace. The other landholder lad and a local voice, Gil thought, perhaps from somewhere over into Angus like Rattray himself. 'That's a fine wolfhound, maister. Is he a good hunter?'

'Never mind that the now, Adam. I'm Patey Simpson,' said the last, a lean young man with a Fife accent. He pushed dark hair out of his eyes. 'What d'you want wi us, maister? Is it about Andrew? He was our freen, we'd no ha hairmed him.'

'It's about Andrew,' Gil agreed. 'If it was none o you, then who was it? Somebody slew him, and then set fire to the infirmary to hide it.'

'Oh!' said Munt. 'You mean, so they'd think it was the same as what happened to—' He gestured over his shoulder in the general direction of the corrodian's house.

'Wasn't it the same?' said Calder, staring in surprise. 'I thocht it was.'

'That's what I mean,' Gil agreed. 'So I need Andrew's friends to tell me about him. What was he like? Who did he get across? Did he have any enemies?'

They looked at one another, and shook their heads blankly.

84

'He was a member o the community,' offered Calder. 'One o the limbs, like it says in the Epistle.'

'He was just ordinar,' said Munt.

'Och, Sandy, he wasny!' contradicted Mureson. 'He was away the best scholar o the five o us, for one thing. But no made up wi it,' he assured Gil. 'He'd as like to help any o us wi learning by rote, or debating questions, or rhyming Our Lady.'

'He was right good at that,' said Simpson.

'I'm no,' said Calder. 'I canny do the rhymes. Andrew was helping me.'

Gil nodded. He knew of the Dominican leisure occupation of composing impromptu rhymes to the Mother of God, hailing her in gilded terms and capping each other's efforts.

'So he was a good fellow, then?' he asked.

'He was,' said Munt, his round face distressed. 'It's – I canny believe he's dead. He's no been wi us for a few days, right, no since Faither Prior put him away, but it's like he'll be back as soon as, as soon as—' He stopped abruptly, and hid his face in his beaker.

'I think you were in the infirmary last night,' Gil said. 'Complaining o the rheum?'

'Sandy, you never!' said Mureson.

'We were forbidden,' said Calder in disapproval. 'All the limbs ought to obey the head, St Paul says it. You'll ha to confess that.'

Munt emerged, reddening.

'Aye,' he admitted to Mureson, ignoring Calder. 'I'd a daft notion, I thought – I thought maybe I'd get a word wi Andrew, so I went when Brother Euan wasny there, but Faither James kept a good eye on me just the same. He gied me a couple o cherry pastilles, mind, but I had to thank him and leave. No chance o nipping along to where Andrew was.'

'He'd no ha spoken to you,' said Mureson. 'No if he was ordered to keep solitary. He's – he was like that.'

'Very proper behaved,' confirmed Calder. 'Which was why—'

'He'd his moments, mind you,' Simpson interrupted. 'Wi hair that colour, ye ken, maister. He'd his moments. But we'd leave him be, and he'd come round again in no time.'

'He'd words now-and-now wi Sandy Raitts,' said Munt, 'but so does all of us. Even Faither Henry crosses him. Even Faither Prior crosses him, it's that easy.'

'Were you surprised when Andrew confessed to causing Pollock's disappearance?'

'Oh, that was a right tirravee!' said Simpson. The others nodded.

'He'd no been right for a day or two,' said Munt. 'Brooding a bit, like, and no joining in the crack. We're no supposed to sit and chatter,' he confided unnecessarily, 'but if you ken where's out of the wind and out of hearing – anyway, the last few days he was wi us Andrew wasny for joining in, just hung about at the edge o things.'

'Looking like someone stole his bannock,' offered Simpson. 'We asked him what was the matter, but he wasny for telling us.'

'How long had he been like that?' Gil asked carefully, setting his beaker down for the dog to finish the last inch or so of ale.

'Och, a day or two,' Munt repeated.

'So before the corrodian disappeared?'

They looked at one another again.

'That's right,' said Munt after a moment. 'Before Pollock vanished.'

'No idea what was wrong? Word from home, discipline from your superiors, that sort o thing?'

'Nothing like that,' said Mureson.

'He's–he'd no kin,' said Munt, 'that he ever mentioned. Parents deid a year or two, afore he was ever tonsured, by what he said. Nor he never spoke o his home or where it was.'

Simpson said, 'Well—'

Gil raised his eyebrows, and the young man went on, 'I saw him speaking wi Pollock, ae time. It was after that he was kinda mumpish.'

'Wi Pollock?' said Munt. 'Where?'

'Here in the guest yard.'

'He should never ha been out here,' said Calder in shocked tones.

'Aye,' said Simpson shortly. 'They were . . .' he paused, considering his words. 'It didny look friendly.'

'When was this, Patey?' asked Mureson.

'That should ha been told to Faither Henry,' pursued Calder, 'or even to the Chapter o Faults.'

Ignoring this, Simpson thought deeply, counting on his fingers as he did so, and finally said, 'Three days afore the man Pollock vanished. Aye, that would be right.'

'Can you describe it?' Gil asked. 'Where were they? Where were you, to catch sight o them?'

'I was passing the slype,' said Simpson, 'and I looked down it, see, the way you aye do, in case there's anything from the outside to be seen out here.'

Gil nodded, recalling his own enclosed years at the college in Glasgow, where the youngest students were not allowed out into the town without express permission.

'And here was Andrew, maybe ten paces from the end o the slype, head to head wi Pollock. He was kinna,' Simpson pondered, searching for a word, 'braced, like. I could see his fists ahint his back, man, and I could tell he was trying gey hard no to haul off and strike the fellow. Then Pollock grinned and clapped him on the shoulder,

87

and Andrew took a step back, and I heard him say, *I'll see you in Hell first*. Then he turned away, and I moved on quick for fear he found me watching him.'

'You heard no more?' Gil asked. 'It's no longer spreading gossip, you understand, it's giving me information that might lead me to discern what happened.'

'Aye, I see that,' said Simpson. Munt was hiding dismay, not very well, Calder was frowning; Mureson simply looked serious. 'But I'm no right sure I heard what I heard, if you ken what I'm saying. Maybe it was from afore he professed,' he said, brightening. 'Aye, maybe that – for there's naeb'dy like Pollock for digging in a fellow's past. The Deil kens how he learned the most o't. He was at me about a book missing fro the library at St Andrews.'

'Was he?' said Munt. 'What did you say to him about it, Patey?'

'Tellt him it was confessed and paid for, and my faither beat me for it and all. And Faither Prior kent all about it, for it was him that confessed me for it when it was lost. Wasny my fault, even,' he added sourly. 'How was I to ken that fleabag o a dog would take a fancy to the thing?'

'That's bad,' said Calder. 'That's a sin, to destroy a book. Brother Sandy would be angry if he kent it, and no wonder.'

'Brother Sandy's aye angry,' observed Simpson.

'He was on at everyone, Pollock was,' said Munt. 'I seen him talking to Sandy Raitts one time, making signs wi his hands, smirking the way he did, and Sandy shaking wi passion. And Tammas Wilson, and even the Infirmarer once.'

'Sandy, that's gossip,' said Mureson in warning tones, and his friend subsided.

'So what did you hear?' Gil asked. 'What did Pollock say to Andrew?'

'That's just it. I'm no right sure I heard it,' said Simpson, going red. 'But I thought he mentioned a lassie. No by name. It was *I'm sure she wouldny like* – something or other. And Faither Prior was mentioned. But he didny have a lassie, did he?'

'No Andrew,' said Munt firmly. 'He's,' he swallowed, 'he *was* away too serious about all this.' He gestured at his novice's habit. 'Now me, I've no objection if some lassie wants me to help her bring in the May *in nomine Domini*, but Andrew would never even ha noticed if he was asked.'

'Sandy,' said Mureson again. 'That's unbecoming.'

Munt looked away, rather uncomfortable.

'Aye, I suppose,' he muttered. 'But all the same.'

'Andrew hadny a lassie,' said Simpson. 'Unless it was from away back.'

'He did and all,' said Calder darkly. 'He went out into the town, regular, and he wasny drinking, for he never smelled o drink. Must ha been a lassie.'

'Into the town?' Gil queried. 'How do you ken that?'

'I seen him go a few times,' said Calder, blue eyes very round. 'See, my cell's opposite his in the dorter,' he explained, 'and whiles it takes me a good bit to drop asleep. I seen him go out, after Compline when he thought all was quiet and Faither John was snoring. And one time I followed him, to see what he was at, for he was gone far too long for it to be a call of nature,' he went on primly, 'and he went out across the yard here and out by the barns and through the wee postern there, and right out the house. I turned back, no wishing Brither Porter to see me, but I taxed him wi't – Andrew, I mean – the next day, and he made believe I was dreaming.'

'Maybe you were,' said Mureson.

'I wasny!' said Calder indignantly. 'I ken what I saw, and for one that pretended he was the maist devout o all o us it was no way to carry on, I tell you.'

89

'He never pretended that,' said Munt. 'He was a good fellow, aye ready to help. You said yoursel he helped you wi the rhyming.'

'That was afore.' Calder poked with his foot at the ashes fallen out of the fire. 'It doesny do, I tell you. We're a limbs o the one body, and for one o the limbs to be rotten, well, it poisons the whole. I waited for Faither Prior to deal wi't, but he never.'

'Och, you and your limbs,' said Simpson tolerantly. 'Leave it, Adam.'

Gil had drawn breath for another question when Socrates scrambled to his feet, ears pricked. There was a commotion outside the building, beyond the heavy door of the guest hall, with much bustle and shouting and a familiar yapping.

'That's my lord Bishop,' said Mureson.

'The Bishop?' Gil rose, just before quick footsteps heralded Nory, raindrops spangling his plaid and bonnet, his hands red and raw with cold.

'You're asked for, maister,' he said, and patted Socrates, fending him from the door. 'Bishop Brown's here, wanting to hear all.'

'We'll be wanted and all,' said Munt with regret, and tossed off the last of his ale.

'If any of you,' said Gil, rising, 'thinks of anything else that might aid me, come and tell me as soon as you can. And my thanks for this.' He looked from one to another of the four. 'It's hard to lose a classmate, I ken that mysel, but keep in mind Andrew had been shriven no so long afore, and he was dead by the time the fire took him.'

'And he's likely under Our Lady's cloak now,' said Simpson. The others nodded, and all four crossed themselves, and followed Gil to the door.

'You'll no go afore the Bishop like that, maister,' said Nory, capturing him. Quick expert gestures with the chilled hands straightened Gil's garments, brushed ash from a sleeve, altered the set of his short gown. Three of the young men slipped past with a murmured word, but Mureson said softly by Gil's ear, 'I'll come back later, maister.'

Gil nodded, without speaking, and the young man followed his fellows. Nory stood back and surveyed his master critically.

'Aye, you'll do,' he said. 'I'll attend you, will I, seeing that Ersche gomeril's away up the town?'

'You'll stay here and warm yoursel,' Gil said. 'I'll tell all over the supper, never fear.'

The guest-hall yard was full of the Bishop's men. Pausing to offer them room by the fire alongside Nory, Gil made for the Prior's chamber, where he found the Prior himself, the subprior and Maister Gregor, all facing Bishop Brown in full flow.

'I couldny credit your letter!' the Bishop was saying as Gil entered. 'Who would do sic a thing? Surely it's been someone got over the wall, maybe to steal—'

'What do we have to steal, Georgie?' said Prior Boyd wearily. 'I'd as soon believe it was someone from the outside, but it's no the answer.'

'One of your community?' said Brown in disbelief. 'I've aye admired the fellowship, the brotherhood, in this house.' Jerome, on his lap, growled at Socrates and he tapped the animal's muzzle. 'Bad dog! Quiet! But how? Why?'

Boyd turned to Gil.

'What have you discerned this far, Gilbert?' he asked in Latin.

'Little enough,' said Gil in Scots. He summarised most of what he had learned, making some judicious omissions. The two Dominicans heard him out in impassive silence, Bishop Brown in increasing distress, Maister Gregor with little bleats of disbelief and shock.

91

'Och, there must be some mistake!' he said before his master could comment. 'You canny have it right, Maister Cunningham, it's surely been some terrible accident!'

Jerome growled again. Socrates, by Gil's knee, turned his head away.

'Rob, you're a fool,' said the Bishop. 'The laddie's throat was cut. That's no accident.'

'Aye, but their skin splits wi the roasting,' argued Maister Gregor. 'You mind, after Monzievaird, burying all those Murrays, how they—'

'Aye, where it's stretched. On the brow and the elbows and the like. No under the jaw.' Brown turned to Gil. 'What like kind o weapon, would you think?'

Gil shook his head.

'No way o saying, sir. A knife, for certain, and no a penknife. It was done wi one cut. It seems possible it was this missing kitchen knife – a boning knife Brother Augustine calls it – which hasny turned up yet, but beyond that . . .' He shrugged.

'Hmm.' The Bishop frowned. 'It's a bad business, Davie. A Chapter o Faults, maybe?'

The subprior nodded, silent in the corner, but David Boyd raised his chin and said, with a nip of frost in his tone, 'That's an internal matter, Georgie, and I'm still Prior o this house. I've already convened a Chapter of Faults for this evening, after supper and afore Compline. The break in the routine ought to shake the brothers, maybe shake loose something we need to hear.'

# Chapter Five

'You should ha been there, maister,' said the novice Mureson, and sat down heavily on the side of the bed. The black cat appeared from under the other bed and rubbed against his legs.

'Clearly,' said Gil, handing the young man a cup of spiced ale. 'I wish we had something stronger to offer you. Tell me it again.'

'I shouldny be here out my place.' Mureson scrubbed at his eyes with the sleeve of his habit. 'But we're all at— Christ aid me, I think I'll ask to transfer to the Charterhouse.'

'They have their disagreements, too.' Alys entered the chamber, a steaming beaker in one hand, a second candlestick in the other. 'Drink this. It will settle you.'

'Aye, I suppose they must.' Mureson took the beaker, looked helplessly from that to the ale, then set both on the floor and buried his face in his hands again. 'But to hear Auld Harry accused!' he said from behind them. 'It's no to be borne!'

'Tell me again,' Gil prompted.

After a moment, the young man emerged from hiding, and took a cautious sip of Alys's draught. Surprise crossed his face, and he took another.

'It began the usual way,' he said shakily. 'Auld Harry, Faither Henry, read the chapter, and Faither Prior led us wi the prayers we aye use, and minded us it's our duty to *confess all faults and wickedness, from the least to the greatest, in ourselves or our brothers.'* He was using the Latin phrases unconsciously. 'So a couple o the lay brothers confessed to gossip and argument, and then afore they could withdraw, afore we novices could speak – I mean, Adam aye finds something to confess – afore he could start, Sandy Raitts and Thomas Wilson rose both at once, on opposite sides o the chamber, and began, *Accuso*. Faither Prior tried to make them speak one at a time, and wait till we'd left, but they shouted him down, the both o them, accusing one another first and then Faither Henry as well, and there was all the folk about them shouting, and us novices trying to defend our teacher.' He scrubbed at his eyes again, took another mouthful from the beaker, and gulped it down.

'Accusing him of what?' Alys asked. She set the candlestick down on a kist and sat beside Mureson on the bed, at a modest distance. The cat jumped onto her knee and settled down, watching the young man. 'What are they all supposed to have done?'

'Of killing Andrew,' said Mureson, as if it was obvious. 'And burning the infirmary. And burning Pollock. All of it.' He gulped another mouthful, and licked his lips. 'And then, and then, I've no notion who started it but they was all fighting, and Brother Dickon got his men thegither and swept all us novices out wi him, and bade me let you ken, so I cam here.' He sighed, and sat back, peering into the empty beaker.

'How did each react to the accusations?' Gil asked. 'Raitts and Wilson denied what each other had said, I take it.'

'Oh, aye. Shouting about it all across the Chapter House. And Faither Henry, he rose when they accused him, and then he just stood there. Shook his head a couple o times but said naught. No that he'd ha been heard, save he went into his lecturing voice.'

94

'They were still arguing when you left?' said Alys.

'Arguing? Arguing it out wi their fists, they were. It was a rammy like a market day. Never seen sic a thing, mistress. I should transfer to the Charterhouse,' he said again.

'Our Lady may counsel you differently,' she said, leaning forward to lay a hand on his sleeve.

'Did either man adduce any evidence?' Gil asked. 'Claim to have seen or heard aught that might back his accusation?' He considered Mureson's face, and his more composed posture. 'Drink your ale, and go over it again for me if you can. Start where they both stood and said *Accuso*. Did they point? Name one another?'

The young man's fists clenched. He looked down at them, and carefully opened them out and laid his hands flat on his knees.

'Aye. They rose, in the same moment, and pointed, and said each other's names. And then turned and pointed at Faither Henry, accused him by name and all. The rest o us began shouting, and Faither Prior bawling for silence over it all, and Faither Henry rose and said naught, just stood there. Then Raitts and Wilson both started denying it, saying, *It was you was abroad in the night* and would gie no reason.'

'They both said that?' asked Alys. Mureson glanced at her and nodded.

'And then – it was Wilson, I think – pointed at Faither Henry and said, *You and all, abroad in the night. What were you both at, whispering in corners?* And Raitts turned on him and all. I thought they two was friends,' he said, and scrubbed at his eyes again. 'Auld Harry spends as much time in the library. They've aye seemed at ease thegither.'

'And then what?' prompted Gil. 'Did they say anything more about the accusations?'

95

'No.' Mureson thought a moment. 'No, I think they didny, for that was when the fighting began. And then Brother Dickon whistled his men thegither, and—' His face twisted, and he turned away from the light.

'I've met your teacher,' said Gil, 'and the librarian, but no the man Wilson. Tell me about him. Does he bear office?'

'Aye.' Mureson drew a deep breath, and accepted the change of subject. 'He's sub-factor, collects the rents from the town and sees to the maintenance of the properties the house holds there. Oversees an altar in St John's Kirk, that we have the gift of. Deals wi Andro Pullar about the rest o the rents.'

'You're very clear on all that,' said Gil.

'Oh, aye. I've been assisting him these two month, till Yule there. It's how we learn all the workings o a house like this.'

Gil nodded. That made good sense.

'And the man himself?'

Another deep breath, and a check, and Mureson said defensively, 'You canny expect me to say ower much about my fellows.'

'So you have little good to say of him?'

'I never said that.' Henry White's teaching suddenly showed in the young man's manner. 'He's a punctilious member of the House, does his duties assiduously, conducts himsel modestly at the Office—'

'But what sort of man is he?' Alys asked. Mureson's mouth twisted, and he turned his face away again. 'We are investigating murder here, brother, you ken that. We need to hear anything that might be relevant.'

'Aye, but if I tell you something – about Brother Dickon, or Patey, say – and it's no relevant,' said Mureson a little desperately, 'then I've slandered a friend to no purpose.'

'We canny tell,' said Gil, 'whether a fact's to the purpose or no, till the matter is ended. We need all the information.'

The young man shook his head, still keeping his face averted.

Alys said gently, 'You must pray over it. Our Lady will show you the rights of the matter, I am very sure of that.'

He turned back to look at her, and after a moment nodded.

'You're wise, mistress. I'll—'

There was a tapping at the door. Gil, the nearest, opened it, and found Jennet outside.

'If you please, maister,' she bobbed a curtsy, 'here's some more o the novices, saying this fellow's sought for, to say Compline wi the rest o them.'

'Sandy?' It was Munt, behind Jennet, looking as shaken as Mureson and peering over the girl's shoulder for a sight of his friend. Socrates, beside him, nudged his hand, and he petted the dog's soft ears absently. 'We're to, we're to, we're to say Compline. Now. And an Act o Contrition afore it. The whole o the house, never mind how hoarse some o us are yet. I doubt we'll be on our knees most o the night.'

'It's deserved,' said Calder out of the shadows behind his friend. The cat jumped down off Alys's knee and slipped under the bed again. 'We should never ha come to sic behaviour. It's no worthy.'

'Aye, so we should be on our knees,' said Mureson. He rose, but hesitated. 'You two go ahead, I'll be right ahint you.'

'Are you fit for it?' Munt asked, rather anxiously. 'There's, there's, there's one or two'll be absent by what I hear. You'd never be missed if it's too much.'

'No, he should be there,' said Calder. 'The whole o us needs to ask forgiveness.'

97

'I ken my duty,' said Mureson. 'I'll be right ahint you, never fear.'

Munt withdrew unwillingly, the dog following him, Jennet following the dog. Mureson turned to Gil and gestured to him to close the door. When the heavy planks thudded into place he produced, from within his habit, a linen bundle.

'This is Andrew's,' he said simply, holding it out. 'He asked me to take it, keep it safe, when he was confined. It's— we're no supposed to have personal possessions, let alone . . . well, you'll see when you look at it.'

'Where was it?' Gil asked, taking the folded linen. It was warm from contact with the young man's body; there seemed to be papers in the bundle, and one or two small objects with hard corners.

'He'd a hiding place. Under the planks o his bed, right cunning. I think you should have it now.' Mureson edged past Gil towards the door. 'I need to go, maister. Thank you for – for all you've said. And you, mistress. And for the draught, whatever it was, it was right helpful.' He ducked in an embarrassed bow and slipped out.

Gil followed him, saying, 'If you think of aught else, come back and tell me as soon as might be.'

'I will, maister.' Mureson bowed again, and hurried across the wide chilly hall of the building to where Munt waited with a lantern in each hand. 'God send you all rest the night.'

Another of the penitential psalms arose deep-voiced in the cloister, broken by coughing, and figures moved in the shadows beyond the dark windows of the hall. The two novices looked up in alarm, and left hurriedly; Gil assumed they could join the procession from the end of the slype, probably unnoticed except by their immediate fellows.

'What's amiss, maister?' It was Tam, in the doorway behind him, hand casually near his dagger. 'They didny seem happy. Is it another body?'

'No this time,' Gil answered. 'I dare say you'll hear soon enough – the Chapter meeting turned to fighting, scandalous behaviour in a house o religion, and there's three o the brethren accused by their fellows o killing the novice.'

'Three?' Tam whistled. 'A conspiracy, like? Will you question them? I suppose you'll no be wanting to persuade them,' he said with faint regret.

'Likely no,' said Gil, 'but if I do, I'll call for you.'

In their chamber, Alys had already unfolded the linen bundle and was contemplating what it held in some dismay.

'Look at this,' she said in French as he entered. 'The young man did indeed have a girl in the town. See, here is a fairing, one of those badges lovers buy, and these documents seem to concern a house and payments of money. How should he have money to give her?'

'I hate to think.' Gil lifted a paper she had not yet unfolded. 'Does it locate the house? One of us could call on her.'

'Indeed, one of us should,' she said seriously. 'She may not yet know of his death. The name of the dead is not at large in the town.' She leafed through the open documents. 'It names her here as Margaret Keithick, and there is no mention of a husband, present or late.'

'Ah!' said Gil, turning the sheet he held to show her. 'Here is where the money comes from. I'd know Andrew Halyburton's hand anywhere. Your father is right, it gets worse every time one sees it.'

'Andrew Halyburton? The Scots factor in Middelburg? You mean the young man has been trading into the Low Countries?'

'Yes, and to some purpose. This has been a profitable venture, whatever he sent.'

'Clearly his fellows did not know,' she said, 'by what you told us at supper.'

'Nor did the Prior.' Gil reached for another folded paper. 'Aye, this is the same, from six months ago. Not quite such a profit, but still well worth the venture. Halyburton is an excellent factor. He knows the market there in the Low Countries. He can turn a pretty penny for a venturer.'

'And then there is this strange collection of oddments.' Alys poked at them. 'A stone with a cross painted on it, a mount from a bridle with someone's badge on it, and this.' She unwrapped a scrap of brocade, like the oddments a church might use to wrap its relics in. 'See, a pilgrim badge of St James, and silver at that. Someone has been to Spain and back.'

'Curious.' Gil turned the bridle-mount in his hand, but failed to make out the crest in the candlelight. 'A collection of treasures, I suppose, with meaning for Andrew if for nobody else.' He smoothed the document on his knee and looked at Alys. 'I think we keep all this to ourselves meantime. The Prior will have to know of it eventually, but for now it may give us an advantage over someone.'

She nodded, and lifted the remaining folded paper. It seemed to be a smaller sheet than the others; she opened it out carefully, and stared at it.

'*Ah, mon Dieu!*' she said. 'Look at this, Gil.'

A drawing showed faint in the candlelight. A woman, modestly dressed, her head bent tenderly over the infant on her lap, another child by her knee.

'The Virgin and Child with St John?' Gil offered. 'We know Andrew had a great devotion.'

She frowned.

'I wonder. There is far more than six months between these children, more like three years, I should say, and the drawing has been kept hidden, although such a subject could be displayed without discredit. Could this be his mistress?'

'With two children? He started young, in that case. I suppose he was twenty-two or three.'

'Perhaps they are not his.' She was studying the faces. 'We never saw him, of course.' Gil repressed the thought of the sight of Andrew Rattray as he came out of the ashes of the infirmary, and leaned over to see the image better. 'This looks like a real woman,' she went on, 'rather than an ideal. Her hands are not perfect. See how short this little finger is?'

'Many limners prefer to use models, rather than draw from imagination,' he observed.

'Yes, but they would draw Our Lady perfect.' She began folding the papers. 'We should visit the man of law who acted in this as well, I think.'

'So Andrew was breaking the Rule, by keeping a mistress, by trading on his own account without turning the money over to the Order, though how he managed any of that as a novice, confined to the house, is beyond me. But is all this sufficient reason for anyone to kill him?' Gil added the papers he had looked at to the bundle.

'You said one of the novices mentioned that he left the priory at night,' Alys pointed out. 'I suppose we know now where he went.' She began to fold the linen round the little collection, and paused, looking at the finely hemmed margin. 'This is a kerchief, and good quality linen, at that. I suppose it must be hers, whoever she is. Poor woman, she will grieve for him.' She tucked in the last corner to secure the package, and pulled up the hem of her gown to reach her purse, hanging between gown and kirtle. 'Shall I keep it for now, or will you?'

'You keep it.' Gil got to his feet. 'I have more papers to deal with, or at least tablets.' He kicked lightly at the kist on which she had set the second candle. 'I should have studied Pollock's effects before this.'

'There has hardly been time,' she observed, straightening her skirts. 'Do you wish help, or shall I hear what else the servants have to say? Perhaps Euan is returned by now.'

'I doubt it.' He moved the candle and opened the kist. 'Aye, the men may have learned more from the lay brothers. Alys?'

'What?' She turned from the door, and the candlelight lit the razor's-edge outline of her nose. He held out a hand, smiling at her.

'Kiss me first.'

Armed with the lingering memory of the kiss, he began to sort through Leonard Pollock's property. It was a task he generally enjoyed, when faced with an array of documents from which he could piece together an individual's life and activities; but when, as now, the documents were entangled in a mass of clothing and other effects, none of it very clean, it was less to his taste. The clothes he slung over the raised lid of the kist, thinking he would get Nory to tend to them later. They were all of good quality, and would certainly have kept their owner warmer than the other members of the community, though the moth had got into some of the furs. They seemed to him to represent a considerable sum of money, perhaps invested over a number of years.

By the time he reached the bottom of the kist he had a total of ten sets of tablets laid on the floor beside him, together with a bundle of five or six folded documents. He tapped round the sides and base of the kist to check for hidden compartments; finding nothing he rose from his knees, drew the candles more conveniently, and sat down to study his finds, supervised by the cat.

'He's kept all his records,' he said in French. 'Ten years' worth of notes of extortion and favours, identified by initials, with one or two names in full. Young Rattray was one.'

'I remember,' said Alys suddenly. 'You had just mentioned him when the dog found – found the man's foot.'

'Indeed, yes.'

They were seated together by the sinking fire, to talk over the day's findings. The servants had been despatched to bed, Socrates was sprawled by the ashes, and the moment of privacy seemed very sweet.

'So who else was named?' Alys asked, tilting her head on his shoulder to look up at Gil's face. 'I recall two others. Brother Dickon said they were men of Perth, I think.'

'Those two, yes. There were some I recognised, members of this community. I must ask the Prior for a list of the brethren, so I can establish whether he had any victims outside the walls. He kept no record of the alleged misdeeds, I suppose that was all in his head, but the returns are listed. Candles, small sums of money, items like a chicken or a haunch of beef which he sold on.'

'He sounds a very unpleasant man.'

'That seems to be the consensus.'

'What are the names he mentioned?'

Gil drew his own tablets from his purse, opened them and tilted them to the single candle. The lines of writing showed up palely in the dark wax, more of a prompt than a script.

'Billy Pullar and Jaikie Wilson,' he recalled. 'Dickon said those were men of Perth. Certainly Pullar is a local name. Young Rattray, Thomas Wilson and Sandy Raitts were all named in full.'

'Oh!'

'Quite so. And there were payments under their initials, all three.'

'Henry White is not named?'

'No. But there were also James Anderson, Edward Gilchrist – the Infirmarer, the Cellarer – with no payments noted either by name or by initial, and a P.S. whom I take to be the novice Simpson, who said he resisted the extortion.'

'Yes,' she said thoughtfully. 'His secret was merely a lost book, serious enough but hardly a great misdeed. In a community like this,' she paused, ordering her words, 'the person challenged I suppose would have to set the initial demand, at least, against the possible penance if the misdeed was revealed.'

'Pollock would have pitched his demand to take that into account.'

'Yes. But then, if one succumbed, gave him what he asked, that is a further misdeed, and the longer it goes on, the deeper one is mired. And one can tell no one, because that is to risk making public whatever it is he has discovered.'

'I need to pursue Pollock's acquaintance in the town tomorrow. Today has been chiefly devoted to young Rattray. Do we know, is he any kin to Sir Silvester?'

'Sir—? Oh, Mistress Buttergask's friend? Gil, I never thought to ask her.'

'You were thinking of Pollock at the time.' He tightened his arm about her shoulders. 'I would have expected the Prior to mention it if they were connected. Did she say Sir Silvester was away? I should probably get a word with him when he returns, but her statement was quite definite, you think?'

'She described what she thought she saw very clearly,' Alys agreed. 'It sounded to me like the smoke from the – the burning – towering over the house and then blowing away.'

'Yes.' Gil considered his notes in the flickering light. 'I wonder what really happened? How could someone

104

have got in to set the man on fire? The whole house was sealed, one way or another. I'd have said barely a draught of air could enter.'

'If we continue to ask questions,' she said with confidence, 'we will find the answer. So tomorrow you will look for these two men in the town?'

'To begin with, at least. Likely Brother Dickon can tell me where to find them. And you? What will you do?'

'I return to the Greyfriars. I hope Brother Michael may have more advice.'

He looked down at the black woollen crown of her head in puzzlement, but did not pursue the matter. She drew herself out of his clasp and stood up, reaching for his hand.

'Jennet will be asleep by now,' she observed. 'You will have to unlace me.'

Gil tucked his tablets away with the free hand, and got to his feet.

'I expect I can manage that,' he said.

'The entire house,' said Prior Boyd. 'Wi the exception o the lay servants and the outdoor men, a course. If they're holding silence they canny be accusing each other o breaking the Rule. At least, no so easily,' he added sourly. 'My apologies, Gilbert, if it makes your task the harder, but the health o the community comes first. If you're needing to question a man, we can have him in here and he can speak afore me.'

'As you wish, sir,' said Gil, preserving his countenance with some difficulty. This would indeed make his task harder; the entire community had been sentenced last night to dwell in silence, when not reciting the Office, until the Prior should lift the ban. He had been summoned after Chapter to hear the news, but it had already been brought to them with their morning bread and ale by one of the kitchen men, who was nearly as dismayed as Gil.

'How Brother Augustine's to get by, I canny tell,' the fellow had said, rubbing his jaw. 'I've a thick ear already, only for asking what he was signing me about, and he's broke a platter ower Billy's head for fetching him oatmeal instead o rye flour.'

'Since the outdoor *conversi* are not included in the injunction,' continued the Prior now, switching to Latin, 'I have instructed Brother Dickon to give you all possible assistance. I hope with this support you may pursue your investigation with due haste, which is now become essential.' He paused, and Gil raised an eyebrow. 'I have received a letter from Stirling. The Crown is taking an interest.'

'It had to happen,' said Gil. 'The man was a Crown official, after all. Just who is taking an interest, sir? Surely not the King's Grace himself?'

The Prior crossed himself, an expression of alarm on his face.

'Our Lady forfend! My correspondent does not say, only that there have been inquiries from the Treasury about the matter.'

'Inquiries?' said Gil. 'More than one?'

'More than one.'

'Pollock would ha been there in Knollis's time,' Gil said thoughtfully in Scots. 'Maybe I should go ower his papers again, see if there's aught in them that might interest the Treasury.'

'Aye, afore they send someone to see for theirsels,' agreed his kinsman. 'How long will this take, Gil? I need the matter settled, whatever the cost, and I'm aware that will be high. But once we ken which of us is guilty and all's dealt wi, maybe the house can quiet down again and we can address oursels to God's work as we're charged.'

'I'm nowhere near finding the answer,' said Gil. 'I need to ask more questions. How long will you keep the community silent?'

The Prior spread his hands in acceptance of the point, then rose as the little bell began to ring for Terce. Feet scuffed in the cloister outside as the brothers moved in silence towards the church. Gil held the door for the older man, bent his head for the blessing, and watched him pace off after the last of his flock; then, pulling his plaid up round his neck against this morning's biting wind, he made for the infirmary courtyard.

He remembered this place in high summer, with bees buzzing in the lavender hedge and a rosebush bending over the path; it was set between the infirmary itself, the side of the Chapter House, and a high wall over which he could see bare apple trees tufted with grey lichen, and he recalled that it had seemed to collect the sun's warmth and hold it, distilling it into a healing peace. Little of that remained now; the garden was ruined, hidden under stacks of half-burned timbers and broken roof-tiles, and the dismal smell of burning still hung over everything. He picked his way through the various obstacles to the well, and leaned on the parapet to peer in.

The water surface was perhaps five feet down, but the well seemed to be deep; beyond the reflection of the sky, with his head black against it, he could see the first course of the stonework, but below that all vanished into darkness. He stood for a while, thinking what a suitable metaphor this made for his situation, and considering what to do next. A trip into the burgh of Perth seemed inevitable, but the question was whether to deal first with the man of law named in young Rattray's papers, or with Pollock's mysterious visitors. None could be approached until he had a direction for them, which would have to wait until the

Office was ended and Brother Dickon and his cohort were free.

'Maister?' It was Nory, on quiet feet. 'Maister, that's that Euan come back fro the town. Claims he's got word for you.'

'Has he, now?' He straightened up. Nory came to his side, looked in disapproval at the smears of soot on his hands and shirt-cuffs, and glanced into the well.

'Leckie in the kitchen was saying that's twenty foot deep,' he observed. 'Likely that's where the missing knife is gone. He'd no hang onto the thing, after he'd slain the laddie, and it's the handiest place to put it.'

'My thought and all,' Gil agreed. He wiped his hands on his hose and turned away. 'Let's hear what Euan has to say for himself.'

Euan was seated in at the fire, a mug of ale in his hand. He rose when Gil entered the chamber, grinning.

'Your good health, maister! Here I've learned all sorts, and found the man Pollock's accomplice and everything you need.'

'And where were you last night?' Gil enquired.

'Och, no, I wasny intending that, and I'm sorry for it, so I am. See, maister, I was on my way back here when who should I meet, in yon street wi all the leatherworkers, but Alistair MacIain that's an Ardnamurchan man, and him a good fellow, even if he is from Acharacle. And afore we knew it, it was nightfall and the gates was shut, so I was going home wi him, and we were talking the most o the night, what wi all the doings from Ardnamurchan I had to tell him.'

'Did you get Brother Euan's simples?' Gil interrupted.

'Och, yes, I did that, and they are waiting for him now in that wee house where he was yesterday. I told Brother George, that's there watching the old man, what I had fetched. But I was telling you, maister, I've been hearing all sorts that you need to ken, and one of Alistair's neighbours was a friend o the man Pollock and was forever visiting him here and talking of how he was an important man and kent all kind o secrets.'

'Was he, now?' Gil sat down. 'Go on, then. What's his name?'

'It's a Jaikie Wilson, that's a journeyman leather-worker to a saddler in the town, and cousin to the rent collector here. So that's likely his accomplice, see, and probably set fire to him and all,' said Euan earnestly. 'And I can be taking you there, at least to Alistair's house, and he can direct you to the other fellow.'

'Never heard o him,' said Jaikie Wilson firmly.

'Och, the leear!' exclaimed Euan. 'When there's the whole o Perth telling us you visited the man regular.'

Wilson was an unprepossessing scrawny individual in an out-at-elbows doublet and stained hose; tracked down at his employer's workshop, he had come reluc-tantly to talk to Gil. Now he scowled at Euan and said, 'I'll no take that from a filthy Erscheman that canny tell the truth himsel!'

'That's enough,' said Gil before Euan could reply. 'Wilson, you're named in Pollock's papers and notes, and Brother Dickon tellt me you were there often visit-ing the man.'

'Oh, *that* Pollock!' said Wilson ingenuously. 'I thought you meant another one. Aye, I suppose I did call on him now and then. My faither served him one time,' he divulged. 'But I gaed to Maister Tammas at St John's Kirk after the – the fire, and he dowsed me wi holy watter and that, and he says I'm no contaminate.'

'And what did you do for Pollock?' Gil asked. 'Carry messages? Carry errands?'

Wilson shrugged thin shoulders.

'Aye, now and then,' he said again. 'Nothing important.'

'Like what?' Gil prompted.

109

'Like nothing much.' Gil leaned against a rack of oxhides and continued to watch the man; after a moment Wilson looked uneasily aside and said, 'Maybe like carry papers to one or another in Perth, and one time a word to some man o law in the High Street.'

'And what else?'

Another shrug.

'I'd to take the answers, hadn't I?'

'What was in the papers?'

'I wouldny look at them,' said Wilson indignantly. 'They was all sealed, forbye.'

'And the word to the man of law? Who was it? What had you to tell him?'

'Oh, I canny mind. I carry that many messages for my maister.' The man looked across the workshop to where his master and another journeyman were conferring over a cutting-board strewn with scraps of leather, and trying to pretend they were not listening to the conversation. 'It was Maister Andro Pullar at the sign o the Pestle, just up from the Speygate.'

'And you said to him?'

'I tellt you I canny mind.' He was still not looking at Gil. 'Here, I better get on wi my work.'

'So if that's all you did,' said Gil, 'why did you visit Pollock so often?'

'Likely he would be carrying all the gossip o Perth to the man,' said Euan. Wilson threw him a dirty look and said nothing. 'Or so I was hearing,' added Euan airily.

'Hah!' said Wilson, and gathered up the bundle of leathers he had been working on when his master had summoned him to speak to Gil. 'Believe an Erscheman, you'll believe anything.'

'And how about Billy Pullar?' Gil asked. 'D'you ken him?'

110

'Is that his accomplice, maister?' said Euan with enthusiasm. 'Likely they both set fire to the man thegether, and—'

'I never!' said Wilson in alarm. 'I never had aught to do wi that, I tellt you, Sir Tammas at the kirk sained me and I never heard o this Billy Pullar any road! I've tellt you all I ken, maister.'

'He must have visited Pollock when you were there,' Gil commented. 'The burgh's no that big, I'd ha thought you'd ken the other journeymen well enough.'

'Well, I don't, then.' Wilson clutched the stack of leathers closer and turned away. 'I need to get on, maister.'

'And I think you're kin to the factor at the Blackfriars,' Gil said. 'He's another Wilson. Is that right?'

'Oh, him,' said Wilson in disparaging tones. 'Aye. My da's second cousin, he is. Good day, maister.'

'You don't sound as if you welcome the kinship,' Gil said, straightening up.

'Him?' said Wilson again. 'No likely. Aye round the door after money, for all he's—' He bit off the words.

'For all he's what?' Gil prompted.

'I need to get on. Good day to ye, maister,' said Wilson firmly.

'For all he's what?' Gil said again, refusing to be dismissed. 'For all he's stealing the convent's money? For all he's raising the rents beyond reason? What's he doing, man?'

'I never said that!' said Wilson. His master looked hard at them across the workshop, then moved towards them in a casual way. 'I ken naught about the fellow. I've never spoke to him, saving he's been in the house after money.'

'So what were you going to say about him?' Gil pressed. He nodded at the saddler, who had been named to him as Maister Richie Henderson, but returned his attention to Wilson, who was now staring down at the

111

armful of leather he held. 'Tell me about Brother Thomas Wilson,' he invited.

'I can tell you about Brother Thomas,' said the saddler, a grim set to his jaw. 'More than Jaikie, I'll warrant, for all he's kin.' He jerked his head towards the far window where a litter of papers and a rack of drawers suggested accounts and records. 'Come yonder, maister, and hae a seat, and I'll tell you all you wish to hear. Jaikie, you can get on wi that harness for Sir Silvester, as I bade you earlier.'

It was a sorry tale Maister Henderson unfolded, but one Gil had encountered before; as the Blackfriars' factor Wilson handled coin on a daily basis, and some of the thin, slithering slips of metal were prone to slither into his sleeve rather than into the convent's strongbox.

'He'll say the rent's gone up,' said Maister Henderson, 'so you find the extra coin, and next quarter the same again, but somehow at the year end it's still the old rent on the parchment. Or he'll demand an extra in kind, say a mart beast or a dozen fowl, and it's never recorded.'

'Have you complained to Faither Prior?'

'I complained to Wilson, said I'd take it to the Prior, and he says, *Take it if you like, he kens all. He signs the accounts,* he says.'

'Does he now?' Gil wondered. 'Myself, I'd not adhibit my handwrit to accounts I hadny verified, but there's some are more trusting than that.'

'Aye, well,' said Henderson resentfully. 'I tried to argue the matter, and got, *If you don't like the rent, you can find another workshop.* Which is no so easy, let me tell you, maister, what wi the light you need for the work and the storage for the skins and that. It's no just every place you can walk into and set up shop.'

'I'll look into it,' said Gil. 'You keep a record, I take it?'

'Oh, I do.' Henderson glanced at the rack of drawers. 'Mind, it's my word against his, but you'll get the same tale from the most o the Blackfriars' tenants in the town.'

Extracting Euan, who had got into a discussion about the best cattle to supply the hides the business used, Gil stepped out into the Skinnergate and looked about him.

'Will we be going back out to—' Euan said hopefully, and shut his mouth on the convent's name. 'It will be time for dinner, maybe.'

'No,' said Gil, turning towards the centre of the burgh. 'We'll find this man of law.'

# Chapter Six

'Are ye making broth, or what, brother?' asked Jennet, surveying the items on the broad table in the centre of the chamber.

'Broth? No, no, it needs heat, not moisture,' said Brother Michael. He moved one of the crocks aside, and drew the gory package towards him. The second Franciscan, a small man with lank fair hair who had been identified as Brother Dandy, bridled at the sight.

'Brother!' he said in shocked tones. 'And this a fast day and all!'

'*All things must be verified by the path of experience,*' Alys quoted in the Latin, and translated for the servants.

Brother Michael nodded, but Tam said warily, 'What path would that be, mem?'

'Trying things to see if they work, as Friar Roger Bacon recommended. You know he was a Greyfriar too, don't you? I think Brother Michael plans to try whether a piece of meat can burn to ashes.'

Brother Dandy crossed himself, and took another step backwards. Rain rattled on the horn windows, and Alys drew her plaid closer about her.

They were in the kitchen of the Franciscans' guest hall, a wide, cold, vaulted space somewhat diminished by the presence of the table, on which Brother Michael had assembled a curious mixture of items. Six – no, eight – covered crocks, a dripping parcel of meat, a mixing bowl and a poke of flour, a tangle of small trivets, a bundle of rags, a handful of candle-ends.

'Recreate the conditions in the man's own chamber,' Brother Michael said, indicating this hoard, and taking Alys's understanding of his experiment wholly for granted. 'Seal one, part seal another, maybe set the candle closer—'

'What, and summon the Devil into the crock?' said Jennet in alarm. 'Won't he burst free from it and carry us all off?'

'The man wasny carried off,' Tam reminded her. 'His ashes was all there – he was burned to a cinder, just. Like the mistress said.'

'Aye, but that woman yesterday,' Jennet argued, 'she seen the Devil clear as daylight, in the very act o taking him away.'

'She's right, you ken that, brother,' said Brother Dandy nervously.

Brother Michael, ignoring this, opened out the package of meat.

'Fat pork,' he said. 'Since the subject was well covered, by what they say.'

'Jennet,' said Alys, nodding at this, 'we'll want paste to seal the crocks. Can you see to that?' She reached for the bundle of rags, and shook it out. 'We should use one of these cloths to dry the collops, perhaps, brother, and the rest to wrap them.'

Jennet, hauling at the pump in the corner of the chamber, said, 'What for d'you want to wrap them? That's a new way to bake meat, surely, mem.'

Tam was already wiping one of the collops dry.

'If ye'd a bit chalk,' he observed, watching Brother Michael setting the crocks out in a row, 'or maybe charcoal, ye could mark on the table by each what you'd done wi it. Do ye want this wrapped close, or a bit slack, brother?'

116

'Some of each, surely,' said Alys. 'And would it be good to turn one of the crocks upside down?'

'Upside down?' Brother Michael paused, frowning at her.

'Set the candle on the lid,' she said, 'and the trivet over it, and the meat in that, and then put the crock over. Then the flame can draw air if it needs. We'd have to use that one,' she pointed to the one crock with a flat lid, 'so it would stand up.'

'No, no, surely,' said Brother Michael, 'the candle draws all the air it needs, supposing we don't seal the lid. No need for that.'

'I'd like to try it,' she said. He frowned at her again, then nodded.

'Aye, I suppose,' he said. 'Making trials is aye good. You can set that one up, then. Here!' he said to Tam in alarm. 'What are you doing?'

'Wondering what's on this rag,' said Tam, lowering the cloth from his face. 'Kind o an odd smell about it. Where'd they come from, any road?'

'No dichting your neb,' said Brother Michael in some relief. 'No idea. Had them from our kitchen. They likely had them from the rag market.'

'Here's your paste done,' said Jennet, shaking flour from her fingers. 'See us one o they rags, Tam, till I wipe my hands. Is that thick enough, mem?'

Brother Dandy, backed into a corner, was muttering anxiously and crossing himself.

Alys smiled at him and said, 'It's an experiment with fire, brother, no a spiritual matter. Our souls are in no danger.'

'Danger?' said Brother Michael. 'A course it's dangerous! All trials is dangerous, you never ken what will happen.' He turned to look at his fellow, and shook his head. 'Never mind that, Dandy, make yoursel useful. Get your tablets out and write this down that I tell you.'

Alys wondered later whether it would have been more expeditious if she had sent her two servants to wait beside Brother Dandy. Despite their very competent help, it was more than an hour before all the experiments were set up. This was largely because Brother Michael persisted in checking everything himself, the wrapped collop of pig-meat, the trivet, the candle-end stuck to the bottom of each crock and carefully lit before the trivet with its burden was lowered in and the lid placed on top and sealed, part sealed, left unsealed, as he decided and dictated to his record-keeper.

'No so fast, brother!' complained Dandy as the list of attributes of the first jar was rattled off. 'I canny scribe that quickly!'

'My mistress can,' said Jennet, looking sideways at him. Alys was already opening her own tablets and drawing the little stylus out of its holder. Brother Michael, ignoring this exchange, began a description of the second crock. The pause while he worked a strip of flour-and-water paste into the rim of the lid enabled her to catch up; she had already set up her own inverted crock, at the other end of the table, and made notes of what had gone into it.

'Did you decide what was on that cloth?' she asked Tam quietly. He shrugged.

'Kinna like lamp-oil or the like, but no so strong.'

'It's left your neb all black,' Jennet observed pertly. 'Here, see us another rag and I'll take it off for you.' She dabbed at the dark smudge on Tam's nose, and he reared back. Brother Michael began his description of the next assemblage, and Alys hastily turned her attention to his words, but was aware of a brisk argument behind her.

'There's sand, or glass, or the like on that rag! It's scratched me!'

'Nothing o the sort. See? This one's clean.'

Outside the kitchen a bell began to ring. Brother Dandy said anxiously, 'Michael, that's the bell for Nones. We need to go. Michael, that's the bell!'

'Sealed halfway around,' said Brother Michael, ignoring him.

'Aye, it has. Look – it's drawn blood!'

'It's naught but a wee scratch. There must ha been sand on your neb a'ready, it was never on this cloth. Here, can you smell burning?'

'Crock number four,' continued Brother Michael. Alys dragged her awareness back to the tablets in her hand and made another note.

'A course I can smell burning, we've just been setting light to all sorts. It's wee specks o dark stuff. It must ha been on that other cloth,' said Tam. He stepped over to the light of the horn window, inspecting his forefinger. 'See, it's wee grains—' He tasted carefully. Then: 'St Mungo's garters! Get away fro that crock, man, afore it explodes! Get down, mem!'

'What—' Brother Michael broke off his enumerations and turned to stare at him. Brother Dandy, taking Tam's word for it, cannoned past Jennet to the door, knocking her flying as he went, Tam seized Alys and threw her to the floor, Brother Michael exclaimed in irritation, and the fourth crock exploded with a bang.

It was not a large explosion, but it was quite spectacular. Alys was aware of a bright, brief light, a sizzling, a rattling sound as fragments of pottery landed around them, though she could not have said in what order these things happened. She squirmed out from under Tam, and got to her knees, feeling a little shaky.

'Are ye hurt, mem?' he asked anxiously, scrambling up to give her his hand. 'I'm right sorry about knocking ye down.'

'I'm not hurt,' she assured him, brushing dust from her woollen gown. 'That was quick thinking. What

– was it gunpowder on the cloth? Brother Michael, your face!'

Jennet was getting to her feet too, rubbing her elbow, glaring at the open door. Brother Michael stood in the midst of his experiment, staring about him, blood dripping down his jaw from several small cuts. Jennet seized another rag, checked it briefly, and tried to apply it to the wounds, but he jerked away from her, still staring at the table. The base of the fourth crock was present, cracked in three pieces, and in their midst the trivet shattered in several more; there was no sign of the wrapped collop. The two crocks nearest the demolished one had fallen over, and the lit one had lost its lid, disgorging a lightly singed bundle and a strong smell of scorched meat. The candle was out.

'Now I canny tell,' he said discontentedly, 'whether that had gone out afore the crock fell over, or no.'

'Does it matter?' asked Tam. 'Can you no set it up again?'

'Aye, I suppose. Make a note, lassie,' he added. 'Gunpowder no a good idea.'

'Are ye just going on wi it?' said Jennet. 'What if the rest blows up and all?'

'There was no more rags like thon,' said Tam. 'Likely it'd been used for cleaning a harquebus or some such thing.'

Running footsteps heralded the arrival of two lay brothers, who stopped at the doorway, peering in suspiciously.

'What's blew up now, brither?' said one of them. 'Is that burning meat? It's a fast day, isn't it no?'

'Nothing to concern you. Nothing to worry anybody,' said Brother Michael irritably.

'There's Brother Dandy come blundering into Nones, interrupting the Office –'

'There was no need for that!'

'– and saying you're all blown to pieces and three others along wi you, and Faither Prior sending us out to look, but it doesny appear like that to me.'

'Dandy's a fool,' said Brother Michael. He took the cloth from Jennet and dabbed ineffectually at his face, glanced at the bloodstains and looked surprised. 'It was a crock. No great matter. Nobody's hurt.'

The two lay brothers looked at one another, and at Alys; she smiled, and nodded reassuringly, and after a moment they withdrew. Brother Michael began picking up the singed experiment, his booted feet crunching on the broken pottery on the floor.

'Where's the lid o the broken one went?' Tam wondered.

'Never mind that, where's the collop?' Jennet said.

'There,' said Tam, looking upwards. Alys followed his gaze and saw, directly over Brother Michael's head, a palm-sized piece of raw meat adhering to the stonework of the vaulted ceiling.

Jennet began to laugh, and the fragment peeled away with a faint sucking sound and dropped onto Brother Michael's tonsure. He clapped a hand over it, looked blankly at the result, wiped his palm on his habit and said to Alys, 'Read me the notes, lassie. What all was in this one again?'

Ignoring Jennet's giggles, Alys obeyed, and carefully took notes as the remaining crocks were assembled. As she worked she became aware of a smell of burned meat, of hot fat, of soot. The servants were both aware of it too, she realised, and were trying to identify which crock was the source.

'Makes you right hungry, and all,' said Tam. 'No, it's none o these.'

'It's that one!' said Jennet finally. 'The mistress's one. Look at your crock, mem!'

'And this one unsealed,' said Brother Michael, paying no attention. Alys wrote down *No selit* and looked round

121

at her own experiment at the far end of the huge table. For a moment she thought it unchanged; then she saw that something was oozing from the gap between the lid and the crock inverted on top of it, something yellowish, which congealed as it touched the well-scrubbed wood. Hot fat.

'The floor,' she said. 'The floor of the house was greasy.'

The crock was giving off heat; she could feel it when she approached. Brother Michael, his own experiments settled, came to join her, put a hand close and drew it away again sharply.

'Still at work, whatever's happening.'

'The floor of the man's house was covered in grease,' she said again. He nodded, without looking at her.

'The fat feeds the flames. Melts wi the heat, and burns like a tallow candle wi the clothing as a wick, and the excess runs off. Wouldny ha happened if he'd been naked.'

'He'd no ha sat there naked on a winter's night,' said Tam.

'He'd never ha sat there naked,' objected Jennet. 'It's no decent!'

Alys looked longingly at the crock, but before she could speak there was the tramp and scuffle of booted feet outside, and a little group of Franciscans appeared at the open door, a small man at their centre with clipped silver hair and very black eyebrows. She curtsied, aware of Jennet bobbing beside her and Tam bending his head. There was no mistaking Father Prior, even before he spoke.

'Michael!' he said, and sniffed suspiciously. 'What are you at now, brother?'

'An experiment,' said Brother Michael, in a less irritable tone than he had used for the lay brothers.

122

'And what does the experiment consist in?' Father Prior stepped into the kitchen. Behind him one of his entourage held a smoking thurible, another bore a basin and aspergillum. The smoke of the incense wafted into the room, fighting with the reek of burned pork. 'Are you putting these good folk at risk? Is anything else like to explode?'

'No,' began Brother Michael, and was interrupted by a sharp crack.

Tam flung himself and Jennet to the floor, Jennet squeaking indignantly. Two of the brothers in the doorway ran away. The man with the basin dropped the aspergillum, but Father Prior said, with a grim note in his voice, 'I think you may rise, man. Michael has cost us anither crock, no waur than that.'

Tam climbed to his feet with a sheepish grin, and bent to help Jennet. Brother Michael was already frowning over the broken crock; it had simply split into two unequal parts, revealing another bundle of singed rags in its soot-blackened interior.

'I should pay for the crocks,' said Alys hastily, 'seeing they're broken to answer my question.'

'That would be generous, daughter,' said Father Prior, although his tone said, *The least you can do*. 'And what question would that be?'

'Fire,' said Brother Michael before she could speak. 'Will fire work within a closed space. Whatna conditions will it require.'

'And?'

'Mostly it doesna,' he admitted. 'Thon one seems to be in action, but we need to wait till it cools enough to open it. If we had some glassware,' he said to Alys.

'God forbid!' said Father Prior. 'Understand me, Michael, I willny have this kitchen nor any other part of this priory covered in broken glass. I never heard that our brother Roger shattered glassware in his experimenting, and I see no need for you to do so.'

'Aye, Faither,' said Brother Michael with reluctance.

'And,' said his superior in the same tone, 'you willny leave this chamber until all is straight again and these potsherds swept up and put on the midden.' He eyed Alys and the two servants, and went on, 'I'll send Doty wi a mess of food to the four o ye, for the dinner has waited long enough a'ready.'

He delivered a brief blessing over Alys's murmured thanks and swept out, his cohort scattering to let him pass. Tam closed the door behind them and whistled, but Brother Michael merely looked along his depleted row of experiments and said, 'This one's cold, and that. We can open them up.'

The food, brought by a wary lay servant, was simple but hot and welcome: a big bowl of bean and lentil pottage, with roots chopped into it, a whole loaf of that day's rough bread to eat it with, a jug of thin ale. Brother Michael looked at it blankly, but when Alys asked him if he was hungry he waved her away.

'No the now, lassie! Eat if you must,' he added in a kinder tone, 'I'll see to these first.'

'It's right tasty,' said Tam, scooping up a generous portion of the thick concoction on a lump of the bread.

'You should eat while the food is hot, brother. The experiments will still be there when you have finished,' Alys prompted. 'And then I can make notes for you.'

'Hmf!' he said, but came to join them.

'But how does this show you what happened to the man?' Jennet said suddenly, as if continuing a conversation. 'Even if you can set fire to a lump o meat, and you've no done that yet, it doesny prove that's how he burned up. He'd never ha sat still waiting to catch alight, he'd ha jumped up, for sure.'

'Good question,' said Brother Michael, tearing off another hunk of bread.

'Maybe he was asleep,' said Tam, 'and his clothes was well alight afore he knew it.'

Jennet shuddered, and crossed herself.

'Our Lady send sic a thing never happens to me. What a way to go!'

'Flares up quickly,' said Brother Michael, through a mouthful of bread and pottage. 'Well alight, as you say.' He closed his eyes to think, chewing, and after a moment added, 'Too fast to smother them yoursel. Need help.'

'And there was none to be summoned,' said Alys.

'Aye.'

'We all meet our end some time,' said Tam philosophically, and took a pull at the jug of ale.

By the time the food was finished, all the experiments had ceased working. When Alys approached hers she found the crock cooling, with little ticking noises, and the fat beginning to congeal round its rim. Brother Michael threw it a glance, but began at the other end of the row of crocks and worked his way methodically along it, dictating notes on the state of each.

'It's no learning you anything,' said Jennet, when the friar had uncovered a fourth container of barely scorched cloth, cold meat and snuffed-out candle. 'None o it's doing aught, save the two that exploded.' He frowned in irritation, but she went on, 'No that that's a bad thing. I'd as soon no more o them explode afore we've left here.'

'Jennet,' said Alys, 'see if you can find a broom, and start sweeping up the broken pot.' She wrote, *Clout scaldit, meat no brent* against the last of Brother Michael's experiments, and turned to her own. He gestured to her to uncover it herself; setting her tablets and stylus down, she took a deep breath and laid hands on the upturned crock.

It came away from its lid readily enough, being still rather hot to handle. She drew it up, and looked at what it revealed.

'It hasny worked,' she said in disappointment.

'What, yours and all, mem?' said Jennet, emerging from the scullery with a broom and shovel. 'Here, Tam, gie's a hand here.'

'It has,' corrected Brother Michael. 'See?' He poked at the blackened bundle which still lay on the trivet, then drew his eating-knife from his purse and used it to prod the unsavoury object. 'Burned all round. Cloth's all gone, meat's been burned. Fat's run down.' He scraped at the lid between the feet of the trivet. 'See, plenty fat left.'

'But it's no burned to ash,' objected Tam. Alys was staring at her experiment.

'Fire needs air. Common fire. I've proved it,' said Brother Michael offhandedly. 'Starved o air it goes out, every time.' He looked at his row of failed assays. 'Those are proof it's common fire we're dealing wi. But this,' he prodded the crust of the burned meat again, 'this has begun to burn up afore it ran out o air.'

'Why's this one different?' said Tam. 'Was there a hole in the crock, or what?'

'The flame could draw air in at the bottom,' said Alys. 'Until the fat running out blocked the gap.'

Brother Michael nodded.

'Aye. And the bit o meat was a sight bigger within the crock than a man is within his bedchamber. He burned to ashes, but this ran out o air and ceased burning. We need a bigger crock.'

'I think Father Prior might object,' said Alys.

'What about a bread-oven?' said Jennet, bending to sweep under the empty charcoal range. 'That's just a big crock, is it no?'

'Like mistress, like maid,' said Brother Michael obscurely. 'But no the day.'

'No,' agreed Alys.

*     *     *

126

'How do I find Mercer's Land?' Alys asked the porter as he swung the outer door of the priory open for them.

'The Mercer's Land, lassie?' he said, and scratched the back of his head within his hood. 'It's right the other side the town. See, you go in at the South Port here, and right through the town and out the Red Brig Port, and then you cross the Town Ditch, and it's . . .' He paused to reckon, staring absently at a group of riders emerging from the port. 'Third or fourth on your right, it would be. Canny miss it.'

'Thank you, brother,' Alys said, and curtsied. He raised his hand in the conventional blessing, and she stepped out into the drizzle to find the riders had halted before the door, a mounted woman with a whip in her hand, three men and another woman riding pillion. Their horses were trampling in circles while the woman gave orders in a loud, harsh voice.

'Ask at him, Thomas you great fool, he has to tell you. Is there any Alexander Stair dwelling here, ask him. And he'll tell you true or it will be the waur for him.'

The man addressed answered inaudibly, and she cursed him and tugged on her reins so that her horse swung round, its hindquarters narrowly missing Tam.

'Here, watch out!' he objected.

She turned her head and cursed at him too, and when he did not step back fast enough, cut at him with her whip. The thong missed, but Alys said briskly, 'Madam, permit my servant to pass, if you please.'

She found herself inspected briefly by a hot, dispassionate gaze like a hawk's, and dismissed; the rider turned away as her own servant returned from the priory door.

'None? Well, we'll lie up here anyway, and learn if it's the truth. Go back and tell him we'll lodge here.'

'What a termagant!' Tam had slipped past the horse, and Alys made haste to remove them all from the scene. 'I'll wager she gets plenty use of that scurge.'

127

'I wonder who she's after,' said Jennet. 'D'ye suppose it's a servant, or her man ran away, or the like?'

'Whoever it is, I hope he sees her first,' said Tam, grinning, and followed Alys through the South Port's shadowy tunnel.

'Where are we going, mem? Are we no going back to the Bl—' Jennet began, and stopped as Tam nudged her in the ribs. 'To our own place,' she finished.

'No yet,' Alys said.

It was well after midday, and the light was beginning to fade, but the Watergate was bustling with shops and stalls dripping in the rain; apprentices bawled their masters' wares, merchants and stout burgesses paraded about in furred gowns. Opposite the row of shops stood the mansions of the wealthy, backing onto the river. What had Gil called it? Ah, yes, the Tay.

'I hope it's somewhere warmer than thon kitchen, then,' said Jennet, pulling her plaid tighter about her.

Alys had to ask her way twice more before she found the house she sought. It was out past the dyeworks and tanners' yards of the northern suburb, one of several small timber-framed buildings on a strip of land running down to the river. It had a pair of flowerpots by the door, one with a straggling clump of lavender in it.

'That'll no do well this weather,' said Tam.

Alys rattled at the pin. Inside the house a child's voice called, 'Door, Mammy! Door, Mammy!' and a woman answered, 'I hear it, my lamb.' Light footsteps approached, and the door opened.

The woman who stood there was so different from what Alys expected that for a moment she could only stand, open-mouthed, her tactful greeting silenced. Young, not so much slender as thin, decently dressed, her head clad in good linen, a baby of eight months or so on her hip and an older child clinging to her skirts, she would have been pretty were it not for the scar across her eye and the badly broken nose which had set crooked and flattened. Her expression suggested she was braced for the onlookers' reaction, whether it was revulsion or pity.

Alys swallowed her words, and just in time spied a curl of red hair escaping from the linen undercap. Enlightenment struck her.

'Mistress Margaret Rattray?' she said.

'None by that name here,' said the other woman, and began to close the door.

'That's a pity,' Alys persisted. 'I have sorry news for her.'

'News?' The tone was apprehensive. 'What news would that be?'

'From the Blackfriars.'

The woman seemed to brace herself even further, and stood aside.

'Aye, you'd best come in.'

They stepped into a modest chamber, adequately furnished, with cushions and a brazier to make it comfortable. A spinning wheel, the baby's cradle, some toys, were scattered about. A spider-legged baby walker stood by the settle. The woman closed the door behind her and leaned against it, holding the baby protectively.

'Is he—?' she began. 'Is Andrew—?'

'Andrew Rattray is dead,' said Alys gently.

Margaret Rattray's gaze dropped. Studying a wooden animal with deep interest, she said in a thread of a voice, 'Well, he's wi Our Lady now, for certain.'

'His friends have told us how great a devotion he had for her,' Alys said.

'Mammy?' said the older child. 'Mammy, is it folk?'

'It's folk, my lamb,' said Mistress Rattray. 'Three folk come to talk wi Mammy. Come, you go in your walker till I heat some ale for them.'

'Can I do that for ye, mistress?' offered Jennet, just as Alys realised with a chill of dismay that the child was blind.

'Aye, my wee brither,' said Mistress Rattray, still dry-eyed, clasping the drowsy baby against her shoulder. 'There was four year atween us, and our parents both dee'd the year after I was wed, just after Drew was born.'

'That's hard,' said Alys, and Jennet added a murmur of sympathy from where she knelt by the hearth. Tam, across the room playing with Drew and a ball with a bell in it, nodded agreement.

'And then Andrew would go for the Blackfriars. Skene was against it, but then he was against near everything—'

'That was your man?' said Alys, detecting a bitter note in her voice.

'Aye. Nicholas Skene, burgess o Montrose, weel kent and weel respectit. You'd no think a man like that would do this to his wife—' She gestured at her face with her free hand, and Tam jerked round to stare at her in horror. 'It took Andrew a year to get by the objections Skene raised, about the money and the property. Mysel, I think he'd hoped to come by the lot some way, or at least manage it for Andrew whether he liked it or no, and once it was wi the Blackfriars he couldny touch it, a course.'

'Was there much?' Alys asked.

'Two houses in Montrose, that the rents paid for his schooling, and a bit land in the township our mother came fro. It was after Andrew left this began,' she gestured at her face again, 'quarrels and beatings, and then when I was six month howding wee Maimie here he cam home drunk one nicht fro a banquet and did this to me. And he struck . . .' She gestured at small Drew

130

across the room, and then at her eyes. 'That was his doing.'

Over the other woman's shoulder Alys saw Tam bend his head and clench his fists, as if dealing with strong emotion. The child asked him a question, and Tam straightened up and turned to him with an effort.

'Is your man dead?' she asked. Mistress Rattray looked at her, away again, then down at the floor, rubbing her toe along the broad boards.

'Aye. And now Andrew and all. What came to him? Was he sick? I never— I've had no word from him, these ten days or more.'

'Ten days?' said Alys. 'Are you sure o that?'

Mistress Rattray paused, reckoning on the fingers of her free hand.

'The day after Epiphany,' she said finally. 'He cam to me late that evening, after they was all supposed to be abed. He did that often,' she divulged, 'maybe once a week or so. He said he couldny rest easy, save he knew all was well wi me and the bairns. So that's two weeks now. I've been kinna anxious, but Annie says there's never been any o them about in the burgh, and I couldny ask her to speir for him any road, she'd be certain to gie me away. And now you tell me he's deid right enough.'

'Annie is your servant?' Alys asked.

'Aye, she cam wi me from Montrose. A good heart, but a light head. She's out to the market the now.'

Alys did not comment. Instead she said, 'You mind about the man that vanished?'

'Aye,' said Mistress Rattray warily. 'You said your man's asking questions about it.'

Jennet rose from the hearth with two wooden beakers.

'Here's your ale, mem,' she said. 'Will I put that wean in her cradle, and let you sup?'

'They're saying in the town, by what Annie tells me,' Mistress Rattray went on, allowing Jennet to lift the sleeping baby from her arms, 'the man was carried off by the Deil himsel. But that's naught to do wi our Andrew, surely?' She looked anxiously from Alys to Jennet.

'The day after it happened, Andrew confessed to causing the disappearance,' Alys said.

'Oh!' said Andrew's sister in a different tone.

'So he was confined, though he couldny explain how he caused it.'

'Oh!' she said again. 'But how did that bring about his— he would never dwine and dee just for being confined, no Andrew. Oh, I canny believe he's deid! My wee brither!' Finally there were tears in her eyes. 'What came to him? What are ye no telling me, mistress? Has your man found something to his discredit?' she asked, her tone sharpening. 'Did he have aught to do wi the one that's dead?'

'Not a thing to his discredit,' Alys assured her. She paused, biting her lip. 'Forgive me, mistress. It's no an easy thing to tell. Andrew,' she drew a deep breath, 'Andrew was lodged in the Blackfriars' infirmary, where he could be kept confined. The night before last, the infirmary burned down.' Mistress Rattray opened eyes and mouth wide in a horrified gasp, but Alys pressed on. 'He never burned to death, mistress. Someone had cut his throat afore the fire was set. Andrew was murdered.'

'Murdered?' repeated Mistress Rattray, and crossed herself. 'Our Andrew? But why? He'd never – he'd no – it wasny Skene, was it?'

*I thought you were lying*, Alys said to herself, hearing the panic in the tone.

'They don't think it was anyone entered the convent. It was someone within the Blackfriars,' she said. 'Did he have enemies in the community? How did he speak of the other brothers?'

Mistress Rattray shook her head disbelievingly.

'None, that he named. Och, he got across this one and that, he named the man that guards the books a few times, but none o them was enemies. And his fellows, that he studied wi, they were right good friends by all he tellt me, the two o them that's cried Sandy in especial. His throat cut, mistress? But how? Did nobody hear? Did he no cry out? Are you certain it was some one o the brothers?'

'The Infirmarer is an old man, and very deaf,' Alys said. 'They fear the shock and guilt are like to be his death and all. My man thinks, from the way he was lying, your brother was killed while he slept, likely never knew a thing. There's no sign anyone else got into the place, it must ha been one of the community. There's a kitchen knife missing.'

'Who would do a thing like that?' Margaret Rattray crossed herself again, and looked from the sleeping baby to Drew, now listening avidly to a story Tam was telling him. 'And my bairnies and me wi none to protect us now,' she whispered.

'I think some of these things are yours.' Alys reached for her purse and drew out the bundle Mureson had given them last night. Mistress Rattray stared blankly at it, but when it was put into her hands she accepted it, and slowly unfolded the fabric, rubbing the fine hem between finger and thumb.

'One o my mother's veils,' she said. 'I didny ken he still had it. And—' She put a hand to her mouth. 'Our Lady be praised! It's the title to the house. And the dockets from the Low Country.' She closed her eyes in passionate relief. 'Och, it's ower worldly, to be thinking o sic a thing when my wee brother's just met his end, but—'

'Your care must be for the living,' Alys said gently. 'And these other things, they are his as well? Is the drawing of you and the bairns?'

'It is. Andrew's— he was good at the limning.' She turned over the oddments in the folds of the cloth. 'The stone we found by the river one time. A trinket off my da's horse-furniture. Grandpa's St James badge. I'm right glad to have these, mistress, sorry though I am that they're to me rather than to Andrew.' She looked up at Alys again. 'But here – you were saying, he was confined for that he confessed to causing the man's disappearance, is that right?'

'So Father Prior said.'

'I wonder.' She crossed herself, looking anxious. 'I wonder, could it be right? Surely he'd no – no, no my Andrew.'

'He could never explain how it happened,' said Alys, 'how he caused the man to vanish.'

'Aye, he wouldny bring himself to say.' Mistress Rattray crossed herself again.

'Do you ken what made him think that?' Alys asked. 'It was impossible he'd aught to do wi it. The house was locked fast.'

'Aye, well, it's happened afore, or something like it.' She smiled sadly. 'When he was ten or so, the priest that taught him his Latin dee'd when his house went on fire. Andrew would have it he'd caused it, for that he hated the man and he dreamed o him burning in Hellfire. He wasny,' she tightened her mouth, 'he wasny a good man, but Andrew's aye felt the guilt o his death, since the man would never be confessed o his sins. He tellt me, one time we spoke o't, he tellt me he'd wished him deid many and many times. I tried to tell him, that's no guarantee it will happen. *Look at Skene*, I tellt him, *have I no wished him deid many and many a time?*'

'I see,' said Alys. 'That would fit. I'm agreed, wishing is no enough, we haveny the power, only God can order

134

things to His will. But Andrew was . . .' she selected her words carefully, 'I think he had very strong feelings.'

'Oh, aye.'

'Strong enough to think his wishing someone deid might—'

'Aye,' said Andrew's sister. She looked down at the jumble of things in her lap, and covered her eyes, her fingers automatically cupping the scar. 'Oh, my wee brother.'

There was a step outside the door, the latch lifted, the door swung open. A plump middle-aged maidservant stepped in, outlined for a moment against the light, a basket on her hip, her plaid wet with drops of rain.

'Mistress?' she said, peering suspiciously at the visitors. 'I got the kale, at a bargain just while he was putting the shutters up, and a wee bit mutton will make us a nice broth. Who's all these, then?'

# Chapter Seven

Enquiring on the Highgate for Maister Andro Pullar's place of business got Gil first a disparaging, 'Oh, him! He's along that way.' The second citizen he asked spat copiously on the cobbles, just missing Gil's boots, before he jerked a thumb at the next forestair and said, 'Yonder, in the grand house, like an honest man.'

'It's a grand house indeed,' said Euan, impressed. 'There's a good living for a man o law in this town, that's plain.'

Gil, climbing the stair, said nothing, but rattled the pin at the oak door. Euan had a point; it was a very handsome house, tall and narrow in the Dutch style, and recently built by the look of the stones of the lower floor. A clerk answered the door, and bowed them into a neat chamber where a liveried servant was kicking his heels on a bench along one wall, but rose as they entered. Besides the bench there was a table, a tall desk and a hearth with a fire in it. The furnishings were all new, locally made by a good craftsman, Gil thought. A door at the far side of the chamber was firmly shut, but voices were audible through it.

'You'll no mind waiting,' the clerk announced officiously. 'My maister's got someone wi him the now. Hae a seat on yon bench if you wish, maister.'

He took up a pen from the desk and returned to copying something. Euan retired to a corner, conveniently close to the fire. Gil shook the rain from his plaid, nodded at the servant and sat down, wondering whether he needed a clerk to admit clients to his own house. Lowrie or one of the servants usually answered the door, and his notary's practice was hardly profitable enough to keep a clerk as well as Lowrie. He occupied the time reckoning how much work he would need to bring in to make it worthwhile, and was concluding that he had no wish for that much extra work, when the voices from the inner chamber became suddenly louder.

'I assure you, Mistress Trabboch—'

The clerk looked up, and the waiting servant flinched and braced himself.

'You'll assure me o nothing, you handless, shilpit wee sumph!' declared a loud harsh voice. 'Six weeks you've had to find him, in a place this size, and what can you tell me?'

'I doubt you've been misinformed, mistress, for I—'

'I wasny misinformed. Isabella Newton kens him as well as she kens me, she'd no mistake him.'

'It's a pity she couldny recall what habit he was wearing. But I assure you, mistress, there's none o that name in any o the houses hereabout.'

'Useless, you are! You'll no see a penny piece for this, for I'll no believe you've stirred yoursel off your arse in the matter at all. I'll see mysel out, man. I'd no trust you to convey me to your ain stair.'

The door flung open, and a tall woman stalked out, her wide skirts swirling round her, a harassed maid-servant hurrying after her.

'Thomas,' she said sharply as she crossed the chamber, elbowed the clerk aside when he would have opened the door for her, jerked at the latch and flung the heavy boards back. The door, rebounding, caught her servant's shoulder as he hurried to accompany her, then crashed shut behind the party.

138

'*Dhia!*' said Euan from the corner. 'You would take her for Scathach herself!'

The man of law who appeared from the inner room was not an imposing figure. A foot or so shorter than Gil, narrow of face and form, one shoulder higher than the other, he glared after Mistress Trabboch, then sniffed disparagingly and turned to Gil.

'Aye?' he said.

Gil bowed, and said in Latin, 'Good day to you, brother. May I have a word?'

Maister Pullar stared hard at him for a moment, then turned back into his chamber, saying in the same language, 'Hah! Come in.'

'A difficult client,' Gil observed, closing the door behind him.

'Difficult!' said Maister Pullar. 'Aye, very difficult. How may I help you, brother?'

Gil introduced himself and they bowed again, the formal recognition of one man of law for another. Pullar sat down at his elaborate desk and waved at the nearest stool.

'Have a seat, maister. And what brings Blacader's quaestor into Perth? The Archbishop of Glasgow has no authority in Dunkeld diocese.' His Latin had the accent of St Andrews rather than Glasgow.

'I know that,' Gil agreed. 'I am lodged at the house of the Dominicans.'

'Ah. In the matter of the disappearance of Leonard Pollock, I must suppose.'

'Indeed.' Gil was watching the man, maintaining his friendly expression. 'I am told you had some dealings with him. I hoped you might be able to tell me a little, seeing he is now known to be dead.'

'Dead, is he? That is certain?'

'The fire which was thought to have carried him off in fact destroyed his body absolutely. We have found his ashes.'

139

Maister Pullar crossed himself, murmured something conventional, and folded his hands on his desk.

'What proof do we have that the ashes are Pollock's?' he asked.

'Circumstantial only,' Gil admitted. 'The house was locked and barred from the inside, and we found the key melted among the ashes. It's hard to say who else they might represent.'

Pullar's eyes widened briefly.

'Melted?' he repeated, and whistled. 'Surely that must have been Hellfire.'

'There was no smell of sulphur, nor other signs of demonic presence,' Gil assured him. 'I am working on the assumption that the fire was caused by some human agency, and seeking to learn who might have had cause to wish the man dead. The list is not short.'

'Oh.' Pullar contemplated his folded hands for a moment, a frown creasing his brow. Then he said, 'I did indeed have some dealings with Pollock. I acted for him in one or two land transactions, very profitable to himself, and he has a strongbox deposited here.' He fell silent. Gil waited, still watching; the man's face gave away nothing further, and after a pause he continued, 'I do not have the key, nor can I think it would be appropriate to open the box without some written authority.'

'Father Prior?' Gil suggested. 'I am certain he would give you a letter over the convent's seal requiring an inventory of the contents of the box. And I believe there is a key among the man's effects at the Priory, which may be the key to the box.'

'That might be suitable. Aye, that might be very suitable. Perhaps you would assist me to make such an inventory.'

'That would be possible.' Gil sat quiet, curious to see if any more information would emerge, and reflecting that he would not wish to play cards with this man; his expression did not alter for some time.

Finally Pullar appeared to come to a conclusion, and sat back, saying in Scots, 'Aye, well, that'll all be assopat now. You'll be aware o his various sources o income, I take it, maister.'

'I've found one or two,' Gil admitted. 'If you can show me any more I'd be glad of it.'

'Aye. He'd the corrody, a course, a good sum lodged wi the Blackfriars by the Treasury to see to his keep as long's he required it—'

'Why was that?' Gil interrupted. 'D'you ken what prompted it? The Crown's more like to set up a pension or a benefice than buy a corrody, by my observation.'

'I asked him that myself,' said the other man, 'but I'd no answer. He himself wished the corrody, I believe, and it might well ha been to annoy someone, by one or two remarks he passed at other times.'

'Another difficult client,' Gil commented.

'Aye,' said Pullar flatly. 'So he'd the corrody, but he'd brought a well-filled box wi him, and invested it wi care while he was still getting about. He's a good income in rents, no within the burgh, a course, him no being a burgess, but from the lands outwith the town, about the Blackfriars and the like; there's a good few properties scattered about there. He'd a couple o ventures overseas,' he added, 'but they wereny successful. Maybe if he'd taen Maister Halyburton's advice—'

'Interesting,' said Gil. 'Is there coin in the strongbox, then? For there wasny a great sum in the kist in his lodging.'

'No, no,' said Pullar. 'For it's all sent away, or at least the most o't.'

'Sent away?' Gil repeated, aware of his eyebrows climbing. 'Where to?'

'I never enquired,' said Pullar, in that flat tone. 'It began two–three year ago. Every six month or there-about, a fellow turns up bearing the key, shows me a jewel, collects what's lying here and goes off again, and I send the key back to the Blackfriars. The last time or two it's been an Irishman, afore that it was a Fleming, a different fellow every time, but they all had the jewel right enough. There's one about due. I've been wonder-ing what's like to happen.'

'What kind o a jewel?' Gil asked. 'I take it it's easy identified.'

'Oh, it's that all right. An enamel badge on a chain, shaped like a white rose. A bonnie thing, but perilous.'

'Perilous indeed!' said Prior Boyd. 'The badge o the Yorkist kings o England, that Harry Tudor overthrew in '85. What's that doing here in Perth? What's the House o York to do wi Pollock?'

'My thought and all,' Gil agreed. 'It's, what, near ten years since Bosworth Field. There are plenty o their adherents still about trying to get a revolt thegether, and Margaret of Burgundy's trying to get back at King Henry for the death o her nephews in the Tower wi every breath she takes, which will all take money like it's going out o fashion. But why should a former Treasury man suddenly begin funding the Yorkist cause? Had he letters from abroad? Visitors?'

The Prior shook his head.

'No that I ever saw,' he said. 'It's only the last year or so he's been confined to the House – to these premises,' he amended. Gil nodded. 'He might ha met anyone out in the burgh – he spent a good part o his time there. Could some agent of Burgundy have caused his death, maybe?'

'I thought of that,' Gil agreed, 'but if he was sending them money, a good sum every time by what Pullar told me, why should they suddenly weary o him? It makes no sense.'

'So we're no closer learning by what agency the man dee'd.'

'It's less than two days since I got here,' Gil pointed out, 'and the trail was cold. I'm still gathering information. Once I've got it all, it'll maybe make sense.' Or maybe it won't, he thought, but did not say. 'Meantime, sir,' he went on, 'I'd as soon pursue young Rattray's killer, if I can. The boy deserves justice.'

'Aye.' The Prior crossed himself, and heaved a sigh. 'No member of the community has presented himself to confess,' he said sadly, changing to Latin, 'and I have not so far questioned those who accused one another, feeling that some delay might be beneficial in giving them time to reflect, and also that you might prefer to be present when I do so.'

'I would value the opportunity,' Gil replied in the same language. This was exactly what he had hoped for. He would have preferred to question the various members of the community privately, but since that was impossible this would be the next best thing.

He had returned to the Blackfriars in time for the midday meal, to find Alys still absent about the town somewhere and the men with no idea where she had gone. After they had eaten he had set all three of them to talk to the lay servants and the outdoor men, hoping that Brother Dickon would enlist Euan's help at something backbreaking if he approached him, and repaired to the Prior's study to report what progress he had made. It seemed remarkably little, particularly since he had suppressed any mention of the contents of Andrew Rattray's linen bundle.

'Should we have them in together?' he continued now. 'This would avoid any appearance of favouring one party or the other.'

143

Thomas Wilson and Alexander Raitts, summoned by a servant, jostled each other through the doorway, glaring sideways and both breathing hard, but they were sufficiently wise in their Order to maintain the silence they had been commanded to keep. Gil studied them as they took up an appropriately humble stance before their Prior, heads bent, hands tucked into their sleeves. He recognised Wilson now as one of the friars he had seen about the place, a broad-shouldered, broad-faced man with a pleasant smile and calculating eyes, who seemed much more composed than his companion. Raitts's fingers were twitching inside his sleeves, perhaps drumming on the opposing wrists, making the heavy wool quiver. His nostrils were twitching as well. Both men were somewhat battle-scarred; Wilson bore a scabbed bruise on his cheekbone, and Raitts sported a magnificent black eye and a split lip.

Prior David delivered himself of a brief but pungent speech, reminding them of the value of truth, brotherly affection, and the stability of the Order, and instructing them to speak one at a time in answer to Maister Cunningham's questions. Raitts shivered at that, and clasped his hands tightly; Wilson raised his head and looked at Gil, frowning slightly.

'Gentlemen,' said Gil, arranging his thoughts. 'You mind I'm here to investigate the matter of Leonard Pollock's disappearance.' Wilson nodded. Raitts scowled. 'I'm asked of your Prior,' he bowed slightly towards his kinsman, 'to consider the death o Andrew Rattray as well. I wasny at the Chapter of Faults when I'm told you accused each the other o causing these events. I want to hear all you ken that prompted you to say sic a thing.' He pointed at Raitts. 'In the order o the alphabet, you first.'

Wilson stiffened, and swallowed, but said nothing. Raitts stared from Gil to his Prior and back, looking appalled.

'I – I – I –' he began, and gulped like a carp. 'Is he to question us, Faither? On a Priory matter? It's no appropriate.'

'Answer the question,' said Prior David.

'Murder and arson,' said Gil deliberately, 'are pleas of the Crown, and hanging offences. It's gone beyond your walls now, brother. What prompted you to accuse Thomas Wilson o murder?'

Wilson turned his head and glared, but held silence. Raitts gulped again, and said in a whisper, 'He was about the place in the night, creeping out o the kitchen in the dark, whispering in corners wi Henry White, for I saw him. What else could he ha been at?'

'And how did you come to see him?' Gil asked. 'I take it you were creeping about the place in the dark and all?'

'I wasny creeping!' said Raitts indignantly. 'I went out to the – to the necessarium, all openly. You canny just step out in the dark. The stairs is as worn, you need to watch your feet and go by the wall, even wi a lantern, so I was going slow and quiet and here was this one—'

'A moment,' said Gil. 'When was this?'

'Why, the night the infirmary burned. The night the poor laddie was murdered.' Raitts tried to look sideways out of his bruised eye at Wilson and flinched at the attempt.

'Where is the necessarium? You've no privy at the same level as the dorter?'

'It's in the corner o the cloister,' said the Prior, 'at the foot o the day stair. Far from convenient, especial when it rains, though at least it's under the cloister roof.'

'The day stair.' Gil tried to envisage the cloister. 'So it's at the other end o the refectory from the kitchens.'

'Aye, and here's this one, ganging along the cloister walk from the kitchen, talking wi Henry White, all in whispers.'

145

'How did you identify them?' Gil asked. Raitts stared at him. 'What time was this? I take it it was full dark. How were you so sure it was Wilson and White?'

'Well, it – well, it was obvious,' said Raitts. 'Who else would it be?'

'It's far from that, Alexander,' said the Prior sternly. 'If you accuse your brothers you must bring good reason, you ken it as well as I do, and all you've shown so far is that you were out your bed in the night and detected two others doing the same.'

Wilson stirred restively, but his superior looked hard at him and he bent his head. The librarian broke the clasp of his hands so that they seemed to leap out of his grubby white sleeves, gesturing wildly.

'I took it it was Henry and this one talking about me at first,' he said, 'for that I'd to deny Henry a book that afternoon – there was another reading it – and he wasny best pleased; and this one's been asking about me in the town to my discredit. I took it they were speaking o how I must be put out from here, *He has to go*, they said, but then it was, *Secret knowledge*, and *Secret fire*, and what should that be but witchcraft and burning the infirmary?'

'It could be many things, my son,' said the Prior sadly.

'Did you hear those words?' Gil asked. 'You're sure o them?'

'Aye, I'm sure,' said Raitts indignantly, in a tone which failed to convince Gil.

'You heard nothing else? Only that?'

'Is it no enough? Conspiring in the night, creeping away from the kitchen—'

'I never!' burst out Wilson, finally unable to contain himself, then dropped to his knees as the Prior gave him another adamantine look. 'Forgive me, Faither,' he said, head bent.

'You'll get your moment,' said Prior David. 'Maister Cunningham, have you more questions for Alexander?'

'I have.' Gil studied the librarian, who captured his hands one with the other, tucked them into his sleeves again, and waited apprehensively. 'Let me be quite clear here. You came down the day stair, at what time?'

'I've no idea the time,' said Raitts irritably. 'Afore midnight, likely.'

'Afore midnight, and saw two persons in the cloister walk outside the refectory. Did you see them when you came down the stair, or when you came out of the privy?'

'I've no doubt they were there as I cam down the stair,' began Raitts. Gil raised his eyebrows. 'But no, I didny see them till I cam out.'

'They never heard you?'

'I was moving quiet, so's no to wake folk.'

Wilson grunted in disbelief, but kept his head down. 'Then what did you do?'

'I stood and listened, wi my light held low ahint my cloak, see, and heard what I tellt you, and then I thought, best get out o here, so I got away up the day stair again and back to my bed, and I sat in the dark and thought to talk it ower wi Our Lady and St Dominic, but they wereny answering me, and then Henry cam past me going back to his bed.'

'You're very sure it was Henry White,' said Gil.

'A course it was. He's next me, see, the last on our side of the dorter, and Archie McIan opposite him, and I could hear Archie snoring all through. And I heard this one moving about and all,' Raitts added bitterly, jerking an elbow at Wilson. 'Fell ower his bed-end, so he did, as if he was drunk.'

'Did you see a weapon of any sort? Did they have lanterns the same as you?'

'They'd just come fro the kitchen,' said Raitts with a flicker of indignation. 'They'd just stole the knife from there, a course they had a weapon.'

'But did you see it?' Gil pressed.

'No. He must ha hid it in his sleeve, or his belt, or the like. And aye they had lanterns, but held low, same as I was doing, to see the flagstones. Right treacherous they are, a man can trip or stub his toe as soon as step on them.'

Gil thought about this briefly, but continued: 'You accused Wilson of being responsible for the death of Leonard Pollock and all. What grounds do you have for that?'

'Well, it's obvious,' said Raitts. 'If he's slew one o the community, he must ha done the other. I've seen him, talking wi the man, likely being asked to pay for keeping his secrets hid, telling him other folk's secrets and all. He'd plenty reason to do away wi him!'

Wilson stirred restively, but Boyd shook his head and said sternly, 'That is no matter for you to speculate on. A question o secrets is one for me to deal wi, not you.'

Gil considered the librarian for a moment, wondering if he himself believed what he was saying. Having unburdened himself of all this he seemed calmer, but still trembled, and a muscle twitched beside his eye. He met Gil's eye hardily enough, and suddenly said, 'I'll swear to it, on anything you ask o me.'

'I've no doubt o that,' Gil responded. He rose, excused himself to the Prior with a brief bow, and went out into the cloister walk. None of Raitts's statement rang true somehow, but he felt it incumbent upon him to check the positions the man had described.

Two passing friars eyed him with faint suspicion as he located the day stair. The door to the necessarium, readily identifiable by smell, was next to it; standing at the foot of the stair Gil looked out into the cloister walk, along the row of slender columns which supported pointed arches and the red-tiled roof of the walkway in front of the refectory. As he had suspected, anyone

148

approaching from the far end of the refectory would be clearly visible, but a watcher standing here, or even two paces to his right by the necessary-house door, would be equally clearly visible to those approaching. In the dark midnight, the small candle-lanterns the friars carried would show up well.

What did the man see, he wondered. One or two persons abroad in the cloister at dead of night, probably, but who were they and what did they discuss? Or perhaps they were all tiptoeing about with their lanterns, failing to see one another, like Romans in a scene of the Betrayal of Christ.

Back in the Prior's study, the three Dominicans were as he had left them, silent as statues. Prior Boyd appeared to be praying. Gil sat down again, waited in equal silence till the older man looked up, then said, 'Wilson. What did you see, that led you to make sic an accusation?'

Wilson straightened up, glanced at his Prior, and said firmly, 'Brother Alexander is lying in his teeth.' Raitts drew an indignant breath, but subsided under the Prior's gaze. 'About all o't. I may ha passed the time o day wi the man Pollock, but no more than that, and I—'

'Answer the question, my son,' said Boyd sternly. 'That isny what you were asked.'

'What did you see?' Gil asked again. 'What hour was it, for a start? Are we talking o the night the infirmary burned?'

'Aye, that night. About an hour afore midnight,' said Wilson, 'I rose wi a bellyache, and since I found no relief in the necessarium I went to see if I could rouse Brother James at the infirmary, but he never woke to my knocking, so I cam back here to the cloister. Then I tried the kitchen, hoping maybe for a bit peppermint or a clove or the like, but Brother Augustine keeps all secure. There was naught to be seen. So then I was making for the day stair, to go back to my bed, and here's your man here

149

talking secrets in the corner at the foot o the stair wi Henry White.'

'No!' said Raitts on a sobbing breath, shaking his bent head.

'Alexander,' said the Prior in warning tones.

'So I stepped back into a shadow,' continued Wilson, 'and shut my lantern, and—'

'Why?' asked Gil. Wilson stared at him. 'Why did you hide? You had no reason. You're as entitled as they are to be abroad in the night.'

'Which is to say, not at all,' observed Prior Boyd disapprovingly.

'Aye, well,' said Wilson. 'That's why. If you're about in the night on a – a private matter, and see another fellow, you assume he's on the same kinna errand, no seeking fellowship and brotherly discourse. But these two was talking away, in whispers you could hear at St John's I'd wager, so first off I thought I'd wait till they moved on up the stair and then I found they'd maybe no wish me to hear their words.'

'And those were?'

'*Secret*, they said, more than once, and *None must hear*, and the like. And then *Fire*, quite clear. I thought little o't at the time, save to wonder what was so secret, and I wasny that long back in my bed afore the cry o *Fire!* went up, and see, next day – that's only yesterday, Our Lady save us – I waited and waited for someone to confess, and then when they hadny confessed by the time we cam to Chapter o Faults I, well, I made certain o't.' His voice tailed off as he took in his superior's expression.

After studying him for a long moment, Boyd turned to Gil.

'Have you more questions, maister?'

'I have,' said Gil. 'Was the infirmary in darkness? Did you try the door?'

'Aye, it was still as the grave,' said Wilson, 'and the door was barred, else I'd ha got in and roused Brother James mysel.'

'Barred?' said the Prior. 'I never kent James to bar the door. Brother Euan does, by what he's said, but no James. In case somebody needs him, like you're just saying.'

'Well, I couldny shift it,' said Wilson positively.

'And then you went straight to the kitchen?' Gil went on.

'I stopped to think a moment, and then I minded the kist o spices, and made my way to the kitchen. But there was naught to be had there, Augustine keeps it all locked down, like I said, only the cat playing wi a couple mice, so then I cam back out into the cloister and that's when I heard the two o them, whispering away in the corner.'

'And when did you go back up to the dorter?'

'No till after they'd gone up, you can believe me.' Wilson grimaced. 'That's about the one true word your man here uttered, I did trip ower my bed-end, for that my lantern went out just as I cam to the top o the stair. It meant I could better see their lights still burning, mind you, Henry's along by the far end and this one's next to him. Which is how I kent who it had been talking out in the cloister.'

Gil considered this information.

'When you heard the whispering,' he said, 'you didny ken yet who it was, am I right?'

'Aye, I suppose,' admitted Wilson.

'So there's no knowing who said what.'

'Aye.' The tone was reluctant. 'I suppose.'

Gil turned to Raitts.

'I ken who I heard,' said that individual resentfully. 'I'd swear to it.'

'How did you ken? Could you make them out?' Gil asked. 'It's no easy to identify a whisper. I'd no trust my ears in sic a situation, and you could hardly say the light was good.'

'Oh, well, if you're no to believe me,' said Raitts, increasingly sulky. 'I suppose you've made your decision, who's right and who's in the wrong .'

'Alexander,' said Prior Boyd. Raitts bent his head, his expression thunderous. Wilson looked briefly smug, until his superior said, 'It's clear to me that neither one o you has an ounce o cause for the accusations you brought yesterday. Accusations, let me remind you, which led your brothers into grievous behaviour and disturbed the peace o this cloister in sic a way as will take years to mend, which have wasted my time and Maister Cunningham's listening to a catalogue o mishearings and misdeeds, and which have slandered each o you the other and worse still, have slandered Henry White, who is an obedient member o the Order.' He paused for breath, while Gil admired his facility with words. 'I'll announce your penance the morn's morn in Chapter, for I must pray over it. It'll no be light, I warn you.'

Almost simultaneously, without looking at each other, both miscreants dropped first to their knees and then flat to the floor, face down, arms spread out in a cross shape. Gil felt a shiver go down his back: this was the most solemn form of the *venia*, the appeal for forgiveness and mercy, the version employed after a serious misdeed. He stared at the sprawled figures, aware of how substantial Wilson was even in abasement like this, and of how slight a creature Raitts was inside the layers of heavy woollen cloth.

Prior Boyd also considered the two bundled habits, the pale tonsures, the clenched fists.

'Rise and go,' he said. 'Report to Brother Dickon, see what labour he can set you to, and maintain silence. I'll speak to you afore Chapter.'

152

As the door closed behind his sons in religion, the Prior stood, and went to the nearer window. It looked out on the infirmary garden, but he seemed not to see the grey devastation, nor the handful of lay brothers and others working in the fading light.

After a long silence Gil said, 'That was some help, in fact.' His kinsman made a questioning sound, without turning. 'They contradicted one another, but it's clear enough they each saw two people talking in the cloister, and took it for one another and Henry White. I'd wish to ask him if he was also abroad in the night, and if so who he spoke to. And what about.'

'Aye.' The Prior finally turned away from the window, and looked searchingly at Gil. 'I was thinking o their history. Those two. Sandy came late to the Order, he was a man grown when he was tonsured, but he should ha learned to think more clearly than that. It would be,' he paused, reckoning in his head, 'four or five year ago, I suppose, he turned up, wi naught to his name but forty merks and a bundle o books. Which were right welcome in the library, I'll admit, he'd a copy of Pierre d'Ailly's sermons Henry and I were very glad to see, but for all his reading he's no a good thinker, and he'll never make a preacher whatever we do. There's even less excuse for Thomas, we've had him since he left the school. Errors in logic, suppositions taken for established facts, conclusions wi no foundation – that was what set off yesterday's stramash. It grieves me sair, Gilbert.'

'The whole community's owerset,' Gil observed. 'First what happened to Pollock, now what's happened to Andrew Rattray – it's no wonder if they're no thinking clearly.'

Boyd grunted, but came to sit down at his desk again.

'You wish to question Henry,' he said. 'Will we send for him now?'

'I'd sooner hear more o those two,' said Gil. 'Would either ha had cause to harm young Rattray?'

'No!' said Boyd, startled. 'I've no idea that either o them had much acquaintance wi him. Thomas had the boy Mureson to his assistant the last six-month, I think he's never had Rattray wi him. Sandy would know him, a course, in the library, but that's no like to cause him to . . .' His voice tailed off.

Gil preserved silence on this point, and said instead, 'And Pollock? Has either o them mentioned dealings wi him?'

'No,' said the Prior, shaking his head.

'I heard something in the town the day,' Gil pursued awkwardly, 'no greatly to Wilson's credit.'

Boyd looked at him.

'How does that no surprise me? Spit it out, son,' he said. 'You'd be the first to remind me, this is a matter o murder, secrets must out. It's no clyping, it's uncovering the truth.'

Carefully, naming no names, Gil relayed what the saddler had told him. Boyd heard him out, his face darkening, and finally said, in some dismay, 'Aye, and if our corrodian had learned o this, here's a good reason for Thomas to find himsel his enemy. I need to talk to Brother Thomas at more length.'

'His name was in Pollock's notes,' Gil observed, 'and also his initials in a list of what I take to be payments.' Boyd nodded, but did not answer. 'Can you recall Wilson's demeanour when Pollock's disappearance was discovered?'

'He was amazed, like the rest o us. If he felt aught else, he concealed it from me. I tell you, Gilbert,' said the older man, suddenly forceful, 'if the Deil didny truly carry off our corrodian, he has visited this house none the less. Lies and deception, murder and discord, stealing, suspicion one o another, these are all his work. It

154

will take the community years to recover.' He paused, considering the future bleakly. 'I'll stand down once the matter's settled. It will take another hand than mine to steer this vessel to quiet waters.' And then, in what seemed like a natural progression of thought, 'Shall we have Henry in? And best send for candles.' He reached for the little bell on his desk.

Henry White, warned as his colleagues had been and given permission to speak, simply bowed and stood waiting in silence.

Gil studied the man for a moment, and then said, 'On the night the infirmary burned and Andrew Rattray died,' White turned a penetrating gaze on him, 'were you abroad earlier, after the community was abed?'

White appeared to consider the question with care, and finally nodded.

'I was,' he agreed.

'Did you meet anybody else moving about the place, or see any others?'

'I did.'

Gil waited, but no more was forthcoming, so he persisted, 'Can you name them? How many were there?'

'There was more than one, but I canny name them.'

'Had you no conversation wi any?'

There was a brief hesitation.

'No.'

Gil eyed the lector principalis with some misgiving, a faint suspicion creeping into his mind.

'Did you learn anything that night,' he said carefully, 'that bears on the question of who killed Andrew Rattray?'

'How can I tell,' White parried, 'whether a matter bears on the question or no? All things are linked under God's eye,' he crossed himself, 'that sees a sparrow fall.'

'Aye, very pretty,' said Gil. 'Now tell me what you learned, sir.'

'I canny say that I learned anything,' White said.

'Why were you abroad in the night, Henry?' demanded the Prior.

White turned that sharp gaze on his old friend and said mildly, 'I heard something outside, so I rose to see what it was.'

'And what was it?' Gil asked.

'Why, I found the two who accused me, both about the place, quite separate. I'll no compound the symmetry by claiming they were whispering one wi another. And once I'd found what was about, I went back to my bed. Does that answer you?'

'Insufficiently,' said Gil. 'Who did you speak to, sir?'

'I spoke to neither Thomas nor Sandy Raitts.'

'So who did you speak to?'

'I canny say that I spoke to any.'

'Then how did you recognise Wilson and Raitts?'

'I see better than most by night,' said White. 'Both men are conspicuous in build and manner. I formed certain conclusions, which were confirmed when I returned to the dorter and recognised who had been out his bed lately.'

'And when the infirmary burned,' said Gil, 'it never occurred to you that anyone,' he stressed the word slightly, 'that you'd seen outside might know something about it?'

'Oh, it did,' said White. 'But, like David here, I was willing to wait for the miscreant to confess on his own.'

Despite being pressed to answer, White would give no more information. Nor would he offer any about the death of Leonard Pollock, merely reminding Gil that they had discussed this matter before. When he had left, Prior Boyd sat silent for a little while, the candlelight flickering on his face and folded hands; then he turned to Gil and remarked, 'You never asked Thomas nor Sandy about the man Pollock.'

156

'Pollock was in the habit of extortion,' said Gil. 'I should prefer to question folk in private on that subject.'

'The man o law,' said Boyd obscurely. 'Yet you questioned Henry.'

'As he said, we'd discussed it before.' Gil rose, as Boyd had done earlier, and went to the window. With the light behind him, he could see little through the small panes; work had ceased, and the ruins of the infirmary formed dark shapes, vaguely threatening in the twilight. His back still to Boyd, he said, 'Who does Father Henry confess, can you tell me?'

'Ah. You saw that.'

'I did. I've met those forms o words afore this. I'm all in favour o the seal o confession, but there are times it makes my task the harder.'

'Aye.' Prior David appeared to consider, and after a moment said, 'I can tell you who he confesses, I suppose. You could learn it from any in this house, after all. It's the first-year novices, Munt, Mureson and Calder, Simpson and,' the level voice checked and continued, 'Rattray, poor laddie. Our Lady receive him under her cloak.'

'Amen,' said Gil, crossing himself. 'And where do the novices sleep? No in the dorter, I take it.'

'There's no enough room in the dorter. They sleep above the sacristy, next the night stair. It's no ideal, I admit. John Blythe the novice-master sleeps there along wi them.'

'He sleeps sound, does he?'

'Aye.' The Prior grimaced. 'He has a sleeping draught the now, since he'd complained o waking the entire night. He didny waste the time, he spent it in prayer, he said. Prayer has great value, but so does keeping awake to teach your classes in the morning. So aye, he sleeps sound, times the novices has to wake him for Matins.'

'Who sees to the second-year men, George and his fellows?'

'John confesses them. He and Henry have aye taen alternate years in charge, ever since I can mind.'

Gil turned away fro the window and sat down. His kinsman was still at the desk, looking as if he could not move under the burden now on his shoulders.

'Tell me about the novices,' he said. 'Munt, Mureson, Simpson, Calder. I've met them. A mixed load, I'd ha said.'

'You'd ha said right.' Boyd sighed. 'We don't get the same laddies we did when I was young, keen fellows eager to take God's Word into the country places. I mind the men in my class . . .' His voice tailed off, and after a moment he shook himself. 'Aye, well. These five. Four. Good laddies, well intentioned, but it was only Rattray and Mureson had a true vocation I'd say, and two more simply felt the life would suit them.' He smiled crookedly. 'Simpson at least will make a good preacher, a good Dominican, when he settles down. He's a sharp mind, a clear thinker, well able to open matters to those less able than himself. Munt will be happy enough once he learns obedience, never a jewel o the Order but no disgrace to it I expect.'

Gil, thinking of Munt's remarks in the guest hall, preserved silence on this point, and said only, 'And Calder?'

'A difficult laddie,' said Boyd after a moment. 'He thinks he has a vocation, and it may indeed be God's will for him, but the Order isny what he thinks it is. Teaching him is,' he hesitated, and then said, 'no easy. He will argue even against Brother Thomas at times. There is freedom o thought, Gil, and there is wilful foolishness.'

Gil nodded in sympathy. A Dominican who argued with the statements of Aquinas, the great theologian of the Order, would need to be a very deep thinker.

'*Sall never of sa sour ane brand ane bricht fire be brocht,*' he quoted.

Boyd looked blank for a moment, then said, 'Ah, the tale of Rauf Coilyear. Aye, times I feel like that about the laddie. Mind you, he may make a preacher yet. He has a hold of St Paul's thought, that we are all a part of the one body, and sees everything in those terms, and it makes a good foundation for a sermon. We can hope. But Rattray and Mureson. I think I've spent as much time in prayer ower them, Gil, as the rest o the community thegither.'

'Why's that?' Gil asked cautiously. 'You told me Rattray was devout, and Mureson seems a serious young man, very conscious of what's due to his calling.'

'He's settled a lot, the last month or two. He found the Feast o the Incarnation a great comfort. He's— he lacks patience wi those less observant than himself, has little charity for those who find the road stony or the Rule hard. I hope in time he'll come to see that Our Lord loved sinners equally wi the good.'

'One of those who *lives by sense rather than reason*?' Gil prompted, in Aquinas' own Latin. Boyd shot him a startled look.

'I did not know you were acquainted with our Brother Thomas,' he said in the same language. 'No, that describes Sandy Raitts well, he's no one for reason as you discerned the now. I think Mureson tries to apply the Rule to every aspect of life within this house, and expects others to do the same.' Once again, Gil preserved silence, reflecting that this was, after all, the purpose of a Rule. That was why he had not sought a monastic career. 'He is nearly as devout as was poor Andrew, and has a good understanding of the works of our Brother Thomas. I hope to make something of him in due time. As, indeed, I did of Andrew.'

# Chapter Eight

'I'm glad you never disabused Prior Boyd,' said Alys, shaking the rain off her plaid. 'About the lady in the drawing,' she elaborated, as Gil looked blankly at her. 'Her name is Margaret Rattray, not Keithick. She's his sister.'

'You found her!'

'Led us straight there, so she did,' said Jennet with pride. 'And we've learned why the poor laddie thought he disappeared the other fellow, and all.'

'Christ aid her,' said Tam, his face darkening.

'Come and tell me.' Gil patted the bench beside him, and Alys hung her plaid on the finial at its end and came to join him before the fire.

Leaving Prior Boyd, Gil had returned to the guest hall to find it deserted apart from the cat and a resentful Socrates who had demanded out with some urgency. Exercising the dog in the dark courtyard, watching the members of the community come and go from the makeshift infirmary across the way, he had been joined by Alys and her escort, with a borrowed lantern, but there was still no sign of the other servants. Since it would soon be suppertime, he was not much concerned.

'I spoke to the man of law as well,' Alys was saying now in her accented Scots. 'Mistress Rattray gave me a token for him, and a signed permission on a set of tablets. He's acted for the two o them these six or eight months, sending to the Low Countries and dealing wi the property and so on.'

'That's well done,' he said admiringly. 'Tell me about it.'

She recounted her visit to Mistress Rattray, with comments from Jennet interpolated. Gil heard her out, frowning.

'There's still a lot of this goes against the Rule,' he said at length, 'even if he was keeping no mistress. Leaving the house by night, keeping property back, transacting business abroad – these are all misdeeds for which Pollock could have threatened to expose him.'

'Very likely,' Alys said. 'And I think by what one of the novices told you – was it the one called Simpson? – that Pollock knew of Mistress Rattray and assumed she was Andrew's mistress, and believed that Andrew would be afraid of the truth getting about. She's still hiding from her husband.'

'And no wonder,' muttered Tam.

'Yes. I can see the boy would have wished Pollock dead,' Gil said, 'but I don't like this tale of the priest who died before, and by fire at that.'

'It could look very like witchcraft, to the wrong hearer,' Alys said, looking sideways at him. He nodded. 'Mistress Rattray told me the Sheriff found it to be arson, and the man guilty was found, and confessed at the Assize at Montrose, and hanged.'

'Nevertheless,' Gil said, 'I think we don't mention that afore the Prior or the Bishop. Tam, Jennet, you hear me? No mention of the boy's past. Nor of his sister, I think, unless we must.'

'Are you sure of that?' Alys asked. Gil looked directly at her.

'Unless we must,' he repeated. She bit her lip, then looked away.

'I wonder how much his fellows kent of this,' she said. 'I wish we could talk to them, but I suppose it would hardly be proper to try to question them just now, when the community is in silence.'

'There are more reasons for talking to them,' Gil said. He recounted what he had learned in the day, to exclamations from Jennet and cynical nods from Tam.

Alys listened closely, and sat back as he finished, saying, 'Very strange. I agree, it sounds as if Father Henry protects someone who has confessed to him, but surely if someone confessed murder, his confessor should set a very great penance?'

'Aye, and in a community like this the penance at least would be known, even if the cause was kept secret. He did say he was waiting for the miscreant to confess of his own accord. But to what? Arson, or murder, or both?'

'And what about the factor farming on the rents?' burst out Jennet. 'That's a crime and all, even if it's no murder, cheating honest men o their coin. And I'll warrant it goes into his own purse, no the Blackfriars' kist.'

'If that's what Pollock knew,' said Alys, 'the man Wilson also had reason to wish Pollock dead.'

'Several people wished the man dead,' Gil said. 'Wilson, Rattray, Raitts I know of, and I've little doubt there are others. The Prior kens about Wilson now,' he added to Jennet. 'We'll hope he'll deal wi the matter appropriately.'

The other men, Nory and Dandy and Euan, straggled back just as the supper was carried in from the kitchen by the lay servants. The conversation was general over stewed kale and stockfish with a green sauce, but once the dishes were cleared and the broth from the dish of kale poured onto a broken loaf for Socrates, as the deep-voiced processional singing of Compline floated from the cloister, Gil drew his stool to the table again. 'Time to set what we've learned all thegither. There's still much to discover, but if we know what we've got we can direct the search better. Nory, have you got anything new the day?'

His body-servant grimaced.

'Little enough, maister,' he said primly. 'I was working in the great barn, mending nets for the stables along wi Brother Archie, who can talk without drawing breath let me tell you for all he's still coughing, and heard all about how easy this or that friar is to work wi and how the kitchen men gets a loaf to take home wi them every week, and the like. He'd no a lot to say about the laddie that died, the novices and the lay brothers don't come across one another that often, but he'd a fair bit to say about yesterday's stushie, mostly lamenting that Brother Dickon had got the lay brothers out afore it got going. He did say Faither Henry was no for joining in, just stood there in silence wi the battle brewing about him.'

'So young Mureson said,' Gil agreed. 'Did he mention any others by name?'

'The two that begun it, that accused one another, he named them. Wilson and Raitts. And he said, one o the novices was right distressed by it, he'd thought he was like to swoon away wi horror, which is the reason Brother Dickon rounded them up and got them out wi his own men. So Archie said,' Nory finished, scepticism in his tone.

'If it was the boy Mureson,' said Alys, 'he was still very shaken when he came to tell us.'

'And he'd a deal to say about the man Pollock, Archie had. Seems there's been one or two enquiring for him the week after he vanished away.'

'I wasny told that,' said Gil.

'Aye, well, maybe it never reached the Prior's ears. If it was someone came to the gate, or spoke to one o the lay brothers working in the yard, they'd maybe turn back when they heard he wasny here. One o them was a fremit kind o fellow, so Archie said.'

'Fremit? What kind of foreigner?'

Nory shook his head.

'Just no from here. Archie's no a travelled man himsel for all he was a soldier – he'd reckon anyone from further than Glasgow or Aberdeen was a foreigner – but I think this one had some kind o accent, spoke funny, and he'd a badge wi a rose on it on his jerkin.'

'Oh!' said Gil. 'And this was after Pollock disappeared? How long after, did Archie say? Had he seen the man before?'

'He never said,' Nory reported with regret.

'A red rose or a white?' asked Alys.

'I never asked him. I could ask him the morn,' Nory offered.

'Aye, do that.' Gil frowned. 'Odd that the messenger never called on Pullar. He said he'd been expecting one about now.'

'What messenger's that, maister?' Nory asked, and Gil recounted his visit to Andrew Pullar. The man listened, and offered, 'Likely he went away again, never spoke to the man o law, thinking there'd be no money, when he found Pollock wasny here.'

'You'd think he might check with the other contact.'

'Unless Pollock was to give him the direction to Pullar's place of business,' Alys suggested. 'I wonder where the coin is going?'

'It will be going into Ireland, to the O'Neill,' said Euan. 'It will be for the new Duke of York, that is certain.'

'Of course!' said Gil, and Alys nodded. 'This fellow that's maybe, or maybe no, the Duke o York. Claims to be the son o Edward Fourth, or the like – one o the two boys that were prisoned in the Tower at London,' he explained to the two grooms, who were looking blank.

'There's more than one o the monarchs of Europe friendly to him, if only to annoy Henry Tudor. I've heard he's some friendship wi the O'Neill, but I suspect we'll see him in Scotland afore too long, if this has been the Treasury sending him money.'

'Och, no, he is planning to go to England and fight King Henry,' said Euan confidently.

'In any case,' said Gil, 'it looks as though Pollock was supporting the man's cause, for whatever reason. Thank you, Nory.'

'How are your hands?' Alys asked. 'I have a cream for your finger-ends, if the rope has chafed them.'

'Dandy,' said Gil over Nory's murmured thanks, 'did you learn aught to the purpose? What did you do the day?'

'Dod and Jamesie was redding up the plough-harness,' said Dandy, 'so I gied them a hand, did a couple wee mends, we got it all greased and laid out ready for the ploughing. So natural enough, working at that, we spoke o where we'd come fro, and then where others were raised and all. Seems Wilson's a local man, Henry White's from Lanarkshire though he's been here for years, and the man Raitts is out of Ayrshire they think, though he's very close as to his history. As Nory here says, they'd little knowledge o the novices, though they both had a liking for the laddie that's slain, thought him a decent fellow, like to make a good friar and a good preacher.'

'Did they say aught at all o the others?' Gil asked.

'No a lot. Calder's ower serious and just as like to report you to Brother Dickon, though to be fair they say Brother Dickon doesny like his men reported to him. He sees to their discipline hissel, says there's no need for some youngster owerseeing them. Munt and Simpson, is that the names? They're aye good for a laugh, it seems, and up to all the kind o tricks laddies that age gets up to.

It'll no last, they reckon, they'll be as solemn as the rest by the time they're done. The one, Mureson, is ower solemn already, they said.'

'And Andrew?' said Gil. 'The dead laddie? Was he lively and all, or was he serious?'

'Kinna in atween, by what they said. Certainly up to tricks, they reckoned he'd a lassie in the town, covered for him a time or two when he'd been out and shouldny.'

Gil nodded.

'Very useful. Thanks, Dandy. Had they any notion how he died? Who might have cut his throat and burned the infirmary to conceal it?'

'Oh, they reckon Sandy Raitts. They all hold him to be a pirlie, ragglish fellow, liable to all kinds o cantrips. They wouldny put it past him to do an orra thing like that.'

Jennet muttered agreement, but Alys said, 'No, surely no. He's a poor creature, I'll admit, but he's no destructive.'

Gil looked at her.

'What, you think he would kill but not set the fire?'

'I think he would not kill, and certainly not set a fire. That's a thoughtless action.'

'Arson always is,' Gil agreed. 'Well, perhaps. And you, Euan, have you learned anything of use?'

'Och, indeed,' said Euan proudly. 'I was sitting with the old man again, the one that's deeing, to ease Brother Euan's work. He's a dispensation from the silence, Brother Euan has, seeing he must question his patients, so we was chatting away in the Gaelic whenever it was quiet. He's been telling me all the history of the folks here, and who gets on wi who, and what their quarrels are. You'd never know the wee things they quarrel over, what wi being shut in and obedient.'

'So what have you learned?' Gil prompted.

167

'Well, well, the man Raitts has quarrelled with the most of his brothers, saving maybe Henry White, over his books. This one has ill-treated a book, that one has put one back wrong, all those sorts of things. *You'd think they was his own books*, says Brother Euan. The brother called Thomas Wilson has been farming the rents, though Father Prior doesny ken yet. The second-year novices has been brewing ale in one o the barns, and put all sorts into the mash and gave theirsels some bad dreams. It's a wonder what the Infirmarer knows about the folk in the place, so it is.' He paused, closing his eyes to think. 'The one Raitts is accusing Wilson of talking about him in the town. Seems he told someone he was spreading tales o him, though he never said what sort of tales—'

'Ochtaway, this is all just well-head clash!' protested Rob. 'There's no purpose in any o't!'

'And how is it any different Jamesie telling you tales o the same man?' demanded Euan, firing up.

'Be at peace, both of you!' said Gil. 'You've both done what I asked o you, and it's a matter o fortune whether simply talking to folk raises useful information or no. Tell me more about the novices, Euan. What did the sub-Infirmarer have to say about them?'

'Och, they're good enough laddies, by what he tells me. They've called at the infirmary daily to ask after their friend while he was shut away, though that's had to cease now, and sent him messages and words o comfort each time. That would be the first-year novices, a course. Euan never let them in to see him, so he says.'

'Did he mention John Blythe?'

'Him that's novice-master? Do you know, he did, now – and what was he telling me o him?' Euan closed his eyes again, the better to recollect. 'Och, yes, he's no been sleeping well, the poor man, and has had a sleeping-draught to him the last few weeks or more. Euan was just making up

168

some more the day.' Despite much racking of his memory, he produced no further useful recollections.

At length, giving up, Gil said, 'Very well. We'll brew up a stoup of buttered ale and put all thegether, see if we can work out what's been happening. Where did that jug of ale go? Should we send into the kitchen for another?'

Once they were gathered round the fire, watching Jennet pour the hot spiced brew into wooden beakers, Euan remarked airily, 'It will not be any surprise that the O'Neill has disposed of the man Pollock.'

'Why would he do that?' Tam asked in sceptical tones.

'Why, if Pollock had learned some secret of his, the way he was finding out things to everyone's discredit, the O'Neill would certainly have him killed.'

'What, an old man here in a priory in Perth?' said Tam, the scepticism even stronger. 'How would he do that, when he never left the place?'

'The man was having folk call on him here,'said Euan, 'and who is to say what secrets they brought him? And the O'Neill has a long arm, I can tell you that.'

'That's speculation,' said Gil firmly. 'What do we ken for certain about the man?'

'We ken how he died,' said Alys, grimacing. Socrates put his head on her knee, and she stroked his ears. 'Burned up by fire behind locked and barred doors.'

'He was given to extortion,' said Gil. 'So there are a good few folk who disliked him, possibly enough to kill him.'

'Was he not writing down the reasons for his extortion?' asked Euan.

'No,' said Gil. 'Names, initials, but nothing about the original misdeeds. I've no doubt he feared it getting into other hands.'

'Now that's a pity,' said Euan. 'Interesting it would be, to know what misdeeds might be in a house of religion like this.'

'Who do we ken was on his list, maister?' asked Tam. Gil hesitated.

'I'll not name the living,' he said after a moment. 'Better if that doesny get about.' Tam grinned, his glance flicking to Euan and back in the firelight. 'We ken he had a go at Andrew Rattray, thinking the lady in the town was his mistress no his sister, and he had a go at one o the other novices and all, and was denied.'

'And what was that about?' asked Euan avidly before he could go on.

'A book from the college library at St Andrews, all confessed and dealt wi,' said Gil repressively, and Euan subsided.

'There are others, then, maister?' said Tam. Gil nodded. 'But did you no say the doors was barred? How would anyone get in to set fire to the man, whoever it was?'

'Down the chimney?' suggested Dandy.

'Blocked,' said Alys. 'So is the window to the inner chamber, and the inner door was locked and the key in the man's purse, or so we assume,' she glanced at Gil, 'since it was found among his ashes.'

'It's impossible,' said Dandy. 'He might as well be in a lead coffin, and how would you get at a man in a lead coffin?'

'No, but a lead coffin's well sealed,' said Tam. 'Naught can get in or out, that's its purpose. Even wi the doors barred, there's plenty can get into a wee house like yon.'

'Like what?' challenged Dandy. Euan was silent.

'Rats. Mice. You ken as well's me they can get anywhere. Fire, a draught o air, rain down the chimney – unless it's sealed off complete, mistress?'

'So you're saying a trained rat ran in wi a wee firebrand in its mouth?'

'There was fire in the house already,' Alys said over Tam's indignant response. They stopped arguing to look

170

at her. 'He had a brazier to keep him warm, and he must have had a light in that chamber, for he had been looking in his kist.'

'We never found a candlestock,' Gil said.

'Likely it was wooden,' said Tam. 'It would burn up wi the rest.'

'But how did the fire consume the man completely?' demanded Dandy. 'I've been and looked in the kist where they're praying ower it, there's just wee bits o ash and bone. The other laddie wasny consumed, and that fire was hot enough, Our Lady kens. If your clothes catches alight, all you do is, you put it out. You don't just sit there and burn, do you?'

'If you're bout-fou you might,' argued Tam. 'You might no notice till it's well alight. Happened to my auntie's good-faither. He'd had the most o a jug o Bordeaux-wine he'd won in a wager and fell asleep by the fire, except she noticed and tossed the dishwater ower him. He wouldny ha minded,' he added thoughtfully, 'but she never took the crocks out first. The great one caught him a wallop in the cods, had him limping for a week.'

'Was the man a drinker?' Alys asked.

'Brother Dickon said not,' said Gil. 'I asked him.'

'So how did he catch on fire?' Dandy persisted.

'This is unsatisfactory,' said Alys. 'On the one hand,' she held one hand out, 'we have a man dead in a locked chamber, locked from the inside, and no way to tell which of his enemies might have had a means of getting into the chamber. On the other,' she withdrew her other hand from Gil's clasp and held it out too, 'the means by which he died is not clear. How did the fire start and why was it so fierce?'

'Aye,' began Tam.

'That sums it up well, sweetheart,' said Gil, retrieving her hand, 'but—'

171

'But that's my point!' she broke in, gesturing again with the free hand. 'It seems like nothing done by a human agency, nothing started by a mortal hand, given that we saw no mechanical contrivances, no artificial hearth or the like. And no trained rats,' she added, 'though I suppose those would hide from Socrates.'

The dog beat his tail on the hearth a couple of times in acknowledgement of this. Gil said, 'Go on. Where does this lead?'

'If it's not a human action,' she turned to look earnestly at him in the candlelight, 'it must be either a wholly natural one, some sort of accidental occurrence, or a supernatural one. Are you agreed?'

'Aye,' he said, and Tam murmured something. Dandy seemed less convinced.

'The supernatural happens very rarely,' she went on. 'We know there are supernatural events, Holy Church teaches us so, but I never witnessed such a thing as the Devil coming into this world—'

'There was what that woman saw, mem,' objected Jennet. 'Wi his great wings rising up, and his red een.'

'I think she saw the smoke from the great fire,' said Alys. 'No, it seems to me so much more likely that Pollock died by some natural occurrence that I have been trying to make it happen again, in a small way. I hope we know more the morn.'

'Oh, is that . . .' said Tam, then fell silent. Gil considered this proposition cautiously.

'I'd need something solid enough to convince Blacader,' he said at length. 'No to mention Brown and the Prior.'

'That should be possible,' said Alys, with equal caution. 'If I can make it work once, I can do so again with witnesses.'

'Aye,' he said, unwilling to question her further in front of the servants. 'Well, we'll look at this again when we've a bit more to go on. Now, what about the young man Rattray? What do we ken about him?'

'He was well liked,' offered Tam.

'Someone didny like him,' said Dandy.

'Aye, but he'd no enemies that anyone'll name,' argued Tam.

'He thought he had killed the man Pollock by hating him,' said Alys.

'Aye, but what's that to say to his death, mem?' Jennet said. 'I'd ha said they were all glad to be rid o that man.'

'It's something we know of him,' Alys said. 'Until we have solved the matter, every detail may be important.'

'He was asleep in the little chamber where he was confined, at the end of the building,' said Gil slowly, 'and Father James was also asleep in another chamber nearer the door. Someone crept in without waking the old man, which seems to have been no sort of a problem, but also without waking Rattray, I suppose, and cut the lad's throat, then set a fire and left.'

'I suppose he could hardly waken the old fellow,' said Tam. '*Here, wake up, brother, I've set your infirmary alight.*'

'Quite so,' said Gil. 'Then we have the Chapter of Faults which descended into a battle, and the community was silenced, and the first I've been able to question any of them was the day.' Quickly he outlined what he had learned from Wilson and Raitts. 'I tried to question White, but he gainstood me. I suspect he's protecting someone, but the question is who? We've not been able to find that the lad had any enemies, nobody wi a grudge against him. Why kill him?'

'Maybe he kent something?' Dandy suggested.

'Maybe the old man, the Infirmarer, had an apoplexy and cut the boy's throat and then forgot he'd done it,' Tam said.

'There's no chance he cut his own throat?' asked Nory, breaking a long silence.

'Unlikely, I'd say,' said Gil. 'He was laid in his bed, and for all the changes to the body from the fire, it seemed as if he'd been lying quietly afore it – afore it happened. There was no sign o a razor or knife or the like anywhere near him, either.'

'Brother Augustine's knife has still not been seen,' Alys said.

'If it's like killing a pig,' said Nory thoughtfully, 'there'd be a deal o blood. They're all in they bonnie white habits, a wheelamageerie colour for a muddy country like Scotland, and none o them that I've seen's ower blood.'

'The trick is to strip yoursel first,' said Euan. 'Likely he would be leaving his habit by the door, and putting it back on when he was done.'

'And therefore,' said Alys, leaning forward, 'he barred the infirmary door, not wishing to be interrupted in his body-linen.'

'That would fit,' Gil agreed. 'Boyd said he had never known Father James bar the door. That would fit well.'

'That's the how,' said Dandy. 'But who was it?'

'Whoever Father Henry was talking to?' said Alys, and answered herself, 'No.'

'No,' Gil agreed. '*Thys may ryme well but it acorde nought*. If Wilson had just found the infirmary barred, and then saw White talking to someone, and some time later the infirmary went up in flames, there must ha been at least two people. Other than White,' he added scrupulously. Euan frowned over this, but after a moment Dandy nodded.

'But if it's a matter of confession,' said Alys, 'if he's protecting someone who had confessed to him, I mean, I suppose we have to guess who it might have been and confront that one direct. I wonder what they really discussed?'

'Anything other than what either Wilson or Raitts claims to have heard, I suspect,' Gil said. 'I'd not trust

174

either man's account. Well, we can do nothing until Prior Boyd releases the community from its silence. I wish he had weighed up the drawbacks afore he imposed it. There must ha been another penance would have done as well.'

'We could make them all strip to their linen,' said Nory, still thinking deeply. 'There's likely bloodstains in the inside o his habit, no to mention his shirt.'

'They wear shirts?' said Jennet. 'Och, I suppose they must, they'd freeze to death otherwise, never mind the wool chafing at their skins.'

'That's for the morn,' said Gil. 'Nory, you find out what happens about their wash and see if there's been any bloody sarks sent down. I wish we'd thought o that sooner, there's no knowing when the laundrywomen will come. Dandy, you did well the day, see if you can get any more the same way. Euan.' He looked at the Erscheman, who gazed innocently back at him. 'I'll maybe want you to attend me, but if no, you can talk some more wi Brother Euan. See if you can find out where more o the brothers are from, what kind o family, are they country folk or townsmen.'

'Och, yes indeed, I can be doing that,' said Euan cheerfully.

'Maister Gil,' said Tam, craning to see past Dandy, 'is that someone in the yard? There's lights out there.'

Gil turned to look at the narrow windows. The lower portions were firmly shuttered, but the glazed upper sections showed dim lights moving, and now there were voices calling. Away through the high hall someone hammered on the outer door with a sound like thunder.

'What's amiss?' he wondered, getting to his feet and lifting one of the candles. Tam followed him out into the hall, where they met a liveried manservant stumbling in out of the night, another behind him. Horses trampled,

175

lanterns bobbed, and a harsh familiar voice sounded from the yard.

'And don't take no for an answer, Thomas! Go on, ask them!'

'Oh, it's you, maister,' said the man in front, and swung his bonnet in a servant's bow. 'It's my mistress outside, looking for the Prior.'

'You've found the guest hall,' Gil said. 'Come in out the cold a moment. You'd need to knock at the gate to the slype, and whether any will hear you's a good question. Did the porter no—'

'My mistress wouldny wait for the porter to come back,' said Thomas without expression.

'Thomas!'

'I'll come out,' said Gil. 'Wait till I get my plaid.'

The rain had stopped, but a bitter wind blew between the buildings. Mistress Trabboch sat on her horse in the midst of the yard, glaring about her by the light of two lanterns. Gil approached her stirrup, and she scowled at him and said, 'You're no the Prior. Where is he? He's got my man here, I want to talk to him.'

'This is the guest hall, mistress,' said Gil. 'Will you step in and wait in the warm till the porter comes back?'

'No,' she said curtly. 'I'll wait here. He'll no slip past me and out the gates afore I set my hand on him.' It was not clear whether she meant the Prior or her husband.

'The friars have sung Compline,' Gil observed, 'and are likely all abed by now. It may be a while.'

'I'll wait.' She drew her furred cloak closer against the biting wind. The other horses in the yard fidgeted. 'Thomas, can you no hold they beasts quiet?'

'Have you come far?' Gil asked politely. 'It's bitter season for travelling.'

'None o your mind,' she retorted. 'But you can tell me, if you've been here any length o time, is there a friar here by the name o Alexander Stair?'

176

'None that I've met, mistress,' said Gil. She grunted in what might not have been disbelief. 'Your husband?'

'Aye.'

'When did he leave you?'

'I'll talk wi the Prior,' she said curtly. Gil took a step backwards out of the light, and a dark form emerged from the slype and appeared as a lay brother, hurrying towards them across the courtyard.

'Mistress?' he said. 'The Prior's retired for the night, but he's just rising. He'll be wi you in a short time. Maister!' He had caught sight of Gil. 'I'm to ask if you'd be present.'

'You will not,' said Mistress Trabboch. 'The idea! This is a private matter, no for discussing afore the marketplace.'

'Prior Boyd may wish me present as his man of law,' said Gil.

This was indeed the case. Boyd, blinking in the light of a branch of candles held by young Brother Martin, was polite but very firm.

'I've no idea what you want, mistress,' he said, 'or why it canny wait till the morn, but I will have Maister Cunningham present while we discuss it.'

'Hah!' she said, and after a moment, 'I suppose a witness. Eppie, get down.' She swung her leg over the pommel, paused to disengage the wide skirts of her riding-dress, and slid to the ground, ignoring Gil's hand. Her maidservant materialised out of the shadows and straightened the heavy folds of cloth. 'Where do we meet?'

'The guest hall is warm and light.' The Prior nodded to Brother Martin to light the way. Mistress Trabboch, ignoring his arm as she had Gil's, stalked into the hall behind the young man. In the light she was as tall as Gil, probably broader in the shoulder, with a jaw like a nutcracker. She sat down on the nearest bench.

'Put those lights there,' she directed, 'and you sit there where I can see your face. As for you, I've no use for men o law. If you're staying you can keep out my sight.'

Gil, ignoring this, set a stool for the Prior with all the courtesy of which he was capable, nodded to Tam, who had appeared again out of the shadows, saw Brother Martin and Mistress Trabboch's maid suitably disposed, and sat down himself at the Prior's elbow.

'Thank you, Gilbert,' said the Prior quietly. 'Now, madam, what is this about? What brings you to our door at this unseasonable hour?'

'You've a man here by name o Alexander Stair,' she said, without preamble. 'Which is my husband, that deserted me five year since, leaving me the speak o Ayrshire and my whole lands to manage mysel. A man o medium height, wi grey een and dark brown hair, legs like windlestraes, sees a boggart ahint every bush. I want him back.'

'We have no man by that name here,' said Boyd, 'whether as friar or lay brother, nor have we ever had that I ken.'

'Don't tell me that,' she said. 'He was seen here in Perth, in a monk's habit, no three month since, and I've spoke to every one o the houses o religion round the burgh, and they've denied me. This is the last, so here's where he must be.'

'I assure you, mistress,' began Boyd.

'I want him back,' she repeated.

'Why?' Gil asked. She paused, staring at him with her mouth open. Beyond her he saw the maidservant put up a hand to cover her eyes. 'If he's deserted you, and left you wi your own lands, why do you want him back?'

'Because he's my husband. You're no wedded yoursel, I take it,' she said scathingly. 'I wedded him for consolation and companionship in life and I've had none o that in five year. He'll come back and supply it, or I'll see him hang for it.'

'Desertion's no a hanging offence yet, mistress,' Gil said. 'Can I ask, how much consolation and companionship had you o him in the years afore he left?'

Her mouth fell open again. Behind her, the maidservant's hand slid down as if to conceal a grin. Tam was also grinning, and gesturing graphically; Gil ignored him.

'That's no to the point,' said Mistress Trabboch, recovering. 'The point is, you're concealing my man here, that's a married man and no to take religion without my consent, which I will never gie him, let me tell you, and I want him back.'

'And I tell you, madam, we are concealing no such person,' said the Prior.

'Why did he leave you?' Gil asked. Though I can guess, he thought.

'No reason at all,' she averred. 'I've been a good and faithful wife to him all the years we've been wed, put up wi all his nonsense and his dreaming and studying and that, never said a word about all his papers, and what's my reward for it? He runs off, only for cause that I sellt a few o his books, and never a trace o him till Isabella Newton seen him in the town here, and it would ha been more help if she'd kent what habit he was wearing.'

'How can I convince you?' said the Prior rather helplessly. 'I'll not rouse my brothers at this time o night. We have to say Matins in a few hours and—' He stopped. 'If I show you a list o the men present at the moment, will that convince you?'

'No,' she said, 'for I canny read. There could be the King himsel on a paper and I wouldny ken.'

179

'What if I read the list out to you?' Gil suggested. 'You can look over my shoulder to make sure I don't skip any o the names.'

'Aye, I suppose,' she said grudgingly after a moment's thought.

Brother Martin was sent to fetch the great book out of the press in the Prior's chamber. While he was absent Mistress Trabboch stared about the hall, looking at the high carved windows which disappeared into the shadowed roof, the elaborate chimneypiece, the fine proportions of the place.

'You do yourselves well,' she remarked sourly. 'Take a deal o alms and legacies to pay for this lot.'

'This is the royal lodgings,' said Prior Boyd repressively. 'It was built for the first Jameses, so it's little wonder it's a fine building.'

'Hah!' she said in that tone of disbelief. Gil felt it was fortunate that Brother Martin appeared at this point, clutching a lantern and a substantial leather-bound book.

'Find me the list we made for the Provincial Chapter,' said the Prior. The young man sat down and picked his way through the heavy pages, tilting them towards the light, until he came on a list of names, written slantwise down the page in a shaky, elderly hand. Prior Boyd glanced at it, and closed his eyes briefly.

'I'd forgot, it was Brother James writ it for me,' he said. 'There, Gilbert. Take and read that page for the lady. It's a true copy o the record we took to Edinburgh last autumn, madam, wi all the lay brethren and the servants and all.'

'We'll hear all o't,' she said in that sour tone. 'You'll no conceal him from me disguised as a kitchen-man.'

Gil took the book, tilted it to the light as Brother Martin had done, and began at the top of the page in Scots.

*Yhe talye o yhe freres dominican att Perht, 7 day octobre 1494. Dauvit boyd, priorus. robt Park, subpriorus, jhon blyhte lector principalis, henricus whyt, the samyn.*

He worked his way down the page, pointing at each name as he read it so that the angry presence at his shoulder could see that none was omitted, down to the list of the lay servants and associate tradesmen.

'Hah!' she said in disgust as he finished. 'I'll find him yet. Thomas, where are you, you dolt? Get the horses. Eppie!'

She swept out, without a further word, her servants hastening after her, leaving Gil and his kinsman to look in amazement at one another.

'Well! *Whanne she was gone the kynge was glad for she made suche a noyse,*' Gil quoted after a moment.

'You may well say it,' said Boyd. 'I'll admit, if I had her man here I'd be tempted to conceal him. What a targin scauld! May Our Lady lesson her in humility,' he added dutifully, and crossed himself.

'I encountered her in the town earlier,' Gil said. 'That's an Ayrshire name, and so's her husband's. I wonder if that's where she's from?'

'Well, she's no from hereabout,' said Boyd, 'nor I never encountered her when I was in Ayrshire, Our Lady be thankit for both.' He rose, stretching his back, and pulled his black cloak closer about him. 'Martin, wake up. You'll get a couple hours afore Matins if you get back to your bed the now.'

Outside the windows, lights, horses and people were moving about uneasily, Mistress Trabboch's harsh voice resounding over all with contradictory riders to her men. Through this came hurrying feet, another light, a voice calling, 'Faither? Faither Prior!'

Gil strode to the hall door and jerked it open just as one of the lay brothers raised a fist to hammer on it. Startled, the man reared back, saying, 'Is our Prior here?

He's called for. Faither!' he exclaimed, seeing Boyd behind Gil. 'You need to come. It's our librarian.'

'Sandy?' Boyd said. 'What's wrong, Archie? What's he at?'

'I think he's killt Faither Henry!'

# Chapter Nine

The cloister was dark and filled with the bitter wind, the bulk of the church looming against a ragged sky dotted with stars, but in the corner of the walkway by the library a cluster of candles and lanterns revealed confused patches of white, which resolved into sleeves, cowls, habit hems, appearing and disappearing against the black cloaks of a number of Dominicans. Many voices offered advice: the order for silence had clearly been forgotten.

'No, don't move him yet.' Brother Euan's soft voice cut through the hubbub. 'Lay that over him, that's right.'

'What's happened?' demanded Prior Boyd. 'How bad is he? Is it Henry indeed?'

Brother Euan looked up, and sat back a little, so that over Boyd's shoulder Gil could see the patient, sprawled on the flagstones under two cloaks and a blanket. Henry White's long face and thick dark hair showed in the light, with a dabble of dark blood on his cheek.

'He is breathing well,' said the sub-infirmarer. 'No! Don't move him!' he repeated sharply to the man at his right. 'I am not knowing how long he has been like this, but the blood is sticky on his head rather than wet.' He indicated a patch on his own long skull, behind the left ear.

'I found him like that,' said another voice. Raitts, standing by the wall, sulky and resentful, with his hands bound by what looked like his own belt. 'He was lying there and I heard him snoring, and came to see if it was some gangrel body seeking alms, and it was him. I never struck him, no matter what you say,' he added to the man at his side. One of the second-year novices, Gil thought. Tam moved quietly from behind Gil and took up a stance at Raitts's other side.

'What is going on?' asked Prior Boyd, in more authoritative tones. Several people began to answer him, but he held up one hand, pale in the flickering light, and pointed to the novice. 'You. David Brown, is it? I canny see you in this light.'

'No, Faither, it's Robert Aikman.' The young man ducked his head in a bow. 'Archie and me was watching wi Brother Euan, and he sent us to find you, and as I cam through the slype I heard a noise, and came to see what was up, and here was our librarian, and Faither Henry on the ground. So I shouted, and he ran, and Archie and me caught him, and Archie fetched Brother Euan—'

'Aye, and I should be sitting with Faither James,' said Brother Euan, 'to let these laddies be getting some sleep. There is too much the now for one Infirmarer, Faither, we will need to be choosing another to learn beside me.' He looked down at Father Henry, his hands gentle on the man's inert shoulder, at odds with the irritation in his voice.

'I found him like that,' said Raitts again. 'I cam by here and there he was, and then these two come shouting at me and a course I ran, who wouldny, but I never struck him down.'

'Can he be moved?' the Prior asked Brother Euan.

'I've sent Archie to fetch a hurdle,' said the sub-infirmarer obliquely. 'I'd as soon carry him steady on that as lift him wi his head falling all about. We could do wi a couple folk to be going ahead, make up the other bed, fetch hot stones from the kitchen. And you need to see Faither James, Faither,' he added significantly.

'Is this where he was lying when you found him?' Gil asked Raitts.

'He was closer to the wall,' said Raitts. 'I rolled him over to see who it was and why he was snoring like that. He's stopped the snoring,' he added unnecessarily. 'He stopped when I moved him.'

'Good,' said Brother Euan.

'How long ago was this?' Gil asked. Raitts shrugged.

'The half o an hour? No as much as an hour. I cam by here . . .' He checked, and shuddered, 'I cam by here to go into the kirk for that I heard voices in the guest yard, and there was *women* there. At this hour o the night! What's women doing here the now? It's no right!'

'The woman who was in the yard has left,' said Gil soothingly. 'How come you were about? Where were you when you heard her?'

'More to the point, why was Faither Henry here?' said the Prior. 'Who has struck him down, and why? This community is cursed, I begin to believe it.' He crossed himself.

Brother Archie arrived with a wicker hurdle. Gil, looking around him, wondered if the whole community was now awake and here in the cloister. There seemed to be at least ten people milling about, though it was hard to count in the darkness. Brother Euan took over, issuing orders, getting his patient moved carefully onto the hurdle, directing four men to take the corners. The Prior firmly ordered everyone else back to bed, reminding them of the imposed silence, and followed as the small group with its burden moved off towards the door.

From his post Tam said, 'An accident, maister? Or was he struck?'

185

'I'm no certain.' Gil moved towards the wall, where Raitts and his captor still stood, apparently uncertain of what to do. 'Bring that light, would you? About here, you said he was lying?' he said to Raitts, who looked up and nodded numbly.

'Maybe a bit along. I canny mind.'

Faced with this level of precision, Gil resorted to inspecting the wall over a length of two or three ells, holding the light close and peering at the warm-coloured stone. He was rewarded; not far from where White had lain he found a dark sticky patch about shoulder height, with dark hairs caught in it. He touched it and sniffed his fingers.

'Blood,' he said aloud.

'What's that?' said Raitts. And then, as if he could hold the question back no longer, 'Maister, is she really gone?'

'I saw her leave,' said Gil.

'What brought her here?' he demanded fretfully. 'How did she come here, out o all places?'

'She's seeking her man,' Gil said. 'Some friend thought she saw him here in Perth.'

'Oh.' The tone was dismayed. Raitts subsided, staring into the dark garden, or perhaps into some hell of his own. Brother Robert edged away a little.

'You think he fell, then?' said Tam.

'I do.' Gil straightened up and looked about him. 'Though it's hard to see what he might ha tripped over. And he hit the back o his head.'

'These stones is slippy when they're wet. Maybe he just couped ower.'

'It's stopped raining,' Gil observed.

Robert Aikman quietly leaned forward, unbound Raitts's wrists and held the belt out to him. The librarian looked down at his freed hands, then picked up the nearest lantern, and made for the doorway into the church, ignoring the belt. The novice watched him go, then looked helplessly at Gil.

'Maybe you should go back to the infirmary,' Gil suggested.

Left alone with Tam, he lifted the remaining lantern, looking about him.

'It makes no sense,' he said. 'What was White doing here at this hour, when they should all have been abed? What was Raitts doing? And why should White fall over and strike his head, here where the flagstones are level and dry?'

'That one they were holding for it,' said Tam, 'said he cam past here acos he heard women in the courtyard.' He chuckled briefly. 'You could hear that woman at Glasgow, I'd wager. As if he was planning to hide in the kirk,' he elaborated.

'Aye, it's possible, though why he was abroad in the night at all—'

'Maister Cunningham!' Hurrying feet, a light at the doorway. A Dominican, his lantern picking the white sleeves and hem of his habit out of the night. 'Maister Cunningham? Faither Prior sends for you, as soon as may be.'

'What is it?' Gil made for the door, Tam following hastily.

'It's Faither Henry. He's — his habit's a ower blood. He's been stabbed!'

'He's living,' said Brother Euan in his quiet voice, 'and will live yet, by God's grace. But aye, he's been stabbed.'

'Where?' Gil demanded, keeping his voice down in turn. 'Can I see the wound?'

'Here.' Brother Euan turned to the bed where the second patient lay, his head and shoulders on a backboard, a heap of bloody linen and wool discarded by his feet, one of the infirmary assistants just removing a basin of reddened water. Across the chamber, Prior Boyd had assumed his stole and was murmuring softly over Father James, whose face had changed in a subtle way Gil had seen before. 'Our Lady has had our brother in her care, truly,' the sub-infirmarer went on, drawing away the blankets over Henry White. 'See, no great injury. I am thinking it has missed anything vital, and we found it afore he was bleeding to death.'

There was a long gash skidding down the left side of the man's ribcage, oozing blood again after having been washed. There was blood still caked in the mat of black hair over the belly. Despite his words, the injury looked extensive, and Gil said as much.

'Aye, but none so deep,' said Brother Euan. He reached for a roll of bandage. 'The knife has caught the ribs, I would say, and slid off. It goes only into the flesh here, not so deep as the vitals.' He scooped something green from a tub onto a piece of linen and slapped it on the wound. 'And St Dominic be praised I had Billy make up some of this the day. Will you take an end o that back-board, maister, till I get him wound up?'

Gil obediently helped the assistant to support White's head and shoulders off the bed, so that Brother Euan could roll the bandage round the man's muscular ribcage, strapping the wound securely. He fastened the end with a pin, nodded to them to lower the board, and turned his attention to the head injury, snipping away the hair round the contusion with a small pair of shears. His assistant quietly moved the linen-wrapped hot stone nearer to White's other side and pulled the blankets up about the broad shoulders.

'I'd thought he simply fell,' said Gil, 'cracked his head on the wall – in fact, I found where he struck – but this is another matter.'

Brother Euan threw him a look, but said simply, 'Aye.'

'It's hardly an expert thrust,' Gil went on, thinking aloud. 'I suppose it could have been some kind o argument, then an unexpected blow, he went backwards and struck his head, the other fellow ran off . . .'

'Or no.' Brother Euan was smearing more green ointment on the head wound.

'What, you reckon . . .' Gil began. Their eyes met, then the sub-infirmarer looked down at his work.

'Why was he abroad in the night?'

'Why was Father Henry abroad in the night?' Gil countered. 'And now everyone's been ordered back to bed, which hardly helps me find who was abroad and who wasny.'

'Has he said nothing?' asked Alys.

'He's still in a great swound from the blow to the head,' said Gil. 'Brother Euan felt he was best left like that meantime. Until he rouses and can tell us, if he will tell us, we've no idea who is to blame.'

'And a knife,' she said. 'So the kitchen knife is not down the well.'

'It looks like it,' Gil agreed. 'The Prior was determined we should not search for it just now, in the dark. It can wait until the morning, he says.'

'What will you do?' She was frowning. 'Will Father Prior let you question them all now? He has really been little help so far, has he?'

'More of a hindrance,' said Gil drily, 'though I hope it isn't deliberate. When he finished ministering to Father James he heard what Brother Euan and I had to say, and agreed to call an early Chapter meeting after Terce and permit me to speak to it. Whether I'll be able to question any alone, without him present too, we'll see in the morning. Somehow I doubt it.' He stretched his hands and feet to the dying fire. The black cat, taking exception to this, rose and stalked out of the room, tail flicking.

Socrates watched it go, then lay flat again. 'I suspect he'll have to announce Father James's death to them, he doesn't look long for this world, which won't help.'

'What an evening,' Alys said. 'Indeed, what a day it has been. Gil, that woman. I saw her earlier, I think she is staying at the Greyfriars.'

'I saw her earlier too,' Gil said. 'She expected the man of law Pullar to have found her husband. I wonder why she wants him back? Five years' desertion is a long time.'

'She seems like a woman to hold onto her possessions,' Alys said. 'A pity she and Mistress Rattray's man could not make a match of it, they'd be better suited.'

'The symmetry would be pleasing,' he conceded.

She ignored this, biting the back of a finger thoughtfully. 'Gil, this is very strange about Father Henry. Why was he talking to someone there, and at that hour? What was he talking about that would end in such an argument? There seem to have been a great number of the friars about, when they should all have been abed. What raised the alarm, I wonder?'

'They may have been roused by Mistress Trabboch's visit,' Gil speculated. 'She made enough noise, after all.'

'Yes,' said Alys inattentively. 'I wonder, could he have been out about the place for the same reason as the other night?'

'Whatever that is,' said Gil.

'You said he had heard something outside,' Alys recalled, 'and rose to see what it was. You also said he sleeps at the far end of the dorter.'

'So Raitts said,' agreed Gil.

'His hearing must be good. Nobody else heard what he heard? He roused nobody to go with him?'

'Secrecy,' said Gil. 'Whether he genuinely heard something, or simply went out to pursue something, someone, he suspected, he won't tell us.'

190

She nodded. 'It seems very like it. I suppose tonight he might have heard Mistress Trabboch and come out to see what was afoot, but it could equally well be the same reason, as I said.'

'It hardly seems like the man to indulge simple curiosity,' Gil said. 'And we won't know the answers till he recovers enough to tell us, if he does.' He got to his feet. 'Time we were abed and all, sweetheart. I'm past thinking clearly.'

'In the *library*?' Gil repeated in astonishment. 'Why was I not woken?'

'Aye,' said Brother Dickon flatly. Across the table Alys was looking dismayed. 'I'd ha woken you mysel, my son, but Faither Prior was determined I wouldny, said you'd hear all in the morning.'

'And nobody heard anything?' said Alys. 'Noticed anything? When did it happen?'

Dickon shook his grizzled head.

'He's likely been lying there while all the tooraw about Faither Henry was going on. And how Brother Archie never thought to fetch me to that, I canny tell,' he added.

Jennet set her spoon down in her porridge bowl and said, 'Surely there's a curse on this place. We ought to be getting hame, maister, it's no a good idea to wait about here. We'll all be murdered in our beds afore we go.'

'I hope not, lass,' said Brother Dickon.

'Tell me again,' said Gil. 'Wilson was missed when?'

'At Matins. He was out o his place, and after the Office Faither Prior sent to the infirmary to see if he was there, and when he wasny he set up a search. We were roused to help, and it was Archie and me found him in the library. Which by rights should ha been locked, save that our librarian says he lost the key a month ago.'

191

'And he'd been stabbed,' said Gil. 'You were right, sweetheart,' he said to Alys, 'the knife is clearly not down the infirmary well.'

'But how,' said Alys in puzzlement, 'how did he come to be there? Why would anyone meet another, alone in the dark, when there has been one death already? It makes no sense.'

'He's – he was a brawny fellow,' said Gil. 'It must ha been someone he trusted, to get close enough wi that knife. Assuming it's the same knife.'

'Aye,' said Brother Dickon. 'He'll ha been stripped and washed by now, you'll can get a look at the wound by daylight. But it's no so like there'd be two knives at liberty about the house, it's like to be the same one. And where was it hid when we searched the place last? I looked everywhere, desks and dorters and ahint the books in the library.'

'You'll have to show me where he lay,' said Gil. 'And I'll need to see the body afore Chapter. Let me get my boots on.'

There was a lay servant on his knees with a bucket and scrubbing brush just inside the door of the library. Brother Dickon used an unsuitable expression under his breath, and hurried forward.

'Gie's a moment, Attie, lad,' he said. 'Maister Cunningham needs a look at the marks.'

'It's no lifting,' said Attie, sitting back on his heels. 'You can see it clear.' He pointed. 'Is this where he was stabbed, then, maister?'

'It's where he died, certain,' said Dickon.

'How was he lying?' Gil asked. Dickon looked about him.

'On his back, wi one arm out. You'll see him, he's set like that. As if he'd gone ower backwards, knocked that desk out the way, gone down off it.'

Gil studied the scene.

'And the bloodstain? Under him when he was lifted?'

'Aye, it must ha soaked into his cloak and then into the wood.'

'So he'd ha been standing here,' Gil moved into position, 'just within the door at any road, and was stabbed – where?'

Dickon put out a broad hand, the fingers stiffened, and prodded Gil in the breastbone.

'Got him in the heart this time. I reckon he didny die immediate – there was blood at his mouth and plenty soaked into his clothes, but it would ha been quick.' He pulled a face. 'We'll need to move the furniture; naeb'dy's going to want to stand here to study.'

'Right,' said Gil, and stepped back. 'I want a look at him now, and then I suppose it's Chapter. You can carry on,' he said to Attie, who had been listening avidly.

The murdered man was laid out in the little house between Pollock's and the makeshift infirmary, candles burning at his head and feet and two of his brothers in religion kneeling beside him with their beads. Gil, wondering briefly what had happened to the remains of Leonard Pollock, drew back the linen sheet to uncover Thomas Wilson, washed and stretched on a board in the attitude in which he had died, a narrow wound over his breastbone. His eyes were open, an expression of astonishment on his face, as if he felt so small a gash in his flesh should not have been wide enough for his life to escape by.

Hunting about, Gil found several straw mattresses rolled in a corner of the inner chamber. Drawing out a length of straw he inserted it carefully into the wound, and found it nearly a palm's-breadth deep.

'Likely nicked the heart, or one o the big vessels next it,' Brother Dickon said. 'He'd no last long once it happened, even if there had been help at hand.'

'This is an expert blow,' said Gil. 'Someone kent what he was doing.'

'I thought that,' said Dickon. 'Same's Andrew Rattray, though if you've killt a pig or two you can cut a throat.'

'No other marks on him?' Gil was feeling the skull, checking the arms and hands. 'Help me roll him till I see his back.'

'No marks that Archie mentioned,' said Brother Dickon, obliging. 'He said, it looked as if he'd been taken by surprise.'

'Like Faither Henry,' said Gil, setting the body back as he had first seen it. 'And the boy Rattray was sound asleep, I'd ha said. It's been nobody he saw as an enemy.'

'Aye,' said Dickon. 'It's an internal matter, right enough.' He drew the linen over Wilson's surprised face and turned to leave the chamber. 'Doesny seem right, leaving him staring like that, but we'll no get his een closed till he softens.'

'So he was well stiffened when he was found,' Gil stated.

'Oh, aye. The most o him was set solid, though his legs was still limber. He wasny that cold, either.'

'Is that so?' said Gil.

When they emerged from the slype, such members of the community as were not engaged in praying over the dead or caring for the injured could be seen filing quietly into the Chapter House on the far side of the cloister. Following them, Gil found the chamber already nearly full, but young Brother Martin was lying in wait, bowed politely and led him in silence to a stool near the great chair which awaited Prior Boyd.

He sat quietly, watching the friars gathering in their silence under the vaulted roof, observing how companionship and sympathy of thought could be expressed without word or gesture simply by the angle of head or shoulders, the turn of the neck. The brothers took their seats on the wall-bench, the novices stood in one corner near the door, the outdoor lay brothers in the other. The librarian sat isolated in the midst of the crowd, every face turned away from him. The first-year novices might as well have been leashed together like hunting dogs, looking about them but moving as a tight group.

The great door swung open again, the subprior entered, all rose and David Boyd paced in, the length of the chamber, and nodded to Gil. Turning to face his flock, he raised a hand and pronounced, '*In nomine Domini.*'

All responded with *Amen*, and they sat down with a ruffle and hush of heavy woollen fabric, a shuffle of booted feet. The Prior held out a hand and the subprior set a book into it; opening it at the marker Boyd said in Scots, 'I'll no read from the next chapter following yesterday's reading. This is more apposite to our case.'

Gil, seated beside him, could see the round Latin script and the painted decorations on the page, simple curlicues and the occasional leaf, but found he was listening to a clear, confident Scots version.

'Hae nane disputes, but if ony should arise, bring them to ane speedy end, lest anger grow into hatred, the mote into the beam, and your saul into a murderer's. For he that hates his brother is ane cut-throat, ane slayer.' The Prior paused to clear his throat. 'If ye hae injured another . . .' he continued.

The excerpt from Augustine's Rule was lengthy. Gil, watching the faces as the rich Scots washed over them, could not feel it was reaching its target. Raitts sat solitary, shivering from time to time; the outdoor men with Brother Dickon in their midst stood at grim attention near the door; the novices in another group all seemed to be hanging attentively on the Prior's words. Other faces were serious, anxious, dismayed; a few men were watching Gil, glancing away as he looked at them.

The Prior, having reached the end of his chapter,

offered a prayer for guidance and protection in troubled times, sat back and considered his audience.

'Likely you'll all ken by now,' he said, 'that disaster has visited us again. Our brother Thomas Wilson was found this morning, cruelly done to death in the library. Afore that, our brother Henry White was stabbed. One o our number has sinned grievously against the whole community. We'll ha to call in the Sheriff, but afore that Maister Cunningham, that has practice in sic matters, will help us order our thochts and maybe find the sinner in our own way, rather than give any brother ower to the Sheriff's questioning. If Maister Cunningham asks a question and any o ye has an answer, he's to raise his hand, and I'll call on him to speak. Understood?'

Not the introduction I'd have wished, Gil thought, and leaned forward.

'*Let him not imagine that his sin will pass unnoticed,*' he quoted, using the original Latin. '*He will surely be seen, and by those he thinks not of.*'

A small stir of surprise went round the chamber: laymen did not usually have knowledge of the Rule. No need to mention that he had just read that sentence in the copy held by the Prior. Gil glanced from face to face and said carefully, 'Right now, we canny tell just what happened. But each of you kens some wee bit of the picture, and if we put them all thegither we can learn more, and maybe enough, as Faither Prior has said, to save one o the community from torture.' He paused, but nobody spoke. Well, they were still under an order of silence. 'Think back to the end of Compline last night. It's my understanding that you go from Compline straight to your beds, is that correct?'

'It is,' said David Boyd beside him.

'At that point, was anyone out o his place? Does anyone recall noticing a gap where one o the brethren should ha been?'

There was a certain amount of shuffling, of looking from side to side, of shaking of heads. One of the lay brothers raised a hand.

'Brother Archie,' said the Prior.

'Me and Brother George was helping in the infirmary,' said Brother Archie diffidently. In the other corner of the chamber Brother George nodded agreement.

'So you wereny in your bed, but you were in your place,' said Gil. 'Anyone else?' Nobody else stirred, so he went on, 'The next thing to happen, I think, was someone knocking at the gates demanding to see Faither Prior. Who was porter last night?'

Another of the lay brothers raised his hand.

'Brother Jamesie,' said the Prior.

'It was me,' said Brother Jamesie, 'and what I did was, I let her into the yard wi her folk, seeing she wouldny take No for an answer and kept shouting at me, and I went through the slype and up the dorter to wake Faither, and he said he'd come out to the guest hall and to ask Maister Cunningham if he'd be present, and when I'd done that I went back to the lay dorter to wait in the warm till she'd to be let out the place.'

'And she left in due time?' said Gil.

'Aye, she did, and a face like a skelped arse on her and all. I'm right sorry for her servants, so I am.'

'Jamesie,' said the Prior in reproof. Brother Jamesie bowed and muttered something apologetic.

'While Mistress Trabboch was in the guest hall,' Gil continued, 'I think Brother Archie and Brother Robert Aikman,' the two looked up from the midst of their respective groups, 'crossed the guest-hall yard from the new infirmary and came through the slype into the cloister here. Were Mistress Trabboch's horses still in the yard?'

'Aye, they were,' contributed Archie, 'for one o them let fly a kick at me. We went through the slype, see,

197

intending to go and waken Faither, since we didny ken he was a'ready awake, and just by the library door we cam upon our librarian bending ower Faither Henry—'

'We didny ken it was Faither Henry,' said Aikman. 'He was bent ower something on the ground, and when he seen us he ran, so I ran after him and I brought him down, and Archie said, here was Faither Henry and he was deid, and Brother Sandy was shouting at us and we was shouting back, which brought Andrew Jackson and Patey Simpson both out the church where they were praying for Andrew Rattray, and they joined in and that fetched a good few folk out the dorter, and—'

'Stop there,' Gil said. 'Now, we ken Henry White isny dead. When did he rise from his bed? Does anyone mind seeing him? Did he go to bed after Compline, or did he wait up?'

There was an expectant hush, with heads turning to see if anyone had any knowledge.

After a few moments Raitts straightened up, looked about him, and said dully, 'I saw him go past my cell.'

'When was that?' Gil asked, taking this in.

'Once all was asleep?' said Raitts vaguely. 'I canny mind. I was – I was thinking.'

One or two of the friars stirred restlessly, as if they would have made an immediate accusation.

Gil said, 'When did you leave the dorter?'

'Maybe an hour after Henry?' said Raitts after another pause. 'Maybe longer, I canny mind. Thomas went down and all,' he added.

'Afore or after Henry White?' Gil asked.

'Afore,' said Raitts on reflection.

'Was this afore or after Jamesie came to wake your Prior?'

'Oh, long afore it,' said Raitts, suddenly quite clear about something. 'And when I heard Jamesie name

198

Agnes Trabboch I thought a bit longer and then I went down and all.' He caught himself up, looked about in alarm, and went on hastily, 'To hide, you ken, for that there shouldny be women in the place. Two dwelling in the guest hall's bad enough, at least those two's civil and shamefast,' *I must repeat that to Alys*, Gil thought, 'but more o them demanding to come in at sic an hour o the night, it's no right at all. I thought I would hide in the library, but I fell ower something by the door, and I was just seeing what it was when these two cam out the slype and shouted at me. So I ran, in case it was that woman, and there was no need for knocking me down,' he ended with resentment.

Gil looked at the faces turned towards him.

'Can any confirm that?' he asked. 'Did any hear White or Wilson leave the dorter?'

Further round the ring of seated brethren a cautious hand rose.

'Brother Bernard,' said the Prior.

'Thomas is next me,' said Brother Bernard, a round-faced man with a pair of wire-framed spectacles tied onto his face with a black ribbon. 'I thought I heard him moving about, early on, no so long after Compline. I took it he'd the bellyache again, same as he complained o the other night. I never heard him come back up, but—' His face changed as he recalled why, and he crossed himself.

'Anyone else?' said Gil. A few heads were shaken. 'Well, it's something. Where were we? Arguing over Henry White in the cloister out there,' he recalled. 'What happened next?'

'We bound Brother Sandy,' said Robert Aikman diffidently, 'and Archie went for Brother Euan to see to Faither Henry, for we could see he'd hurt his head, and folk brought lights, and then Archie fetched Faither Prior and yoursel, maister.'

199

Gil nodded.

'That's clear enough. While you were all arguing over White, did anyone try the library door? Or see anyone else try the library door?'

'I'd ha had plenty to say if they did,' said Raitts angrily. 'There's nobody allowed in there if I'm no there.'

Looking at the man, Gil thought he was quite unaware of what he had just said. He glanced about the room; one or two expressions suggested their wearers had had the same thought, but nobody seemed inclined to admit to trying the door.

'What happened then?' he asked. 'Mind me.'

'Faither sent us to bed,' said someone, without putting his hand up.

'Did all go there?' Gil pursued. 'Two went to pray over Andrew Rattray, I'd ha thought.' Two hands were raised, two heads nodded. 'There were several in the infirmary, as I recall.' Another three hands went up. 'Anyone else?' After a moment he looked directly at Raitts. 'I think you went into the kirk. How long were you there?'

'I stayed there till Matins,' said the librarian sullenly. 'They two can tell you that.'

One of the two bedesmen nodded. The other looked blank. Making a mental note to question them privately, Gil went on, 'Those o you that were moving about at that time, did any o you notice anything or anyone out o place? Anything at all, even if there was a good explanation for it,' he added. There was a silence. Finally he drew out his tablets and continued, 'I'll not keep the meeting by questioning each o you the now, but I'd like a list o all those that were about at that time, so I can get you later.'

'Raise your hands,' said Boyd, 'any that were out their beds between Compline and Matins.' He looked about the chamber, and began dictating the names to Gil.

200

'That's about right,' he added when he had finished. 'I canny recall that I saw any others at that hour.'

'Thank you, sir,' said Gil. 'And one final question afore we move on to Matins. Did any set eyes on Thomas Wilson atween Compline and the time you were all sent back to bed?'

There was a long silence, into which someone muttered, 'One o us must ha done.'

'And I could name him,' said another voice.

'Who said that?' Gil demanded. Perhaps wisely, the speaker did not identify himself. After a moment Gil went on, 'Now, when you rose for Matins, was all as usual apart from the absence o Wilson and White?'

'I thought so,' said the Prior beside him. 'Did any notice aught amiss?'

Heads were shaken, there were murmurs of *No* and *No, till we were in our places.*

'Everyone else was present that should ha been?'

'Apart from those occupied in the infirmary,' qualified the Prior, 'I saw no gaps in the stalls other than Henry's and Thomas's. We sought Thomas immediately the Office was over, and he was found as you have seen him, I think.'

Well, not quite as I saw him, Gil thought. 'Who found him?' he asked. There was a pause, and several heads turned, looking at one place on the bench.

'Archie and me,' said Brother Dickon from his corner. 'Brother Sandy said we should search there.'

'I did,' admitted Raitts reluctantly, under the stares of his brethren. 'I thought maybe he'd sneaked in there wi'out permission, and there he was, blood all ower the floor, the reading-desk couped ower. Archie and Dickon were there ahead of me,' he added.

'I'm told the library wasny locked.'

'I lost the key,' said Raitts defensively. 'I canny tell

201

where it went. I've no had it these three weeks or more. Since afore Yule.'

'Is that generally kent in the house?'

Murmurs of agreement suggested that it was.

'And what did you do when you found Wilson?'

'He yelled out,' said Jamesie. 'And they all cam running.'

'Who decided he was dead?'

'It was obvious,' said another brother. 'Lying staring like that, never blinking in the light. I tried his pulse,' he demonstrated at his own throat, 'but you could tell, any road.'

'What state was he in?' Gil asked.

'Well, he was dead,' offered the friar. 'No a very good state.'

'I mean,' said Gil patiently, 'had he begun to stiffen? Was he cold, or still warm? When you found the blood, was it still wet?'

'He was stiff as a board,' said another man.

'No, his legs was still limber,' said someone else, 'for they were a ower the place when we put him on the hurdle.'

'His arms was set, just the same. And he was cold.'

'No that cold. No as cold's the floor, say. No very warm, mind.'

'So he'd been dead a few hours,' said Gil.

'Aye,' said someone.

'Aye,' said Prior Boyd. 'Slain in secret by one o his brothers. One o us here in this Chapter House. This is no dwelling together in unity. This is no honouring God whose temple each o us is. This is foul murder, and though we may love the sinner we must hate the sin. I call upon the man who murdered Thomas Wilson to confess now, afore us all.'

There was a silence, which grew and grew. One or two heads turned, to see if any looked like coming forward; a few sat back, to emphasise that they would not.

After what seemed an eternity, the Prior said in weighty tones, 'Well, if you will not confess, it seems I must name you mysel. Alexander Raitts, I accuse you o—'

'No!' Raitts sprang to his feet. 'No, you canny, it wasny me!'

'—enticing Thomas Wilson secretly away from his proper place into the library o this house—'

'No, I never, I canny, I've no knife nor any weapon!'

'—and there stabbing him to death. And I think it likely you slew Andrew Rattray and all.'

'No!' shouted Raitts. 'I did no sic a thing. I'm innocent!'

The men nearest him hastened to seize his arms. He struggled, and more friars joined him, with a couple of the lay brothers. The first-year novices were staring, the second-year men looked appalled. Gil himself was deeply dismayed: this was not the outcome he had hoped for.

'Take him out and confine him,' said the Prior. 'There must be a storeroom to the purpose.' He turned to Gil. 'Maister Cunningham, Gregory says, *if scandal arise from truth, the scandal should be borne rather than the truth be set aside.* You've made the truth right clear to us, and I thank you for it, though the outcome grieves me sair.'

# Chapter Ten

'No, I agree,' said Alys. 'That man could hardly kill twice, and nearly a third time, and not show it. But could he have done it otherwise? What reason could he have?'

'Plenty for Wilson,' said Gil, 'to judge by what I saw yesterday. Sweet St Giles, was it only yesterday? Less for White – they are reputed to have got on well, but I suppose encountering him after killing Wilson, he might have stabbed him to prevent him talking of it. In which he is successful so far,' he added. 'White is still in his swound, though I suspect Brother Euan is keeping him that way.'

'And the boy Rattray?' Alys bent to throw another log on the fire. It spat and sparked as the flames licked at the bark.

'Raitts had as much opportunity as any in the place,' said Gil slowly, thinking about it, 'but I cannot tell that he had any reason, any more than he had reason to kill the other novices.'

'He had more reason to kill the one named Simpson,' Alys observed wryly, 'if he misused a book. I suppose he might be protecting whatever secret Pollock had discovered about him, if any of the others had learned it. He did say Wilson was talking about him in the town?'

'Aye, though he said he was talking about him, not asking questions about him. And I suppose either of the others could have learned something by accident.'

'What other reason could there be for killing the two who are dead?'

'You don't think Pollock was killed?'

'Not deliberately, no. And not by the same person, I am certain. I should have more to tell you later.' She glanced at the light through the high windows. 'I hope Tam comes back soon. What do Rattray and Wilson have in common?'

'Little, I'd have said.' Gil considered the two. 'They're an essay in contrasts, indeed. The novice a promising man, a good scholar, ardent, devout. Wilson not one of the world's learned, known to be peculating in the matter of the rents, not greatly devout. What did the other boy say of Wilson?'

'He was careful to say nothing,' said Alys, 'though he was less clever than Father Henry about concealing the fact.'

'We can assume he at least knew about the rents,' agreed Gil.

'Why was the man in the library?' Alys wondered. 'Was he looking for something, or meeting someone – the person who killed him, perhaps – or hiding from someone?'

'No sign that he tried to run, by what they described who found him,' Gil said. 'That's a good point. Why was he there? I suppose, with the rule of silence at the moment, any wanting to have a conversation would need to use secrecy.'

'Yes,' she said thoughtfully, 'so it must have been someone he had no reason to fear. I should not think he would meet secretly with the librarian. How would you persuade such a man to meet with you in private?'

'Ask for pastoral advice?' Gil suggested.

'Yes, that would work. He would have been flattered, I suppose. But who? Nobody else admitted to being out of his place.'

'Nobody we've not accounted for, and I'd checked with Brother Euan that none of his helpers vanished for any length of time.' Gil sighed. 'The trouble is, because he has Raitts locked up, Boyd sees no purpose now in my questioning the rest. He has sent to the Provost, to say there has been a death and the man responsible is taken, and also to the Bishop, and refuses to lift the injunction of silence. I suppose I can still speak to the servants, the outdoor men, the folk in the infirmary, who are not enjoined, but not the others.'

'What will you do?'

'Now I've warmed up?' He looked about him. 'Take the dog for a walk, outside this place, and think. Will you come with me?'

'No,' she said regretfully, 'for if Tam has been success-ful I have something to do.'

Bundled in his plaid over the leather doublet, his hands encased in thick woollen mittens, Gil strode briskly along the banks of the Town Ditch, nodding to the occasional passer-by, with Socrates loping happily around him. There seemed to be interesting smells and trails everywhere, to judge by the way the dog's long nose twitched and snuffled near the ground. At least one of us has something to follow, Gil thought, and glanced to his right where the Blackfriars' easternmost outbuildings sat behind their wall. What was going on in that place? Who had killed two men, injured a third, for no reason he could make out? Raitts made an uncon-vincing villain, though his protestations of innocence were not wholly convincing either. What was he up to, Gil wondered, wandering about the place in the dark, hiding in the library from strange women.

No, the answer had to lie somewhere with what linked the three dead or injured. All were Dominicans, though one was a senior man, one an ordinary friar, one a novice. That was hardly the answer; it did not single them out in their community, and failing the work of the Devil their attacker must be a member of the same community. Two were able scholars, the third must be a cunning man if he had practised the deceit over the rents for any length of time. White was a priest, he did not know about Wilson, and he could probably assume the young man Rattray was not yet priested. In most ways he could think of, the three men were different rather than similar. So what linked them?

He paused, looking about him. The path he had followed along the bank was about to join the muddy network of tracks and roadways through the next patch of suburban building, clustered about the northwest port of the burgh. Several dogs of mixed size and type were surveying Socrates warily from a gap in a fence, and a handful of hens scurried for cover in the damp bushes. He whistled to Socrates and turned back, passing a man with a stout kist on his shoulder, a smell of new wood drifting after him. Probably delivering it somewhere, Gil thought.

Working his way back along the Ditch, he reviewed what he knew of the three men, trying to call each to mind, though the image of Rattray as an eager, ardent young man sat badly with the thought of his smoke-blackened, contorted remains. Put them together, he thought, and how do they act? In his mind's eye the three drew together into a group, heads bent, manner quiet and decorous. Father Henry appeared to be praying aloud, the other two paying close attention, their beads in their hands.

Then the image of Rattray turned and looked straight at Gil. He could see the bright red curls about the boy's brow, the earnest pale face, the freckles across the cheekbones. Blue eyes met his, and the lips moved.

'I took him for my brother,' the young man said, his voice hoarse and intense. 'Get him. Mak him confess.'

208

'I'll get him,' he answered aloud. '*Trouthe the shal delivere, hit is no drede.*'

'Mak him confess,' said the hoarse voice again as the image in his head was dispelled.

'Maister?' said another voice entirely. 'What are you at?'

He looked about him, blinking, and found he was standing at the very edge of the Ditch, with Tam at his elbow and Socrates at his knee both staring anxiously at him. Rapid red-brown water, thick as lentil broth, gurgled coldly a few inches from the toes of his boots. He stepped back in some alarm.

'A wee bit close,' said Tam. 'Lucky I seen you, maister. What were you about, so near the edge?'

'I – I was thinking,' said Gil. 'Wasny looking where I was going. Thanks, man!'

'Aye, well.' Tam cast a look at the Ditch. 'You couldny rely on the dog to haul you out o that.' He turned to walk along with Gil. 'I'm glad I found you, but.'

He fell silent. Gil looked along his shoulder at the man. He had known him for years; Tam was not a lot older than Gil, had run at his stirrup in the hunting grounds of Lanarkshire, and it was clear now that his henchman wanted to ask something.

'Out wi't,' he said. 'What is it troubles you?'

'No *troubles*, maybe,' said Tam awkwardly. 'No troubles so much as – aye, well, I'm troubled. See, I ken the mistress mentioned this lassie to you.'

'Lassie?' Gil searched his memory, and then recalled Alys's tale of yesterday's encounter. 'You mean the young man's sister?'

'Aye.' Tam stared hard at a flock of chaffinches squabbling under a bush, until Socrates loped over to investigate and the little birds flew up. 'See, I'd to take back the lantern she lent us, the day, and I got talking wi her. She's – she's in a right uneasy position, maister, wi her brother deid, and the two bairns to protect, and she's feart her man catches up wi her.' He stopped speaking, biting his lips. Gil made an encouraging noise. 'I was wondering, maister, if you'd maybe ha a word wi her. Advise her, maybe. She's no certain how the law stands, and nor am I.'

'You've a notion to her,' Gil said. Tam coloured up under his fair thatch of hair.

'I have,' he admitted. 'I've little hope, she's outside my station in life, but I canny think when I was as taken wi a lassie. She's valiant, she's true, she's stalwart. Her man scarred her face, sic a sight as it is, poor lass, but she doesny hide it. And the wee laddie – did the mistress say he's blind? His faither did that to him, but he's a merry wee boy. Minded my voice as soon as he heard it, asked straight off for another story.'

'What d'you want me to say?' Gil asked, reflecting that his uncle, whose servant Tam was now, would not be pleased if his groom suddenly left to support a family in Perth, and would be even less pleased if he brought another man's wife to Glasgow.

'I'm no right certain,' said Tam. 'What is there to say? You're the man o law, Maister Gil, no me. Could her man insist she brought the bairns home? Can he order her back to him? It's that kind o thing she's fretting on.'

'Aye to both,' said Gil, 'if the wee one's still nursing.'

'I thought that,' said Tam grimly. 'He'll ding her to death if she goes, and likely the bairns and all. Hah!' he said, without humour. 'Yon woman last night wants her man back, will he, nill he, and here's this lassie hiding from her man. It's a strange world, this.'

'Where does she dwell?' Gil asked. 'Can you take me there now?'

Despite Alys's description and Tam's warning, Gil had difficulty hiding his dismay at the sight of Mistress Rattray's face. The thought of a man who could do this having charge over the two infants in the room was a chilling one.

'It's right kind in you to spare me the time,' she was saying now. 'Your man tells me you're a man o law yourself? I suppose you'll ha seen sights like this afore.' She indicated her scars.

'There's nobody seen the like o't,' said her maidservant unhelpfully. She was seated by the other window with a basket of mending and was putting stitches in a small shirt; she had become quite flustered by Gil's arrival, and Mistress Rattray had had to deal with the buttered ale herself while Tam introduced Socrates to the little boy, encouraging the child to feel the soft ears and long nose; the dog bore all with patience, dignity and the occasional friendly swipe of a long tongue, which made Drew giggle.

Keeping the pity out of his voice, Gil said honestly, 'No. No where it showed,' he qualified, thinking of Bess Stewart's missing ear.

'Aye, well,' she said, pouring buttered ale into cups, 'he did a bit o that and all.'

'Have you witnesses,' he asked, accepting the wooden beaker, 'who could swear to you having those marks afore you left your husband?'

'Andrew—' she began. Tears started to her eyes, and she clapped a hand over her mouth. 'I canny keep it in mind,' she said, turning her head away, 'that he'll no support me mair.' She swallowed, and straightened up. 'Annie would swear to it.' Annie nodded, looking up from her mending. 'Those that were servants in the house afore I left it might speak for me and all.'

'Eppie Craigo,' said the maidservant.

'Aye, you're right, Annie. There's maybe one o my neighbours, sir, Eppie Craigo that's mairriet on Will Guthrie the apothecary, it was her Annie fetched to me

211

that night once Skene was in his bed. She'd mind that, I think – it was the middle o the night.'

Gil nodded.

'That might be enough. I'd recommend, mistress, that if he resorts to the law to get you back, you offer to return and walk about Montrose openly telling folk how you got the marks.'

'Och, no, she couldny do sic a thing!' exclaimed Annie. 'And make him the speak o the town? I never heard the like!'

Mistress Rattray flinched, gritted her teeth, nodded reluctantly.

'But mostly,' Gil went on, 'I'd suggest you keep out his sight. Is Perth far enough away, do you think? I take it you cam here because your brother was here?'

'Aye.' She looked round the chamber, drew a deep breath and let it out. 'There's naught to keep me here now, I suppose. I've neither kin nor acquaintance anywhere further afield, though. I'll need to gie it thought.' Tam, across the chamber, now playing finger-games with the boy, looked up at that, but did not speak.

'You were close to your brother, I think,' Gil said gently. 'My wife tellt me he would come to you here once a week or so.'

'Aye. He said he couldny rest without he knew I was safe. I've no notion how he got out the place, I'd ha thought it would be all barred and bolted, but he never got caught.'

'Did his friends ken where he went?'

She shook her head.

'We reckoned to tell nobody I was here. I go by Margaret Keithick, was my mother's name, and it's Annie does the most o the marketing.' She stopped speaking, gazing at something Gil could not see. In the cradle by her feet the baby snuffled, stirred, found her thumb and fell asleep again. 'It seems hard,' she said at length, 'when I'm in the same town, that I shouldny get to his burial. D'you ken when—?'

'It's no arranged yet.'

'And madam your wife said,' she went on, recollecting something, 'that you're looking into how he – into who – have you discerned anything yet? Who was it killed him?'

'I've no discovered that yet,' Gil said. 'It's certain it was one o the community, for there's no sign any stranger got in, and there's been another death and a man injured and all.'

'Lord ha mercy on us!' she exclaimed. 'Is one o the brothers run mad, or something? Are they all taen to quarrelling like dogs? What's ado, maister?'

'I wish I knew,' he said. 'What can you tell me about the place? What did your brother say about the other men?'

'Madam your wife asked me the same,' she said, 'and I could tell her nothing, but it set me thinking. I mind a wee bit more now.' Gil made an encouraging noise, and she sat back, gathering her thoughts. 'He spoke a lot o the fellows he studied wi, Patey and two called Sandy and another. They seemed to be good fellows, aye good-humoured and helping one another con their books. There was what he called second-year men – is that right? – that he got on wi and all, though one named Robert annoyed him a lot, he said he asked daft questions. There was the man that guards the books, whatever his name is, Andrew got across him a time or two, whether he wanted to look at a book he shouldny, or what, I'm no certain. His tutors, he'd a great respect for them, thought the sun rose and set in Faither Henry, and Faither John was near as important. Faither Prior he spoke well o and all.'

'But?' said Gil as she slowed down. 'Did he mention others?'

'I asked him about that one Wilson,' said Annie without looking up. 'Seeing I'd heard o him in the town, how he keeps asking more on the rent than's due, so I asked the laddie, and he laughed.' She sounded resentful. 'It's no a laughing matter, that.'

'Och, Annie, he said as much himself,' said Mistress Rattray. 'What he said was, he'd heard the same, and one o his fellows better no hear o't afore the Prior did, for that he reckoned all Dominicans should live perfectly by the Rule. That was what he laughed at, no the cheating on the rents.'

'Still,' said Annie. She bit off her thread, shook out the little shirt and folded it. 'Will I make a start on the dinner, mistress?'

'Did Andrew speak o any more? Any other names?' Gil asked, when Annie had stumped out through a door in the far corner. Tam and the little boy were now playing with the ball that jingled. Mistress Rattray looked at them and smiled wearily.

'The factor, what's his name, Paterson? Patonson? One like that – he was assisting him a while afore Yule, found him honest enough but easy confused wi reckoning coin, was what he said.' She grimaced. 'I said, he wasny put in there to pass judgement on his fellows, and he said, no, but when the judgement was thrust at him he couldny help it. That's about all I mind, maister. I hope it's some help.' She scrubbed at her eyes with the cuff of her kirtle. 'I still canny take it in, that I'll never see him mair.'

The fire in the guest hall was burning low. Gil kicked the logs, sending out sparks which flew up the broad chimney, and threw some more wood on. There seemed to be nobody about, so he sat down to wait for dinner, Socrates leaning against his knee.

On leaving Mistress Rattray's house, he had gone into Perth, to spend a fruitless hour before the statue of St

Giles in St John's Kirk, turning over the two puzzles in his mind and coming to no sort of conclusion about either, other than to strengthen his conviction that the Prior was holding the wrong man. Whatever Alexander Raitts had been doing skulking about the cloister in the dark, it was not meeting Thomas Wilson in secret, nor knifing Henry White in an accidental encounter.

And where was the knife? It was an ordinary kitchen knife, with no sheath, no belt, no means of securing it to one's person; whoever used it must carry it in his hand, perhaps hiding it in his sleeve until he came to use it. When not using it, he must presumably conceal it somewhere, but Brother Dickon and his men had searched the place, even to the point of looking behind the books in the library. So where was it hidden?

Out across the chilly great hall, the door to the yard opened. Socrates scrambled to his feet and Brother Dickon's voice said, 'Maister Cunningham?'

'In here!' he called, rising. 'Come and warm yourself.'

'I'll no deny that'll be welcome.' The lay brother entered the small chamber, paused to return Socrates' greeting, and drew a stool to the hearth. 'Thocht I seen you come in,' he added. 'Drifting about like a boat wi no rudder.'

'I'm not certain what to do now,' admitted Gil. 'My wife's about some work she reckons will tell us what happened to the man Pollock. I can do little more there until she completes it, and it seems as if my other task's done.'

'Is it, now?' asked Brother Dickon, without looking at him. The black cat padded in, raised its tail in greeting to Socrates, and jumped onto the lay brother's lap.

'You're no convinced either?' said Gil after a moment.

'Convinced? I'm convinced we've got the wrong man.' He turned his head to meet Gil's gaze. 'Aye, you and all. Sandy Raitts never killed anyone, no wi a knife any road. I can see him going wood-wild and battering a man's head in wi a rock or the like, but no a knife.'

'Was he in the library when you searched it, after Rattray was killed?'

'He was.'

'How did he behave?'

'Better than I expeckit. He tried to chase us out, a course, Jamesie and me, wi our big boots and dirty hands, but when I showed him our hands were clean and minded him we'd a knife to seek, he let us proceed. *A knife? In here?* he said, and looked right troubled for the idea. *Oh, you need to find that! Heaven forfend it's in my library!* he says. Sat there like a hawk on a perch and watched every move we made, especial when Jamesie laid hands on any o the books, but that was all.'

'And when you finished?'

'That was the odd thing. I said to him, *We're done, we've found no knife, brother, your library's no been used as a hiding-place,* and he crossed himsel and said, *Our Lady be thankit.* As if he'd really been feart it might be.'

'I wonder . . .' said Gil. Then, as an idea came to him: 'Who searched the novice dorter? Was it you yoursel?'

'No. Likely it would be Archie and Dod. Never fear, they've searched a house afore this, they'd ken to look under the mattress, feel the pillow, that kind o thing.'

'Would they look for a hiding-place under the boards o the bed?' Gil asked. What had the boy said? No, that was all, he had given them no more detail. 'I ken one at least had something hid there.'

'Had he, now?' said Dickon, stroking the cat. 'Right. I'll ask Archie. And I suppose we'd best search the brothers' dorter and all.'

'It might be wiser,' Gil concurred. 'Is there any way you can search without folk noticing? We'd not want to spread alarm.'

216

'No, I'm agreed there,' said Dickon ambiguously. 'Leave it wi me. And I'll no be arranging to meet any o the brethren in secret, either.' He stared into the flames for a space. 'I might get a word wi the prisoner, but. Ask him what he meant by that. Had he maybe seen something made him suspicious, or the like, made him think there'd been someone in the library.'

'What, is he still locked away here?'

'Aye, and two o my lads told off to watch he doesny get out. Seems the Provost's depute sent to say he's from home the now, spent Yule at his landward property, can we keep Brother Sandy till he gets back. They'll no want to pay for feeding and guarding him, likely. And the Bishop rode out early to one o his other properties, though likely he'll come back when he hears o this. It's no Father Prior's best day.'

'It gives us a bit of time, though. Aye, get a word wi Raitts if you can. I wondered,' said Gil slowly, 'whether he did stay in the kirk until Matins. One o the two that were watching over Andrew Rattray agreed he'd seen him, the other didny. Do you mind who they were? Was it Pullar and Simpson, or was that when they changed over?'

'I can find out, get a word wi them,' said the lay brother. 'Though I think it's no matter. Likely Thomas was already stiffening when we found Faither Henry.' He jerked his head at the windows. 'Any word from the infirmary?'

'I called in there,' Gil said. 'No change, in either. One hanging on by a thread, one still asleep. Brother Euan seems confident Father Henry will wake, though he won't say how clear his head will be when he does.'

'Aye,' said Dickon. A small bell began to ring outside, and he gathered himself to rise. 'I thocht it was about dinnertime. Get away back to your kitchen, cheetie-cat, and catch some more mices. I'll report, maister, soon's I learn aught worth the telling.'

Alys came in from the kitchens, Jennet behind her, as he crossed the hall, and he paused to greet her and went out. The women came to join Gil by the fire.

'I don't see why they all complain about Brother Augustine,' Alys observed. 'I find him most obliging.'

'I thought you had gone out,' he said, taking her hands in both of his. 'You're cold.'

'I've been making more of the cough mix. Tam isny returned, so I wished to be occupied.'

'That's my fault,' he said guiltily. 'I kept him back.'

The other men came in as he was explaining, stamping their feet and complaining of the cold, and the kitchen servants appeared to set up the table just as Tam entered.

'That'll be fine, mistress,' he reported to Alys. She nodded, but did not clarify matters to Gil, from which he concluded that he was not to be forgiven yet for causing a delay.

Settled over a hot platter of fresh fish with braised turnips and, inevitably, stewed kale, the men began to report their morning's work, and Gil recalled that he had had no chance to rescind last night's instructions. Well, no harm done, he thought. Better than leaving them idle.

Euan got in first. 'You would be astonished, maister,' he began, dipping his bread in the sauce, 'if you was hearing how many different parts the brothers is coming from. Three from Aberdeen, four from Caithness, there is even a man from Galloway that is an Ersche speaker and all, though his accent would strip paint off a door, says Brother Euan. The most o them are coming from the burghs, so he says. Only one or two are off the land, and Faither John that is novice-master is an Edinburgh man himself.'

'That's what I've heard too,' Gil admitted.

'So I was asking what quality of folk they might be,' Euan swept on, 'and it seems they are not mostly o baronial stock like yoursel, maister. Faither Prior is of high degree, indeed, and Faither Henry, and Edward Gilchrist that is the cellarer,' he counted off the names with the fingers of his free hand, 'and one other he said. Och, and the one they have locked away for stabbing folk and all, their librarian, he said. I said, was he certain, for it hardly seems a noble thing to be stabbing folk in the dark and in secret, and he said, indeed, you had only to look at the man's manner to see he was used to servants and a household.'

'That Brother Augustine, that's in the kitchen,' said Jennet, 'he's from Dunkeld, like the Bishop, so one o the servants tellt me.'

'That's interesting, Euan,' said Gil. 'I hadny thought of that. So there's no that many would ha learned to kill a pig or use a dagger as part o their upbringing.'

'Och, now, that would be a different matter,' said Euan airily, helping himself to another portion of the fish. 'For when they were killing their own pigs last autumn, there was four or five of the brothers stepped forward to the task when Faither Prior required it. And one o the novices is the son o an armourer and is not the only one, so Brother Euan was saying, that kens which end o a dagger is the sharp one.'

'If they're out on the road collecting alms,' offered Dandy, 'I suppose they'll ha to drive off robbers now and then.'

'A staff's the more usual weapon,' said Gil. 'That's a great help, Euan. Was there much custom for Brother Euan's ministrations? Were there many visitors to the infirmary?' he elucidated, at the man's blank look.

'Och, indeed there was, and no all o them coming as patients. All the novices happened by one time or

219

another to ask how was their teacher, and half the brothers was there asking for him and for Faither James. He's at peace, is Faither James, just lying quiet, sinking slow. An easy way to go. Faither Prior sat wi him a good while.'

'I hope you wereny in Brother Euan's way,' said Alys.

'Och, indeed no, mistress!' protested Euan. 'I was a great help to him, so he said, watching over the sick and tending a pannikin he had on the fire and that, and mixing an ointment to him. It was making a nice change, so it was, working wi all that herbs. Maybe I could take to that.'

'Ah, you'd get them all mixed up, you daft Erscheman,' said Dandy.

Gil broke up the argument which promised to develop by saying, 'Did you learn anything, Dandy?'

'No a great deal the day,' said the man, reddening. 'We turned to the horse-harness, seeing we got the ox-graith ready yesterday, and mostly it was tales o the beasts they'd kent, and the days they were under Brother Dickon as men-at-arms to the old King. Jamesie was saying Brother Dickon minded the man Pollock from yon time, and had no good to say o him. Nor did any o them. They said the same as you heard yesterday, Nory, that there was a couple o different folk asking for the man since he dee'd, and one wi a white rose badge on his breast and an orra way o speaking. That's about it,' he said deprecatingly.

'It's worth something,' Gil said. 'You canny catch a fish every time you cast in the river. Thanks, man. Nory? Did you learn aught?'

'I did,' said Nory, with quiet pride. 'I found how their wash is managed, and spoke wi the chiel that deals wi't. Seems there's a couple women come in once a fortnight, and it's all done in the outer yard where the beasts is kept, and this time o year it's dried in the great barns. So we howkit through the bags o wash, and a savoury task that was, let me tell you, and we found this.' He leaned down and lifted a bulging scrip which Gil had vaguely noticed when he came into the chamber, and from it produced, like a juggler in the marketplace, a bundle of stained cloth. Shaking it out he revealed a shirt of greyish linen, rusty-brown marks blotting its cuffs and breast.

'Oh, well done, man!' said Gil.

'I'd say,' Nory commented, 'he's stripped to his drawers, as the gowk here said, and put his sark back on after he's done his work. These marks is more like they came off him, rather than if it caught the fresh spray.'

'I think you're right,' said Gil, considering the stains. 'Some o those are smears rather than full marks. There wasny a pair o drawers the like?'

'No, though we looked,' said Nory, grimacing.

'May I see it?' said Alys, and Nory handed it across the table.

'I wonder that he never thought to burn the sark, with the fire there to hand,' said Euan.

'He'd have to account for it if he did,' Nory pointed out. '*Why have you no shirt, my son? I burned it in the infirmary, Faither. And why did you do that, my son?*'

'To burn away my sins, Faither,' offered Dandy, with an assumption of piety.

Across the men's laughter Gil said, 'And whose is this sark? When did it come down for the wash?' And that's the crux of the matter, he thought.

'It was in a bag wi the indoor lay brothers' shirts,' said Nory, 'but Barty, that's the chiel at sees to gathering in the wash, reckons it's more like one o the novices', though he canny say which o them.'

'Is it marked in any way?'

Alys turned the garment before handing it to him, with the inside of the neckband visible.

'Aye, you've found it, mem,' said Nory. 'No a lot o help, is it? I'd say he's picked it out, mysel.'

221

Taking the bundle of coarse linen, avoiding the stains, Gil turned the neckband to the grey light from the windows. Two or three smudges and tufts of red thread stood in the linen, caught in the weave, where one would expect to find initials or a press number. He knew his own shirts and Lowrie's, like the rest of the household linen, were carefully numbered and initialled by Alys, and could see that it made sorting the clean linen far easier; it seemed reasonable to assume that the friars used some similar system to identify their linen, but it would be easy enough to check.

'Can I see it, maister?' said Dandy. Gil handed him the bundled shirt, and he rose and went to the window. Alys followed him and they bent together, peering closely at the neckband.

'And when was it put in the sack, do you reckon?' Gil asked Nory.

'Now that,' said Nory regretfully, 'I couldny well make out, maister. It seems they get the wash done once a fortnight. They change their linen weekly, on a Saturday, to be clean for Sunday, and their beds once a month, but they put the soiled linen in a bag in the dorter, which isny collected till the Monday, and lies in the washhouse waiting till the women comes in, seeing they've other washes to do in the week. Likely they do for some o the other friars and all. There's enough work about here for a whole guild o laundrywomen.'

'When were they here last?' Gil asked.

'They're due the morn.'

'So the bag you found this in could ha been lying in the washhouse since last Monday? Ten days?'

'It could,' agreed Nory, 'and Barty reckoned it for one o the ones that cam down last week no this week, though he did say he thought there'd been someone at the heap. So if our man brought this down himsel privily, rather than put it in the bag in his own dorter, he'd ha plenty

222

sacks to choose from to put it into, and it did kinna look like that. It was right at the top, as if he'd just pushed it in the neck o the bag and pulled the cord tight.'

'And the infirmary burned on Monday night,' said Gil thoughtfully. 'No, he'd not want to put this out in the dorter, have it lying for a week afore the bag was collected, risk someone seeing the stains and commenting. Very good work, Nory.'

Nory accepted this with a prim smile, and Alys said, 'Gil? We think we can see what this mark is.'

'It's no very clear,' agreed Dandy, 'but you can see where the needle went in, maister, where the stitches has been. You get the same kinna thing on a bit leather when it's come unstitched, though this is away finer work, a course. It's letters right enough.'

'We think an A and an R,' said Alys.

'Oh, *Dhia!*' said Euan. 'So they have locked away the right man indeed, have they? What could that be but Alexander Raitts?'

Alys glanced at him, but did not comment.

'Andrew Rattray,' said Gil. 'Robert Aikman.'

'What, he was not content with cutting the other fellow's throat, he had to be stealing his sark and all?' said Euan in shocked tones.

# Chapter Eleven

'This is right kind in you, mistress,' said Alys. The dog Roileag, sniffing at her shoes, made her whining growl, and she tucked her feet under her skirts.

'But what is it you're wanting to do?' asked Mistress Buttergask, blue eyes very wide. 'Your man just said you craved the use o our oven for a time, but no to fire it, if we wereny using it ourselves. Which we're no, because we made bread yesterday, and two pies and all, for that we're expecting Sir Silvester back the night by what he sent.'

Alys opened her mouth to explain, and then closed it, suddenly realising just what an exercise in tact this would be. Jennet, with no such qualms, said proudly, 'My mistress is trying out what really happened to the man Pollock. Making trial how he could have all burned up like that.'

'But I saw him carried off,' objected Mistress Buttergask. 'He never burned up, he vanished away.'

'I think,' said Alys, picking her words carefully, 'what you saw was maybe his soul being carried off by the Devil, because we found his ashes in the house. He was all consumed by the fire, every bit, and yet the rest o the house was unharmed.'

'Excepting his foot,' said Jennet. 'The dog found it under a stool.'

'His *foot*?' repeated Mistress Buttergask in amazement. 'Why would he – how would he leave his foot behind?'

They were in the little chamber at the back of the house, with its view of the January garden and the Blackfriars' wall. The two young servants had been given leave to visit their mother for the afternoon, so Jennet had been invited to prepare buttered ale, which she was swirling in its jug just now over the brazier. Alys sat back on the cushioned settle and recounted first what they had found in Pollock's house, to many exclamations of astonishment from her hostess, and then how she and Brother Michael had made trial of the ways in which fire might consume flesh.

'I think we need a bigger space,' she concluded, 'like a bread-oven, and I hoped you might let us use yours.'

'Oh.' Mistress Buttergask considered this, looking doubtful. Alys wondered if the woman was consulting her voices, but she finally said, 'I'm no certain what Rattray will say. One o the Greyfriars, did you tell me?'

'He directed the trials,' Alys said, exaggerating slightly. 'A very holy man he is, Brother Michael Scott. Do you ken him?'

'I do,' said her hostess, still dubious. 'Though I'd no ha said he was holy, exactly, more kinna, well, wrapped up in his own head. But if he's in it, I suppose it's no harm. Maybe he'll can sain the oven after you're done, just to be certain?'

'Oh yes,' said Alys, cheerfully committing Brother Michael. 'I'm sure he'd do that for you.'

'And how long will it take? I'd no like the oven to be out o use just when Rattray's coming back.'

'It took us all yesterday morning,' said Jennet, swirling the buttered ale again. 'But now we ken what we're at, it should go quicker, shouldn't it no, mem?' She laid her hand to the side of the jug. 'This is about ready, mistress, will you have me serve it out?'

'Indeed aye, lassie, and some for yoursel and all,' said Mistress Buttergask, clearly still turning the whole idea over in her head. 'And what would you do, exactly? Set fire to the joint, did you say? But meat doesny burn up, it just blackens, it's a thing a'body kens.'

Before Alys could arrange her thoughts to counter this argument Roileag shot out from under Mistress Buttergask's chair growling, and a rattling at the house door proclaimed Tam, with Brother Michael and a basket of raw meat wrapped in rushes to keep the flies off. Several stray dogs were following them hopefully, but remained out of range of Brother Michael's staff.

Their hostess set to, much flustered and accompanied by a shrill descant of yapping, to welcome the Franciscan, offer him refreshment, and discuss the weather, the state of the market, and possibly matters spiritual, all of which he ignored.

'Let me see this oven,' he said abruptly, 'till I resolve whether it's big enough.' After a moment's thought he added, 'And the trivet. You've a trivet? Aye?'

'Aye, there's a trivet,' said Tam tolerantly over the Franciscan's shoulder, following Mistress Buttergask and her expostulations out to the kitchen. 'I seen it mysel when we was here the other day. I tellt you afore we reached the flesher.'

Alys, about to follow on, found Jennet's hand on her shoulder and the beaker of hot spiced ale thrust into her hand.

'Drink it up, mem,' said the girl, 'and take one o her wee cakes and all. Saints alone ken when we'll get a bite to eat if he's to get started now. I ken it's no very good manners, but it's common sense.'

Alys had to admit the truth of this. She accepted both, and bit into the sweet cake as she pursued Mistress Buttergask's exclamations across the other front room of the house and into a commodious kitchen, whitewashed clean and with ample storage and racks for hanging herbs, cheeses, and what looked like most of a salted pig in neat joints. There was a wide fireplace, the fire carefully banked while the maids were out; there was a big iron cooking-pot beside it which must be the source of a very savoury smell, and next to that a small charcoal range, presently unlit. This last caused her a pang of envy and the resolve to instal one this spring in their own kitchen at home.

'Never noticed any smell o burning the day,' Brother Michael was saying, 'and the crocks washed clean, they tellt me.'

'Them that survived,' muttered Tam, and flinched as Jennet kicked his ankle.

The oven was built in by the fireplace, where it would lose the heat more slowly, and was as handsome as Tam and Jennet had reported to her, with a solid well-fitting wooden door which Mistress Buttergask was now demonstrating.

'You just need to fasten it tight wi the paste,' she said, 'and there's never a draught gets in to spoil the bread. I had the best builder in Perth to make it, there's no an oven in the road like it.'

Brother Michael grunted, and turned to survey the rest of the chamber, nodded briefly to Alys and propped his staff against a convenient press.

'It's your trial, lassie,' he said. 'Y'have a protocol?'

'But brother,' said Mistress Buttergask more urgently. He turned to look at her. 'Is it safe, brother? No the oven, it's – at least aye, it's the oven, but it's the—' As he frowned, and turned away again, making nothing of this, she burst out, 'You're no like to conjure the Deil in my kitchen, are you? Or Mahoun or Termagant or any spirits like that?'

'Mistress, I'd never do a thing like that in another woman's kitchen,' said Alys, 'or my own either.' She took the older woman's hand. 'We made a trial o this in the Greyfriars' kitchen yesterday, and there was no conjuring anything, no words or cantrips or signs made, these two will tell you.' She indicated Tam and Jennet, who made haste to agree with her. 'I'm sure Brother Michael will ask a blessing on the work afore we begin, won't you, brother?'

'Mm?' He looked up from peering into a bowl of dried lavender on a shelf. 'Oh – aye. Better get on.'

'A blessing, brother,' she prompted him.

'Oh.' He raised his eyes to the ceiling, adopted a pose of prayer, and pronounced resonantly, *'Benedictionem velit, habet benedictionem, per Dominum nostrum, Amen.'* As Mistress Buttergask crossed herself with a devout *Amen*, and Alys bit her lip to prevent herself from giggling, he took off his heavy scrip and began to unload the contents onto the table in the middle of the kitchen. As yesterday morning, a bundle of rags, several candle-ends, two small trivets emerged, along with a poke of flour and a small flat dish. Mercifully he had left the mixing-bowl behind. Mistress Buttergask was inclined to take umbrage at the presence of the flour.

'As if I wouldny have flour in the house, that you're as welcome to. There was no need to carry that all the way from the Greyfriars!' she protested as Alys, retrieving her sacking apron from the basket Jennet had carried, began to pin it to her person.

'Mistress?' The kitchen door had opened, and the two young maids stood there, the one in front staring open-mouthed, the other on tiptoe to peer over her shoulder. Roileag bustled across the floor to greet them, dancing on her hind legs and yipping in excitement. 'Mistress? What's ado? Who's all these folk in our kitchen?'

'Jennet,' said Alys hastily, but Tam was already at the door, edging the girls out. They went reluctantly, hardly listening to his promises of explanations, trying to see more of what was happening. The dog scurried out along with them, and as the door closed Jennet asked Mistress Buttergask for a bowl, and Alys unfolded the bundle of rags, seeking a suitable piece of cloth to use for a wrapping.

Brother Michael stood back, making an occasional note on a worn set of tablets, scrutinising her work in silence. Mistress Buttergask, on the other hand, kept up a spate of questions and wondering remarks, which Jennet answered as best she might while Alys swaddled the lump of meat. It was a piece of fat mutton on the bone, with a good layer of lard under the skin, just as she had instructed Tam to ask for. She said as much to Brother Michael and he wrote that down as well, without comment.

'Here's your paste, mem,' said Jennet as she finished.

'And you'll put that in the cold oven?' said Mistress Buttergask in amazement. 'What'll that do? Will you say a prayer over it? You tellt me there would be no cantrips,' she said suspiciously.

'I'll put a candle to it, only,' said Alys, looking around her. 'May we use your trivet, mistress? The great one there?'

'A candle? To set fire to a piece o mutton that size? Surely no, lassie!'

Brother Michael stirred.

'Use mine,' he said. 'The two o them. One each end.'

'Not the great one?'

'More support,' he said. He laid aside his tablets, lifted the small flat dish and one of the candle-ends, and bending to the banked fire lit the candle and set about securing it to the dish with drips of wax. Alys arranged the bundle of meat across the two trivets, inside the cavern of the oven, and slid the candle into position under the meat so that the flame just licked at the layers of cloth. Brother Michael lifted the door and set it into its aperture, and watched while she sealed its edges with the paste Jennet had kneaded up.

'Now we wait,' he said. Elsewhere in the house, the dog began barking furiously.

'How long?' asked Mistress Buttergask. 'How long will it take? When will we ken if it's worked?'

'An hour?' he said. 'You saw, mistress. Nothing else in the oven, only the flesh and the candle.'

'Oh, yes, I saw,' she agreed. 'I still canny understand what you're about, mind.'

The kitchen door opened to admit Tam, with one of the maidservants pushing past him.

'There's a—' he began, but the girl went to Mistress Buttergask, saying, 'If you please, mem, it's the maister back! He's just dismounting afore the door this moment! The wee dog kent he was there, the clever thing.'

'Rattray!' her mistress exclaimed, her face lighting up, and then, transparently, 'Oh! Oh, I'll need to tell him – explain all this.' She bustled out, leaving the maidservant to look sidelong at the sealed oven, the items still lying on the table.

'Is that all you need to do magic wi?' she asked boldly. 'A bowl and a poke o flour and some candle-ends? Maybe I could set mysel up for a necromancer and get rich wi making gold.'

'No magic, lassie,' said Brother Michael repressively. 'Making a trial o something, is all.'

'He said,' she jerked her head at Tam, 'you were seeing how the man got carried off wi the Deil, just ower the wall there.'

'He never got carried off,' said Jennet.

'Aye, he did! My mistress saw him.'

Out in the other room Roileag was barking hysterically, men's voices could be heard, booted feet stamped, Mistress Buttergask embarked on an explanation over which someone said, 'Sorry I've been as long, Bessie.

I've been at Montrose trying to sort this will. What's that you're saying? Necromancy? In our kitchen? Bessie, you fool! What are you about?'

Three swift, heavy footsteps brought a big man to the kitchen doorway, dark-haired and unshaven, still booted and bundled in furs, Roileag leaping about his knees. He stared fiercely round the chamber. His gaze lighting on Brother Michael, he said forcefully, 'What are you at, persuading Mistress Buttergask to take part in your filthy practices? We'll ha none o that in this house! Be off, or I'll fetch the Bishop to ye!'

Brother Michael, taken aback, gulped like a carp in a pond and produced no coherent words. Alys summoned all she had learned from her mother-in-law and stepped forward, and Jennet and Tam both straightened up, their attitude watchful.

'Good day to you, sir,' she said, and curtsied. 'You must be Sir Silvester Rattray.'

'Aye, I am,' he said, staring at her. He was older than she had thought at first, perhaps as much as sixty, but confident and vigorous. 'And who the Devil are you?'

'Oh, Rattray, I'm just telling you,' protested Mistress Buttergask. 'That's Mistress Mason, that's wedded on Blacader's quaestor, and looking into the man we saw carried away in the night, only he wasny, for he left his foot behind.'

'Bessie,' he said, and she fell silent. 'Mistress?' he added to Alys.

'Alys Mason,' she confirmed. He nodded acknowledgement of this. 'We're trying to establish how the man could have burned to ashes—'

'All save his foot,' supplied Mistress Buttergask.

'And Mistress Buttergask has kindly let us have the use o the oven here. There's been no necromancy, no conjuring of spirits, nothing like that at all.'

'Aye, so you say, but what's this—' he bit off the word, 'doing here?'

'Brother Michael has been overseeing the trials. I do assure you, sir, there's been no ill-doing here.'

He stared at her, and then round the kitchen, noting the same things the maidservant had seen. Roileag, who had been pawing impatiently at his boots, chose the moment to start yapping again, and he snatched the little beast up and muzzled it with one big hand.

'Aye, well,' he said, still suspicious. 'We'll hear more o this. Just let me shift my gear and get a wash. Is there water hot, Bess?'

There was a flurry of activity, involving Mistress Buttergask and her maidservants and one of Rattray's men; Alys took refuge in the corner by the oven, and found Brother Michael beside her, clutching his staff in a casual manner which did not deceive. She became aware that the oven was giving off a significant heat, and a faint hissing crackle like a hot frying pan, and turned to look at the sealed door.

'*Nihil dice,*' said the friar quietly.

Washed, shaved and combed, clad in a clean shirt and hose and the doublet which had been hanging in the bedchamber, Sir Silvester Rattray presented a much more polished aspect to the world. Seated by the brazier in the solar, with a platter of bread and meat and a jug of ale on a small table before him, he considered Alys and finally said, 'Mason. It's no a name I've heard.'

'My father is French,' said Alys. Mistress Buttergask, across the room, looked up from her needlework at this, her blue eyes widening.

Rattray pushed Roileag away from his chair with a slippered foot and went on, 'Aye, well. But I have heard o your man. The Bishop had a bit to say o him a year or so back. So he's back in Perth, is he?' Alys nodded. 'What's he found, concerning the man Pollock? I ken the

Bishop and Prior Boyd were well exercised about the fellow, and the Treasury and all, as one o theirs.'

'No a great deal,' said Alys cautiously. 'He's been held back by the other deaths, a novice called Rattray and the friar Thomas Wilson.'

'Rattray?' he repeated sharply. 'Jockie was saying when he shaved me, they've had more trouble ower the wall, but he never named names. What was the laddie baptised? Andrew!' He looked at Mistress Buttergask. 'Here I've been scouring Montrose for the boy, and he's lying dead ower the wall from you.'

'You're seeking him?' Alys said. 'What for, sir?'

'Money. Never mind that the now, what about Pollock? What's Maister Cunningham found, then?'

'No a great deal, as I said. The man was in the habit o extortion, he sent money to the Yorkist party abroad, he was little liked.'

'No a great deal? I'd no want to be the one he discovered a lot concerning! So what's all this to do wi our kitchen? Aye, I ken, Bess,' he added as she began to speak, 'but I'll ha Mistress Mason's tale to it and all.'

Alys explained, yet again, what they had found in Pollock's house, what had led her to think of experimenting, what the trial presently in the oven was intended to demonstrate. He heard her out, frowning, chewing on the food, asking a couple of sensible questions. When she had finished he paused to take a long pull at the jug of ale, ignoring Mistress Buttergask's further assurances, and finally said, 'And when should it come out the oven? When will you ken what's come o't?'

'We should let the oven cool,' Alys said unwarily. He shot her a look, but did not comment. 'Perhaps another half an hour?'

'Then tell me what's this about Andrew Rattray. Did you say there was two deaths?'

'Two deaths,' she agreed, 'and one man stabbed.'

Beginning with their arrival, she summarised the wider events of the last few days, while he fed the scraps of his meal to the dog, which begged importunately for every mouthful and produced its squeaky growl if he did not hand it over fast enough. Sir Silvester was paying more attention to the tale than appeared, for when it was ended he said, 'There must be some link. If one o them had run stark wood he'd never trouble to call a secret meeting, he'd simply run about stabbing folk openly. Or so you'd think,' he added, 'though I'm aware you canny tell what a madman will do.'

'There must be a link,' Alys assented, 'only we cannot find it.'

'And your man thinks they've the wrong fellow locked away.'

'He does,' she agreed. 'We both reckon he's no one to use a knife, least of all to plan ahead enough to steal one out the kitchen and keep it hid.'

'But the poor laddie,' said Mistress Buttergask, tears in her eyes. 'To be killed in his sleep like that, never knowing his end.'

'Better than some, Bessie,' said Rattray. 'He'd been at his prayers, he'd confessed lately, he'd never ken it happened. No like thon fellow in Montrose.'

'You keep talking about Montrose,' she said, wiping her eyes with the linen she was working on. 'What took you there, any road? I began to think you'd never come back.'

'Never think that, you daft woman,' he said with rough affection. 'I'd a letter afore Yule there from a man o law at Montrose, concerning the will o one Skene o that place, asking did I ken the whereabouts o Andrew Rattray or his sister Margaret.' Alys sat very still. 'And since I reckon they'd be some kinna cousins to me, I writ back asking more detail. Found his answer waiting for me, and little advance it was, so I rade off to Montrose to see for mysel.'

'But what was it about?' Mistress Buttergask asked, round-eyed. 'Why did you need to go there? Is it no a long ride?'

'Fifty mile,' he said, shrugging, and pushed the dog away with his foot again. 'Away wi ye, it's all done. All done! Turns out this Skene deceasit last autumn, was pulled out the harbour, took a peripneumony o the lungs, survived long enough to confess and make his will, and got his man o law to that rather than the priest.'

'Och, yes, indeed!' said Mistress Buttergask. Alys nodded her understanding. One's man of law would write down one's own wishes; a priest would set about persuading one to remember Holy Kirk, to the disadvantage of one's own kin.

'I've seen the document. Seems the lassie, Margaret, was his wife, and ran off, taking the bairn wi her. The will gied directions for the return o the conjoint fee and her dowry, and a bit for the bairn's inheritance, and the rest to Andrew Rattray on condition he sees his sister right.' He eyed Alys. 'So what d'you ken o her, mistress?'

'Me?' she said, alarmed.

'Aye, mistress, you. I saw your face change when I said how Skene dee'd. What way did you think he went?'

'I ken nothing o the man,' she parried, wondering how much to say. Mistress Buttergask leaned forward, giving her a significant look, so that she wondered if the other woman's voices had spoken.

'You can tell him, lassie,' she said. 'Whatever it is, you can tell him.'

'But what will you do now,' Alys asked, avoiding the issue, 'seeing Andrew Rattray's dead?'

'I'm none so certain,' he said slowly, his attention still on her face. 'Skene having predeceasit him, Andrew dee'd in possession o all that was left to him, but I'm

236

assuming he made no will, and he'd already gied all his worldly goods to the Blackfriars, I'd suppose. It's a nice question who it devolves upon, which I'd hope your man would turn his thoughts to, seeing he's a man o law and all, I believe.'

'Are you no a man of law yoursel, sir?' she asked. 'You're knowledgeable in the subject.'

'I studied it,' he said. 'So how far is she from here?'

'You think she's in Perth?'

'I think she's in Perth.'

'You can tell him, lassie,' said Mistress Buttergask again.

'I've nothing to tell,' she said. For it's not my secret, she was thinking.

Rattray was still looking intently at her, and she hoped she was not blushing. He drew breath to speak, but Roileag scurried out from her mistress's skirts growling, as quick footsteps in the other chamber heralded Jennet at the door.

The girl bobbed a general curtsy to all three, but said to Alys, 'If you please, mem, Brother Michael is wishful to open the oven. He needs to get back for Compline, he says, and he thinks it's about time.'

She jumped up, hoping her relief did not show too clearly.

'Certainly!' she said. 'And Mistress Buttergask needs her kitchen cleared and all.'

'There's been wee noises coming out it,' Jennet confided. 'We'd as much trouble keeping the men from keeking in there to see what was at work.'

'What kind of wee noises?' Alys led the way out towards the kitchen, trying not to trip over the dog, who was clearly convinced there would be food involved.

'Like something tapping? Or maybe like a branch tapping on the window, that kind o noise. No very loud. And sic a stink o burned meat!'

As Jennet had said, the kitchen was full of the smell of burned meat. Brother Michael was still on guard before the oven, staff in hand. When he saw Alys he visibly relaxed, and the group of people round him fell back a bit, one of the men laughing self-consciously as if he had been the most importunate about opening the door.

'Cooled now,' said Brother Michael.

'Was there any smoke?' she asked him, suddenly apprehensive. 'Did anything—?'

'Nothing to see,' he said. 'Heat, you felt that, the smell, no other outward sign.' He gave her an approving look. 'Open it up.'

'Och, aye, open it up,' said the man who had laughed. 'Let's see what sort o magic you worked, or whatever it was.'

'There was no magic,' said Brother Michael wearily.

'Are we to see what's happened, or no?' demanded Rattray.

The Franciscan turned his shoulder on him and leaned on his staff, keeping the multitude at bay. Alys, taking a deep breath, got a grasp on the oven door and dislodged it. Flakes of paste fell away at her feet, and a waft of dark smoke emerged from the gap. One of the maidservants shrieked, and the other began muttering an *Ave*.

'Oh, Rattray!' said Mistress Buttergask. 'What is it? What's in there?'

Alys lifted the wooden door from its socket and set it aside. The burned-meat smell was even stronger now. Flapping her hands to clear the smoke, she peered into the cavity of the oven.

'It hasn't worked!' she said in disappointment.

'Look closer,' said Brother Michael.

'But there's still—' she began, then as the smoke cleared, 'Oh! We need to get it out of there. Is there a shovel or the like?'

'Wait,' he said. 'Need witnesses.'

238

'Oh! Aye, you're right.' She stood aside. 'Mistress? See what has happened?'

Mistress Buttergask came forward with reluctance, clutching her beads for protection, glanced warily into the oven, then leaned forward to look closer.

'Oh, my!' she said in amazement. 'Saints preserve us, who'd ha thought it? It's all burned up save the two bits at the ends.'

'What?' Rattray stepped up behind her, looking over her plump shoulder. 'Well, I'll be . . . and you really put nothing in there but the meat and a candle?'

'And two trivets,' Alys said. 'Which are half melted.' She found herself looking as proudly at the heap of ashes, the shrivelled fragments of meat and bone, the two twisted metal structures, as she had done at her very first meat pie.

'Christ on a handcart,' he said. 'I'd never ha believed it if I'd no seen it mysel.' He looked about him. 'Here, you two, see what your mistress has wrought. Jockie, Ned, you get a look and all.'

'Is there a shovel?' Alys asked again, as Tam and Jennet elbowed one another to inspect the interior of the oven. 'I'll not use the bread-peel. The ash would cling to it. You'd never get it clean.'

After some searching the shovel was located by the back door, and a rake fetched from the hearth in the other chamber. Carefully, with much advice from Mistress Buttergask, Alys manoeuvred the fragments of her experiment onto the metal-edged blade of the shovel, raking round the floor of the dark cavity to be certain she had found everything. The smell of burned meat was almost overpowering, but she thought there was also a trace of the strange, sweetish smell she had noticed in Pollock's house. Reminded, she looked closer at the oven floor, and realised that as well as the ash from the meat the bricks were coated in grease.

'Aye,' said Brother Michael when she commented. 'Like your experiment yesterday.'

'Is that all it is?' said one of the maidservants as Alys drew the shovel out of the oven. 'Just some burned meat? I thought it was some great work, maybe wi gold at the end o't.'

'Well, if it was to be gold, it's no worked,' said the man who had laughed.

'It's worked well,' said Alys. 'It's done exactly what I hoped it might.'

'Well!' said Mistress Buttergask. 'I still don't see what you've proved wi't, lassie, but if it's what you hoped for I'm right glad of it.'

'Let me set this down.' Alys looked about her, and someone pushed a stool nearer for her to set the shovel on. She bent over it, poking among the ashes and lumps of material she had extracted. Brother Michael joined her, picked out the little dish the candle had stood on, now completely blackened, and isolated two twisted pieces of metal.

'Is that your trivets, man?' said Tam over Alys's head. 'St Peter's balls, it's as well you didny use the mistress's great trivet here. They's all melted.'

'Like Pollock's key,' Alys commented.

'Like the key. It's successful,' said Brother Michael. 'No proof o what happened, a course, but proof o what might ha happened. Good work.'

She had the feeling this was not an encomium he bestowed lightly. She gave him a complicit smile, and said quietly, 'It was all in the supervision, brother.' Then, louder, 'See, the meat has all burned up, save for the end parts, as you said, and the bone has burned and all.' She turned one of the cindery lumps, and prodded the bone where it projected on one side. 'That looks exactly like – like something we lifted in Pollock's house,' she observed, just preventing herself from identifying the

240

fragment concerned. 'The cloth has all burned away, even on the ends, though I wrapped it around carefully, but it's only in the midst of the joint that the meat has caught.'

'Aye,' said Brother Michael.

'So what do you have here?' demanded Rattray. 'Tell me again what went into the oven.'

'Och, that's a disappointment,' said one of his men, and turned away as Tam began to rehearse the preparations they had made. Alys straightened up, and looked at Mistress Buttergask.

'Might I beg the loan o a box, or a basin, or a wee poke? I'd like to take all this back to show to my husband.' She put a hand on Brother Michael's brown woollen sleeve. 'And, brother, thank you for all your help. It's been an education.'

He smiled at her, in an unaccustomed sort of way.

'Been a pleasure. And an education, for me and all,' he expanded hastily. Then, glancing at the darkening window of the kitchen, 'I should go. The Red Bridge port.'

'Aye, they'll shut the port any time now,' agreed Mistress Buttergask, returning with a green-glazed pottery basin. 'Better get on your way, brother, and safe home.'

He nodded, delivered a perfunctory blessing, this time in Scots, and strode out. She thrust the basin at Alys and hurried to see him out, the dog scurrying at her heels. Alys carefully tipped the ashes and debris into the basin, making sure she had all the fragments.

'So this proves,' said Rattray, watching her, 'that the man burned up, wi no harm to his house or the rest o his goods.'

'No,' she said, dusting the last flakes off the shovel, 'but it proves it could have happened like that.'

'Why?' he said bluntly. 'Why are you wishful to prove that?'

241

'It's a simpler explanation,' she said. 'Simpler is aye better, d'you not think?'

As always, it took far longer than she would have liked to get herself, her servants and the bowl of incinerated meat out of the house. Part of this delay was caused by her own offer to clean out the oven, which was refused firmly by Mistress Buttergask.

'As if you could start a task like that at this hour!' she exclaimed. 'No, no, never concern yoursel, lassie, we'll sort it the morn when it's plenty time to dry after.'

Despite argument, she would not be persuaded, so Alys withdrew from the kitchen, to the clear relief of the rest of the household. Further delay was brought about by Sir Silvester, who led her back into the solar and demanded a complete rehearsal of what he had just seen.

'You're trying to show it could ha had a natural cause,' he said when she had gone over the reasoning behind the trials, the procedure and the result.

'That's right,' she agreed, wondering how he had failed to grasp this before.

'Why?'

'My husband doesn't believe in witchcraft.'

'Do you?'

She opened her mouth to say, *Of course not!* then closed it again and considered.

'No,' she said finally. 'Not witchcraft as spells and cantrips and magic ointments. I have encountered . . . things I couldny explain. So has Gil,' she added. 'But neither one o us thinks it possible to kill someone at a distance by witchcraft. There needs to be a corporal agent.'

'Does there, now?' he said. She had the feeling he was laughing at her, and raised her chin defiantly. 'Do you believe in the Deil?'

'Of course I do!' she said indignantly. 'Any Christian must!'

'So why could it no ha been the Deil carried the man away, same as Bessie saw?'

'Did you ever hear of anyone else carried away like that?' she countered. 'I never have in this day. A hundred years or more ago, maybe, in stories, but no in our times. It could be what you saw was the man's soul being carried off: we all ken that happens.'

'I'm certain that's the answer, Rattray,' said Mistress Buttergask earnestly. 'And it's away less fearsome a thought, surely.'

'Aye,' he said. And then, abruptly, 'Where does Margaret Rattray stay?'

She had been warned by the slight change in his expression.

'I can tell you nothing o Margaret Rattray,' she said.

'Hah!' he said. 'Gil Cunningham's well cled in his wife. Tell him I'll gie mysel the pleasure and honour of calling on him the morn, if it's convenient.'

'I will, sir,' she said, and rose to leave. Roileag jumped off Mistress Buttergask's lap and began barking.

'Bessie, can you no keep that wee beast quiet?' Rattray asked, scooping the dog up and muzzling it again.

'Och, she's no so bad,' said Mistress Buttergask, in defiance of the evidence. 'Lassie, can I get a word wi ye?'

'Yes,' said Alys, startled. Her hostess fixed the man of the house with a pointed stare, and after a moment's indecision he wandered out into the other room, pulling the door to behind him. 'What is it?' Alys asked, half expecting to be asked for some assurance about what the woman had seen.

'Did you say your mammy was a French lady?' said Mistress Buttergask. 'I've had a French lady in my head these three days, bidding me tell her daughter all sorts.'

243

Alys stared at her in the candlelight, too astonished to speak. 'She says, do you mind the flowered kirtle?'

Alys groped behind her to find the stool and sat down again, still staring.

'I—' she began, and her voice croaked. 'I do.'

The kirtle was made of a piece of embroidered silk she and her mother had found in the market when she was seven. She had worn it until it could be let down and added to no longer. How could this woman know about the flowered kirtle?

'She says,' Mistress Buttergask tilted her head, eyes closed, as if she was listening, 'do your duty by your faither. It's no that easy to make her out. I've no French. She's aye watching ower you, I've got that bit. You're to – no, you've *got* a good man – she says you must honour him.'

'I do,' Alys said again, and felt for a moment almost as if she repeated her marriage vows for her mother. But could it be her mother? How could her mother be speaking to Mistress Buttergask?

'And you're to bide your time. The bairns will come in their own season. She's showing me a picture, lassie. There's you and a wee boy wi dark hair and two bairns smaller.' Mistress Buttergask opened her eyes. 'She's away. They do that, you ken, once I've tellt their messages. Was it your mammy, do you think, my dear?'

'I . . .' Alys began yet again, staring at her, and suddenly found she was weeping. There was a clatter and rattle of furniture and the other woman was seated beside her, drawing her head onto a capacious bosom, murmuring endearments which her own mother had not used because they were the wrong language, though the tone was unmistakable.

It seemed a long time later that she straightened up, wiping her nose and eyes on the sacking apron.

'A wee bit better?' said Mistress Buttergask.

'Better,' she agreed shakily. 'I – I beg your pardon, I can't think what—'

'Well, it was needing to come out,' said the other woman sagely. 'Folk do that often, when I pass them a message. Even when it's good news. You miss your mammy, then, lassie?'

She nodded, biting her lip.

'They watch over us, whatever the priests say. You'll maybe find something's settled, by the time you've slept on it. Just mind what she told you.' Mistress Buttergask glanced at the window. 'Will you stay here for a bite supper? I doubt you've missed the Blackfriars' mealtime. They'll all be at Compline by now. I heard the wee bell.'

# Chapter Twelve

'Well, maister, you were right,' said Brother Dickon. 'Aye, you're a fine dog,' he added, clapping Socrates firmly on the shoulders.

Gil, who had deduced this from his triumphant expression as soon as the lay brother slipped in at the guest-hall door, made an encouraging noise.

'Brother Augustine's missing knife, just where you said it would be,' the other said, 'and I'd Jamesie wi me as witness. A right cunning place, a pouch o cloth nailed onto the bottom o the planks in his bed, you could hide all sorts in there. We'd to get down on our knees to see it – well, Jamesie did – and then you'd to reach halfway under the bed to get to it.'

'The boning knife?' Gil questioned. 'Where is it now?'

'Aye, the boning knife. Blade this wide.' Brother Dickon held out a knobbly-knuckled hand, the little finger extended. 'Well sharpened and a point like a needle. I had Jamesie put it back where we found it, but we can easy get it if you're wanting it.'

'A good thought. And where is that?'

'Whose bed was it under, d'you mean? That's just it, maister. It was under young Andrew's. His bed's bare now, but I mind perfectly well which was his.'

'Makes sense, I suppose,' said Gil. 'Once his friends kent it was there, one o them was bound to make use o the hiding place. But it gets us little forward.'

'Well, it's one o the novices,' said Dickon. 'Or John Blythe, I suppose,' he added fairly, 'though I canny see him knifing his friend Henry White.'

'Men do strange things,' said Gil, 'but I'm agreed. What puzzles me is why, short o simply running mad, one o the novices should kill Andrew Rattray and Thomas Wilson both.'

'I can think o one reason,' said Dickon after a moment, 'though I canny say I'd heard it o either man.'

'You'd know more about that than I would,' said Gil, 'given that I think your men pick up all that's going on.'

'I keep warning them o gossip,' said Dickon. 'They might no pick that up, it would be kept close secret after all, but I've no seen aught that would suggest it mysel either. And then why would he go on and knife Faither Henry?'

'No, that's easy enough. I'd guess Faither Henry suspected what was afoot, and went out to find and challenge the man responsible, maybe to persuade him to confess.'

'Aye, that would fit,' said Dickon. 'And he was at the same the other night and all, when two men each thought he was whispering in corners wi the other. They must ha seen him wi the – the man responsible. And that's a joke,' he said without humour. 'Responsible! No very responsible, to go about killing your brothers.'

Gil, who had not suspected Brother Dickon of a sententious streak, preserved silence, and after a little the lay brother went on, 'Could it be some reason from afore they all were tonsured? Some common secret out in the world?'

'I wondered about that,' Gil said. 'We'd have to dig into their pasts, Wilson and White and all the novices, which is none so easy without Faither Prior's assistance.'

'Aye,' said Brother Dickon thoughtfully. 'I'd tell you what I ken, gladly, but there's maybe other matters, things only kent by those that accepted them for clothing.'

'We could make a start,' said Gil. 'Have you time the now?'

The other man glanced at the window, judging the light.

'An hour or so,' he said.

'Right,' said Gil. 'Fetch us a jug o ale from the kitchens, and let me hear it all.'

By the time Dickon returned, Gil had listed the three victims in his tablets, and noted what he already knew of them.

'Aye, that's right,' said Dickon, drawing a stool up to the table opposite him. 'Thomas Wilson's a local man. Was, I should say. His faither's living yet, he's in the almshouse down by the haven, what's it cried? St Barbara's, that's it. There's a couple o brothers and some other kin in the burgh – you'd find them if you asked about. Likely Faither Prior's let them hear o his decease so they might be in the place the day. What was his faither's trade? Now you're asking. I'd need to get Jamesie onto that, he's a Perth man and all.'

'And he never travelled? Wilson, I mean.'

'Might ha been as far's St Andrews or Edinburgh. Never overseas, I'd swear to that.'

Gil made a note, and went on, 'And speaking ill o the dead it may be, but I hear he was cheating on the rents in the town.'

'Lord love you, son, that's no new,' said Brother Dickon. 'The most o us kens that, or suspects it, though it's not got to Faither Prior yet.'

Gil absorbed this comment, made another note, and Brother Dickon said, 'And while I mind, I've learned the prisoner stayed in the kirk the whole time till Matins.

One o the lads that was praying had, er, meditated for a bit wi his een shut, but the other would swear to Brother Sandy being there on his knees afore Our Lady all the while.'

'I never thought he had killed Wilson,' said Gil, 'but that makes it even less likely. Did you ask him about the knife?'

'I did, but he never made much sense. Mumbled something about a library being no place for sharp steel, a course he was relieved that we never found a knife there.'

'Well, it was worth asking. Thanks, man.' Gil looked down at his tablets again. 'Henry White's a Lanarkshire man, so I'm told, though it's no a name I can place.'

'It's his mother's name,' said Dickon significantly. 'I'm told his faither was a lord, recognised young Henry, paid for his schooling.'

'Ah. D'you ken where?'

'Lanark itsel, I think. Then I suppose he'd join the Glasgow house, and I ken he's studied overseas, Cologne and like that.'

'How long has he been here?'

'Longer than me. Me and the lads took the habit in the autumn o '88,' he added helpfully, 'after Sauchieburn. I think he's been here eight or ten year.'

Gil noted that, and stared at the gouges he had made in the wax, willing them to make some kind of pattern. He could see no connection. Not that it was essential to connect Father Henry to the others, he recalled.

'Andrew,' he said. 'I think he was o good family, by what Faither Henry said. From somewhere north o here, out towards Montrose, aye?'

'Aye. They held land near Brechin, I think it was. He'd been at the college at St Andrews, I ken that, for he once said, *At St Andrews they teach Bible studies, no Theology.* No that I'd ken the difference, and the most o them's been at St Andrews, seeing we're the nearest house to there.'

'Any kin living?'

'Parents deid, I believe. There might ha been a sister, but she'd likely be wed by the time he joined us. I've a notion he'd a, er, friend in the town here,' Dickon continued, 'for that he was out at night a time or two that I kent.'

Gil did not comment on this. Turning to the opposite leaf of his tablets he said, 'And the other novices? How many are there, for a start?'

'Four the same year as Andrew, four second-year men.' Dickon leaned back, took a pull at the ale jug, and wiped his mouth and beard. 'Where from? Now that's another matter.' He held up one broad, callused hand, marked off a finger with the other forefinger. 'George Spens. Fife, I think, him and David Brown, aye, they're both from Dunfermline. Robert Aikman from Aberdeen, Andrew Jackson from Arbroath. That's no so far from Brechin,' he commented. Having counted off four fingers he started counting on the other hand. 'Mureson. Munt. Simpson. Calder. Calder's from somewhere in Angus, Montrose or the like, cam wi a good settlement in coin to the house, no to the Order, I'm no just certain why the distinction. Mureson's daddy's a baron, I think, somewhere down the Spey. Munt and Simpson are both merchants' sons, one in Dunfermline, one in,' he paused for thought, 'Dundee.'

'But which o them,' said Gil, looking at this list, 'has any connection wi any o the men who were attacked, let alone all three?'

'Aye, that's the question,' Brother Dickon was saying, when Socrates sprang to his feet growling, and there was an eruption of noise in the yard.

Hooves clattered, harness jingled, Brother Archie's voice rose protesting uselessly, and over all a familiar, unpleasant voice declaimed, 'I'll see him as soon as he likes, and no argument!'

'Our Lady save us!' said Brother Dickon. 'She's back! What's she after this time?'

'I thought she'd got what she wanted last night,' said Gil, stowing his tablets in their brocade pouch. 'Best go and see, I suppose.'

Mistress Trabboch was no more prepossessing a sight by daylight than by candlelight. Her wide-skirted gown was dark red, the furred short gown she wore over it was a staring tawny the colour of rust, the boots which she was just freeing from the stirrups as Gil emerged from the guesthouse were of green leather, but none of the bright colours did more than emphasise the heavy jaw, the dark brows, the hot angry glare like a mewed hawk's. She scowled at Gil as he approached to hold her stirrup.

'You again!' she said, spurning his offered hand, to slide down from the saddle herself. 'You taken up residence here, or what? Where's that Boyd? I want another word wi him, and he'll no refuse me or I'll fetch him out o there mysel, *and* tell his kinsman Boyd o Naristoun o his disobligement and all.'

'Aye, Brother Archie,' said Brother Dickon behind Gil. 'Maybe you'd let Faither Prior hear the lady would wish another word wi him.'

'Me?' said Brother Archie in alarm. 'Why me, Serj – brother?'

'Can I ask your business wi my kinsman?' Gil enquired.

'You can,' she said, smirking triumphantly at him, 'but I'll no answer, for it's none o yours. Fetch Boyd, will you, man?'

Gil bowed, caught Archie's eye, and made for the slype. The lay brother scurried after him, saying with open gratitude, 'He's more like to hear it fro you than me, maister.'

Prior Boyd was discovered in the library, in the throes of a discussion with John Blythe on the interesting topic of the precise meaning of *quotidianus* in the *Pater noster*, with reference to the vocabulary of the Greek original. It seemed the injunction to silence did not cover such learned discourse. Gil waited politely while Father John, a rotund, bald fellow with bone-rimmed spectacles and a red nose, soliloquised, with perfectly audible marginal notes, on the two possible meanings he could discern, but when the paragraph reached its conclusion, he broke in before the Prior could launch an equally scholarly response.

'Forgive me, fathers,' he said in Latin. 'There is a guest at the door asking for Father Prior. It is the lady who visited last night,' he added, and Boyd flinched. 'She seems determined that she must speak to you, but will not reveal her business.'

'Ah,' said Father John, and stepped backwards, saying in Scots, 'I'll leave you defend us, Davie. This is where I'm right glad it's no my turn at being Prior.'

Boyd, tucking his hands resignedly into his sleeves, nodded to the two friars nearest him, and they obediently left their books and followed. Brother Archie would have slipped away to safety, but was called back by a quiet word, so that the Prior was attended by a decent retinue on this occasion.

Mistress Trabboch was seated in the guest hall, tapping one booted foot impatiently. When Prior Boyd swept in and bowed to her she looked him up and down, ignoring his courteous greeting, and said sourly, 'Took you a while. I want a look at all your monks.'

'A look?' he repeated in amazement. 'Why? And we are not monks,' he added. 'We're friars.'

'Nae difference. A look at all your monks, a look at their faces, now in daylight. It came to me last night, there's no certainty he was tonsured under his right name. He could ha called himsel anything he pleased, I suppose. I don't imagine you ask for certificates o baptism when a man rattles a purse o money at you.'

'No,' said Boyd rather faintly. 'It – I suppose it's a reasonable request. It could take a wee while to sort,' he warned. 'At this hour, folk are all at their studies, save for those in the infirmary or the kirk.'

'I'll wait,' she said, and reached for the jug of ale which Gil and Brother Dickon had been sharing. 'Maybe you'd get that list out that you had last night, so we can be sure I've seen them all. I'd no wish for any to get owerlooked, by accident.' Her emphasis was not pleasant.

Gil, wishing desperately that Alys was here to share in this scene, said, 'Will I ask for a bit more refreshment, mistress?'

'You might as well,' she said ungraciously. 'I've a thirst on me like a carter's, for I'd sic an argument wi the Franciscans, and all for nothing. He's no there. So we'll have another look for him here.'

As Boyd had said, it took a little time to organise a procession of all the able-bodied men in the place. Once again, Gil sat by with the book, this time marking off each man as he entered the guest hall, faced Mistress Trabboch, and was dismissed with varying degrees of disgust or disparagement.

'It's a right collection o shilpit studiers and lectours,' she commented as the novices were led out in a group by John Blythe. 'Is that the lot?'

'There's the fellows in the infirmary,' Gil said, 'who canny be moved. One's on his deathbed, one's injured. There are two corps in the chapel, if you want to be thorough, and a man locked away for slaying one or both o them.'

She stared at him for a moment, as if suspecting him of joking, then said, 'It's a right peaceable community, this, I can tell. I'd best see them and all. Where's your infirmary?'

'No, we canny have that,' said the Prior. 'Faither James is slipping away, he'll no need to be disturbed, and Faither Henry needs to sleep the now.'

'I ken what to do at a sickbed,' she retorted, and rose. 'Where's your infirmary, then? I'm determined I'll see every man that dwells within these walls.'

Rather to Gil's surprise, she did indeed know how to behave at a sickbed. Led into the infirmary by Prior Boyd she inspected Brother Euan with that direct, disparaging stare, dismissed him as of no account, and swept past him into the inner chamber of the little house. There she glared at the gallowglass who was sitting by the fire again, inspected the two sick men and then dropped to her knees by Father James and recited two *Aves* and a prayer for the dying in a soft murmur quite at odds with her usual manner. Rising, she crossed herself, peered suspiciously at Father Henry as if he might have changed identity while she was occupied, and strode out again. The Prior and his entourage hurried to keep up with her; Gil brought up the rear, enthralled.

'Neither o them,' she said, pausing in the courtyard. 'Where's these two corps?'

'One o them's no very—' began the Prior.

'You'll no conceal any o your monks fro me,' she said. 'Deid or alive, I'll be certain you're no hiding my man here.'

'Have you ever seen a corp brought out o a burned house?' Gil asked. She threw him a black look.

'No. I'll get by.'

'We must enter by the west door,' said Prior Boyd, giving up the unequal struggle.

The church was dim, and the chill struck to the bones. Led in by Prior Boyd, Mistress Trabboch strode up the

255

nave, looking about her, and remarked, 'I canny be doing wi the way the Blackfriars runs a kirk. No pictures, no carving, no colours. Dreich, to my way o't, so it is. Where's these corps?'

'In St Dominic's Chapel,' said Boyd, turning that way.

'One thing, you'll no need to worry about them going off, in this cold. Preserve a corp for a lifetime, it would.' She paused to curtsy in the direction of the tabernacle in the chancel with its ever-burning light, and followed him into the chapel, her skirts swirling about her.

The two friars praying over the biers looked up in alarm, and Boyd said soothingly, 'Mistress Trabboch wishes to pay her respects to the dead. She'll no interrupt you.'

Wilson, stretched on a board under a linen sheet, was beginning to settle into his death, the face relaxing and turning waxy. Gil wondered briefly why he was not yet shrouded, then realised that most of the body would still be stiff, and also that the Provost's men might wish to see the injuries. Brother Archie held the sheet back, crossing himself with his free hand, and Mistress Trabboch approached, looked closely, turned away.

'No,' she said briefly. 'Where's this other?'

'He's already coffined,' Gil said, 'and no a bonnie sight. He's the one that burned.'

'You're no hiding any o them from me,' she reiterated. 'We'll have the cover off him.'

The coffin lid was not yet nailed down, and Gil and Brother Archie lifted it off between them, releasing a waft of the spices which had been tucked in beside the remains of Andrew Rattray, to sweeten the bedesmen's task a little. Mistress Trabboch took a step closer, got a sight of the blackened, contorted corpse, and rocked back on her heels.

'Body o Christ!' she said. 'You wereny joking, were you?'

'Hardly, on sic a subject,' said Gil politely. 'The laddie had red hair, you can see some of it there.' He touched the singed curls delicately, and she stepped backwards with obvious relief.

'No. Stair has brown hair, I tellt you that yestreen. Dark brown.'

So have half the men in Scotland, Gil thought. Prior Boyd was saying, in equal relief, 'Now are you convinced, madam, that we areny concealing your man here?'

'No,' she said baldly. 'You said you'd one locked away for killing another one. I want a look at him.'

'Aye, madam. It could mean you entering the convent, the retired part o the priory. It's no proper.'

'I've no wish to linger, believe me,' she said. 'The sooner you cease to gainsay me, the sooner my task's done, but I'll no leave without I see every man o your monks.'

'Friars,' said Prior Boyd wearily, and turned to Brother Archie. 'Where is Brother Sandy held?'

'Next the infirmary, Faither,' said Archie, head bent in ostentatious meekness. 'He's shut in the inner chamber, and two men to watch in the outer one. He's in the guest-hall yard, Faither, no need for the lady to—'

'Is he a danger?' demanded Mistress Trabboch. 'What's he done, any road?'

'There are two men dead and a third stabbed,' Gil reminded her.

'One slain in the very library itsel,' said Boyd.

'Hah!' She was making for the west door now. 'Canny be my man then. For one, he's feart for sharp things, couldny abide even my broidery snips, faizart poltroon that he is. For another, he'd never slay a man in the presence o his books. Thought more o them than he did o me, I can tell you. Let me get a look at him, just the same, and then we're done.'

In the outer chamber of the house between Pollock's and the infirmary, two lay brothers were working on more harness. To judge by the size of the yokes, the plough-oxen must be massive beasts, Gil was thinking, as the two rose and bowed to Prior Boyd.

'Brother Eck, Brother Tammas,' acknowledged Boyd. 'Is Brother Sandy quiet? How has he taken his imprisonment?'

'Quiet,' agreed Brother Tammas. 'Very quiet, he's been. Just sitting there. Whiles he's been at his prayers, he recited the Office when the rest o you were in the kirk. He's been little trouble. Did you want a word, Faither?'

'Mistress Trabboch wants a sight o him,' said the Prior. Then, apparently realising how that sounded, 'The same as she's had o the rest o us.'

'If we open the door,' said Brother Eck, 'maybe the lady can look in. Or should we bring him out?'

'That might be best,' said the Prior, 'in case he decides to fight, or run away, or the like. If the two o you bring him out, one on either side, we can get a good view o his face. Will that suit, madam?'

'Aye,' she said shortly.

Gil drifted casually round the small room, moving behind the three Dominicans attending Boyd, until he was well placed to see both the inner door and Mistress Trabboch's face. Tammas opened the door from one side, Eck looked through it from the other, nodded and stepped in, his brother in arms at his back. Brother Dickon's company must have been well disciplined, Gil reflected.

'Right, my laddie,' said Tammas briskly, 'on your feet. You've a visitor. There's a lady out here to see you.'

'A lady?' Raitts sounded alarmed. 'That's no right, there should be no women in this place! It's no right!' he exclaimed, in increasing anxiety. 'I canny – I canny be – I'll stay here. I need to stay here!'

258

'You'll come out,' contradicted Tammas. 'Faither Prior's instructions. On your feet.'

'No, I—'

'Right, Eck?'

'Right, Tammas.'

Feet shuffled, and the lay brothers reappeared, moving sideways through the doorway, Eck first, Tammas last, with a protesting Raitts between them grasped by the elbows, his feet barely touching the ground. They achieved the outer chamber and set their burden down, though they maintained a grip on the librarian's elbows.

'The prisoner, sir. Faither,' said Tammas crisply.

Raitts's despairing gaze had found Mistress Trabboch. What little colour the man possessed washed away, his mouth opened helplessly, and he stared at her in horror like a man awaiting his death blow. Gil looked at the woman, and found her staring back at Raitts, equally fixed but quite expressionless.

There was what seemed like a very long silence. Then Raitts closed his mouth and whimpered slightly, a small defenceless sound. As if it was a signal, Mistress Trabboch took a step backwards.

'I never saw him in my life afore,' she said levelly, turned on her heel and swept out into the courtyard.

Gil, staying behind as Boyd and his retinue hurried after her, saw Raitts close his eyes and relax, so much in fact that he feared the man was about to swoon. He stepped forward, but the two lay brothers had a firm grasp.

'Bear up, man!' said Tammas. 'We'll ha none o that now! You can go back in your cell and sit quiet, you're no wanted longer.'

'Is she gone?' Raitts demanded, his voice shaking. 'Is she really gone?'

'No, hold up a moment,' said Gil. 'Wait.'

Out in the yard, the harsh voice was drowning anything the Prior might have attempted to say.

'Well, if he's no to be found, he's no to be found. I'll need to get back to Ayrshire and see to my daughter's wedding, get it ower afore Lent.'

Raitts was staring at the door. Boyd said something which might have been conventional good wishes for the marriage.

'Aye, well, she's done better than she deserves. Stair would teach her to read, but Mungo Schaw o Coilsfield doesny object to that. Says it keeps a woman out o trouble.' Boyd made another indistinct comment. 'Aye, well, I'll away then.'

The voices receded. Gil relaxed slightly, and looked at Raitts, who was still staring at the door.

'She's gone now,' he said. 'Did she sell all your books?'

'H-half,' said Raitts distractedly. 'Nearly the half. Mungo Schaw, did she say?' There were tears glittering in his eyes, but he allowed his guards to ease him back into the inner chamber without resistance.

'I think she'll not be back,' Gil said.

'As God wills it,' said Prior Boyd, crossing himself. 'But I hope you may be right.' He caught Gil's eye and nodded slightly. 'I am aware of what she said.'

'Two-edged,' Gil said elliptically.

'Aye. Though the character reference might not have been a defence in any case,' said Boyd, retreating into Latin. 'You wished to see me, Gilbert?'

'I did, sir.' Gil lifted the scrip at his feet and drew out the folded shirt. 'We discovered this, among the linen waiting for the wash.'

Boyd watched as he opened the garment out, his face crumpling in distress as he recognised the bloodstains.

'What are you showing me, Gilbert?'

260

'The shirt someone wore when he cut Andrew Rattray's throat, I believe,' said Gil. 'Unless there's been an animal slaughtered lately.'

'The slaughtering was before Yule,' said Boyd, 'and it is to be hoped that it would have been done more neatly.' He touched the stains delicately, and crossed himself again. 'So you think this is the boy's blood? Andrew's?'

'I do, sir.'

The Prior closed his eyes to murmur a prayer, then said, 'Tell me the rest.'

Choosing his words with care, Gil laid out the discovery of the shirt and the knife. His kinsman listened in mounting distress, and when he had done rose abruptly and went to look out of his window at the darkening infirmary garden with its ruins.

'We have the wrong man,' he said.

'It seems likely, sir.'

'I was certain I understood where your discourse led us.' He leaned on the low sill. 'Lessons in humility are rarely welcome. What should we do, Gilbert? How do we discover which of my flock is a killer, without reason, even attacking his confessor who should stand as a father to him? It will be a man I ken well, a man I have taken for my brother. How do we find who he is?'

'What I should like to do,' Gil said, thinking of his vision of Andrew Rattray, 'is set a trap for him, tonight.'

'A trap?' Boyd turned to look at him. 'What kind of trap?'

'A baited trap,' said Gil, 'but first I may need to talk Brother Euan round. Have we time afore supper, do you think?'

'I don't like it, Maister Gil,' said Tam. 'It's a daft plan, and dangerous. What if we're no quick enough? What if he gets by us?'

261

'You have a better one?' Gil asked, settling himself in his corner.

'As for letting the mistress in on it, that beats all, so it does.'

'Tam. Be quiet, man.'

'Aye, I ken. Wait who kens how long, for who kens what, armed wi a knife and like to slay someone this night.'

'Tam, if you canny be silent, you can go to your bed.'

The man subsided, with a few more grumbles, but Gil had retired into himself, into the quiet watchful state of mind he had been taught as a boy by his father's huntsman, waiting in such a way that the quarry would not be alarmed, and found it easy enough to ignore him.

Brother Euan, tackled in the infirmary, had been readily persuaded to take part, once he had accepted that he was not required to move his patient.

'Indeed, it's better he stays where he is,' Gil emphasised. 'We want to convince the—' he paused, selecting a word.

'Killer,' said Brother Euan, with a most un-Ersche directness.

'Aye. We want him to believe that Faither Henry will wake the morn and be able to talk, and that he's sleeping in the guest hall the night, untended, save that you will be going in and out, because Faither James is so near his end it's better he has absolute quiet.'

'Och, no, that is a nonsense,' said Brother Euan, 'though I think they hear more than we can tell, and feel touch too, the dying.'

'I ken it's nonsense,' Gil persisted. 'Just so the killer believes it.'

'I canny be telling folk that,' Brother Euan said. 'They would never be believing me.'

'No need, Euan.' Prior Boyd took a hand in the discussion. 'I'll announce it at supper, that all are to stay away

262

from the guest hall and to be quiet passing it, and Brother Dickon can spread the word that Henry is there. All you'll ha to do is cross the courtyard once or twice in the night, go into the guest hall, wait there long enough to be convincing and then come back here.'

'Oh, I see!' said Brother Euan, suddenly understanding. 'You wish to – och, yes, that is easy done. I will help all I can.'

'Thank you, brother,' said the Prior. 'How is Faither James? How long has he—?'

Brother Euan shrugged. 'A few hours? A day or two? No longer, I should say.'

Shifting his feet in the dark to ease stiffening muscles, careful to make no noise, Gil hoped now that Father James would hang onto life until this matter was dealt with. The passing-bell and the resulting commotion would not be helpful additions to his plan.

It had been more trouble to persuade his own men the scheme would work, that they would not have a wakeful night to no purpose, and Alys's reaction had been disapproving too, though he suspected that was because there was no place for her in it.

Why had she come back to the Blackfriars so late? She was in a strange mood, a mixture of triumph, almost elation, and the tearstained resolute behaviour he associated now with her hearing that another neighbour was pregnant, though he thought she knew nobody in Perth likely to have such news. They had been unable to discuss her day, though she had had time to tell him that she had found what might have happened to Leonard Pollock, and to show him the contents of the cloth-wrapped basin she had borne back as if it was an original copy of Aristotle, and also to warn him that Sir Silvester Rattray would call tomorrow.

Not too early, I hope, he thought, and eased his position again. And what was that in the basin? It did appear uncommonly like what they had swept up in Pollock's inner chamber, but after letting him look briefly she had wrapped the fragments up again, stowed the bundle in a travelling kist out of the dog's reach, and retired to their bedchamber with Jennet, leaving him to set the watch.

'What time is it, maister, d'you think?' Tam breathed, his voice carefully pitched now to carry no further than Gil's ears.

'Near midnight?' he guessed.

They were not in complete darkness. The door to one of the lesser chambers, the easiest to reach when one stepped into the hall, stood ajar, and a light burned within as if the sick man slept there. Gil and Tam lurked in the shadows of the hall, within sight of both doors; Dandy and, at his own insistence, Nory, were in the lit chamber. Euan had been set to guard Brother Euan and the infirmary, just in case their trap was ignored. Gil was torn between the hope that this would be unnecessary and the fear that one man was not enough protection. No doubt Brother Euan can fight, he thought. Two determined Erschemen ought to withstand an army.

Brother Euan had made one trip across the courtyard already. He had done it very well, pacing across the wide space with his small lantern, quite as if he was on the errand he pretended, staying in the lit chamber for five minutes or so and emerging with a blessing which sounded genuine and heartfelt.

The gate from the slype creaked, and Tam drew a sudden sharp breath.

'Aye,' Gil answered, on the edge of sound.

Quiet, cautious footsteps approached across the courtyard. Gil straightened up, flexed his legs, settled the leather doublet in place, made certain he could reach his dagger. A hand brushed the outside of the great door, the latch clinked. The door creaked open slowly, and against the slightly lighter sky beyond it a head moved, a shadowy figure slipped into the hall and made for the lit doorway. A second figure followed it, turned to close the door quietly —

Two of them?

As both figures were outlined against the candlelight, Gil shouted, 'Get them! Tam, you get the left one!' he added, springing forward. There was a squawk of alarm, both intruders whirled, one putting his fists up in a very businesslike way, the other lifting a dark bundle which was certainly not a knife. *Cloak*, Gil thought, dodging sideways to come in behind the elbow, grab the arm and carry the movement on upwards. The swathe of fabric unrolled and entangled his opponent. There was a scuffle of feet as the two men in hiding emerged to join in, making for Tam. Gil let go the arm he held, shifted his grip to put a forearm across the man's throat, and dug his thumbnail into the folds of wool where he judged the small of the back might be.

'Quiet now,' he said. 'Quietly.'

The other man was putting up more of a fight. Someone had already fallen back, blowing and gasping from a kick in the belly, and a handy blow produced a curse from Tam. At his words, Gil's captive stood very still.

'Maister Cunningham?' he said, in muffled tones, under the blanket. 'Is that you, maister?'

'It is,' Gil agreed, close to his ear.

'Let me go, sir. It's Sandy Munt. Me and Patey came to guard Faither Henry. Patey!' he said, more loudly. 'Patey, it's Maister Cunningham's men. It's all right!'

'All right, is it!' Patey Simpson leaned sideways from a swinging fist and backed against the wall, hands up, the sleeves of his habit pale in the dimness. 'All right, all right, *pax*, I've stopped. We've no weapons, maisters. You can search us, we've no knife on us, neither o us.'

'You came to guard Faither Henry?' Gil repeated, letting go of Munt. 'Who else kens? Who did you tell?'

'Nobody,' said Munt, struggling out of the folds of cloth. 'We reckoned two was enough.' Nory emerged from the small chamber again, bearing the candle in its candlestick, and in the increased light both young men looked embarrassed. 'Some guards we'd ha been, if you could surprise us like that, but I never thought o you being involved.'

'Nor me neither,' agreed Simpson, sucking his knuckles, allowing Tam to check his person for concealed weapons. 'How is he – Faither Henry?'

'Well, so far as I ken. Asleep. Brother Euan's happy enough wi him for now, though it's to be seen how he is when he wakes.'

'Can we see him?' Munt asked. Then, after a moment's thought, 'He's no here, is he? Is it a trap, and we've sprung it?'

'Keep your voice down.' Gil gestured at the doorway beside them. 'Come in here. Let's get that light away from the windows. Aye, it's a trap, and though you've sprung it, we could say it's worked well. Dandy, are you hurt, man?' He perched on the end of the empty bed, peering at the groom in the light.

'I'll live,' said Dandy, dabbing at his nose with a sleeve. 'You've a wechty nieve, man, for a religious.'

'I've brothers,' said Simpson briefly. 'What can we best do, maister? We'd planned,' he looked at Munt, 'we'd planned to go into Matins, rather than be sought the way we all sought for, well, for Brother Thomas and for Faither Henry.'

'We thought, if we waited by the slype, we could slip in at the back o the procession,' supplied Munt. 'They'd likely just think we'd been longer getting our boots on.'

Gil, with longer experience of the omniscience of those who dealt with the young, doubted this, but did not comment, saying only, 'If you stay, you'll need to keep quiet.'

266

In fact, he was not convinced the trap would catch anyone else this night. The killer need not have seen these two stealing about the cloister to be wary; anything or anyone out of place could cause him to think twice, to abandon his intentions.

'What did Faither Prior give out at supper?' he asked quietly, over the assurances of silence and stillness. The two looked at each other again.

'About Faither Henry?' said Munt. 'That he's improving, that Brother Euan thinks he may be able to speak the morn, that he's to lie here the night. Was any o that true, maister? He's – he's – he's been out o't a long time, is he ever to waken?'

'Certainly that he's improving,' Gil said. 'The long sleep's deliberate treatment for the head wound. I've met it afore, and my wife's read o such things.'

'Ah,' said Munt, relief colouring his tone.

'I'm sorry, maister, if we've owerset your plans,' said Simpson, accepting the folded blanket from Nory. 'It seemed like a good idea, that we cam down to keep watch by our teacher, but I see now it's no so clever at all. Thanks, man,' he added to Nory, who nodded and slipped out into the dark hall again.

'If we hadny been here,' said Gil, 'it would ha been a right good idea, and you'd no way to know my plans.' He got to his feet. 'You two bide here wi Dandy, Nory can come out in the hall—'

'Maister!' It was Tam, in a hissing whisper. 'Maister, can you come out here? Something's afoot,' he added as Gil hastened to join him. 'Listen?'

There were raised voices, somewhere outside, a confused shouting. Gil made out panicky cries of 'Murder! Who's dead?'

'Tam, wi me!' he said sharply, stepping to the door. 'Dandy, bring a light and follow us. Nory, you stay here wi the lads. The women are still in their chamber.'

Out in the courtyard it was much easier to find the direction of the shouting, which was definitely coming from somewhere in the cloister. Gil made his way cautiously through the slype, dagger in hand, Tam at his back, and peered out into the open space beyond. The raised voices were over to his right, towards the day stair, where a group of cloaked Dominicans were arguing fiercely, lantern-light catching white sleeves. It was not clear what was happening. Gil, relaxing a little, moved round the walkway towards them, Tam still behind him, and Dandy caught them up with a handful of lanterns just as they reached the group.

'Nobody passed me!' Brother Martin was saying. 'He never went that way, any road!'

'Nor into the kirk,' said someone else. 'I'd swear to it, that door makes sic a noise.'

'What's amiss?' Gil asked. 'We heard you in the guest hall. Is someone hurt?'

'Maister Cunningham!' It was one of the novices. Taking a lantern from Dandy, Gil held it up, and recognised Mureson. 'Oh, maister, we've seen the murderer! Adam and me, we saw him just the now!'

# Chapter Thirteen

'They did!' agreed Brother Martin, and two more men agreed with him. Beside Mureson, Adam Calder was shivering, his teeth chattering, whether in shock or with the cold was not clear, for he was not wearing his cloak.

'I saw him,' he said, nodding eagerly. 'I cam out the privy and there he was in front o me, all in shadow in one o our habits, and I yelled and he ran. That way,' he gestured along past the Chapter House and the Prior's study.

'Did you see him?' Gil asked Mureson.

'We should hunt for him,' said someone. 'He must be in the kirk.'

'I tell you he's not,' said someone else.

'What, hunt for a madman wi a knife? In the dark?'

'I was right behind Adam,' said Mureson. 'It was him got the bigger fright, but I near— I louped like a lassie when he yelled.' His voice trembled, though he was not shivering. 'Dear God, I think I'll go to the Charterhouse the morn.'

'Did either of you recognise him?' Gil asked.

'If we all go thegither we'll be safe enough.'

'N-no, I didny get a sight – it was all so quick!' Calder's teeth were chattering again.

'You want torches for that,' Tam said to the incipient search-party. 'You aye need torches for a search like that.'

'Will you come wi us, maister?' someone asked.

'I will not,' said Gil. 'If the fellow has any sense, he's hastened up the night stair and he's back in his bed and warm by now, and I'd advise all you gentlemen to do the same.'

'Sound advice, Maister Cunningham,' said the Prior, appearing behind Brother Martin. The young man yelped in alarm, and staggered back against his neighbour. His ghostly father glanced at him, than surveyed the rest of the group by the light of his small lantern. 'What is this unseemly assembly about?' he demanded from behind the light. 'Why are so many of our community out their beds at this hour, making so much noise when you are supposed to be observing a strict silence?' There was some shuffling, and a general murmur of apology and requests for forgiveness. 'Brother Martin, can you explain?'

'Brother Adam and Brother Sandy saw the murderer, Faither,' supplied Brother Martin. 'And the rest o us came down when we heard them yelling. We were just going to hunt for him when you—'

'He went that way,' said someone else.

'He must be in the kirk, there's naught else there!'

'There's the night stair, like Maister Cunningham said.'

'The more talk there is the now,' said Boyd, raising his voice a little, 'the longer will the imposition of silence last.'

A silence fell immediately, into which Calder said, 'But Faither, I was face to face wi him!'

'Did you see him too, Brother Sandy?' asked the Prior.

'I was just behind Adam when he – no, I . . .' Mureson tailed off.

'Very well. You and Brother Adam, come wi me, and the rest o you, go back to your beds, and try to sleep between now and Matins. Unless anyone else feels he has anything to add?' he finished, in a chilly tone which was far from encouraging.

'Should we no hunt for him?' said someone from the shadows. 'He must be somewhere about!' Several voices agreed with him.

'As Maister Cunningham has said,' the Prior pronounced over the objections, 'the fugitive is likely back in his bed by now and getting warm. You'll all do the same, if you please. Maister Cunningham, do you wish to question these two?'

'I'd be glad of the chance,' Gil admitted. 'In your study, sir? I'll follow you. I want a look round first.'

Boyd peered at him in the lantern-light but did not question this. Instead he waited while the gathering dissolved, its members slipping away one by one with murmurs of, '*Mea culpa*, Faither,' and when the last had gone, turned and paced off down the length of the cloister. The two novices followed obediently.

Gil watched until they vanished into the Prior's study, and said, 'Dandy, see us those lanterns over here. Something went down, something metal.'

'Metal?' Dandy obediently approached with the light. 'Did they really see the madman, Maister Gil?'

'Something like this?' Tam's booted toe nudged an object on the flagstones. Gil swooped on it.

'Indeed! And look what we have.'

They stared at the knife in his hand. A wooden handle, a long narrow blade, its edge curved with much sharpening, the point like a needle.

'So he was here,' said Tam. 'I thought they'd just managed to fright themselves, maybe telling stories or the like, and fancied they saw him.'

'No,' said Gil, turning the wicked thing. 'He was here all right.'

Sending Dandy back to the guest hall, with instructions to make sure the two novices still there returned to the dorter, Gil followed the Prior to his study. Here, by the extravagant light of three candles, Boyd was questioning Mureson and Calder. All looked round as Gil entered, but he signed to his kinsman to continue and found himself a seat, prepared to listen quietly. Tam took up position by the wall, the image of a well-trained servant.

'So you were leaving the necessarium,' Boyd said, 'when you encountered a brother wi a knife, is that what you're saying, Adam?'

'Not quite, Faither.' Adam Calder stood in an attitude of humility, hands tucked in his sleeves, head bent. 'I'd just got there, reached the door, when I saw him. He was coming at me wi his knife, all ready to cut my throat. It was Brother Sandy was leaving.'

'I was just opening the door, Faither,' agreed Mureson. He had adopted the same pose, but now raised his head and shuddered in recollection. 'I – I was taking care my lantern didny blow out, and there was this great skelloch outside the door, and afore I could close it this shadow leaped past and I near jumped out my boots, and Brother Adam fell against the door. So I yelled out and all, wi the fright, and Adam says, *Did you see him?* and I says, *Who was it?* and then the others cam down to see what was amiss.'

'I see,' said the Prior. 'So, Adam, you saw the man with the knife, let out a skelloch, and Brother Sandy came out of the necessarium in the same moment, and let out another.'

Mureson nodded, and shuddered again, but did not speak. Calder said, 'Aye, Faither.'

'And then what?'

'He ran off along the cloister, Faither, like I said.'

'Sandy, did you see the man at all?'

'I only saw his shadow, Faither,' said Mureson. 'It was,' he bit his lip, 'it was like a giant's shadow. *Magna atque terribilis.*'

272

Boyd looked at Gil.

'Maister Cunningham? Do you have questions for these two?'

'I do,' Gil said. 'Adam.' Calder turned towards him, head still bent. 'Look at me, Adam.' Calder raised his head, keeping his eyes downcast. 'No, look at me,' Gil insisted. 'This is no moment for custody of the gaze.' He waited until Calder met his eye, rather tentatively, and went on, 'You had just reached the door of the privy when you saw this figure, is that right?'

'It is, maister.'

'What did you see? Can you describe it?'

'Well . . .' Calder hesitated. 'It was one o ours, maister, for he was wearing a habit, and coming at me wi his knife in his hand, all ready to cut my throat, so I yelled out, and Sandy heard me and yelled out and all, and the madman just pushed past me so I fell against the door, and ran off instead o—'

'Could you identify him?'

Calder shook his head.

'No, maister. It could ha been near any o us, save maybe Faither, or Faither John, or Faither Henry.'

'Why none of those?'

'Well.' Calder looked blank for a moment, then expanded his statement: 'Faither was there later, and Faither Henry's lying sick, and Faither John's got his sleeping draught and besides, he's a kenspeckle figure wi's bald head shining.'

'I see,' said Gil. 'So none o those three, but any other. And the knife? What like was that?'

'I never got a right look at it,' said Calder regretfully, 'just a common kitchen knife, I think, wi a narrow blade.'

'How long was it?'

'Maybe so long?' Calder held his hands out, forefingers eight inches or so apart.

273

'So you had got to the door of the privy, and saw this figure coming at you wi the knife,' Gil said. Calder nodded. 'Where from? Where was he?'

'From,' Calder swallowed, and licked his lips, 'from along by the side o the refectory. He was right on me when I saw him, but that's where he was coming from.'

'I see. Then you and Brother Sandy yelled, and the figure ran off down the cloister.' Another nod. 'Why did you not run after him? There were the two of you, after all.'

'I – we'd got a fright, maister,' said Calder reproachfully.

'Adam,' said the Prior in rebuke. Calder bent his head.

'*Mea culpa*, Faither,' he said. 'But I think that was the reason, maister. We were that busy picking oursels up and I was telling Sandy what I'd seen, and then other folk heard us and came down. And then you was there, and then Faither came down and commanded us.'

'You're quite certain you didny recognise him,' Gil said.

'It was ower dark,' Calder said, 'and he just pushed past me, like I said. I'd not know him again, I saw so little. He was bigger than me, and he moved fast,' he offered.

'And he ran off down the cloister. Will you come out and show me how, the now? Where he went?'

'Now? In the dark?' Calder looked dismayed. 'Those flagstones are no safe, maister. It's one thing a madman running, I'd not care to try it wi no light, or even wi one of our lanterns.'

'You don't have your own lantern the now,' Gil observed.

'No, mine's burning low, I wanted to save it for Matins. I just came down in the dark. The steps are easy enough, if you keep your hand to the wall. But as for running in the cloister, maister, I'd as soon not try it.'

'Very well,' said Gil. 'It will do in the morning.' He considered the novice for a long moment; Calder shifted uneasily under his gaze, and then bent his head in that attitude of humility again. Eventually Gil said, 'I think we might let them get back to bed, Prior, do you?'

'I'd be glad to, sir,' said Calder, wriggling a little. 'I never did get to the—'

'Ah. Brother Sandy,' said the Prior, 'see Brother Adam to the necessarium, and then the pair of you get to your beds. There's little enough time afore Matins.' He raised his hand in a blessing, and the two young men bowed and said Amen. He watched them go, and when the door had closed behind them turned a face of exasperation to Gil.

'What was that about?' he demanded.

'You tell me, sir,' suggested Gil.

'Hah! I wish I could! Is the lad deluded, or making himself important, or have they frightened themselves telling tales in the dorter? Does he merely want the attention of his elders and his peers?'

'You saw that too?' Gil shook his head. 'Could be any of those, I suppose. The thing is, we found this, out there where he claims to have encountered the murderer.' He drew the knife from his sleeve and laid it on the desk. Boyd recoiled, staring at it as at a basilisk.

'Is that— aye, it must be, surely! A common kitchen knife wi a long blade.' He tore his gaze from the weapon and looked at Gil in deep dismay. 'Outside? Out on the ground here in the cloister? So he really was there.'

'Aye,' said Gil. 'I think he was.'

'You didny show this to Brother Adam,' the Prior observed shrewdly.

'Never put all your cards on the table at once,' Gil said. 'What I should like to do now, sir,' he went on without looking at Tam, 'is set a watch.'

'Ah. You think the – the killer will come back for it?'

275

'I do. He likely kens where it went down. I know I heard it rattle on the stones, from a few steps away. The rest were too busy arguing to pay attention. He'll come back for it, rather than risk it being found in the morning and returned to the kitchen–'

'With our brothers' blood on it? Surely not!' said Boyd in distress.

'–leaving him without a weapon,' Gil continued.

'Aye, I see. Do you want one or two o the brothers to assist you? Brother Dickon, maybe? A handy man in a stushie.'

'I'll wager,' Gil said. 'No, I'd as soon keep the numbers down. The more men watching, the more likely we are to be noticed, to alert the quarry. I'd sooner you were aware of it, but I can do without anyone else. How do I find you if we do take him?'

'My cell is the first on the left next the day stair, but I'll no be sleeping. I'll admit, I'll be easier for knowing there's a watch being kept.' Boyd shook his head. 'I never heard o sic a thing happening, anywhere in the Order. It grieves me sair it should happen here in Perth.'

'Lightning can strike anywhere,' said Gil. Hark at me, I am just as sententious as Brother Dickon, he thought, as he bent his head for the Prior's blessing.

'So who's standing this watch?' Tam asked quietly, watching Gil as he peered into the shadows under the cloister walk.

'I will,' said Gil. 'Any that wishes can join me.'

'Aye, well, I'd really relish going back to Glasgow to tell the Canon, much less madam your mother, how I'd let you get hurt for the sake o my night's sleep.' Tam moved along the side of the refectory after Gil. 'So how much o that was an invention, the laddies had to tell us?'

'How much do you think?' Gil straightened up and looked at the man by the faint lantern-light.

'If we hadny found the knife,' said Tam after a moment, 'I'd ha said all of it, but that makes it look as though this madman, or whatever he is, really was here.'

'Aye,' Gil agreed, and went back to the refectory door, set deep in its heavily carved archway. 'I think this will have to do. It's dark enough, it ought to hide you, and I'll get beyond the day stair where that buttress is, and we should have him boxed in.'

'I see your plan,' said Tam after a moment. 'As long's he searches where we found the thing, we should have him.'

'Aye, as long as,' Gil said cynically. 'You ken what happens to plans. Tam, go back to the guest hall, making a noise wi that gate, and let the other fellows know what's ado. Bring back my cloak and your own and come as quiet as you can. And bid them get some sleep and relieve us after Matins,' he added. '*Hey, how the chevaldoures woke al nyght*. No sense in two o us freezing our cods off when we can spread the pleasure about.'

'Smells as if it's like to snow,' Tam observed, and set off along the cloister walk. Gil looked about him, standing quietly in the bitter dark, and listened carefully. Out in the burgh a dog barked, another answered, someone shouted at them. An owl screeched and was answered. Closer at hand someone was snoring, muffled behind the dorter windows, and something rustled in the grass in the cloister garden. The owl screeched again, and Tam approached quietly along the walkway, the two cloaks bundled in his arms.

'Brought your gloves and all,' he said, producing the felt mittens from under his arm. 'Right. What's the order o the night, then?'

'I cannot believe how foolish you have been,' said Alys in rapid, furious French, tugging at the bandages on Gil's arm and chest. He yelped, and she loosened them

277

slightly with gentle hands, though her voice did not change. 'To put yourself in such a position, with only Tam to assist you, to catch your man and then to let him disarm you! Is that easier?'

'It is,' he said, attempted to flex the arm, and stopped. 'It was the snow.' She pulled her bedgown closer at the neck, glancing automatically at the window of the bedchamber, where the candlelight caught the flakes of snow whirling past, and snorted inelegantly. 'Help me put my shirt back on, sweetheart.'

'I'll do nothing of the sort,' she retorted. 'You are to drink this and lie down and try to sleep.'

'Not yet,' he said. 'I need to question the fellow. I promised young Rattray I would make his killer confess.'

'Your shirt is not fit to wear,' she said, 'and I am not getting a clean one out of the baggage for you. Also, you are talking nonsense.'

He pushed Socrates' head off his knee and got to his feet resignedly, waited a moment until the chamber stopped whirling, and bent to dig in the nearest of the bags. She watched, with an obstinate set to her mouth, until he turned dizzy again and nearly fell, when she exclaimed under her breath and came to support him back to sit on the bed. Socrates immediately leaned against his knee again.

'You are not fit,' Alys said. 'Lie down, and I will question the prisoner.'

'No, I need to deal with him,' he said. He put his good hand up to touch her cheek. 'Yes, I know I left you out of it and I'm sorry for that. Would you have had me wake you?'

'Perhaps not,' she admitted after a moment, and turned to search for a clean shirt. Jennet, wrapped in a blanket over her shift, came back into the chamber with a tray of steaming beakers. Nory followed her, cast one critical, assessing glance at his master and went to help Alys.

'Here's the buttered ale, mem,' said Jennet, 'and a good drop of usquebae to it and all. Did you no drink your other dose, maister?'

'I'll take that,' he said, reaching for the tray. She held it out of his reach.

'You'll drink the other first.'

Wondering why women all turned into his old nurse when there was an injury to tend, he drank the bitter brew in the other beaker, and was handed his spiced ale as if it was a reward, but had barely tasted it when Nory emerged from the corner of the chamber with a clean shirt.

'Come, we'll help you into this,' Alys said in Scots, 'and I shall help question the prisoner too.'

'Tam's out there heating up his pilliwinks,' said Jennet.

'I hope there'll be no need o that,' said Gil repressively, allowing Nory to ease the shirt onto his bandaged arm. His injuries were not serious, he felt, though they had bled impressively, and Alys had cleaned the cuts well with more of the same usquebae. They were still stinging, despite the salve she had daubed on them before covering all with bandages begged from Brother Euan across the courtyard.

'Drink your ale,' she said, as she tied the strings of the shirt on his chest. 'The spices are to engender blood to replace what you've lost, being hot and dry, and the ale will replace bodily moisture.'

'And here I thought it was for comfort,' he said.

'That too.' She looked at him critically, then kissed him quickly and said, 'You're not so bad as I feared. Will you put on the doublet, or do you prefer a loose gown?'

'The doublet's past wearing and all,' he admitted. 'Nory, d'you think you can patch it? Aye, the furred gown, sweetheart. My *solsicle of swetnesse*,' he added quietly as she helped him into it.

Nory was inspecting the doublet, his prim mouth turned down.

'I'm no leatherworker, maister,' he warned them. 'I'll maybe speak wi Dandy about it, but I doubt you're looking for a new one. Or you could line it wi taffeta,' he added, 'seeing what a thorough job he made o slashing it, and be in the fashion for once. Flame-coloured, maybe, to pull through the slashes in wee puffs.'

'No my colour,' said Gil, equally solemn. Alys giggled, on a faintly hysterical note, and fastened the hooks and eyes down the front of the gown for him.

'Fair takes me back,' Nory added. 'My previous maisters, God rest their souls, ruined a few doublets this way, though they both favoured velvet and brocades ower the leather.'

The doublet was probably ruined right enough, Gil thought, but equally probably it had saved his life, considering the events of the last hour or two.

He and Tam had stood in the cold and dark for a long time, waiting, not moving, before the first flakes of snow flittered out of the black sky. The snowfall grew thicker quite quickly and began to lie, drifting into corners under the cloister walkway, catching on Gil's cloak and boots. He watched it a little anxiously, wondering whether it would make him more or less noticeable here in the shadows. The black cat slipped along the cloister in search of mice, his white patches faint in the little light there was, paused with a paw lifted in a patch of snow to consider him, then padded on into the shadows.

When he finally heard a footstep, it was from the direction he had least expected of those possible. A scuffle, the clink of a latch away to his right, and the door at the foot of the night stair eased open. There was cautious movement; the door closed, very quietly. No point in risking the cold draught waking a brother, Gil thought approvingly. All along this had been done with care and planning; he had never been convinced that the killer was mad, only that he was working, with a warped but definite intelligence, to some deep private plan.

Quiet steps sounded. Standing well back in the corner between the buttress and the wall, Gil kept as still as he might, hoping his face was well shadowed by the collar of his cloak. Even in here in the midnight under the cloister's vaulted roof, a face might be noticed, eyes might glitter in a stray gleam.

His quarry moved quietly past him, a flurry of snow outlining the double blackness of cloak and cowl against the night, past the foot of the day stair, past the necessarium. In the corner of the cloister the footsteps paused, there was a small metallic sound, a narrow beam of light sprang out from one of the friars' small lanterns. The dark figure bent over the light, swinging it to and fro, its weak yellow glow picking up the uneven flagstones. Gil eased himself away from the wall, slid the felt mittens off his hands, drew his dagger. Tam should be about in place by now —

'Looking for something?' Tam asked from beyond the searching figure.

The lantern dropped with a clatter and the searcher straightened up and gasped.

'Oh, brother, you —' he began, took in Tam's un-habited outline in the last flicker of the candle, and turned to make for the day stair, straight into Gil's arms.

Sidestepping a vicious punch, Gil chopped backhanded with the pommel of his dagger at the back of his opponent's neck. Thick folds of black woollen cowl made the blow less than effective; the other's knees gave, briefly, then he recovered and seized Gil's arm, whirling away as he passed. Gil went with the move, spun the searcher round into Tam's grasp, wrenched free and as Tam hoisted the other's arm up behind his back got a good handful of the black cloak and pressed the point of his dagger into the man's ribcage.

'Hold still, will you!' Tam said, but the captive twisted out of his grasp, one knee jerked, Tam slid on a patch of snow and fell back cursing breathlessly.

Gil tightened his grip on the cloak, pushed the dagger point more intently into the man's ribs, and said, 'Be still! Is this what you were looking for?'

He jabbed the dagger again, and before Tam, recovering, could join the fight their opponent twisted about again, moved his arm sharply within the cloak, jerking the dagger out of Gil's hand. It rattled on the flagstones, and all three of them pounced on it. Gil's head collided with someone else's and the world retreated sharply.

When it returned he was kneeling, pain stabbing in his arm and side, a harsh-breathing shadow dark above him just striking again. He lunged sideways, his own dagger whistling past his ear, found someone's knee beside his shoulder, managed to get his arm behind it and yanked hard. The foe collapsed on top of him, and Tam fell on top of all, driving the wind from Gil's chest. This time Tam kept hold of the captive, and contrived to stun him with a punishing blow to the side of the head.

'I've got him! Help me bind him, maister!' he said. Gil staggered to his feet and went to Tam's aid, but his hand seemed to be wet and slippery with something, and the cloister was swinging about badly. They got their captive secured with his own belt, as Raitts had been. Tam drew out his tinderbox and began striking a light, and as Prior Boyd and half his flock emerged from the day stair, succeeded in lighting the candle in the dropped lantern.

'Aye, Brother Adam,' he said, holding the light down to see who they had caught. 'Got a fresh candle, did you? This one's never burnt out, it's all but new.'

'Brother Adam,' said the Prior, staring down at the kneeling prisoner. 'What have you done, my son?'

Adam Calder raised his battered head.

'I did nothing, Faither,' he said, through split lips. 'These two attacked me here outside the privy. See how they've beaten and bound me, Faither.'

'Aye,' said Tam grimly, 'and see how you've let my maister's blood. Maister Gil, you're bleeding all ower the snow.'

Prior Boyd, having led Matins, appeared in the guest hall as Gil emerged from the chamber where he had been washed and bandaged. The Prior came in some state, attended by the novice-master Father John Blythe, the subprior Robert Park, Brother Dickon, and several others, all grim-faced, though one or two were suppressing yawns.

'We have not yet questioned Brother Adam,' Boyd said in his elegant Latin, once he had ascertained that Gil was not seriously injured. 'Before I speak to him, I wish to hear, and for these others to hear, what you witnessed and why you seized and bound him.'

'Indeed, sir.' Gil waited until the Prior was seated, and sat down rather heavily himself. 'He was searching, as I surmised, where the knife had been dropped.'

'But anybody who was there earlier could ha dropped the knife!' exclaimed the subprior in Scots. 'Or maybe he was seeking something else!'

'He came back for the knife,' Gil said. 'He knew it was there. Nobody else did.'

Park seemed inclined to argue, but Brother Dickon said, 'And he ran when you spoke to him, did he no?'

'He did,' Gil agreed.

'And did that to you when you stopped him,' said the Prior, nodding at the sling which supported Gil's bandaged arm. 'That alone is cause to question him, never mind what more actions he is to be accused o committing.'

'Has he said anything yet?' Gil asked.

'No according to my lads,' said Brother Dickon drily, 'other than protesting that he's no guilty, he's much to be commended.'

'Commended?' repeated the subprior. 'Our Lady save us, what's to commend about his behaviour? How is he to be commended?'

Adam Calder, it transpired, was shut away in the space newly vacated by Alexander Raitts, and guarded by a different pair of Brother Dickon's men. While enough seating was found for all who required to be seated, mainly in the shape of the bench for patients, hastily borrowed from the new infirmary, Brother Dickon shook snow off his cloak so that it hissed and whined in the brazier, and interrogated his minions.

'Aye, he was kinna difficult to get shut away,' Brother Eck agreed. 'Fought us like a wildcat, he did, and still crying out that he wasny to be arrested, he was to be commended, Faither would ken when he heard all.'

'That's what we're here for, to hear all,' said the Prior grimly, 'though I doubt I'll be commending him for any o't. The poor laddie must be mad indeed.'

Escorted out of the inner chamber, still bound, Calder gave cause to think the Prior must be right. He seemed elated, lit from within by a fire of confidence in his actions which was proof against the manifest disapproval of the row of senior Dominicans who faced him. Instead of dropping to his knees, or better still onto his face, he stood with his head high and smiled expectantly at them.

'Well, Adam,' said the Prior. 'Can you account for your actions?'

'My every action has been for the good of the Order,' Calder declared, in rather shaky Latin.

'For the good of the Order?' repeated Boyd. 'My son, to begin with the least of your offences, how was the

284

theft of a knife from our kitchen for the good of the Order?'

'A necessary evil,' said Calder, 'trivial in respect of the whole. I required an implement.'

The subprior and John Blythe exchanged glances. Boyd did not look round. Gil, seated at the end of the bench, found himself admiring his kinsman's abilities again; David Boyd was not a natural leader but he was a clear thinker, a powerful intellect, and this was now bent on his novice.

'For what did you require an implement, Adam?' he asked gently. 'And we'll speak Scots, if you please.'

'To prune away the rotten branches,' said Calder, in Latin, as if the answer was obvious.

'In Scots, please, my son. What branches are these?'

'Why, those that bear deformed fruit, or no fruit at all. They must be cut away, before they infect the rest of the vine.'

'Explain yourself,' said Boyd, his tone becoming grimmer. 'Make matters plain to us. What branches have you cut away, my son?'

'Only the two as yet,' said Calder in Scots, with a sudden descent into regrets. 'But those were rotten indeed, Faither. The one was stealing from our tenants in the town, and keeping the usufruct to his own use, and the other presented himsel as a clever student, one you all favoured, one you said was like to be a famous preacher–'

Was that a note of bitterness, Gil wondered, of envy. Was that at the root of his mission?

'Andrew Rattray was one of the most promising novices this house has seen in many years,' said Father John.

'There, you see? He made fools o you all! Andrew Rattray had a mistress in the town. He kept her image in a secret place under his bed, a lewd drawing indeed wi

285

her and her bairns in it, and went out to her every week. How's that for your promising novice?' There was no mistaking the vindictive tone now.

Gil leaned forward. 'The lady whose portrait Andrew kept,' he said, 'was his sister. I've spoken wi her. She's a Christian woman, a widow, and Andrew was her only kinsman.'

Everyone turned to stare at him in a moment of amazement. Calder recovered first.

'And if that's so, how did he no tell Faither Prior about her, and get permission to visit her openly? Why the secrecy?'

'There are good reasons,' Gil said, 'which are not your business. The fact remains you removed a promising branch which would have borne fruit for the Order, and thereby brought grief to a courageous lady and left her bairns unprotected.' And what a chilling way to describe a death, he thought.

'What about setting fire to the infirmary?' asked the subprior. 'Why did you do that, to the great sorrow and hurt o this community, and the loss o our Infirmarer, no to mention all his stock o salves and simples?'

'It had to be done,' said Calder reasonably, 'if the Deil was to come and carry off Andrew's soul the way he deservit.'

'Adam. Are you openly admitting,' said David Boyd, 'that you killed Andrew Rattray, and by that means brought about the imminent death of Faither James? That you killed Thomas Wilson in cold blood, unconfessed, to the danger of his immortal soul? That you stabbed Father Henry, your teacher?'

Calder's face changed, and he looked away.

'Aye. Well. That wasny – he ought no to ha ordered me to desist. I'm about God's work and St Dominic's here!'

286

'Are you admitting that you slew these two of your brothers?' repeated the Prior.

'Aye, I slew them. They had to be removed, you must see that.'

'What gave you the thought that you were fit to judge them?' asked John Blythe mildly, the candlelight gleaming on his bald crown. Calder gave him a glittering smile.

'Why, Faither, it was what you tellt us, right at the beginning. How a Dominican must be obedient to the Rule, and bend all his thoughts to complying wi it.'

'And what makes you think,' said Father John, 'that you understand the Rule well enough to assay anyone's obedience to it, when you areny obedient to it yoursel?'

Calder bridled at that, drew himself up as well as he could with his hands bound before him, and said indignantly, 'The Rule's my dearest companion, the lodestar o my life. *Item, take note,*' he declaimed, going into a better Latin than his own, '*that this office calls for excellency of life, so that just as the preacher speaks from a raised position, so he may also preach the Gospel from the mountain of an excellent life.* How can you say I'm no obedient to that?'

'You dare,' said Father John, with a sudden icy crackle in his voice, 'you who have wantonly, savagely, killed two of your brothers, you dare to quote Humbert of Romans as your guide?'

'I was neither wanton nor savage!' retorted Calder indignantly. 'I made certain that Andrew never kent what happened, though he deserved it, and I executed Thomas at one thrust, wi all possible mercy. You'll never call that wanton?'

Father John bent his head and crossed himself, then turned helplessly to his Prior.

'What can we do, Davie?'

David Boyd looked for the first time at his colleagues to right and left, and then at Gil, who shook his head slightly.

'This is beyond our competence, I think,' said the Prior. 'Adam, you must be confined, for what you've done is no healing surgery but a great blow to the Order and a great wickedness. I'll ha to write to the Provincial Prior in Edinburgh for advice, and to the Bishop. You may pass your time in reflection on the sin o pride, and in praying that you be not released to the secular arm, for they will certainly hang you for murder and arson.'

'Take him within, lads,' said Brother Dickon. Protesting wildly, shouting his innocence and good intentions to the world, Calder was dragged back into the inner chamber and its door closed firmly against him. The Prior rose, and everyone else perforce rose with him.

'I commend you all to your beds,' he said heavily, 'to get what sleep you can afore Prime. As for me, I'll be in the kirk, asking forgiveness for whatever failings, in mysel and in our community, have led our brother into sic misdeeds and foul ways of thinking.'

And Sir Silvester Rattray, Gil recalled with a sinking feeling, was to call in the morning.

# Chapter Fourteen

In fact, it was two days before Sir Silvester appeared in the guest hall. On the morning following the very disturbed night their whole party slept late, and when Gil woke, fretful and uncomfortable, Alys studied him, felt his forehead, sniffed his bandages and announced that he would stay in bed. After a short argument she went off to send a message to Mistress Buttergask's house and to consult in the kitchen about hot stones, pausing to ask Nory to remove all Gil's hose and hide them in his own baggage.

'But I need to speak to the Prior,' Gil said, when she returned with a measure of willow-bark tea.

'The Prior can wait,' she said. 'He has other matters on his mind. They're ringing the passing-bell for Father James now, but Father Henry has roused, and is in his own mind, and though he will not say what was confessed to him or by whom, he was little surprised to hear of Calder's being detained. Drink this.'

'So that young man has caused three deaths,' Gil said, accepting the bitter stuff. 'I wish I'd caught him sooner, but it was only after Wilson died I began to isolate him from the other novices.'

'It seems extraordinary,' she said. 'I suppose it must be a sort of *folie de grandeur*, like those madmen who think they are the Pope.'

She left the chamber, and he lay for a while listening to the little bell tolling for Father James, and thinking over the last few days. It had all been very muddled, he thought, with the two cases confused together and the connection with the English Yorkists as well, which was still unclear.

When he next opened his eyes, Alys was sitting by the window with some sewing. It seemed to be linen work, like the mending Margaret Rattray's woman had been working on. The black cat sat on the windowsill watching her.

'What are you sewing?' he asked. She looked up, startled, and then down at her work again, going a little pink.

'I am making a biggin for my fa— for my good-mother's baby,' she said, not quite managing to sound casual.

'Your father will be pleased,' Gil said, wondering what had brought this about. He had given up trying to make peace between Alys and her stepmother, much less get her to show any concern for the other woman's pregnancy. This was a new departure, and a welcome one.

'I thought that,' she said, picking up the little cap again.

He lay watching her drowsily, and by a rambling train of thought recalled her great experiment of the previous day. It had been badly overshadowed by the events of the night.

'Will you tell me about what you learned yesterday?' he asked. She looked up again, oddly wary.

'You're awake. What — what I learned?'

'I wasn't asleep. About how Pollock died. You said you had discovered something.'

'Oh, about that! Yes, yes I did. It's been interesting, and I think we have proved, not how the man died, but how he might have died.'

'Tell me,' he invited again, wondering what else she had thought he meant. She detailed her efforts of the past few days, making him laugh with the account of the exploding crock and the fleeing Franciscans, and then fetched out the linen-wrapped bowl of incinerated meat to show him.

'And this was a whole piece of mutton?' he marvelled, poking at the cindery fragments. 'It does look very like what we picked up in the man's house. Yes, I suppose if his candle had fallen over, and his gown caught fire, it could have been well ablaze before he knew what was happening.'

'Yes, and then the fat from the man's body would melt and run into the garments, like the wick of a candle,' she agreed, 'and feed the fire until it was fierce enough to consume all. I think he was a very heavy man.'

Gil suddenly remembered Brother Dickon remarking that his boots had not squeaked since he entered Pollock's house, and grimaced at the thought.

'I'm convinced,' he admitted. 'Whether the Bishop will understand it, much less the Provost of Perth, is another matter, but I think David Boyd will agree that the death could well have been accidental.' He gazed admiringly at her. 'I once told the King you were the wisest lassie in Scotland, and you've proved me right yet again. *There is none like to my lady, That ever I saw.*'

Her fleeting smile came and went, and she looked down, going pink across the cheekbones. He put his hand out to grasp hers.

'I'm right weel cled in my wife,' he said in Scots. She turned her hand to clasp his and smiled again, less fleetingly.

'Sir Silvester used the same words,' she said, 'when I would not say if I knew anything of Margaret Rattray. He's seeking her, Gil, I'm not sure why, and her man is dead – the man Skene. He fell into the harbour.'

'Is he now?' Gil tried to address this idea, but found it would not stay still long enough to contemplate. 'You need to let her know that,' he suggested. 'Go to her now with the word, or send Tam. Just be careful you're not followed, if you don't wish him to find her.'

'A good idea.' She looked out of the window at the leaden sky, and began to fold up her sewing. The roofs he could see from where he lay bore a thin layer of snow. 'There would be time before the dinner.'

As soon as she was out of the room the cat came to join him on the bed, curling up beside his feet, and went to sleep. Some time later, Brother Dickon looked round the door. Socrates' long nose appeared at knee level, twitching, then the rest of the dog slipped into the chamber. The lay brother followed him.

'Aye, you'll live,' Dickon said, after studying him briefly. The dog, making a longer, closer inspection, tail waving anxiously, seemed to come to the same conclusion.

'I heard about Faither James,' Gil said. Dickon's beard convulsed as his face crumpled, and he crossed himself.

'Aye. He'd had a good life, mind, all gien ower to the Order, and it was a quiet death, no like some.' He came in, and drew up a stool by the bedside, ignoring as carefully as Gil and the cat the surreptitious ascent of the wolfhound at the other side of the bed. 'You should ha woke me.'

'I thought Tam and I could deal wi him. Turns out I was wrong,' Gil acknowledged.

'I'm no surprised. Seems our man has a bit o a past.'

'What, Calder? At that age?' Gil said, and then recalled that at the same age he had been in Paris, learning street fighting and other skills not generally offered by the Scots College there.

'Oh, he began early. Thing is, he's proud o what he's done. Chatting away to my lads, explaining how it is, how he's recognised his vocation to cleanse the world o sin. Started wi ratting, then he cut his dog's throat for that it wasny an expert ratter, dealt wi a couple o failed hunting dogs the same way. Well, he said they'd failed.' He glanced at Socrates, now extended at Gil's side, and quickly away again.

*Does he hunt well?* Calder had said, looking at the wolfhound. Gil felt a chill down his back, and put his good hand protectively on the dog's head. Socrates rolled a dark eye at him.

'I'll spare you the details o what else,' Dickon went on, 'though I will tell you it turned Jamesie's stomach, but he's boasting o scarring a lassie for life for that she was too free wi her favours, and that was when his family decided he was for the Dominicans, I think.'

'His mother's name wasny Skene, was it?' Gil said sourly. Dickon stared at him.

'How did you ken that?'

'A guess at a venture.' Gil considered what he had just heard, caressing Socrates' ears. 'And yet, called to cleanse the world or no, he had enough sense to go about it in secret, to try to hide what he was doing.'

'Strange, that,' said Dickon. 'Faither Prior spent a long time wi him the day, trying to bring him to see how he'd been guilty o pride and how it had led him to murder and wickedness, but he'll no see it. Maintains it's his vocation.'

'I wonder how he'll react if he ever does see it,' Gil said thoughtfully. Brother Dickon gave him a slantwise look.

'Aye,' he said. 'I'm wondering whether to leave a rope in his cell.'

'It would solve a few problems,' Gil said, 'so long as he doesny make use of it to throttle his guards.'

'We'll see about that,' said Dickon grimly.

\*   \*   \*

293

Gil's next visitor, to his great surprise, was Alexander Raitts. Some time after Brother Dickon had left, the librarian sidled furtively round the door, casting wary glances in all directions. The cat woke and leaped down, disappearing under the other bed, and Raitts closed the door behind him and only then said, 'Can I come in? Madam your wife's no here? No that she's, I mean she's a— I'd not wish to put her out in any way.'

'She's out in Perth, I think,' said Gil, in some amusement, 'and her maid wi her.'

Raitts sagged in relief, and sat down on the stool by the bedside. Socrates studied him carefully, laid his chin on Gil's thigh and relaxed again.

'I came to thank you,' said Raitts, in a sudden rush. 'I think it's your doing they've come at the truth. I never,' he shook his head, 'I never hurt those three, I never had a knife!' He shuddered. 'It's your doing,' he said again. 'Thank you.'

'Wi God's help,' said Gil. 'And my wife's,' he added wickedly.

Raitts looked alarmed, but with some resolution said, almost as if he meant it, 'A clever lassie, and discreet in her carriage. You're much to be envied.'

'Thank you,' said Gil. There was a slight, awkward silence. Then Raitts drew a book from his sleeve and set it on his knee. It was a small thing, bound in worn brown leather, with a design of some sort pounced onto the cover.

He looked down at it, and said, 'Came to ask you a favour.'

'And what is it?' Gil said encouragingly.

'This book. That lassie. The one that's to be wed, I mean.'

'Mistress Trabboch's daughter,' Gil realised. 'Aye?'

'I'd like to send the lassie this. This book. It's a prayer book, as a marriage gift, you ken. Faither Prior said it would be right, and I wondered. I wondered if . . . well, if you'd . . .'

'If I'd see it on its way?' Gil supplied. 'Easy enough done. D'you ken her direction?'

There was another awkward silence, as Raitts stared at him.

'I never – I never thought o that. I could write it for you. The whole o Ayrshire kens Agnes Trabboch,' he added rather bitterly.

'Or it could go to her new home,' Gil suggested. 'Who is it the girl's to wed? A Mungo Schaw? I could see it to his dwelling, wherever that is.'

'That's a good idea. A better idea. It's Coilsfield, hard by Tarbolton. It's a – it's a nice wee property, she should be comfortable,' said Raitts, 'and a sensible man wi the right ideas in his head. Mistress Marion Stair, she is, after her grandam.'

Could the man really be so oblivious to what he gave away with these utterances, Gil wondered.

'Tell me about the library here,' he said, on an inspiration. Raitts's eyes lit up.

'It's no the biggest library,' he said modestly, 'but it's a good teaching collection, wi some excellent texts for further study. It's a right well-endowed house, this, and there's never been any trouble about the buying of books; we've one or two real treasures in the locked case. I'll let you see them when you're on your feet,' he offered generously.

'I'd like that,' said Gil, trying to ignore the softly opening door. Socrates beat his tail on the blankets. 'What kind o treasures?'

'Torquemada's writings, for one, and Vincent of Beauvais' Book of Grace, all neatly printed at Basel,' said Raitts, his heavy eyebrows writhing in excitement, 'and James Forrigon, he's one o ours and all, tales of the saints and the Legenda Aurea and that. There's some precious books coming out o Basel and Strasbourg the now, maister, you've no idea! And we've a History of Alexander, a right pretty thing, wi wee images all through it, hand done.'

'I should like to see that,' said Alys quietly behind him. Raitts gulped, and scrambled to his feet, dropping the prayer book.

As he bent to lift it Gil said, 'Brother Sandy wants to send this prayer book to Mistress Trabboch's daughter for a marriage gift, Alys. I'm sure we could see to getting it to her.'

'Indeed yes, and what a suitable gift. My faither gave me a prayer book as a marriage gift, sir,' she said to Raitts, 'and I value it greatly. I'm certain the lassie will like to have this one.'

He thrust the book at Gil and edged sideways towards the door and away from Alys, looking alarmed. She avoided meeting his gaze, but went on, 'I'll be right glad to get back to Glasgow and see my faither. I've missed him while we've been away.'

'I, I, I wish you joy of the meeting,' he said. 'That's very, a very proper way to feel. I'll, I'll, I'll pray for you, mistress, and for your faither.'

He slid out of the chamber before she could answer, and was gone. Alys looked at Gil, shaking her head.

'Poor man,' she said.

'How do you always know what to say to his comfort?' Gil asked.

'It seemed obvious. Forrigon?'

'Voragine, I suspect. The *Golden Legend*. Tales of the saints, rather gruesome in places. I've seen a copy, and I think Augie Morison once ordered one and it failed to arrive for some reason.'

'Of course, I remember it. Mère Isabelle had a copy for the library in Paris. Do not try to distract me. You

296

will not succeed in making me ignore this dog,' she went on, emphasising *chien*, 'this *dog* who is on the *bed*.' Socrates dipped his ears and thumped his tail at her, but did not otherwise move.

'He's being a doctor. And keeping me warm,' Gil added absently, inspecting the prayer book. It was not so sumptuous as Alys's, which had paintings of the saints, and a riot of plant life in its margins; this was a printed copy with images added, fine ink drawings of fanciful landscapes, animals, birds, and a few tinted woodcuts of good quality. On its first leaf the name *Alexr Stair* had been neatly crossed out and *Marryon Stair* written in below it.

'Well, if he has fleas, you may sleep on that side, instead of me.' She sat down on the stool Raitts had vacated. 'It will be dinnertime soon but I need to tell you this. Gil, we are to send to Sir Silvester to let him know where Mistress Rattray may be found. I thought to send Tam round after the dinner. She was quite *bouleversée* to learn of his existence, and that he is searching for her.'

'Oh, good news indeed!'

'She was doubtful at first,' she admitted, 'but I persuaded her that it could only be a good thing, that since her husband is now dead Sir Silvester can help her get access to her property, and if he knows of her existence it could be some protection for her.'

'Very wise,' Gil agreed.

'And he might help her find someone to teach the little boy. She would not want him to be a harper, I suppose, like our John's father, but there must be something he can do. Unless she has enough property to keep him in comfort,' she added thoughtfully, 'and even then he must be able to manage it.'

'Rattray will advise her,' said Gil. She looked sharply at him.

'You will sleep after the dinner,' she pronounced 'Does it hurt? You had better have some more willow-bark tea.'

By next morning Gil felt a great deal better, and having won the argument with Alys and persuaded Nory to retrieve his hose he left his bed and also left off his sling, though he found it wise to be cautious in movement. So he was present to watch while she rehearsed her experiment to the same group of Dominicans as had witnessed the confession of Adam Calder, along with Sir Silvester Rattray and the Bishop, expounding her method and findings with confidence, answering their questions clearly but without conceit. In effect, he felt, and was consumed with pride in the idea, his wife was successfully defending a thesis. If only women could be admitted to the degree of doctor, he thought, what a worthy admission hers would be.

The examiners had been particularly impressed by a comparison of the twisted trivets from the experiment and the half-melted key from Pollock's house. By the time they went in procession to dinner, served with great formality before a roaring fire in the great hall of the royal lodging, Gil felt she had certainly convinced the Prior and his subordinates of what had happened to Leonard Pollock, though as Boyd had said, it remained to be seen whether the Provincial and the two Archbishops of Scotland would accept the explanation.

'I'm no entirely clear about it,' confessed Maister Gregor in Gil's ear as they entered the hall. 'Is the lassie, madam your wife I mean, saying the man turned into a leg o mutton and burned up? So was that the Deil's work?'

Gil, to his relief, was prevented from replying by the Priory servant who appeared to lead him to his seat. He found himself placed beside Bishop Brown, while Alys, at the other end of the table, had been assigned to share a mess with Rattray as the only man present other than Gil who was not a churchman. He wished he could hear what was being said, but the Bishop was speaking to him.

'I hope your wife isny in the habit o putting hersel forward like that in public gatherings,' he was saying anxiously. 'A bonnie young woman like that, it's asking for trouble to make hersel too noticed. Quiet, Jerome! Bad dog!' he added. 'The big doggie's as much right as you to be here!'

Jerome was inclined to dispute this; Socrates curled his lip, showing several of his white fangs, and lay down on Gil's feet under the elegant folds of the linen cloths which covered the table, with his head ostentatiously averted.

'I've never known her to do so,' Gil said. 'She's the *grein in gold that godly shon*, well comported at all times as well as wise and beautiful.' Bishop Brown looked disapproving, and he belatedly recalled the final lines of that poem, in which the poet wished to hide between his lady's kirtle and her smock. 'It's quite remarkable what she discovered,' he added.

'Indeed, aye. Very original work,' said the Bishop. 'Very clever. A course, if Michael Scott from the Greyfriars was in charge, it would be original.' He heaved a satisfied sigh. 'So it seems as if Pollock's vanishing wasny what we feared at all, but something quite natural. And this other matter, o the novice that ran mad and slew two others,' he went on, as a servant placed a dish of roasted meat in gravy and another of turnips in pepper sauce between them. 'That's been a bad business, a very bad business, but I think we can say it's ended well. You did good work there and all, Gilbert; it was convenient you being here. I'm right glad I had Davie ask for you.'

'Thank you, sir,' said Gil, spooning turnips onto the Bishop's platter.

'Mind you,' said Brown critically, 'I'm no so sure the lad should ha had access to a rope. I'd ha thought better o Brother Dickon, he's usually sharper than that in matters o discipline and custody.' He fed his dog a piece of the meat, while Gil preserved a tactful silence. 'But now Calder's hanged hissel, I think we can assume it was because he'd come to a realisation o his wickedness, which is something, even if he never confessed, and it spares us the trial and all, which would ha been a speak for the whole o Scotland, whether Holy Kirk had handled it or we'd turned him ower to the secular arm.'

'That's a true word,' Gil agreed, thinking that there was probably no point in repeating Brother Eck's account of the last conversation he had had with Calder, in which the young man had railed bitterly against a world which did not appreciate his motives or his worth. Nor was there any point in revealing his own doubts about the position of the knot in the rope which had been convincingly arranged about Calder's neck when he saw the corpse. Brother Dickon's men must all have been trained to kill in various ways, he reflected.

'But it's strange he was never recognised to be mad afore this,' pursued Bishop Brown.

'The insane can be cunning indeed,' said David Boyd, when the tables had been lifted and they had all settled around the cavernous fireplace. At a secular feast, there would have been music and dancing; here, there was wine and candied fruit, and one of the servants by the window with a lute. The Prior seemed to Gil to have aged ten years since he first saw him. 'Our brother Adam managed to hide what he was from all of us, even his fellow novices, even his teachers.'

300

'Is that right?' said Sir Silvester Rattray, in a tone of polite disbelief, and accepted a sweetmeat from the platter the novice Brother George was handing him.

'Most folk prefer to think the best of others,' said Alys. 'It's natural.'

The Prior gave her an approving look. Another churchman conquered, Gil thought, hiding a smile in his glass of the excellent white Rhine wine.

'None the less,' said Rattray, 'my kinsman was murdered here in the safety o this Priory, a young man to whom you owed the duty o a parent, leaving his only sister unprotected, unsupported, in fear o a violent man.'

Yes, you have studied the law, as Alys said, Gil thought.

'Hardly unsupported,' said the Prior, 'if you're taking on responsibility for her.'

'I've a wife and bairnies to see to,' said Rattray unconvincingly, adjusting his velvet gown so that the silver braid on the sleeves caught the dull light from the windows. 'I can lend her countenance, but she needs resources o her own.'

'Indeed,' said Boyd, gesturing to the man with the flagon to pour Rattray more wine. 'I've discussed it wi our factor and our man o law, as it happens, and it seems to us, since the boy never finished his noviciate, it would be reasonable to return a portion o the lands he brought to us when he was tonsured. One-third seems like a good offer.'

'Does it indeed?' Rattray raised his eyebrows.

Gil caught Alys's eye, and she smiled at him. Mistress Rattray was secure, then, though it seemed unlikely Rattray would countenance any approach Tam might make for her marriage.

'This might be better discussed at another time,' he suggested.

'Wi our man of law present,' said the Prior. 'I think you're acquaint wi Edward Gilchrist, Sir Silvester.'

Rattray's face cleared.

'I am that. A reasonable man, Gilchrist,' he said. 'Aye, I'll meet him and discuss the matter.'

'Sir Silvester,' said the Bishop, 'what's your thought now concerning the death o Leonard Pollock?'

'Aye, the man Pollock.' Rattray seemed to increase in height, and his manner became more formal. 'Other than to condole wi you on the recent violent happenings, I would like to say, Prior, that having witnessed Mistress Mason's proceedings in Mistress Buttergask's kitchen, and now heard her expound the whole matter wi sic excellent lucidity, I'm convinced o what happened to Pollock. I believe he was consumed by fire when his garments caught light, and that what I saw that night was the smoke from his burning, though Bessie,' he caught himself up, 'Mistress Buttergask, will maintain it was the Devil carrying off the man's soul.'

'No reason it should not be both,' observed the Prior, and crossed himself.

Rattray bowed in acknowledgement of this, and went on, 'I'll send to the Provost to say the same, and I'll make it clear to any that mention it to me. Likely we'll no convince the entire town, but we'll maybe get them to leave off the talk o witchcraft and devilry.'

'That would be an act o great friendship,' said the Prior.

Later, in the milling about in the chilly cloister while his men were called for and the Dominicans assembled to escort their two noble guests to the gate, Rattray drifted deliberately to Gil's side.

'A word wi you,' he said quietly, and led him aside. Having done so he seemed reluctant to begin, studying the flagstones under his feet with some interest.

Gil said, 'Has Mistress Buttergask contrived to clean out her oven yet?'

'Oh, that!' Rattray laughed. 'Aye, though the bread tasted mighty strange the day, what wi the soap and the mutton fat! I like your wife, Cunningham.'

'Thank you, sir,' said Gil politely. 'So do I.'

'You may well.' Rattray grinned. 'She had me near convinced she kent naught o Margaret Rattray. I was right glad to have your man come yesterday wi the lassie's direction. I was round on her doorstep within the hour, and Bessie's there the day trying to persuade her to move in. Two bairns and their mammy to fuss over, she'd be overjoyed to have her.'

'That would be a good solution,' Gil said. 'At least till Mistress Rattray's found her own feet.'

'Aye.' Rattray gazed across the yard at the drawing on the battered shutters of Pollock's house. 'I'll pass your findings about that business ower yonder to the Treasury. They'll deal wi the rest themsels. No need for you to delve into that at all.'

'What, the man wi the . . .' Gil gestured at his chest where a badge might hang, and Rattray nodded significantly. 'I'd no intention o doing so, but I'm glad the matter's in good hands. If James Stewart or those close to him want to send coin out o Scotland, I'll not interfere, no matter what I think o't.'

'Quite so,' said Rattray. 'And another thing I thought to mention.' There was a pause, in which he dug with the toe of his boot at a weed growing between two flagstones. 'Bessie – Mistress Buttergask,' he began. Gil waited. 'She hears voices,' said Rattray at last. 'In her head. I'm never sure if it's a version o the Sight, seeing she's from north o here, but the thing is, her voices tell her things, and one or two o them she's repeated to me and they've been close to the mark, gey close to the mark.'

303

'I know a couple of folk wi the Sight,' Gil said.

'Aye, well, you ken how what they see, what they tell you, can be right, but no always quite how you expect. Thing is, I think Bessie said something to Mistress Mason, and it worked strong on her. I didny ask either o them about it, but Bessie passed a remark or two to me later.'

'Did she?' Gil said. Could that be what had altered Alys's mood so much the other night?

'Aye. No idea what it was she said, what it was about, but I'd take it seriously if I was you. Bessie seemed to think it was important.'

In the quiet hour before supper, when all the visitors had left, Alys was off brewing a final batch of cough linctus, and Gil and Socrates were sitting quietly by the fire in the lesser chamber, accompanied by the kitchen cat, a tap on the doorframe heralded the three remaining first-year novices, Munt, Mureson and Simpson. The dog got to his feet to inspect them, and they entered diffidently, with a certain amount of nudging and hanging back, until Mureson got up enough courage to speak.

'We thought we ought to ask how you're doing, maister. Is it – were you badly hurt?'

'A few scratches, that's all,' Gil said, oddly touched by this. 'I'll live. Come in to the fire. How are you all?' he asked when they were seated.

They looked at each other, and Munt said, 'Well enough, maister. A bit – a bit surprised, maybe.'

'Surprised?' he repeated. 'About Calder, you mean?'

'Aye, that's it,' agreed Simpson. 'We aye thought he was daft, but we never thought him mad. Brother Archie was telling us how he was boasting o what he's done, making out he was called to it. Called to cleanse the world o sinners? That must be madness. And then to lay hands on himsel and all.'

'The thing is, though, now when you think about it,' said Mureson, 'the signs were there, but it never occurs to you to – to think sic things o someone you see every day and night.'

'It creeps up on you,' offered Simpson. 'He'd got worse lately, since Andrew was confined, more o his stuff about the body and the limbs and that, and he,' he swallowed, 'he tellt us lately how he put his dog away, cut its throat after it let a rat past it. I'm right glad to see your dog safe, maister. He's a bonnie wolfhound.'

'He's safe and well, as you can see,' Gil assured them.

Munt put a hand out for Socrates to sniff, and Simpson nodded at the cat, which was sitting upright gazing into the fire.

'And Our Lady be praised,' he said, 'Brother Augustine's cat never put a foot wrong these last months. We'd ha been eating plain boiled stockfish and dry oatcakes for weeks if anything happened to DominiCattus.'

'It's no catching, is it?' Munt wondered. 'Madness, I mean. Just he seemed right ordinary, right up to the time Faither Prior announced what had happened, who'd killed Andrew and Brother Thomas, and that Brother Sandy was back in the library and no to blame for any o't.'

'Don't be daft, Sandy,' said Simpson, and caught himself up. 'I mean, try to use your intelligence,' he said in Latin, in Father Henry's very diction, and the other two grinned again. Gil recognised the light-headed effect of great shock and release.

'How is Father Henry?' he asked, to change the subject. 'Have you been able to see him?'

'No yet,' said Mureson, 'but he's sent out word to thank us for our prayers, and that he'll be glad to see us when he's permitted.'

'And were we studying the work he gave us last,' said Munt. 'You can tell he's no much harmed.'

'I still canny believe it,' said Simpson. 'That Adam could— och, well. Our Lady have him in her care, bring him to knowledge o his sins.'

'Amen,' they all said.

Then Mureson looked at Gil, hesitated, and went on, 'We brought you something, maister. Sandy, do you have it?'

'Oh!' Munt began searching his person. 'Aye, here it is.' He drew a squarish linen-wrapped object from his sleeve. 'Here it is,' he said again, and held it out. 'It's from us all. We was all three working on it.'

Puzzled, surprised and moved, Gil lifted the package and unwrapped the linen, and stared, transfixed, at what lay within it.

'It's beautiful,' he said after a moment, still staring. 'How can I— It's beautiful.'

'We did it off one o Andrew's drawings,' said Simpson. 'Sandy and me both worked on the carving, and Sandy, the other Sandy,' he nodded at Mureson, 'limned it. We'd been working at it since Andrew . . . I mean, we meant it for when he cam out o confinement, only he . . . only, anyway. Anyway, we'd like you to have it,' he finished in a rush.

Gil looked up, from one to another of the intent, embarrassed, concerned young faces, and back at the little image.

'Thank you,' he said simply. 'It's a gift to remember you all by. I'll hang it by my desk, where I can see it all the time.'

On a panel of wood about the size of his hand was carved, in low relief, an image of the Virgin and Child with St John. It had been painted, with a light delicate touch, and seemed almost to glow in the dwindling daylight; the blue of the Virgin's cloak and the flesh tones of the children were particularly radiant.

It must be some purely fortuitous accident of the brush or the light that gave the Virgin a shadowy scar across one eye.